*The only decent thing growing up in California had ever given Rory was an appreciation for a good pair of sunglasses.*

He now glanced impatiently at his watch; his appointment was forty-one minutes late. That was southern California for you. The weather was unseasonable, the residents were unreliable.

Suddenly, he heard a metallic death rattle of a car coming up the curve of the driveway. This woman, Jilly Skye, drove the world's crummiest car. Rory squinted to get a glimpse of the driver. And once the car's shuddering ceased, the door swung open.

An improbably high-heeled sandal hit the flagstone. Its straps imprisoned a very small foot, arched high by the shape of the shoe. Like the car, the foot's toenails were painted the color of cherry popsicles.

Then the sole of the second sandal hit the flagstone with a *clack. It's just a pair of shoes*, he told himself. The rest of the woman had to get better.

And she most certainly did . . .

D1007965

# CHRISTIE RIDGWAY

# *This Perfect Kiss*

**AVON BOOKS**

*An Imprint of HarperCollinsPublishers*

This is a work of fiction. Names, characters, places, and incidents are products of the author's imagination or are used fictitiously and are not to be construed as real. Any resemblance to actual events, locales, organizations, or persons, living or dead, is entirely coincidental.

AVON BOOKS
*An Imprint of* HarperCollins*Publishers*
10 East 53rd Street
New York, New York 10022-5299

Copyright © 2001 by Christie Ridgway
ISBN: 0-380-81256-8
www.avonromance.com

First Avon Books paperback printing: January 2001

Avon Trademark Reg. U.S. Pat. Off. and in Other Countries, Marca Registrada, Hecho en U.S.A.
HarperCollins® is a trademark of HarperCollins Publishers Inc.

Printed in the U.S.A.

10  9  8  7  6  5  4

## Friend*ship*

How appropriate that the word implies a journey and being kept afloat. This book is for three wonderful women who are traveling through the writing world with me and who keep me buoyant with their enthusiasm, good sense, and undying support. My thanks and love to Teresa Hill, aka Sally Tyler Hayes; Barbara Samuel, aka Ruth Wind; and Elizabeth Bevarly.

# THERE'S SOMETHING
## ABOUT RORY . . .

That's focusing attention from San Francisco to Washington, D.C., on Rory Kincaid, the 32-year-old, gorgeous, self-made software millionaire and scion of southern California royalty. But you'll have to wait until February 14 to find out what that something is—when Kincaid hosts a fund-raising bash for the new Blue political party at his late grandfather's estate, Caidwater.

Expect thunderclaps and lightning bolts in the skies that night when the gods of responsibility battle the gods of revelry. After all, those on the A-list of this trendy political party—the party that promises centrist policies and candidates so clean they squeak—will be mingling at the house once reputed to supply champagne in the swimming pools and willing starlets in the cabanas. The goings-on at past Caidwater parties fed gossip columns throughout the world. Of all L.A.'s magnificent estates, none tops this one for juicy scandals and never-quite-secret secrets.

Speaking of not-so-secret secrets, *Celeb!* can't resist whispering that the word is sexy and single Rory Kincaid will announce his candidacy for the U.S. Senate that night. When asked about Kincaid's chances to win the seat, political pundit Lionel Urbin, the host of CNN's *D.C. Dish,* said, "Pollsters are telling me that the Blue Party and Rory Kincaid are hot, hot, hot." Urbin's wife, bi-coastal celebrity hostess Alana Urbin, added, "He has Kennedy charisma and Hollywood looks. Beyond that . . . there's just something about Rory."

Still, *Celeb!* can't help but wonder how far the apple falls from the tree. After all, there's not a more unlikely family than Kincaid's to produce a squeaky-clean politician. Is Rory truly respectable, or is he really more like those infamous Hollywood legends, his father, Daniel Kincaid (4 wives), and his grandfather Roderick Kincaid (7 wives), who passed away last month at the lusty age of 90? Won't it be fun to find out? *Celeb!* will be watching closely.

**Don't forget, *Celeb!* is always seeking tips. If you catch Rory Kincaid, or any other celebrity, doing the naughty, we want to know! Call us at 1-900-555-0155. ($.99 per minute, average call 5 minutes.)**

# Chapter 1

When a woman stands five feet two inches, a hundred and *ahem* pounds (the *ahem* mainly located below the neck and above the waist), it's a bad idea to attend an afternoon business meeting in a low-cut, flesh-colored evening gown.

Throw in spaghetti straps and a few gold sequins, and the fact that it was the most crucial business meeting of said woman's career—make that her *life*—and the bad idea turned downright calamitous.

Jilly Skye realized this. But she also realized she didn't have a choice. Not if she wasn't going to be unforgivably late.

Still, she hesitated before pressing the intercom button this side of a pair of black, we-mean-business ironwork gates. They were the last in a long line of hurdles she'd scrambled over since early this morning, when Rory Kincaid had agreed to meet with her. Thanks to a buddy's tip, she knew Rory wanted to dispense with a house crammed full of old clothing and costumes. Jilly was a vintage-clothing dealer who wanted into that house. Badly.

1

Madly.

Despite tight-fitting chiffon, Jilly's stomach executed several rabbit-worthy hops. Madness was the word, all right. Because even though the emcee of this morning's charity fashion show had rambled the event into an hour overrun; even though Jilly's assistant had left with *all* the clothing that her shop, Things Past, had brought to the show, including the business suit Jilly had intended to change into, even though her frantic phone calls to Rory Kincaid to explain her holdup had resulted only in a disinterested busy signal, nothing was going to keep Jilly from this meeting with Rory. Too much was at stake.

Determination renewed, she reached through her car window to press the intercom button. But her whole hand was quaking so, she snatched it back. "Calm down, calm down," she muttered to herself. "This is no way to get a job. Take a deep breath." But her obedient inhale turned into a gasp when her *ahems* threatened to pop over the dress's deep décolletage. *Oh, my.* Pinching the top of the bodice to pull it up, she wiggled all the strategic body parts back down. Her cheeks went hot. What had seemed fun and fanciful to model at a for-women-only fashion event now seemed almost . . . scary.

*Darn Rory Kincaid!* Her predicament could be partially blamed on him, too. If she'd been able to cut through those irritating busy signals and reach him this afternoon, she could have made time for a crucial wardrobe stop.

What the heck was he doing on the phone so long? The only thing that kept a number tied up that continuously was a long-distance romance or some heavy Internet surfing.

It was bound to be the Internet. This Rory Kincaid was supposed to be some kind of software mogul. Like Bill Gates, he was young, successful and rich.

Hey. *Bill Gates!* Jilly's heartbeat slowed a smidgen. *Bill Gates*. She mouthed the name to herself again and her nervousness was reduced by a few more degrees.

When she pictured Rory Kincaid as someone like Bill Gates—someone bespectacled, shaggy-haired, and more interested in floppy disks than fashion statements—she could feel nearly confident. If cliché could be believed, techie-nerds lost track of time—well, practically all the time. And certainly he wouldn't care what she wore. If she didn't say anything about the evening gown, he probably wouldn't even notice it.

The Bill Gates idea worked better than Alka-Seltzer. Stomach settling down and heart feeling light, Jilly stuck her arm out the car window and confidently jabbed the intercom with her forefinger. This job was hers. She lifted her chin and threw back her shoulders. As the gates slowly opened, she pressed down on the gas pedal, all the while mentally chanting her brand-new mantra, *BillGatesBillGatesBillGates*.

Her car slowly climbed past the empty gatehouse and up the steep, curving driveway. She shifted in her seat, trying to wiggle herself more securely into the almost-nude evening dress. Yes, she told herself, this meeting was going to be just fine, as long as she held onto that BillGatesian image of Rory Kincaid. *BillGatesBillGatesBillGates*, she whispered silently, willing the idea to take deep root.

Just fine, she assured herself once again. A guy like she was picturing probably wouldn't even notice she was a tad over, or rather, *under* dressed.

Alerted via the intercom at the front gates that his tardy afternoon appointment had finally arrived, Rory Kincaid walked out of the Spanish-style Caidwater mansion and into winter air hovering at an obscene eighty degrees.

He grimaced with distaste.

A dry breeze brushed over him, carrying with it the light scent of orange blossoms and the heavier sweetness of flowering jade plants.

He held his breath.

All around him, birds twittered mindlessly, joining the unceasing good cheer of water bubbling up and over the eight fountains in the eight themed gardens surrounding the forty-four-room house.

The noise grated against his nerves.

Another breath of overhot, too-sweet wind wafted past, and Rory's grimace deepened. It was as close to Paradise as January in southern California could get and Rory hated everything about it.

This was Super Bowl season, for Christ's sake. If he must, he'd forgo rain and snow, but surely a nip in the air wasn't too much to expect in the dead of winter? L.A. took its reputation as the land of fantasies and wishes-come-true much too seriously. It always had.

Shoving his hands in the pockets of his jeans, Rory moved away from the shadows beside the house. Immediately, diamond-hard sunlight assaulted his eyes and he automatically reached for the wraparound Ray-Bans in his shirt pocket.

The only decent thing growing up in Hollywood had ever given him was an appreciation for a good pair of sunglasses.

Descending the wide front steps, Rory mentally nudged the estate's last owner, his grandfather Roderick Kincaid, a little closer to the devil-tended fires of what must be his current abode. The old man deserved to broil for foisting the executorship of his will on Rory. The surviving Kincaid men included Daniel, Rory's father, and Greg, Rory's brother. Had Grandfather passed the hassles on to them? No. For whatever reasons of his own, the old man had named Rory. Rory, who hated Caidwater and everything it represented.

He'd shaken Caidwater dirt off his shoes ten years ago, vowing to never pass through its gates again. But thanks to Roderick's demands, Roderick's insistent lawyers, and Rory's own unignorable sense of responsibility, here he was, weighed down by the opulent estate, all its contents, and a dependent aunt who was left under his protection as well.

The timing couldn't be worse. He should be at home in Atherton—located in sensible, winter-cool northern California—basking in the Blue

Party's gratifying interest in sponsoring his U.S. Senate candidacy. He should be capitalizing on the yet unpublicized endorsement of the state's retiring senator.

Instead, he was stuck here, when the last thing an upcoming political campaign needed was to remind people that Rory was a member of the decadent Kincaid acting family. But thanks to his grandfather and the old man's pack-rat ways, Rory had to waste time waiting around for a woman who bought and sold ratty old clothes.

He glanced impatiently at his watch. The woman was forty-one minutes late.

That was southern California for you. The weather was unseasonable, the residents were unreliable, and the only predictable thing was that he wanted out of L.A. ASAP.

An ominous clatter echoed up the flagstone drive. The skin on the back of his neck crawled. Ignoring the sensation, Rory strode onto the wide curve of the driveway that swung past the house, even though the feeling of doom dogging him deepened.

The metallic death rattle assaulted his ear-drums again. Either the woman, this Jilly Skye, drove the world's crummiest car, or what she *did* drive was screaming for new struts and shocks. Then the vehicle rounded the last hairpin bend in the driveway.

He'd been right on both counts. He believed the vehicle had started life in the carefree 1960s as a "woody" station wagon, but now it was cough-ing up the incline like an aged three-pack-a-day smoker. The car's entire undercarriage shrieked at the abuse, the grating noise making Rory want to shriek, too.

To add insult to injury, someone had thought it a good idea to repaint the thing—wood and all—cherry red.

To get a glimpse of the driver, Rory squinted, but the tinted windows made a clear view impossible. Once the car's shuddering ceased, the driver's door swung open. An improbably high-heeled sandal hit the flagstone. Its straps imprisoned a very small foot, arched high by the shape of the shoe. Like the car, the foot's toenails were painted the color of cherry popsicles.

Rory closed his eyes, biting back a groan. Damn, but he hated this crazy town. Expect a business meeting, find a foot fetish waiting to happen. But he had to look again, and for just an instant he considered throwing over a Senate seat for a position as sales clerk in a chichi shoe boutique on Rodeo Drive.

Then the sole of the second sandal hit the flagstone with a *clack*, bringing him back to reality. *It's just a pair of shoes*, he told himself. The rest of the woman had to get better.

And she did. Get better, that is, and worse, too. Because as he stood watching, from behind the curtain of the red woody door a woman emerged. A short, curvy woman who appeared to be clothed in nakedness. And sequins.

In resigned amazement, Rory closed his eyes again. *Only in L.A.*, he thought, realizing he should have been prepared for this kind of thing all along. The last time he'd been surprised by a woman in an unexpected place had been right here at Caidwater, nearly ten years ago. That was the night Rory had KO'd his father, then torn out of the house to escape north.

The car door slammed, and he risked another look, just in case. Nope, every inch, every improbable inch remained the same, including the winking sequins and stiletto sandals.

As he watched, the woman took a deep breath.

His brain went numb.

Probably from all the blood rushing to the lower half of his body.

He knew he was staring, but then, so was she. He thought her mouth was moving, in some sort of soundless mantra. She stalked toward him—if anyone in that kind of teetery shoe could actually *stalk*—and for an unfathomable reason, he stepped back. Then back again.

But she kept coming and he finally stayed still, taking the time to realize she was clothed in a nude-colored evening dress that clung like packing tape to her small waist and spectacular breasts. Then she stopped before him, a courteous three feet away.

Her hand came out. "Hello, sir. I'm Jilly Skye."

He stared at her, his mind blank of everything but the spangly vision in front of him. Her hand inched closer and he looked at it dumbly, too. What did she expect him to do with it? He looked back at her face for a hint, and thought he detected her lips moving again.

Then her face cleared, her hand dropped. "You're *not* Rory Kincaid," she said, obviously relieved.

He blinked. "No. I *am* Rory Kincaid." At least he was reasonably sure of that much.

She swallowed, her lips moved silently again, and then that hand whipped back out. "I'm sorry. I'm Jilly Kincaid—I mean Jilly *Skye*, Mr. Kincaid, and I'm pleased to meet you."

She had a face the shape of a cat's and green eyes, and he finally realized he was supposed to take her hand. Her small, warm palm and fingers gave his a brisk, impersonal shake. Very quick. Very businesslike.

Businesslike. Jilly Skye. *Oh, my God*, he thought in disbelief, *this truly is my afternoon appointment*.

Her eyebrows rose. "Well?" She smiled uncertainly.

*Well, hell*. What was he supposed to do now?

He once more ran his gaze over the petite woman. She wiggled her toes in those hooker high heels and then adjusted a delicate beaded headband. Beneath it, coffee-brown hair squiggled to her shoulders in a mass of natural curls. He'd already noted the green eyes. Freckles splashed across her face. Her lips moved again, and he guessed she had an unfortunate nervous tic.

Rory mentally shook his head. Unfortunate nervous tic or no, this particular vintage-clothing dealer just wouldn't do. Nearly seventy years' worth of clothes and costumes overflowed every nook and cranny of Caidwater, making the cataloging a daunting task. With the Blue Party fundraiser to prepare for and his own wish to get out of L.A. as soon as possible, he wanted to work with someone professional and efficient.

His gaze flicked over her again and another rush of blood surged toward his groin. He ignored it. From the time he was much too young, he'd witnessed every possible way sexual fascination went wrong. But unlike some of the Hollywood brats he'd grown up with, he'd learned from his famous family's bad examples and boogied out of L.A. after just one major mistake of his own. Now when it came to sex, he always used his brain first.

With the Senate candidacy in the offing, he had a reputation to protect and people counting on him to uphold it. As tempting as it might be, even thinking about dallying with this bosomy little darling spelled disaster in tall tabloid headlines for all the world to see.

A smart man like him would immediately hustle her back into her car and back out of his life.

Just as he was forming the right words to make that happen, her eyes rounded and she swallowed a surprised hiccup of sound. He pretended not to notice, thinking perhaps it was her unfortunate nervous tic in full flower. But then she stumbled backward until her curvy hips met the cherry-red side of her car. Something furry and gray dashed past Rory. With eager paws, it swiftly scaled the woman's dress until it came to perch on her shoulder.

*Oh, hell.*

The woman froze, completely, except for her pretty green eyes, which slid in the direction of the big-eared, long-tailed thing. Which, of course, was an animal. A pet. But this was southern California, so the pet—between the size of a rabbit and a guinea pig—wasn't a cat, a bird, or even a goldfish. No, not any form of animal life, domesticated or wild, that normal people living in a normal environment would expect to find in the normal course of their normal day.

He considered not laying claim to it, but everyone knew he took pride in being a responsible man. "It won't hurt you," he said. Walking toward Jilly slowly, he mentally cursed his brother, who'd been the one to bring the damn thing home. "It's a chinchilla."

He came even closer as her brow crinkled. He gave her big points for bravery, because she kept her body ice-sculpture still. "You're sure?" She was trying to keep *everything* still, apparently, because when she spoke, she hardly moved her mouth. Which, now that it wasn't moving so much, Rory noticed was soft and full. "You're familiar with the little thing?" she asked.

"Kiss," he said.

A pair of green eyes jumped to his. The pink color on her cheeks matched the pink of her mouth. *"What?"*

"It's Auntie's—my aunt's—pet. His name is Kiss. I've suggested we rename him Houdini, but she's not going for it." Face it, his father's sister didn't seem particularly taken with Rory's suggestions *or* with Rory himself. He kept telling himself it would get better once he had Auntie settled at his home near San Francisco.

As if he'd been waiting for this moment all his rodenty life, Kiss the chinchilla gazed adoringly at Jilly, then snuggled closer to rub the top of his head against the underside of her jaw.

She jumped. "Oh!" Then blinked. "His fur is really soft."

Kiss almost appeared to smile, then rubbed his head against that tender-looking skin once more. Rory figured it was only natural to envy an animal he was starting to despise. "C'mon, Kiss." He reached out a hand to grab the beast, but it squealed in protest, then quickly squirmed across Jilly's shoulder to burrow under her hair at the back of her neck.

Jilly squeaked too, and Rory was close enough to see the goose bumps that rushed from her throat toward her low neckline. Before he could start envying those as well, he set his teeth. "Come out with your paws up, Kiss, or it's chinchilla stew for dinner and chinchilla slippers for Christmas."

But instead of surrendering, the sneaky thing wiggled deeper, causing Jilly to gasp. A gasp which in turn caused one—no, make that *two* other spectacular things to happen.

But after a single incredible eyeful, Rory pretended he hadn't seen the sight of her miraculous breasts rising over the top of her dress, or experienced his natural masculine reaction.

Painfully aware that he wasn't going to talk the damn animal out, he sidled closer to the woman, then suddenly thrust his hand behind her, into the curly froth of her hair. Finding the wiggly body of his adversary, he hung on, ignoring Kiss's squeaky complaints and tricky avoidance maneuvers as well as Jilly Skye's big eyes and the way that nervous tic moved her sweet, soft-looking mouth again.

But the warm sensation of Jilly's hair wrapping around his wrist was unignorable. And unacceptable. So when Kiss made a last desperate bid to hang onto his new fascination, Rory set his teeth again and firmly pulled the animal free. With one final squeal, the chinchilla emerged from the new tangle of Jilly's hair, a disgruntled loser.

"There," Rory said triumphantly, stepping back to gauge the woman's reaction.

But instead of being grateful, she was stunned. He couldn't blame her, because now there was even less of her dressed. Apparently the struggle between man and beast had resulted in the barely there gown being barely on. She clutched the bodice with one hand and the end of a broken shoulder strap with the other. Rory knew enough about the law of gravity to realize that her hands were the only thing saving them from transgressing the laws of decency.

Those tabloid headlines suddenly sprang to vivid, career-damaging life in Rory's mind.

"I need to get you inside," he said urgently. It was bad enough when she was wearing the outrageous dress. But now that she was *half* wearing it! Reporters and photographers, eager to cash in on his rumored political aspirations, had been sniffing around for weeks, and telephoto lenses could be powerful, evil things. Forget about getting her back in her car. Until he had her paperclipped or rubber-banded back together, no way could she be seen leaving Caidwater.

Holding Kiss against his chest with one hand, he grabbed Jilly's elbow and started towing her toward the house. "This way."

She came along willingly enough until they reached the bottom of the steps leading to the front door. Then she stopped, tilting her head to scan up, up, up the three stories of pinkish stucco walls. "It's a Moorish castle, for goodness sake."

Rory urged her forward, uninterested in admiring the place. To him it looked just like it was, a self-indulgent, overly luxurious dream palace. "Thirty-six thousand square feet," he said matter-of-factly. "Forty-four rooms including an indoor swimming pool, not to mention the eight separate gardens and acres of undeveloped land. A one-hundred-foot waterfall drops to the canyon below, where there's a canoe pond, a tennis court, and a nine-hole golf course."

Crowning the highest ridge of hills ringing Hollywood, shielded by mature palms and eucalyptus trees from the eyes of the ordinary people who lived in the valley below, Caidwater was a rich man's playground tied with a hangman's noose around Rory's neck.

No wonder he felt like he was suffocating.

His hand on the front doorknob, Rory paused before ushering her through the main entrance. On second thought, it was probably better to avoid the household help, too.

Without explanation, he detoured from the front door and strode quickly through a gate leading to a side terrace, Jilly's elbow still cupped in the palm of his hand. She trotted in his wake, doing okay despite those wacky high heels and the struggle to keep her dress up. He didn't risk letting her go until they reached a side door. When he turned the knob, cool air and the smell of lemon oil and expensive booze oozed over the threshold.

Still grasping the pieces of her dress, Jilly preceded him through the open door, her gaze mildly curious. "Gee, swimming pools, canoe ponds, forty-four rooms," she said. "Sounds like just about everything a despot could want."

Rory stripped off his sunglasses and narrowed his eyes. What it sounded like was that she'd known his grandfather. But he dismissed the thought and followed her into the library he'd taken over as his office. Built-in shelves hugged the walls, filled with miles of never-touched leather-bound books that had come with the house when Roderick bought the place in 1939.

"Wait right here," Rory said, gesturing toward a chair. "I'll be just a minute putting the animal back."

With Kiss safely locked in his cage, Rory could find a way to glue the woman together, thank her for her time, and then get on with finding another way to get rid of the clothes. A hundred bucks should make her happy enough to leave empty-handed.

"Would you mind if I come along?"

Rory paused, halfway out the door that led to the rest of the house. He looked over his shoulder.

And almost choked on his frustration. There'd been no need for such a panic. No need to bring her inside. She had the dress together already.

She apparently noticed the direction of his gaze and half smiled. "An old friend of the family is an ex-Navy man." In no time flat, she'd threaded the broken strap through something inside the top of the dress, then fashioned a knot. "I think he called this one a bowline." She worried her lower lip. "Um, so may I come along?"

Rory dragged his gaze away from her knot, then away from her mouth, and checked the ornate-faced grandfather clock standing against the wall behind her. "Auntie's napping," he said. "I don't want to disturb her." He suppressed a shudder at the very idea. She was cantankerous enough without his interrupting her sleep.

"I'd adore seeing more of the house," Jilly said quickly.

Rory's eyebrows rose. She hadn't seemed all that favorably impressed when he'd described it a moment ago. Still, he wanted to get rid of her with as little fuss as he could, even though he'd made the mistake of bringing her inside. Maybe if he gave her the dime tour, her curiosity would be satisfied—or disappointed.

Caidwater no longer lived up to its reputation. Unlike earlier times, decadent and half-drunk Hollywood brokers no longer lounged around the billiard tables or soaked their overpaid flesh in the steaming whirlpool. And the only deceitful and ambitious wannabe starlets wandering the halls were the bitter ghosts in Rory's own mind.

"Come on, then," he said.

He led the way into the hall and gestured across the tiled expanse toward a massive sunken room. "The cozy living area," he said ironically. There was a gold-leaf coffered ceiling, intricately carved paneling on the walls, and a stone fire-place that could house a small orchestra. If memory served, for one particularly overpacked party, it had.

He didn't stop to assess her response, but instead kept moving forward, pointing out the formal dining room and then the entrance to the hundred-seat private movie theater. "Elevator," he said, indicating another set of elaborately carved doors, but he bypassed it for the curving oak staircase.

Holding the skirt of her dress in one hand, she mounted it beside him, step for step, keeping up with him until he stopped outside a closed door on the second floor. "Auntie's," he whispered. "I'll just slip in and put Kiss in his cage."

She was worrying her lower lip again, but she nodded.

Holding his breath, Rory eased inside. His aunt had a two-room suite, this room and the bedroom beyond the closed connecting door. Picking his way through some of Auntie's things left on the floor—a crocheted throw, two books, and a couple of musical instruments she liked to amuse herself with—he quietly crossed to Kiss's cage. With careful, near-silent movements he inserted the now-squirming creature back inside and firmly latched the door. Damned if he knew how the chinchilla kept getting out. Auntie denied all knowledge.

Sending a furtive glance in the direction of her bedroom—God, he hoped he hadn't woken her—he spun back toward the hall door and walked quickly, silently, toward it.

Silently, until his hasty foot kicked a discarded

tambourine. Though Rory froze, it rattled ominously forward, sliding across the Oriental carpet only to slam into the plaster wall with enough momentum and enough shivery, shattering noise to wake the dead.

*Shit*!

His shoulders tense, he waited for the expected repercussion. And on cue, it came. "Hey," said a voice, querulous at first, then getting stronger. "Hey!"

When there was no response, the voice became even louder, even more plaintive. "Who's there?"

Rory grimaced, trying to ignore the light sweat that broke out on his skin. He pasted a conciliatory smile on his face and, gulping a breath, crossed toward his aunt's bedroom. It didn't surprise him to suddenly find Jilly Skye standing at his shoulder. As he very well knew, that voice was impossible to ignore.

Taking another deep breath, he gently opened the bedroom door to confront his aunt. She was sitting up on a lacy confection of a canopied bed. A pillow mark creased her cheek and a cross expression turned down her mouth. He swallowed. "Iris . . ."

Her cross expression mutated into something monsterish. "I *said* to call me—"

"Auntie," he supplied hastily, one hand lifting to ward off her displeasure. "I'm sorry I forgot."

Her small chin jutted imperiously and he saw her gaze move to the woman by his side. She pointed her finger. "Who?" she asked, like a queen contemplating beheadings.

With a resigned half smile, Rory shifted slightly. Jilly Skye's expression was curious, surprised, and something else he couldn't read. "Ms. Skye, may I introduce you to my aunt, Iris Kincaid. Iris, this is Ms. Jilly Skye."

And as if it were every day that she greeted four-year-old little girls who were the crotchety and commanding aunts of thirty-two-year-old men, Jilly crossed the thick white carpet and shook Iris's hand.

He could hardly believe his eyes. When he'd first met the child a month ago, he'd suspected she might bite him, and that suspicion had yet to disappear. But Jilly didn't seem wary of Iris at all. As a matter of fact, she retrieved and presented an asked-for glass of water without incident.

Rory hovered in the relative safety of the play-room doorway, his surprise turning to bemuse-ment as Jilly settled the sleepy-again Iris back in her nest of light quilts. With a little wave of her hand that Iris drowsily returned, Jilly then led the way back into the hall.

Not taking any chances, Rory shut the play-room door with the lightest of clicks.

Jilly's eyes were bright. "She's adorable."

Yeah, that was what he'd thought at first. Iris was all long golden hair and the famous Kincaid blue eyes. But her personality—at least when it came to him—was more barracuda than baby beauty.

"We're just getting acquainted," he said non-committally, turning in the direction of the stairs. "I never met her before her father—my grandfa-ther—passed away. I'm her guardian now."

"Her guardian?" Curiosity filled Jilly's voice.

"My grandfather left her in my custody," Rory answered. "She's my responsibility now, and believe me, I'm still trying to get used to the idea myself." But a kid needed stability and Rory knew he was the best—and only—Kincaid to provide it.

Of course, his mentor, Senator Fitzpatrick, had rubbed his palms together at the news. He'd crowed that raising a "daughter" would only boost Rory's family-friendly image in the minds of the voters.

Which brought him back to all that needed to be done before the massive fund-raising party next month, including clearing the house of the damn costumes and clothes. That dark sense of shipwreck-in-the-offing resurged.

He slid his gaze to Jilly as he escorted her back to the library. Just one look at her glittery evening gown and the generous upper half that it barely concealed reminded him she was at best a flake and at worst a bad influence on Auntie.

He'd experienced enough of both types to last him a lifetime.

Knowing what he had to do, once in the library he shut the door and then hitched one hip on the corner of the desk. He gestured toward a facing chair and she perched there, her sequined skirt flowing like water over her pressed-together knees. She wore an expectant expression along with that porn-star dress and he shrugged off the feeling he was about to trod on a kitten.

"Listen—" He hesitated, unsure how to begin. "I don't think the arrangement we discussed on the phone will work out after all."

Her green eyes narrowed, a kitten sensing trouble. "Is there a problem?"

"Not a problem, exactly."

She slid closer to the edge of the leather seat. "Didn't my references check out?"

"Your references were fine. Glowing, actually." She'd given him a list. Professors at local universities, curators at two nearby museums, the president of a collectors' organization.

Rory ran a hand over his short hair. "Next month we move out. But before we leave I'm hosting an important party here at the estate. I think it might be too much trouble and take too much time to sort, catalog, and clear everything away before then. One call and some local thrift store will send a few trucks and get it all out in a couple of days."

"You can't do that!" Jilly's voice rose, and then she swallowed and started again, more quietly this time. "I'm sure it's hard to understand the value of what you have, but believe me, it's considerable. Some of your grandfather's things—the costumes—he promised to a museum. As I mentioned on the phone, I'll give you a bargain on my appraisal and cataloging services if you'll let me purchase some of the other pieces from you."

He closed his eyes, rubbing at the headache building between his brows. "Still—"

"It's personal, isn't it?"

His eyes popped open guiltily. "Personal?" he echoed. She looked at him, those pretty green eyes wide, her voluptuous breasts rising above the dress, her hair curling uncontrollably against her shoulders. "No," he lied.

"Then I want to do this," she said firmly.

*Damn.* Couldn't she just let it go? "It'll take too much time—"

"I have the time. You told me over the phone the extent of the collection, but still I'm confident I can get it done by your deadline."

Rory felt like straws were sifting through his fingers. "Your own shop," he said, grasping at the last one he could think of. "How can you leave it unattended—"

"I have a partner. Assistants. And anyway, a lot of our business is off the Web these days."

Before he could come up with another protest, she jumped out of her chair. "Let me show you what I'm talking about."

In a flash of winking sequins, she whipped around his desk and seated herself in the chair in front of his laptop computer. Her small hand cupped his mouse. "May I?"

What could he do but dumbly agree? He walked around the desk to stand behind her, nobly training his gaze on the computer instead of down her dress. She tilted the screen so he could see better, and then expertly point-and-clicked to log on to his Web browser. From there she almost instantly took him to a Web site titled "Things Past," which listed its proprietor as Jilly Skye.

In his ten years in the Silicon Valley, Rory had seen thousands of Web sites and this one wasn't bad, not bad at all. Colorful, but not cluttered, it presented the customer with clear choices such as "Women's Wear pre-1920" and "Victorian Undergarments."

His eyebrows rose. Victorian undergarments? His curiosity piqued, he was disappointed when she clicked on a different button that displayed a page of well-photographed dresses from the 1940s. Below each photo, a caption listed the size and price.

"How many user sessions do you get a month?" he asked, referring to the number of cyberspace visitors who stopped by her site.

She named an impressive figure, then impressed him even more by confiding the dollar amount of Web business they'd collected in the last quarter of the previous year. Smiling somewhat smugly, she did a little more maneuvering with his mouse, and suddenly the screen presented the interior image of a clothing store.

His eyebrows rose again. "A Web cam?" he asked.

She nodded, her small smile reminding him of kittens again, and cream. "A little bit of fluff, really, and, uh, my Webmistress is still working on it, but we thought it might attract more customers."

As he watched, the camera slowly panned the store, and he saw a few people browsing, a young woman behind a cash register, and attractive displays of clothing. "Not bad," he admitted. "And if someone's fancy is taken by an item—"

She pointed a finger toward a box on the screen. "Our toll-free number, or they can e-mail us."

He was still watching the monitor when Jilly Skye suddenly swung the chair around, its rotating seat whining in light protest. "So?" she said, her gaze suddenly intent on his. "Do I get the job or not?"

*Hell.* Rory had been so caught up in the Web site he hadn't been inventing new reasons to refuse. "I . . . Let me think a minute." He rubbed his hand over his hair, rubbed the back of his neck, rubbed his chin, all the while trying to look away from Jilly Skye's admirable assets and pretty little face with its serious green eyes and kissable pink mouth.

She lifted one hand to smooth the tangles from her hair, then glanced down to check the knot on her strap. Oh, sure, remind him that he and Auntie's beast had mauled her less than thirty minutes ago. Then she used the mouse to swim the cursor around the Web cam's image of her shop. Fine, so maybe her business practices weren't as flaky as the rest of her. Finally, her fingertips drifted across the desk to idly touch the edges of the calendar he had opened there.

God, and then there was that. Who else was he going to get to do the job in a timely manner? Her references had assured him she was the best.

Jilly looked back up. "Well?"

"I . . . yes," he found himself saying. *Damn.*

Instantly aware he'd just screwed up, he wanted to thump his forehead against the wall. But he couldn't take it back because, as if she'd guessed he wanted to, she was already out of the chair and smiling and pumping his hand.

She was grateful, she said. She would start the job first thing in the morning. With one more flash of sequins and one more flash of smile, she was out the library door and then out the front door of the house.

The sudden and energetic burst of activity

made his head spin. That and the waft of too-warm, too-sweet-scented air that washed over him once he made it to the front door himself and opened it to watch Jilly Skye steer her junkyard car down the long, winding driveway.

She took it slowly, probably unwilling to push her battered vehicle too hard. Despite her care, the woody wagon popped and rattled, proclaiming, if its owner were willing to listen—which Rory adamantly doubted—that something this old and this odd should have been junked years before. As she rounded the first curve, the second-to-the-last thing Rory saw was a cherry-red roof and a hand lifted in a cheerful farewell.

Only when he saw the very last thing, a final wink of gold sequins, did he realize he should at least have suggested a more modest mode of dress.

Rory shook his head. Only in L.A. Now that he'd involved himself with another of its kooks, something was bound to go wrong.

It was only a question of *how* wrong it would be.

Jilly's heart was beating so fast she wondered if she'd swallowed one of the hummingbirds that flitted about the flowering shrubs lining the Caidwater driveway. Squeezing the steering wheel tightly, she just managed to tamp down her excitement as she drove through the wrought-iron gates and turned in the direction of home.

But she wouldn't make it all the way back without stopping first, not with the news she had to share. Jilly guided the car to a wide, shaded shoulder of the road. With the engine off and the emergency brake on, she reached under the passenger seat for her cell phone. Her fingers shook so hard she couldn't press the buttons, so she held it against her thrumming heart for a moment.

She'd done it! Rory Kincaid had agreed.

*Rory Kincaid.* A funny knot in her belly blossomed, releasing heat that rose to kiss her skin.

Goose bumps broke out on her forearms even as she tried banishing the man from her mind. Whispering good ol' Bill's name at every opportunity hadn't transformed Rory from gorgeous to geeky, that's for sure. He'd turned out to be six lean feet of black hair, blue eyes, and unusual, almost exotic features.

Exotic features that instantly conjured up images of—

*No.* Squirming against her seat, she willed the silliness away. The way the man ignited her imagination not only was unsettling, it was untimely. Hip-hopping hormones had no place in her plan.

Still . . . She sighed. For some unexplained reason, the instant she'd seen Rory, and when she thought of him now, a daydream unfolded in her mind. A most peculiar daydream in which—

*Beep.* Jilly jumped, then loosened her button-pushing clutch on the cell phone. She glanced around guiltily, slightly appalled by this entirely new and almost kinky turn of her mind.

Maybe she needed to eat more vegetables. Or switch to decaf coffee. Certainly she was suffering from some sort of deficiency, because she was mooning over a man when she had more vital things to do. Jilly had wrongs to right.

With her thumb, she flicked the phone on and pressed the first speed-dial entry. A familiar voice answered, reedy with nervousness. Jilly forgot her worrisome reaction to Rory Kincaid and smiled so wide her cheeks hurt. "I'm in!" she said jubilantly. "And I saw *her*."

# $\big\backslash$ Chapter 2

Still brimming with excitement Jilly hurried through FreeWest, the small, offbeat neighborhood where she lived and worked. Named for the two main cross streets of the eight-square-block section—Freewood Drive and Westhill Avenue—FreeWest was cool, it was hip, and if the crowded sidewalks were any indication, it was happening.

Winding around the shoppers, Jilly smiled to herself. In other parts of L.A., her appearance in bedraggled evening dress might cause people to walk the other way. But here it raised only a few curious eyebrows.

FreeWest was famous for its eccentricity and energy. What was one knotted-together sequined gown in the midst of boutiques, a small art-film theater, an astrologer's parlor, and more than two dozen other to-the-left-of-mainstream-but-thriving businesses?

She passed Beans & Leaves, the beverage bar half a block from her store, then French Letters, the store next door to her own. As usual, people jammed its aisles, hovering beside shelves displaying condoms in every conceivable texture, style, color, and flavor. The manager stood behind a countertop, his fingertips drumming impatiently upon it. Jilly sent him a sympathetic look. He complained that most of the store's patrons were voyeuristic looky-loos, not paying customers, and the silent cash register seemed to prove him right.

Outside her own two-story building, Jilly halted. When under stress, some women baked cookies or scrubbed floors. Kim Sullivan, Jilly's twenty-three-year-old partner, dressed the windows of their shop.

Jilly sighed. Her back to the street, Kim stood in the middle of the window's raised platform "floor," props and pieces of clothing in disarray around her. At five-foot-eleven, she looked like an Amazon trapped in a jewelry box. As usual, she wore jeans and a T-shirt over her model's body and had her long blond hair scraped back in a schoolmarmish bun held in place with two yellow Ticonderoga pencils, a style she'd stuck to since beginning her computer studies over three years ago.

Kim draped two red dresses, their colors clashing painfully, over a rocking chair in the corner of the display. Jilly winced. Kim wasn't any better at decorating shop windows than she was at downplaying her beauty.

To put them both out of their misery, Jilly rapped loudly on the window. Kim whirled around, pantomiming surprise, then smiled giddily when she saw who it was. Jilly took a deep breath to clear her mind of any lingering, inappropriate Rory-effects, then grinned back. She'd report to Kim about the meeting, of course, but absolutely not start talking about *him*.

With the way her imagination was working overtime, who knew what might pop out?

Jilly hurried to enter the store. The bells on the door jangled and Kim was already there to meet her. She grabbed Jilly's hands, her fingers cold, and Jilly grabbed back. "Tell me everything," Kim demanded, her voice excited and her grip tight. "Tell me everything *now*."

This was the moment they'd waited for since they'd seen the obituary in the newspaper a month ago. Scratch that. They'd been waiting *four years* for this moment. "She's beautiful, Kim. Blond hair, blue eyes. I think she's going to be tall like you."

"And did she seem . . . happy? Now that her father has died . . ."

Jilly wished she could reassure her friend with complete certainty. "I don't know, Kim. She didn't appear *un*happy. I only spoke with her for a couple minutes. She has lots of toys and a pretty room." Jilly went on to describe the lacy bedcovers, the rose-colored walls, and the kinds of dolls and books she'd glimpsed.

Once she ran out of details, Kim dropped Jilly's hands to press her fingertips against her eyes. "I can't believe it," she said. "I can't believe you were that close to her."

Blinking back her own tears, Jilly breathed in the delicate potpourri scent of the air. She scanned the store. Toward the back, one of the salesclerks was on tiptoes dusting a high shelf.

Another clerk was helping a customer, and several more patrons happily browsed.

She gently propelled Kim away from the door toward the relative privacy of a corner by the window. Her chest tightened and she pitched her voice low. "It's going to happen, Kim," she said. "We're going to find a way to reunite you with your daughter."

Kim slid her hands away from her eyes. "I never dared hope," she whispered.

"No," Jilly corrected her fiercely. "We *always* hoped." She stared up at her friend. Gone was the incredibly beautiful nineteen-year-old who had shown up at the shop Jilly had just inherited from her mother, toting a small suitcase and a soul-deep desperation. Kim was still unbelievably beautiful—no matter how hard she tried to ignore it—but thanks to her success in college, she now exuded a new confidence.

Except when it came to counting on a future with Iris.

"Jilly, maybe I don't des—"

"*No.* Don't even go there." She knew Kim struggled against feeling that her choices of five years ago made her undeserving, even tainted in some way. "Not now, when I have the opportunity to be at Caidwater—to see Iris—every day. The only thing you should be feeling is hopeful."

After another moment, Kim's tight features relaxed. A small smile played around her mouth. "Blue eyes, you said?"

"But with your blond hair," Jilly quickly added.

Kim gazed off into the distance. "Roderick had blue eyes."

Rory Kincaid did, too. Cool, dark blue eyes that made her think of—*No!* She didn't want to think of Rory Kincaid at all.

Kim was looking at her, her brow furrowed. "What?"

Jilly's eyes widened and her face heated. Had she said something? Made some sound? She definitely needed to switch to decaf. Decaf and some big helpings of cauliflower.

She cleared her throat. "I meant to say that Roderick Kincaid was a bastard, a cruel, steel-hearted bastard."

Only the cruelest, hardest of men would exercise the rights a naive teenage girl had signed away in prenuptial papers. Megarich and powerful, he and his legion of lawyers had drawn up a beyond-death agreement that couldn't be cracked. When he threw Kim—his seventh wife—out, he'd left her with nothing and kept everything for himself . . . including their infant daughter.

Kim hugged herself, as if feeling a chill. "I wouldn't have survived at the beginning if it hadn't been for you. You've always been the one with the strength and determination."

Jilly shook her head. "I just get mad better than you and stay mad longer. Anyway, we wouldn't have survived without each other."

The starkness of those times four years ago rushed back to her, too. Still in her black funeral dress, wrinkled and sticky from her furious but determined overnight drive from San Francisco to Los Angeles, Jilly had been wandering the floor of Things Past when Kim had walked in. Her suitcase was full of vintage wear she wanted to sell in order to buy a bus ticket out of L.A. But Jilly hadn't had the faintest idea what the clothing was worth, and was short on cash herself.

At that, Kim had collapsed onto her suitcase and started to cry. Exhausted and emotional, Jilly joined her. But then their tears dried up and their stories started flowing. Understanding followed. An understanding that was the cornerstone of their deep friendship.

And they both understood that Kim's getting Iris back was going to help heal Jilly, too. Or at least bring her some peace.

Suddenly, Kim's eyes rounded and she blinked. "My goodness, I just noticed! What happened to you?" Her gaze ran over Jilly's disheveled evening gown.

Jilly half smiled. "Woman meets chinchilla."

"What?"

"Iris has a pet. She told me Greg gave it to her."

Kim's face went completely blank. "Greg? You mean Rory's brother?"

"I suppose." Jilly shrugged. "I got the impression he lives at the house, too."

There was a moment of silence as Kim seemed once more to retreat into the past. Then she shook her head and her eyes refocused. "I still can't believe you did it, Jilly. So tell me about Rory Kincaid. Do you think he'll be reasonable?"

At the mention of his name, Rory's image roared to life in Jilly's mind. Oh, boy. She pasted an urgent but bright smile on her face. "Give me a moment to run up and change, 'kay? Then I'll tell you all about him." Right. Just as soon as she could reduce him to reasonable proportions in her imagination.

In her tiny apartment upstairs, the one that was a mirror image of Kim's, which lay on the other side of a matchstick-wide hallway, Jilly wriggled out of the evening gown. She reached for jeans and a vintage, pink bowling shirt embroidered with the name "Angel." Then she slid her feet into bubble-gum-colored sneakers. There. Perfect fix-the-window-Kim-bungled clothing. Which was a perfect avoid-the-conversation-Kim-began occupation. Some instinct warned Jilly that if she started talking about Rory, her imagination might—

Clamping down on the thought, she ran into the kitchen, grabbed three baby carrots, and crammed them into her mouth before going downstairs. Maybe Kim would forget the whole line of conversation if Jilly got busy.

As if. Nobody knew better than she that Kim's brains were as awesome as her beauty.

So although Jilly had climbed into the display window while Kim was tied up on the phone, as soon as the receiver slid into its rest, Kim immediately came to hover. Jilly had already removed the horribly clashing red dresses. Her heart sinking and her hands on her hips, she avoided Kim's gaze by pretending to be intently considering the placement of the props—a folding screen, a small hip bath, a narrow rocking chair, and a square-topped table.

Kim sighed. "I shouldn't have tried to do the

window for you. I did my best to follow your sketch, but . . ." She shrugged.

Relief waved over Jilly. "That's okay." She dragged the folding screen to one corner, adjusted the hip bath so it was nearly dead center, then set the small table beside it. The rocking chair she pushed into the opposite corner from the screen.

Good. Now the area looked ready for a lady's bath, especially with corkscrew streamers of iridescent packing material filling the tub to resemble bubbles. Jilly retrieved one of the garments she'd decided to use. As if a woman had just disrobed, Jilly draped the white cotton-and-lace summer dress, circa 1910, over the top of the folding screen. Old-fashioned, white linen high-top boots went on the floor beneath the dress. Over one corner of the screen she balanced a straw, lace-trimmed hat.

"Now tell me about Rory."

At Kim's command, Jilly's hand jerked, sending the pretty straw and lace tumbling. Biting her bottom lip, she retrieved, then carefully rebalanced, the hat before replying. "You know," she said vaguely.

"I don't. I told you, I never met him when I was married to Roderick. What's he like?"

*Nothing like Bill Gates, more's the pity.* No glasses, not even a teeny-weeny pocket protector! Instead, Rory reminded her of—Jilly shivered, then halted her wayward mind from going in that strange new direction it had so recently discovered.

She folded a length of towel, edged with delicate tatting, over the lip of the tub. "He was very, uh, businesslike."

Except when he'd had his hands in her hair. Her scalp had prickled and tickled and she'd almost felt her curly hair twisting in tighter coils. Closing her eyes against the remembered sensation, she dove her fingers into the packing material inside the tub, mindlessly fluffing the "bubbles."

"Businesslike? Well maybe that explains it," Kim said. "The interest the Blue Party has in him, I mean."

"What interest is that?"

"Rumor has it that Rory Kincaid is going to be the new political party's first candidate," Kim said. "For the U.S. Senate."

"Mmm." Jilly moved away from the tub and unfolded a square of ecru eyelet over the top of the little table. She didn't want to think about politics any more than she wanted to think about Rory Kincaid. It was a definite noninterest of hers. Politics was a passion of her grandmother's, which Jilly had come to realize was just one more way for the woman to control people like chess pieces.

With careful movements, Jilly set several brightly colored perfume flasks on the tabletop.

"But come on, Jilly, what did you *think* of him?"

Jilly's hand involuntarily twitched, and the flasks toppled like bowling pins. She sent her friend a harried look. "What *would* I think of him, for gosh sake? I was raised by a Puritan and educated by nuns. I'm not exactly prepared to form an opinion about a man like that."

Which was precisely why she'd banished him from her mind. Though Grandmother wasn't

Catholic, Jilly had attended Our Lady of Peace Academy because it was the most rigorous— make that rigid—kindergarten through senior high to be found in the San Francisco Bay area. Behind the cold walls of a former nunnery, Jilly and her equally cowed female classmates had been taught by Sister Teresa and Sister Bernadette and Sister Maria Guadalupe, but had never learned anything about the ways of men.

The perfume bottles finally just so, Jilly escaped from the table before another awkward movement revealed her silly agitation. She grabbed a pair of stubbed-toe, 1970s Frye boots and set them on the floor of the display beside the rocking chair. Wide-leg jeans of the same vintage went across the seat, and a rainbow-colored, tie-dyed T-shirt over the chair's back. Stepping away, she assessed the display. From left to right, it suggested a demure woman of the early 1900s transforming into the retro-hip gal of the new millennium. Exactly as planned.

With two notable exceptions. Eager to complete the job, she quickly set up a light aluminum ladder. Kim disappeared into the back office and swiftly returned with the last pieces for the new window display. Jilly beamed at her. Already Kim had been quiet for approximately ninety seconds, and with luck, this chore would get her mind off probing any further about Rory.

Jilly mounted the ladder, and then reached toward Kim. Her friend held out a clear plastic bubble about the size of a volleyball, with a small plastic loop on top that had a length of heavy fishing line attached. Inside the bubble was Kim's real contribution to the display. She'd been tasked with finding two appropriate photos off the Internet, one of a turn-of-the-century hunk, the other of a current heartthrob. Each plastic bubble held an enlarged printout of a man's face.

Jilly tied the fishing line on a teacup hook screwed into the ceiling over the tub. She smiled, turning the bubble to appreciate the handlebar mustache and handsome features in this photo. Yes. It looked just like the frothy bubble of a woman's fantasy hanging over her bath.

Jilly reached for the other plastic bubble. Kim cleared her throat, but Jilly didn't spare her a glance as she concentrated on tying this one a bit higher than the first. Satisfied, she was more than halfway down the ladder before she actually looked at the image in the second bubble, the modern female fantasy. She froze.

Kim cleared her throat once more. "Well?"

Jilly blinked, then looked at the image again. In the other bubble was Rory. Rory's face.

"When I was doing my Web research, I ran across his photo."

Kim's explanation floated past Jilly's ears as everything about the real Rory Kincaid burst in her mind, in vivid and unsuppressible living color.

"So, um." Kim waved her hand to break Jilly's trance. "What do you think?"

*I'm thinking I'm in real big trouble.* Because it was getting harder and harder to ignore that funny little fantasy that was sparked by the mere mention of his name. She couldn't figure out why a woman like her would even have such a fantasy, but she couldn't seem to get rid of it. Even now it flowered—

*No.* She couldn't, shouldn't, go there. This craziness she was experiencing just had to be due to some kind of vitamin deficiency.

She looked at Kim. "Broccoli," Jilly said urgently. "Do you have any broccoli?"

Kim frowned. "Are you okay? What happened to you out there?"

Jilly swallowed. She barely noticed that, instead of the platform floor, she had stepped off the ladder and into the tub. Even though she was up to her thighs in faux bubbles, it hardly made a dent in her consciousness. Maybe Kim could help her make sense of what was going on.

She lowered her voice. "I don't know if I'm okay. It's the weirdest thing and I can't seem to understand it. I went there expecting Bill Gates"—she closed her eyes and pictured broad-shouldered, lean-hipped Rory Kincaid striding across the driveway to meet her, the other-worldly magnificence of Caidwater the backdrop behind him—"and instead, I met a blue-eyed, dark-haired desert prince."

"A *prince*?"

"It gets worse." Her eyes still closed, Jilly swallowed again, hot shivers crawling over her skin. "But maybe you can explain it to me. For some odd reason, this daydream keeps playing in my mind. Every time I think of him, I see a desert prince. A sexy, hot-eyed desert prince who leads me into his Moorish castle—a luxurious fortress, actually—where he vows to keep me as his prisoner until he no longer desires me. Next he . . ."

Another shiver ran its heated course down Jilly's back. But then a strange, choked sound caused her eyes to snap open and she looked at Kim. Kim, who appeared one giggle away from peals of laughter. On a wave of embarrassment, Jilly closed her mouth, as a sudden and undeniable realization finally pierced the slave-girl veils she had been about to describe herself as wearing.

*Oh. My. God.*

With a groan, she slid down into the tub, avoiding Kim's knowing, amused gaze by burying her hot face in the mounds of tickling, plastic bubbles. This was Rory Kincaid she was fantasizing about. Rory Kincaid, who had stared at her like she was nuts, and who stood between her best friend and her best friend's daughter.

And she didn't need her best friend to explain what was going on after all. Moorish castles! Hot-eyed princes! Goose bumps, prickly scalps, an awareness of her body she'd never experienced before.

She, Jilly Skye—raised by a Puritan and educated by nuns—*lusted* after Rory Kincaid! Lust. A totally wild and completely inappropriate lust that was no longer a secret.

Even from herself.

# ₯ Chapter 3

The rattle of Jilly Skye's mode of transportation—
Rory hesitated to term it a "car"—pierced the
morning air and even penetrated the thick plaster
walls of Caidwater. He squeezed the receiver of
the cordless phone he was holding to his ear and
peered through the library window.

He must have groaned out loud, because the
man he was supposed to be listening to, his
mentor, California's current U.S. Senator, the
Honorable Benjamin Fitzpatrick, broke off in the
middle of what he'd been saying. "What, son? Is
there a problem?"

By then she'd braked that red monstrosity to a
halt and stepped out. "Everything's fine, sir. You
were saying?"

Oh, but there was a problem. A big problem.
Yesterday's evening-gowned woman hadn't
turned tall, flat, and conservatively dressed
overnight. Not even close. Today, Jilly's curvy
cupcake body was poured into flower-child
revival wear—a white, peasanty blouse and a
pair of jeans gaudily overdecorated with multi-
colored patches and intricate embroidery. He

automatically clapped his free hand over his shirt pocket, feeling for his sunglasses. It hurt to look at the garish, peacock-hued pants.

Worse, even the fact that the blouse's gathered folds hid her heavenly endowments, even though she'd contained her riotous mass of tendrils with a large clip, his mind could vividly detail every inch of her lushness and his hand still tingled from the enticing tickle of her hair. On top of that, now his fingers itched to trace the bright red peace sign on her back pocket and the daisy chain winding around her thigh.

And he had a meeting at Caidwater this afternoon that demanded his undivided focus.

"Rory? Rory? Son, are you there?"

He jerked his attention back to the senator. "Yes. Yes, sir. Right here. I'll be expecting the team at two o'clock."

The older man's voice filled with satisfaction. "Good. You've been stalling far too long."

Rory shifted restlessly. He still thought it was premature to meet with the Blue Party's strategic team about the concrete details of his election bid. "You know I'd prefer to wait until my candidacy is formally announced."

"That's just for show, and you know it. For all intents and purposes, you already *are* our candidate." The senator droned on, going over once more the meeting's agenda.

Rory listened with half an ear. *That's me.* The Blue Party candidate, he thought, waiting for, expecting, a surge of satisfaction. Then he waited some more. In vain.

He frowned. Knowing that the senator believed Rory's own integrity and character were strong enough to overcome both his grandfather's and his father's lifetime of scandals should have him soaring. But instead, unease gripped the back of his neck like a cold hand.

His trepidation didn't make any sense. Last year, when he'd been appointed to a federal committee investigating e-commerce fraud, he'd been pleased when his service brought him to the attention of Senator Fitzpatrick. He'd immediately liked the man and had always admired his politics. They'd moved easily from a professional relationship to a friendship Rory valued highly.

At loose ends due to the recent sale of his software company, Rory had been more than flattered when the older man started talking up the new Blue Party and the Senate candidacy. Not that Rory saw Washington, D.C., through rose-colored glasses. He knew there were egos and power-mongers at work there, but he also believed that with his family background, he was more suited than many to sniff them out.

Yet what had appealed to him most about the whole idea was that the Blue Party aimed to make over politics just as Rory wanted to make over the Kincaid name. The Blue Party and Rory wanted to bring honor back.

In the Senate candidacy, it seemed that Fate had crafted an opportunity made precisely for him.

He gazed out the window, watching Jilly Skye bend over to pull a satchel out of her car. Those worn jeans of hers cupped her sweet, rounded rear end as tightly as a man's palms would. He bit back another groan. Fate, the wily wench, had crafted the opportunity to meet the tempting Jilly, too.

His cheerless mood was all her fault, dammit. Just like yesterday, seeing her made him want to cover his head and duck, waiting for that proverbial other shoe to drop.

Rory cleared his throat, unable to completely tamp down his panic. "Excuse me, Senator, but I have to get off the phone now." With the momentous meeting this afternoon, the one where he'd face the Blue Party's new campaign director for the first time, it wasn't too soon to get the delectable Jilly behind the barricades of his grandfather's collection. With luck, Rory could lock up his mind's devilish thoughts with her.

"Just don't let Charlie Jax spook you, son."

"What? Spook me?" Rory's attention refocused on Senator Fitzpatrick. "What's that mean?"

The senator's chuckle didn't sound all that reassuring. "He's an excellent asset to the Blue Party, even if he is a trifle forceful."

Rory groaned. "Senator, your 'trifle forceful' is everyone else's 'will flatten you like a steamroller.' "

Senator Fitzpatrick chuckled again. "You'll be able to handle him. You swore you were up to new challenges."

Rory groaned louder, resisting the urge to look out the window again. "It's at moments like this that I'm convinced my real challenge is to make you run for another term."

Still chuckling, the senator hung up on the thought.

With the call ended, Rory hurried from the

library and opened the door before his nettle-
some nemesis could press the bell. Her eyes
widened as she took in what he hoped was a for-
bidding expression.

"Come along," he said. With no more greeting
than that, he grabbed the leather bag she carried
and led the way toward the eastern wing of the
house.

"Hello to you, too, Mr. Kincaid," she murmured. "Yes, indeedy, it *is* a fine morning."

He frowned and slanted her a glance.

She peeked up at him from curly, curly lashes
and smiled. In the creamy skin of her left cheek,
something he hadn't noticed before flashed.

*Dammit!*

A dimple. This midget-sized bar of sex candy
had a dimple! It was the kind of disarming decoration that could make some men forget today's
flower-power wear and yesterday's sequins and
everything else that proved she was just another
example of L.A.'s weirdest and wackiest.

He tried to convince himself he wasn't "some
man."

Then he came to a stop at the head of a long
hallway, standing in front of one of several closed
doors on either side. With a speculative glance he
eyed a massive refectory table against a nearby
wall. If he removed the tall Oriental vases collected there and solicited help from the gardeners, maybe—once he got Jilly down that hall—he
could tip the table on its side and shove the thing
across the opening. Locking her up sounded
good.

A slightly gothic idea, true, but Jilly Skye with

a winking dimple in her left cheek and an embroidered begonia on her ass was as seriously dangerous to his "true-blue" Blue Party ambitions as a mad wife locked in the attic.

He gestured in the direction of the doors. "You can start here," he said. The ten rooms should keep her out of his hair for at least several days. In a hurry to return to his office, he waited impatiently for her to move forward. There were notes to make and schedules to consider. Begonias and dimples to forget.

But Jilly Skye wasn't moving at all. "Here?" she said, looking at the closed doors.

Rory stepped forward again. *Just to get her started*, he told himself. He brushed past her and opened the first door, and then he kept walking down the hall, leaning from one side to the other, opening door after door after door.

Jilly still didn't move.

Rory walked back toward her, frowning. Her eyes were wide as they took in the sight of the rooms, filled with rows of clothing on freestanding racks. "Damn," he said. "I should have shown all this to you yesterday. Do you want to back out?"

The fact that he suddenly hated the idea was merely because it would mean additional hassle, of course.

Jilly's feet unfroze, carrying her slowly into the first room. Her fingers caressed the wool sleeve of a man's suit hanging on the nearest rack. "No," she said, sounding dazed. "I don't want to back out."

"Are you sure?" he asked, though he was understandably relieved. "There's another set of rooms just like this one in the other wing."

Jilly's eyes widened. "More?"

"And even more." He raked a hand through his hair. "The stuff is everywhere, Jilly."

She walked deeper into the room, both hands outstretched to touch the fabrics of all the suits, shirts, ties—junk, in Rory's opinion—that the old man had hung onto over the years. Suddenly she whirled, her eyes bright and that dimple of hers threatening to show itself again. "Everywhere, you said?"

He nodded, completely baffled by her eagerness. That clinched it. She *was* nuts.

After leaving Caidwater ten years ago, he'd made it a practice to avoid asylum escapees at every opportunity, so he stepped back, only to find himself pausing. "You *really* like this stuff?"

"Adore it."

He couldn't get over his surprise. "Why?"

She caressed the black velvet of a cape his grandfather had probably donned in some old movie. "Did you ever wear a school uniform?" she asked.

He shook his head.

"I did," she said. "A gray-and-white uniform. I wore it for thirteen years. And my grandmother's house, it was mainly gray and white too. Come to think of it, so is my grandmother's personality. Cold white and controlled gray.

"But this!" She whirled around again and he found himself fascinated by the energy vibrating from her small body. "Linens, tweeds, blues, greens, colors, textures." One arm lifted, as if to embrace it all.

Then something caught her eye. She moved forward, inexorably forward, drawn like other women were drawn to powerful men. Her hand reached out to reverently stroke something filmy and crimson-colored.

Her fingertips swept it caressingly again, and Rory's blood made a southward rush.

"This." Her voice was just above a whisper. "This is about as far from gray and white as I can get. It represents living to me, exciting, no-holds-barred, multihued *living*."

She sighed.

With that wistful, blissful sound, Rory's blood heated again, but for an entirely different reason than a reaction to the sight of her stroking, caressing fingers. He was pissed. This was supposed to be a business arrangement and he didn't want it to include Jilly's husky and intimate little admissions about school uniforms. He didn't want her making him think about his stacks of white shirts and rack of dark gray suits.

She gently pushed aside some other clothing to get a better look at the red thing. It was a woman's ball gown, something that would have been right at home on Ginger Rogers. Hell, it probably was hers, if even one-eighth of the legends about his grandfather were true.

Jilly traced some crystal beading with a gentle fingertip. "I didn't realize there was women's clothing in your grandfather's collection. I know he was a bachelor when he passed away."

"Bachelor?" Rory laughed shortly. "If you can call a man with six—no, seven—ex-wives a bachelor."

She gave him a sharp glance.

*There. That was it*, he thought, cursing his own big mouth. That was his signal to leave. He never talked about his family. If forced, he painted them with the lightest of brushes, no anger or bitterness ever allowed.

But despite all that, he couldn't take his gaze off Jilly. She was slowly drawing the crimson fabric over her arm, and he could imagine it wrapped around her hot little body like a tongue wrapped around cinnamon candy.

*Damn.* His cock went hard again and his feet seemed incapable of moving.

"So these clothes belonged to your grandfather's wives?" she asked. The skirt of the dress slid against the creamy skin of her wrist.

"Maybe." His voice was rough. "Maybe some of my father's wives as well, though he's only had four. So far."

She blinked and was silent for a moment. "That's eleven."

"And she can add, too," he murmured. Eleven women had flitted in and out of this house, eleven wives, though of course there had been countless others who'd made it with his father and grandfather but hadn't made it to the altar.

Then he smiled, an angry and bitter smile, because now he knew why Jilly ticked him off so much. She embodied all the trouble in his life. "Just some of that 'exciting, no-holds-barred, multihued living' for you," he said. It was the kind of carpe-diem crap that he detested. The kind of bullshit his family had used for decades to excuse its excesses.

She blinked again and cut her gaze away. "Well." Her hand trailed over another rack of evening dresses. "They certainly left a lot of things behind."

"Oh, my father and grandfather were expert at finding women who didn't mind leaving things behind." He crossed his arms over his chest. "You name it, they left it. Clothes, shoes, hats." He paused. "Even kids."

There was another charged silence. "Oh. Well. Um. But Iris's mother—"

He made a rough gesture. "Bugged out like the rest of them."

Jilly shivered and he was sure it was due to the chilliness in his voice. But he didn't care anymore about hiding his bitterness. Let her know how it really was.

*Exciting, no-holds-barred, multihued living*! What a load of L.A./La-La Land rationalization for irresponsibility.

She cleared her throat. "I, um, guess your grandfather and father had some bad luck when it comes to wives, then."

"Oh, yeah. You could call it bad luck." Rory chuckled humorlessly and backed away from her. "The truth is, all the Kincaid men have made disastrous choices when it comes to women we've wanted to marry."

Hanger hook squealed against metal bar as Jilly transferred a 1930s-era man's suit from one clothing rack to another. She checked the number on the colored tag she'd clipped to the sleeve, then reached for her notebook to catalog the item number, description, and recommended dispensation. Her hand cramped around the pencil and she sighed, looking up as she massaged her stiff fingers. Tomorrow she'd bring her laptop and enter the information directly into a database.

A thump in the hall outside the room made Jilly grab her pencil again and refocus diligently on her record sheet. Even though the entire morning had passed, she didn't want to talk to Rory again quite this soon.

He was too big, too attractive, too . . . bitter.

She squeezed her eyes shut. Obviously Rory wasn't a big fan of the women who'd married into his family.

All eleven of them.

She brushed that disturbing thought away and focused on Kim. With Rory thinking it had been Kim's choice to leave Iris behind, there was work to be done. Jilly didn't exactly know what kind of work it was, but the reaction to Rory that she'd tried so hard to deny yesterday still remained a *huge* hindrance.

Kim had decided it was a great big joke, but after another round of Rory Kincaid's company, Jilly wasn't laughing. Something about the man's exotic looks—that black hair, olive skin, and blue eyes—set her fantasy world spinning.

One minute she'd be touching a man's fedora, and the next she would find herself dashing over sloping, golden sand dunes pursued by a white-robed man on an Arabian horse. The desert prince's laugh rang out, teasing and delicious, and then he reached her, sweeping her up against him. His heart thundered, heavier than horse's hooves, against her back. His blue eyes burned, hot, hot, hot, everywhere their gaze touched her, and then his lips moved, warm against her ear. "Let me take you to the casbah."

She sighed. What really worried her about that recurring fantasy was the "dashing" over the sand dunes that she was doing in it. Because it truly wasn't dashing at all. As a matter of fact, if she were honest, instead of a hurry, it was much more of a hurry-up-and-get-me.

Her ears picked up another thump in the hall. *Oh, no*, she thought. *The prince—I mean Rory.* But then a light patter followed the thump and the clothes in the rack nearest the door started swaying. Unless he'd shrunk to munchkin size, Jilly didn't think the person who'd just crept into the room was the man she wanted to avoid.

Jilly cleared her throat. "Is someone there? Iris?"

Instead of an answer, the clothes swung more wildly and hangers creaked. Maybe the little girl was shy because she didn't remember Jilly from yesterday. After all, she'd been woken from a nap and drowsy.

Smiling to herself, Jilly finished cataloging the suit, though from the corner of her eye she saw a little figure creep closer. She pretended not to notice that Iris was edging up on her. Jilly didn't know much about kids—her grandmother had never let her be one—but she knew about being lonely.

Lonely little girls liked to observe. Lonely little girls watched people first and participated later.

Jilly reached for a shallow-crowned, wide-brimmed lady's hat that was clipped to a nearby hanger. Of black velvet, it was trimmed with gold ostrich feathers. As bait for a four-year-old girl-child, it didn't get much better. With a sweeping movement of her arm, Jilly "accidentally" let go of the hat, and it sailed miraculously close to Iris's hiding place. "Oops!"

Jilly walked toward the hat, but when she bent to retrieve it, she found herself nose to nose with Iris. The black velvet drooping over her eyes, Iris sat cross-legged on the plush carpet. Holding onto her smile, Jilly gently lifted the soft brim and met the Rory-blue of Iris's gaze. "We meet again."

Iris scrambled to her feet, pushing back the hat as she stood. One of the gold feathers wagged back and forth like a dog's tail. "You're the lady who gave me water."

Jilly stared in surprise at the child's outfit. It wasn't the hat. It was that the hat actually went with the dress Iris was wearing. On a weekday noon, the girl was dressed in a floor-length, black velvet gown. It was long-sleeved and high-necked, and rows of gold lace banded the skirt from the Empire waistline to the hem.

"So you're, uh, playing dress-up?"

Iris looked down. "No. Rory handed this to me."

"Gee. Well. It's certainly fancy." And though Jilly liked to dress up herself, Iris's outfit was completely inappropriate for a four-year-old on any occasion short of an audience with the queen.

Apparently Rory knew less about kids than she did. She smiled. "What have you been doing this morning?"

"Helping Mrs. Mack."

Mrs. Mack was the housekeeper. She'd introduced herself to Jilly shortly after Rory had left her alone this morning. Jilly looked at the dusty smudge along one of Iris's velvet sleeves. "I'll bet Mrs. Mack was cleaning."

Iris nodded, her thumb creeping up toward her mouth; then she snatched it back down.

Jilly silently admired the little girl's self-control. That was something else they had in common—thumb-sucking. Jilly had comforted herself the same way until she was five years old. Then her grandmother had the dentist make Jilly a device she wore at night. If she forgot her grandmother's edict against the habit while sleeping, sharp metal teeth stabbed the pad of Jilly's thumb. She could still remember waking up from the sting.

"Well . . ." Jilly worried her lower lip. The little girl continued to solemnly regard her and Jilly didn't know what to say next.

Iris's stomach growled and she giggled.

Jilly smiled, too. Hunger was a transgenerational language. "It sounds like you're ready for lunch."

Iris nodded.

"Me, too." She plucked the velvet hat off Iris's head. "Shall we go find something to eat? Mrs. Mack took my lunchbox earlier. She said it would be in the refrigerator in the kitchen. Would you show me where that is?"

Iris nodded. "You have a lunchbox?"

Unsure how the day would play out, Jilly had brought her meal with her. "I certainly do. How about yourself?"

Iris shook her head. "I always eat my lunch in the kitchen."

"Of course you do." Jilly followed the little girl down the hallway. "Who makes your lunch? Mrs. Mack?"

"Rory. He says Mrs. Mack has enough to do."

Jilly's eyebrows rose. He helped the child dress *and* he made her lunch? "You don't have a nanny? Someone whose job it is to care for you?"

"Nina got a new job taking care of a baby."

Jilly's heart twisted. The little girl had lost her father and her nanny, only to gain a man who overdressed her in black velvet and gold lace.

Iris led the way down a short flight of steps, then pushed through a swinging door to reveal a kitchen as large as Jilly's store. Bright fluorescent lighting bounced off white floors, granite countertops, and stainless-steel appliances, dazzling her for an instant. She blinked, then noticed, miles away at the far end of the room, a dark-haired man shutting one of two side-by-side Sub-Zero refrigerators.

Rory glanced toward them. "Iris—Auntie. I was just coming to look for you. Your lunch is almost ready." He opened the refrigerator again and reached inside. "And I'll hazard a guess that this"—he turned toward Jilly and held out her vintage *Lost in Space* lunchpail, "is yours."

*Oh, darn.* As much as she'd been hoping to avoid Rory, the only choice she had now was to cross that shiny floor and take it from him. He didn't turn back to the lunch he was preparing, but instead watched her, his gaze steady.

She hesitated. Even from this distance she could feel something tugging at her. *He* was tugging at her, even without a movement of his tall, lean body. As if they had a will of their own, her feet moved forward. Rory kept watching.

As she crossed the floor, Jilly became aware of herself in a strange, new, maddening way. She noticed the rhythm of her steps. Her body moved fluidly, sensually. With each stride, the cotton of her peasant top rubbed her navel with small, soft strokes, but it was enough to tickle goose bumps to the surface. And as quickly as her body temperature was rising, the little prickles ran down her legs, across her arms, and over her chest. Her nipples tightened.

*Oh, my.*

Without thinking, she licked her lips and Rory's gaze sharpened. Jilly stumbled, appalled by her own actions. One minute it was lustful fantasies starring the maddening man, the next it was a wet-mouthed vamp stroll in his direction. She'd never done things like this in her life. What was her problem?

And then it hit her, her understanding sudden and even more appalling. She stumbled again.

*Rory brought out the bad in her.*

Maybe her grandmother was right about Jilly after all.

But even that disturbing thought didn't turn off the supersensitivity. Every time her legs moved, she could feel the rub of denim against the flesh at the backs of her knees, and the rough strokes sent prickles *up* her thighs this time. Her beaded nipples pushed at the cups of her bra.

*Oh, please. Don't let him notice.*

Luck was on her side. When she reached him, he held out the lunchbox, his face expressionless, his eyes focused in the vicinity of her nose. Neutral enough. But when Jilly grasped the handle, Rory didn't let go. Her glance jumped from the box's metallic likenesses of Robot and little Will Robinson to Rory's white knuckles, to Rory's eyes, staring, it seemed reluctantly, in the direction of her breasts.

Jilly's mouth dried, her appetite disappeared, and her goose bumps got goose bumps. Oh, no. She shut her eyes.

Maybe she brought out the bad in him, too.

"I want my lunch."

Rory blinked, then looked away. Iris's voice returned Jilly to normality as well. Her skin was just her skin, her walk just a way to move, Rory just a man who . . . continued to make her skin tingle.

As for him, though, he appeared completely cool and calm. She'd probably imagined the entire holding-the-lunchbox-handle episode.

*Whew.* From the beginning, she had hoped they might come to a sort of friendship, but nothing more than that was safe—not safe or smart at all.

Jilly glanced at the countertop and the plate Rory had prepared for Iris. She did a double take. As big as a platter, the white ceramic was covered with a wide variety of food, from slices of roast beef to miniature marshmallows.

Iris was inspecting the plate, too. She'd climbed up on a stepstool beside Rory that Jilly guessed was there for expressly that purpose. A small finger pointed at the roast beef. "No."

Rory whisked the meat off the plate.

"No," Iris said again, this time pointing to several celery sticks.

Jilly looked at Rory. He swallowed, then nudged the offending celery onto the counter.

"No, no, no." Half a peanut butter sandwich, two pieces of apple, and a wedge of cheese were summarily dismissed.

Rory had paled. Jilly's brows came together as she watched him studying Iris's face. He looked intent, no, nervous, as he waited for her verdict.

Her gaze roamed the plate. "Okay," she finally said.

Rory slowly released a pent-up breath and rubbed a hand against the back of his neck as the little girl stepped off the stool. He handed her the plate and she made a careful path toward a small table set under a window.

Aghast, Jilly looked from Rory to Iris's lunch to Rory again. "There wasn't any food on that plate."

He turned his back on her. "Nonsense," he said. "There was plenty."

She couldn't believe what she'd heard. "What? Marshmallows, pretzels, vanilla wafers, and a red licorice vine? You call that food?"

The refrigerator door shut with a slam. "Haven't you heard of the four C's?"

"The four C's?"

"Calcium, carbohydrates, cookies, and candy."

He opened a cold bottle of Pellegrino and poured two glasses of the sparkling water.

Jilly rubbed her forehead. Licorice was the candy, the wafers the cookies, and pretzels the carbos. Her brain slipped into gear. "Tell me you don't consider *marshmallows* calcium?"

He slid one glass of Pellegrino in her direction and lifted the other. "They're white, aren't they? Like milk."

He couldn't be serious. She opened her mouth. "But—"

"Something to drink," Iris commanded from her place at the table.

Rory quickly poured another glass of Pellegrino. Iris just as quickly refused it.

A thought wiggled to life in the back of Jilly's mind as Rory presented his little aunt with three beverages in succession: lemonade, orange juice, and, at her request, Coke.

Wrong. Iris wanted a *Diet* Coke.

Rory didn't bat an eyelash.

With Iris eventually satisfied, he came back to his glass on the countertop. He took a long swallow, as if the beverage effort had dehydrated him.

Jilly sipped her own water. "What happened to Iris's nanny?"

He cleared his throat. "She found a new position. I'm moving Iris out of here in a few weeks and I decided to wing it until we get settled."

"And is the 'winging it' going well?" He had to know that velvet dresses and marshmallow lunches weren't standard kid caretaking.

Rory shrugged. "We're getting accustomed to one another," he said, his voice neutral.

"It must be difficult, though," Jilly pointed out. Maybe reuniting Kim with Iris could be as simple as appealing to Rory's inconvenience. "A bachelor suddenly taking on a child."

"The difficulty isn't the point," he answered firmly. "She's my responsibility and I plan on raising her well."

Jilly took another sip of water to cover her surprise. Perhaps he really cared about the little girl.

Then his gaze slid back to Iris and he cleared his throat again. "After you finish lunch, it will be time for a rest," he said to her, a forced note of authority in his voice.

"No."

Jilly's lips twitched as Rory hooked a finger under his collar and pulled it forward. Perhaps he couldn't breathe. And though he might plan on raising his four-year-old aunt "well," at the moment, he wasn't exactly aces in the child management department. The thought from before wiggled around some more in her mind.

"Iris," he began. "I mean, *Auntie . . .*"

"I want to go outside and play." Her voice was spawn-of-the-devil demanding and the look she sent him was barbed. "And I want you to play with me."

Rory pulled on his shirt collar again, then sighed. "Fine."

But Iris wasn't quite through. "I want you to take me on a canoe ride."

"Canoe ride?" Rory shook his head. "No. I have a meeting this afternoon. There's not enough time."

At Rory's denial, the little girl's eyes narrowed. She picked up a marshmallow and squeezed, marshmallow guts oozing from between her thumb and forefinger. "Greg always takes me on the canoe," she said, as if daring Rory to disagree again. Then her gaze locked onto Jilly and she smiled sweetly, a normal, nice, four-year-old's smile. "And you. You'll come, too, won't you please?"

Rory didn't seem to notice that the little girl had spoken to Jilly in a tone different from the one to him. His gaze stayed on Iris as he answered for Jilly. "She can't," he said flatly. "She has work to do."

Jilly frowned. No one told her what she could and couldn't do. Not anymore.

"I want her," Iris said, her eyes narrowing again. "Greg's not here and I want someone else besides you to play with."

Rory's voice softened. "Give me a break, Auntie. She can't."

Jilly knew she shouldn't. Not only was there the cataloging to do, but there was Rory himself. The man made her prickle, for goodness sake. Until she devised a way around that and also devised a way to plead Kim's case successfully, she should stay clear of him. Still . . .

"Can't," Rory repeated.

There was that word again. Jilly hated it. Can't, don't, shouldn't. She'd heard them so often, they'd become the theme of her lonely childhood. And they all smacked of control. Of trying to control her.

"Of course I can play, Iris," she said impulsively. This was Kim's daughter, after all. "I don't know much about canoes, so you'll have to teach me."

Reluctant to check Rory's reaction to her rebellion, Jilly kept speaking to Iris. "But you'll need to eat something else first. I have a Swiss-and-sprouts sandwich in my lunchbox. You can have half."

Iris hesitated for a moment. Jilly didn't waver. "Okay," the little girl agreed. "Half."

"And you'll change into some playclothes," Jilly added. "Something like shorts and a T-shirt."

After a moment, Iris nodded. "Okay."

"Thank God," Rory said under his breath.

Jilly still didn't look at him, but turned and set her lunchbox on the counter. The top popped open and she rummaged for her sandwich. "So you didn't pick that dress for her to wear this morning?"

"Lord, no! She commands, I get it off the hanger."

*Commands.* Now Jilly knew her earlier thought was right, and she almost felt sorry for Rory. Almost. It wasn't as if he weren't trying with Iris. But still, this was an opportunity for Jilly to make a small point in Kim's favor. Maybe if he saw he wasn't the perfect guardian for the little girl now, he would compromise on the issue later.

Jilly glanced up at Rory. "Has it occurred to you that you're terrified of her?"

$\wp$ *Chapter 4*

Terrified of Iris? Rory managed not to dignify that question of Jilly's with an answer, even while they waited in silence for Iris to eat her sandwich and change her clothes. Once those tasks were accomplished, the three of them set off toward the canoe pond in one of the estate's golf carts.

As the two females chatted, he didn't try to join the conversation. It irritated the hell out of him that Jilly was along on this outing. She could have picked up on his not-so-subtle hint and stayed at the house. But no.

He grimaced. Not that he found it so easy to deny Iris either. He had a duty—a duty he took very seriously—to her and he had enough kid-smarts to realize she wasn't exactly thrilled with him. Apparently Roderick had nearly ignored the little girl and Iris looked toward his brother, Greg, for caring and parenting. With Greg out of town on a short press junket for his newest film, the little girl's animosity had grown from bad to worse.

Thinking of his brother gave him a little jab of guilt. Greg had been making noises about wanting to take responsibility for Iris, but Rory couldn't take him seriously. Roderick's instructions were clear, and Rory figured the old man had finally wised up and realized that acting and parenting were a poisonous mix. For once, a Kincaid had considered the welfare of a child in his life. Far be it from Rory to counter the single less-than-selfish decision anyone in his family had ever made.

Laughter broke into his thoughts. Behind him, in the backseat of the golf cart, Jilly was playing knock-knock-who's-there with Iris. Her "Orange you glad I didn't say banana?" punch line delighted the little girl. Rory almost automatically smiled at the giggling, but then turned it to a frown.

Jilly. Not one of *his* most intelligent decisions, he must admit.

Though this morning's run-in with her had reinforced his first impression that she was just another wacky L.A. flake, it was also more reason to keep up his guard. A woman aiming for no-holds-barred living was trouble.

Put that together with the first Blue Party campaign meeting scheduled for this afternoon, and the ever-hovering disaster he sensed gained the weight of a two-ton anvil. He rubbed at the tension clamping the back of his neck.

*Dammit!* Flaky woman and important meeting or no, he couldn't—wouldn't—let that anvil fall. No way. Ten years in the cutting-edge e-world had taught him control. It had taught him to analyze problems rather than let them overwhelm him. One weirdly dressed woman wasn't going to undo all that.

To keep control of this situation with Jilly Skye, all he had to do was detect potential problems, then defuse them. At the thought, a bee buzzed by his nose. *Of course.* His mind immediately focused. *There it is, potential problem number one.*

He stomped on the brakes and turned abruptly toward Jilly. "Are you allergic to bee stings?" he asked, meeting her startled gaze.

It was a valid question. See, a bee sting could pose a serious problem. If she was stung and then stopped breathing, he'd certainly be compelled to perform artificial respiration. His mouth meeting her mouth. God. His blood . . . chilled—yeah, that was it—at the thought.

Her brows drew together and she closed her pink lips on whatever she was saying to Iris, then opened them again. "No."

"Fine." Only partially relieved, he turned back, pressed the accelerator, and continued thinking. What else could possibly go wrong in the next hour? Golf cart . . . pond . . . paddle . . .

And the answer, of course, was obvious. Curvy woman, tippy canoe.

Oh, great. Jilly was going to fall into the water.

He could see it now, that paper-thin shirt plastered wetly against her breasts, the jeans that would shrink-wrap her great butt and thighs. He'd have to get her back to the house, probably in his arms, and the Blue Party team would be early and . . .

Damn. Even worse, there was that threat of

artificial respiration again. He stomped on the
brakes a second time. "Tell me you can swim."

She looked at him like he'd lost his mind.
"Yes."

"You're sure?"

"*Yes.*"

He grunted and accelerated again, slower
now, to steer the cart down the zigzagging path
to the bottom of the canyon. When he braked
for the final time beside the boathouse, he heard
Jilly suck in a breath. He ignored the sound and
jumped out of the cart. Jilly and Iris followed
more slowly, and he had enough time to turn
over the small aluminum canoe and grab a paddle and Iris's life jacket.

Jilly stood on the grassy shore, staring up at the
waterfall that tumbled with a muted roar down
the canyon face to feed the canoe pond. Then her
gaze swept over the rippling ribbon of water that
meandered through Caidwater's nine-hole, par-
three golf course. "This is . . . overwhelming,"
she said.

He handed Iris her life jacket. "Overblown's
more like it." Then he dragged the canoe into the
water and stood beside it on the shore, one foot at
the bottom to steady the light vessel. He crooked
a finger at Iris, then assured himself the little
girl's jacket was secure before lifting her in.
"Front bench, Auntie."

Jilly was next. She moved forward as if to step
inside on her own.

"Uh-uh," Rory said. It was a moment made for
a wet tumble. He grabbed her under her arms,

swinging her from shore to canoe. His fingers sank into the soft sides of her breasts.

Rory froze, Jilly's feet six inches off the ground, her frothy hair tickling his chin. He was glad they weren't face-to-face, but even without looking into the no-holds-barred green of her eyes, what he'd been dreading since the moment he met her happened. Energy traveled between them, some kind of crackly, burning life force that surged up the tensing muscles of his legs and through his fingertips to meet electricity, *spark spark spark*, shooting from the soft, warm heat of her body.

Mouthing a curse, he dropped her with a metallic clunk.

She slid onto the seat beside Iris. Gritting his teeth, Rory took his own behind them. From the moment he'd glimpsed her cherry-red toenails, he'd known she was capital-T trouble. He picked up the paddle. It was skinnier than a certain woman's neck, but he throttled it anyway.

Iris pointed ahead imperiously. "That way."

Rory shoved off smoothly, trying to remain calm. So there was a little sizzle between him and Jilly. No need to be rattled. It was merely another reason to keep a sharp eye out for that anvil-trying-to-drop disaster.

"You two move closer to the center of the bench," he ordered, the premonition of a wet Jilly in his arms flashing through his mind. God, with the sparks flying between them, they'd both be electrocuted.

He paddled slowly and easily, making no risky moves, and directed his few comments exclu-

sively to Iris. The pond was stocked with bass
and trout and he pointed out to her the particular
places he and Greg had fished for them as boys.

The two of them had run wild for a time. But
then, even before Rory's voice had changed, *he*
had changed. There had come a day when he
realized that Caidwater needed at least *one* adult
in residence.

As they floated farther from the waterfall, its
noise became a soft hush in the background. His
paddle swished and swished again, and in the
quiet rhythm of the sound and movement, Rory
found himself relaxing. A fish jumped somewhere ahead and the too-warm sun loosened his
muscles and ignited fiery threads in the curly
darkness of the woman's hair in front of him.

"Stop!"

At Iris's abrupt command, Rory jerked. The
canoe rocked.

Jilly gasped, grabbing for the aluminum side.
The canoe tipped wildly again.

"Hold still," he ordered. He held his breath
until their vessel calmed. "Now," he said, "what
is it you want, Auntie?"

She pointed to his right. "The island. Your and
Greg's island."

They didn't have a lot of time. "I don't think—"

"Please," the little girl said.

The politeness was a first, and the parenting
books he'd been reading recommended reward-
ing children for positive behavior. He wasn't convinced it was smart to actually point out she'd
pleased him, though, so he just silently headed in
the direction of the "island." It wasn't an island at

all, really, but an undeveloped pocket of the canyon floor that wasn't part of the golf course.

Once they reached it, Iris scrambled out before he could help her, and Rory had to stab his paddle in the squishy pond bottom to keep both Jilly and himself from tumbling.

She braced herself by gripping the rocking side and peered anxiously in the direction the little girl had taken. "Will she be all right?"

He nodded. "My brother brings her here a lot. It was one of our favorite places when we were kids."

She half turned to straddle the bench and shaded her eyes with her hand to get a good look at him. "You grew up here?"

He nodded and shifted his legs, his knee brushing her calf. She drew hastily away from him. "Believe it or not, my grandfather and whichever wife he was on were more stable than our parents," he said. Which wasn't saying much.

About twice a year their mother had remembered she had sons, her timing based on an intricate formula that factored in the dates of the Paris couture shows and the state of her bank account. Their father's visits had been even more irregular. Rory had never discovered a rhyme or reason to his selfishness. "Greg and I always lived here at Caidwater."

"And was it a good place to grow up?"

Rory flinched, surprised. Most people assumed living in the opulence of the estate guaranteed a happy childhood. "No," he said honestly. "That's why I won't regret taking Iris away from here."

Now Jilly flinched. She swung completely around on the seat. He shifted to accommodate her movement, so that suddenly she was facing him, both of her legs caged by his much longer ones. Her jeaned knee—decorated with a lipstick-red patch that read "GO WILD!"—pressed against the inside of his right thigh like a mouth. Heat arrowed to his groin.

"You're taking her away?" she asked.

"Mm-hmm," he said, staring at her face. "I live near San Francisco. In a few weeks we'll leave southern California and Caidwater for good." Up this close, he found himself fascinated by her skin.

"You seem so eager." She swallowed. "What, is this place haunted or something?"

Rory's eyebrows rose. "Maybe so," he said slowly. By ghosts of scandals and betrayals. "But let's not talk about that."

He watched her swallow again. "What do you want to talk about?" A dash of tiny freckles, just one shade golder than Jilly's complexion, kissed each high cheekbone.

Kisses. Now why the hell did he have to think of that? It made him focus on her mouth. Like the rest of her, it was unconventional. Jilly's lower lip was full, almost puffy, while the upper one had only the shallowest of dips. Really, the greedy little thing had more than her share of sensitive nerve endings. It didn't seem fair that Jilly would possess that riotous hair and those voluptuous breasts and a mouth just made for kissing, too.

Made for him to kiss.

Already half hard, he felt another flaming arrow burn toward his groin.

He glanced around, aware they were completely private. No Iris, no possible way a telephoto lens could catch them here. A disaster-proof opportunity. The sudden thought stunned him. Rory Kincaid, usually the soul of sober responsibility, was thinking about taking a kiss.

A kiss from a woman as diminutive and delectable as Jilly Skye. One who was nothing like the cool, goal-oriented beauties who typically interested him. Instead, she was a knock-knock-joking, lunchpail-toting, mind-blowing combination of luscious, danger-ahead curves.

But what would one kiss hurt? Not when Jilly was made for it. Not when that electricity was charging up again, those sparks lighting in the air between them without anything more than her kneecap against his inner thigh. He leaned forward.

She leaned back.

He almost smiled, the idea of kissing her sounding better and better, even if it made no more sense than before. "Now why are you doing that?" With his free hand, he reached around her and released her hair from the confining clip. She didn't move as it tumbled to her shoulders in those misbehaving curls.

Then he took one of the soft tendrils between his thumb and forefinger. He tugged on it gently, bringing her forward again. Her mouth was still and ripe and he remembered that nervous tic she had and was glad she wasn't nervous anymore.

She licked her lips with her tongue and he wanted to tell her he could do that for her, but that would take too much time, so he tilted his head and lowered it toward her wet, delectable mouth.

"I don't think you want to do this," she said.

He paused. "Strangely enough, I think I do." Yeah, it was out of character for him, but he just *had* to taste her. "Don't you?"

Her eyes widened. "Um. Uh. You don't understand. This is—this is an inauspicious day for new liaisons," she said hastily.

"What?"

Her eyes were nervous, but her mouth was still temptingly wet. "An inauspicious day for new liaisons."

He laughed softly. "Says who?"

"My, uh, chart. I have an astrologer who gives me daily readings of my chart."

His laughter died. "You're kidding."

"No." Her gaze slid away from his. "I'm an Aquarius, February seventeenth."

"That's my birthday, too." The words slipped out.

"Well, there you go," she said. "I'm sure it's a bad day for new liaisons for you, too. I could get my astrologer to make up your chart, though, if you'd like. What time of day were you born?"

He blinked. That staticky energy still crackled between them, their mouths were so close her breath was puffing against his face, and she was talking about what time of day he was born. Charts. Goddamn *astrology*.

But why the hell was he surprised? This was

the land of the weird and unpredictable. This was, after all, L.A. That reality drenched him like a trash pail of cold pond water.

And the electricity between them smoked, went out.

He dropped the corkscrew of Jilly's hair and backed away from her. "Iris!" he yelled. "It's time to go!" It was time to regain his good sense as well.

With Iris in the canoe once more, he paddled swiftly back toward the boathouse. He had that meeting to get to. As a matter of fact, he should probably be grateful to Jilly and her astrology-induced reluctance, because he was already cutting the time pretty close. A kiss might have caused an unexplainable delay. That disaster he'd expected.

Yeah, he should be grateful.

But he wasn't, because as he headed back, that something-bad-is-gonna-happen dread dropped over him again like a suffocating shroud.

With the boathouse, golf cart, and waterfall in sight, he slowed the canoe. He glanced at Jilly's back, her posture straight and serene-looking in that white blouse.

Suddenly another impulse surged inside him, an impulse growing out of some emotion he didn't even recognize—perhaps part kissless frustration, perhaps part just plain sick and tired of waiting for the worst to happen. He tried controlling the dangerous inspiration, he really did, but it was rash and unreasonable and pissed as hell.

The reckless impulse drove him. Drove him to

paddle past the golf cart and paddle past the boathouse and then forward still. Iris shrieked with delight as he flirted with the steamy-looking outer spray of the waterfall.

Then Jilly gave him a look over her shoulder, just one startled look, as if she guessed what he was planning. The spray had sprinkled water-drop jewels in her hair, and her soft mouth was molded in the form of a "No," but Rory thought, Yes. Oh, baby, *yes*.

"You wouldn't dare," she said.

A month ago, a week ago, even an hour ago he wouldn't have. But something about the canoe pond and the memory of the boy who had once played there made him brash. Or maybe it was that Jilly's *Lost in Space* lunchpail had put him in touch with his inner child. That was a fine, south-ern California, psychobabble excuse.

And then there was his gut-deep certainty that something was about to go wrong anyway.

*So just get it over with.* A devilish voice whis-pered sultry temptation in his ear. *Go ahead and drop the damn anvil yourself.*

It seemed like a hell of a good idea. One quick way to dissolve the dread for all time.

Two hard paddle strokes. Three, and then they pierced the cold apron of the water. Iris laughed and the water clattered like a thousand wet tap dancers against the aluminum canoe, and by the time they made it through, all three of them were completely drenched.

Satisfaction waved over Rory, a satisfaction that didn't die even when he brought the canoe back to shore and even though Jilly hadn't uttered one word. Just to be on the safe side, though, he avoided looking at her for the entire return trip in the golf cart. Certainly she'd expect some sort of logical, reasonable explanation, and he didn't have one that would make sense to her. Yet he was glad he'd taken care of the hovering problem himself.

But when they were back on land and within squinting distance of the rear terrace, that satisfaction suddenly evaporated and he felt his gut fall toward his sopping shoes.

Dammit. A collection of suits. Just like his premonition, the Blue Party strategic team, including, most likely, the "forceful" Charlie Jax, was early. They were waiting for him on the terrace. He slid a glance Jilly's way and groaned. Shrink-wrapped clothes, all right. The dousing had made her white blouse nearly invisible and he could see the lace-edged outline of her bra and the rise of remarkable flesh almost bursting out of it.

Beneath his own clammy jeans, his body hardened and he broke out in a sweat.

"Who's that, Rory?" Iris asked, pointing at the dark-suited group.

Jilly pushed a wet, squiggly strand of hair from her face and raised her eyebrows in question too.

"That's some people I'm meeting with. A political team." God. He and Iris looked like wet seals and Jilly the voluptuous mermaid that watched over them. Nothing close to the straight-arrow image the Blue Party wanted for its candidates.

He dragged his gaze away from Jilly's breasts. "They're here for an important meeting and . . . and I'm an idiot." A horny idiot.

Jilly shot him a look. "I'll second that."

He winced. Damn. What had he been thinking? It had seemed inevitable at the time, but now his actions were quite obviously asinine. He drove a hand through his wet hair. Blame these bad decisions and bad ideas on being back at this place. Because he was usually so smart, so focused, so unswayed by a pretty face . . . or a to-drool-for body.

"Listen," he said to Jilly quickly. "These people hold my future in their hands. I'm being considered for candidacy in the U.S. Sen—"

"I heard," she interrupted, frowning as if the idea brought a sour taste to her mouth.

He ignored her expression. "It's really important I make the best impression I possibly can."

"*Dry* would have been a huge improvement, then," she said sarcastically.

*Ouch.* So she wasn't going to be a big help right now. He could hardly blame her.

Still determined to salvage the situation, he gazed in the direction of the wide flight of steps leading up to the terrace and the team, excuses and explanations parading through his mind. "There's got to be some way to fix it," he muttered. If not, the Blue Party strategists might strategize his ass right out of the candidacy.

A thought struck him. "How about this." He paused and turned around to face Jilly and Iris. "What if we say I saved you both from drowning?"

Jilly rolled her eyes. "We'll say you're a big fat liar, won't we, Iris?"

The little girl grinned. "Big fat liar," she repeated gleefully.

He winced again. "Okay, fine. But how about if—"

"Greg!" Iris suddenly shrieked, staring over Rory's shoulder.

Rory turned around. Apparently during the time he had been creating thorny problems for himself, his brother had unexpectedly returned to Caidwater. Greg trotted down the terrace steps toward them.

Iris hurtled past Rory. Greg grinned, bracing himself as the little girl met him halfway and threw herself at him. His arms closed tightly around her as she hit his chest.

Rory moved toward Greg more slowly, with Jilly somewhere behind him. He watched his brother squeeze his aunt in a tight hug.

"Hey, bug," Greg said, and kissed the top of her wet head. He raised his eyebrows at Rory. "Hey, bro." Then his grin widened as his gaze moved on to Jilly.

Rory scowled back, remembering that transparent blouse and those don't-forget-about-me breasts. His brother had no business staring at them. And then there was the way Iris had greeted Greg, while she treated him like burned oatmeal.

He looked away, and his scowl deepened. Now that he was this close, he could see the faces of the Blue Party team and their stunned expressions as they took in Jilly's wet, provocative curves.

He opened his mouth, willing some half-plausible explanation out, but nothing came.

*Damn and damn again.* Instead of immediately smoothing over the moment with the politicos, he quickly stripped off his shirt and shoved it in Jilly's arms. "Put this on," he said, meaning to turn away from her without a word. But she looked irritated and so much like a wet kitten ready to spit that he paused.

"Sorry," he whispered, and tapped her damp, gold-dusted nose with his finger. He sighed, still looking at her as she covered those sweet curves with his dripping shirt.

Oh, yeah, he was sorry, all right. Because, after all, that ill-conceived drenching hadn't changed or solved anything. That dark, doomed cloud was looming over him once more.

With nothing left but to brazen out the situation, Rory hauled in a deep breath and jogged up the steps to face the dark suits. With any luck, the team would just ignore what they'd seen.

But as he introduced himself and damply shook Charlie Jax's hand, Rory quickly deduced the campaign director wasn't the type of man to turn a blind eye to anything. As a matter of fact, *both* his small, dark eyes quickly shot in the direction of Jilly, who was ascending the stairs wearing Rory's shirt and an undecipherable expression.

Jax's thin face was equally inscrutable. "And this is . . . ?" he asked.

*Someone I promise to avoid from this moment on.* "My, um, a, uh, friend of mine." Rory almost groaned out loud at his complete lack of suavity and quickly focused on his brother and Iris, who were also heading up the steps in their direction. "And let me introduce you to Iris Kincaid and my brother, Greg Kincaid." At least Greg's hand was dry.

"The actor," Jax said.

"That's right." Greg walked forward and gave the man's hand a friendly shake, despite Jax's clearly disapproving manner.

Rory quickly greeted the other three members of the Blue Party team. Then he pasted on a rueful smile. "If you'd just excuse me for a few minutes, I'll join you shortly in the library for our meeting."

Rory signaled his brother with his eyes, who thankfully and instantly got the message then guided Iris toward the house. That left Rory with the dripping and who-knew-how-mad Jilly. He clamped his hand around her arm. "Let me see you . . . out." Yeah. Out was the safest place for her.

Charlie Jax's voice stopped them in mid-stride. "Wait!"

Rory swung around reluctantly. "Yes?"

Jax smiled thinly. "You never said what happened. How did you get so . . . wet?"

Oh, there was a wealth of questions in that simple little word "wet." What was Rory doing with a woman who looked like Jilly? What was Rory doing *wet* with a woman who looked like Jilly? "A little—mishap." He didn't dare look at Jilly's face.

"Oh, my," said Jax. He smiled another thin, knowing smile as he assessed Jilly's damp, curvy body. "We'll need to ensure that such things aren't a habit with you, Rory. Though certainly a mishap like this might be . . . tempting, the Blue Party demands more. As our candidate, we just can't afford you any indiscretions."

Rory forced himself to return the smile. The warning was loud and clear. "I understand," he said. Which he did. A rising political career, especially a Blue Party political career for someone with the last name of Kincaid, didn't need the kind of complication a wet woman in "GO WILD" pants provided.

The campaign director studied Rory. "Then I'm sure in future days you'll keep your mishaps to a minimum, or at least more . . . *private*."

Private, his ass. What Jax meant, of course, was that in future days a sweet treat like Jilly must be completely-off limits. Or else.

Or else the Blue Party would rethink its choice.

Rory nodded and took a firmer grip of Jilly's arm, pretending he wasn't the least bit aware of her delectable body or carefully blank expression. It was time to get her out of here.

Out of his sight. Out of his mind.

Except the minute he got her in the house she shook her arm free of his grip and planted her feet on the floor. The carefully blank expression evaporated. He thought maybe she was a little mad.

"I don't like being called a mishap," she said hotly.

Make that *really* mad. He cleared his throat. "Well—"

"And I particularly don't like it after someone makes a pass, then passes me under a waterfall, then tries to pass me off as their 'uh, friend.' I'm a professional—"

"Oh, God, please don't say that!"

She glared at him. "A professional *businessperson*."

He rolled his eyes. "Next time I'll let you hand out your card."

She crossed her arms over her chest. She shouldn't do that. It caused her endowments to rise to distracting prominence. "There better not *be* a next time," she said.

"I hope not," he answered fervently. Honestly.

Oh, God, he *really* hoped not.

A few hours after the campaign meeting, Rory sat in the library in front of his laptop, staring as the screensaver ricocheted a bright red ball through an ever-changing maze. When his fingers found the computer's mouse and stroked it, he wasn't even thinking, really.

His mind was occupied with the last items Charlie Jax had gone over with him—essentially a second round of heavy-handed hinting. Getting wet and half naked with a sexy, voluptuous woman was not the stuff of upright and "true-blue" Blue Party candidates.

The party's plan was to infiltrate Washington and shake it up—by backing politicians who were personally ethical and who would be publicly beyond reproach. It was going to mean something—something honorable and good—to be a national leader again.

As he continued staring absently at the screen, some other part of his mind automatically logged on to the Internet. The cursor swam across the navigational screen toward his bookmarks icon. *Click*. He touched the mouse's button and the addresses of the places he regularly visited on the Web were listed there, including one he didn't actually remember saving.

*Click*. A new screen materialized.

He let out a humorless laugh. An address he didn't actually remember saving?

*Right*.

Why was he lying to himself? This was Jilly's Web site he was looking at, and he remembered very well saving its address. He maneuvered the mouse once more. *Click*.

The screen changed again and he saw the interior of her store as the Web cam slowly panned. Leaning forward, he rested his elbows on the desk, his chin on his hands, and waited. *There*.

*There was Jilly*.

Dry now, she sat behind a cash register, her pose the mimic of his own with her elbow on the counter, her chin on her hand, her eyes pensive. She didn't look mad, like she'd been when she'd left Caidwater. As he watched, she sucked her lower lip into her mouth. Rory's muscles instantly tightened.

Hell. Bad day for new liaisons or not, it didn't even take them being in the same canoe for him to wish he'd tasted that unusual mouth, to wish he'd stroked that dusting of freckles, to wish he'd held those remarkable breasts in his hands.

Despite all the warnings, she was still making him crazy.

Maybe it was a family curse. God knew the

Kincaid men always had women around them who made them crazy.

Maybe Jilly Skye was *his* curse. His downfall.

No. No way would he let her get to him. His anger heated up again and he gulped in a breath of air. She sold old clothes, for God's sake. She dressed and behaved in flaky, weird, and unpredictable ways—everything he hated about L.A. There was the Blue Party to remember, the candidacy, the senator, this chance to be the Kincaid who did something truly worthwhile.

The camera stopped, then panned back in the opposite direction. Jilly lifted her hand and combed it absently through her uncontrollable hair. Rory felt the springy stuff against his palm, as if he were touching it. He closed his eyes, unable to fool himself any longer.

He didn't like her, but, dammit, he wanted her.

And he'd never been any good at not getting what he wanted.

# Chapter 5

Two days after returning home, Greg Kincaid wandered into the kitchen, where Rory sat slumped behind the table, obviously held prisoner by a very black mood or a very bad headache. Since Greg had returned to Caidwater from the press junket, he'd noticed Rory becoming increasingly tense. "Are you all right?" he asked.

Rory straightened. "I'm fine," he said automatically. "Do you need something?"

*Of course he says he's fine.* Greg mentally shook his head. Rory had ever been the strong, responsible older brother. "There isn't something I can help you with?"

Rory grunted. "There's nothing you can do."

Greg tried his best disarming grin. "What about talking you out of this Senate thing?"

"Don't start with me again," Rory warned. "I've heard everything you have to say on that subject ten or twelve times already."

"You're impatient, autocratic, and undiplomatic," Greg said quietly.

Rory rubbed the back of his neck. "Gee, thanks," he said dryly.

"And those are your good points," Greg added, shoving his hands in his pockets. "Maybe if you'd been climbing a ladder in some corporation for the last ten years, I could see you playing dirty political games." But instead, Rory had formed his own software company and kept strict control of the reins—all the reins—until he'd sold it six months ago.

"The Blue Party wants to call a halt to those kinds of games," Rory replied.

But what did Rory want? Greg suspected there were only two reasons why his brother was even considering the Senate candidacy. "You're bored," he told him. That was one.

Rory frowned. "Why are you fighting me on this? Don't you want the Kincaid name to stand for something besides scandal?"

That was the other.

Greg dropped into the opposite chair. "And I'm not contributing in that regard?"

"The Kincaids already have Oscars, Greg."

"Ouch." But Greg already knew his brother didn't understand the passion for acting that had made him follow in the profession of Roderick and their father. Rory didn't respect the business because he didn't respect the men in their family who had been actors. "You really know how to wound a guy."

"Sorry." Rory didn't look the least contrite. "Where's Iris?"

That was something—someone—else Rory didn't understand. "Mrs. Mack took her on some errands. Ice cream was mentioned."

"Ah."

Greg took a breath. "About Iris—"

"No," Rory said flatly.

Greg took another breath to calm himself. Stubborn Ass was his brother's middle name, and getting the Ass's hackles up wouldn't help matters. "Rory—"

"For God's sake, I'm *saving* her, Greg. We lived here, remember? We grew up in L.A., and with an actor for a parent. Do you really want her? Do you really want that *for* her?"

It was the same argument Rory used every time Greg brought up the guardianship. "I'm not our father, Rory," he said.

Rory just stared him down, his face set.

Frustration rising, Greg fisted his hands. He hated arguing with his brother. Ever since they were kids, it was Rory who had cared about him, raised him, and that deserved his loyalty. But this was about rescuing someone else's childhood.

"Rory—"

"No."

Temper flaring, Greg stood up. "Damn it, Rory." He rested his knuckles on the table.

Rory's eyes narrowed. Obviously spoiling for a fight, he jumped to his feet, too. "Damn me, you mean?" He leaned over the table, his eyes hot and his jaw tense.

Startled, Greg jerked back. Though it was true Rory was at the core autocratic and impatient, he was usually also incredibly coolheaded and self-contained. This anger, this pose, was so uncontrolled, so un-Rory, that Greg's own frustration and anger instantly leached away. He sighed. "Forget it," he said, sitting back down.

Time and patience, he told himself. He had to trust that time and patience would untangle the situation, because Rory was unmovable in this mood. Something was getting to his brother, bad. Greg blamed the Blue Party, but it could be Jilly Skye, too. He'd noticed that Rory took convoluted paths through the house just to avoid meeting up with her.

Which reminded him. "Didn't Jilly ask if she could take that black gown with her yesterday when she left?" She'd tracked Rory down in this very kitchen at lunchtime, and Greg had watched with surprise and interest the way the air between them shimmered. He wasn't quite sure if they irritated or excited each other, or some combustible combination of both.

At her name, Rory fell back into his seat, his face shuttered. "Yeah. She wanted to display it at some show this weekend."

"She must have forgotten it. It's on the foyer table."

Rory grunted.

Obviously Rory didn't want to think about or talk about the woman. Greg smiled to himself, itching to poke his brother's buttons. It was so rare that Rory let himself be annoyed, and he was being so damn stubborn about Iris he deserved it. "Maybe you should take it to her," Greg said, his voice casual.

Rory didn't fail him. "Forget it," he answered forcefully. "I have from now until Monday morning free of that wacky woman and her even wackier outfits, and I'm going to savor it."

Greg raised his eyebrows innocently. "I guess that means she'll have to come over and pick it up herself. As long as she's here, I bet she stays and puts in a few more hours." He rubbed his chin. "I wonder what she'll wear. She told me she just bought a dress Marilyn Monroe wore in *Some Like It Hot*."

Rory looked so aghast that Greg almost laughed out loud. It was more than entertaining to see unflappable Rory flummoxed. The free-spirited Jilly—so different from the cold-faced superwomen his brother usually squired—was just the right thorn to pierce Rory's sometimes puritanical hide.

But then Greg thought of the signs of tension written all over him—the testiness, the tired-ness—and he relented. "Do you have her address? I'll take it to her."

Greg was still smiling as he left Caidwater. He'd thought Rory was going to kiss him when he'd made the offer. Despite the Iris-dilemma, it was good having Rory around.

His smile died. God, he'd hate for the mess Roderick had left behind to ruin their relation-ship.

Curse the old man. Curse him, and curse his marquee-sized ego, too. Greg had continued liv-ing at Caidwater with Roderick for the past four years, both of them obstinately refusing to acknowledge the secrets between them. But in the end, damn him, Roderick had won. He'd given the guardianship of Iris to Rory.

The thought so depressed Greg that he forced

his mind from it, concentrating instead on the scripts his agent had sent over the day before. If Rory couldn't be convinced, and actually took Iris north, he would need a new project to fill the huge void in his life.

She'd been like his daughter since the day she was born.

Since before she was born.

Yet Greg wasn't sure how hard and how far to fight for her. Rory would certainly be a responsible father figure for Iris, he had no doubt about that. But would he ever understand her spirit? Would he ever love her?

Greg understood Iris. Appreciated her. Loved her.

But he wasn't sure he didn't have to pay for the past by losing her.

Those thoughts depressed him as well, so he went back to considering the scripts. He'd read through them yesterday, and the one that appealed to him most would shoot on location in Wyoming.

So far he'd been doing "buddy" roles, the kind of character who never got the girl, and this one was no different. But there was something appealing about this part. Ned Smith was the best friend of the hero and a bronco rider, a man in extreme and chronic physical pain throughout the course of the film.

It would be an interesting challenge, and according to his agent, maybe even a break-through role. But only if Greg could realistically portray a suffering man. At eleven, he'd broken his leg while skiing at Big Bear. But that single injury, along with some jammed fingers from beach volleyball, was the extent of the personal experience he had to draw upon.

Once in the FreeWest district, Greg whipped his Land Rover into a parking space down the block from Jilly's shop. His mood lightened as he looked around the area. A condom shop? And the art theater on the corner was showing a film he remembered reading about. From an Indian director, it was said to curl the toes of the most jaded sensualist. Greg grinned. He'd vote for Rory himself just for the chance to see his brother's face the first time he got a load of Jilly's neighborhood.

The image made him whistle a jaunty melody that he saved for only his cheeriest moments. The long string of bells on the front door of Things Past clashed with his musical notes, but he kept right on whistling as he walked a few feet through the store, the box with the dress she wanted in his hands.

He didn't see her or anyone else. "Hello?" he called out. "Jilly?"

At the very rear of the shop was a doorway, presumably to an office, and Greg headed in that direction. "Jilly?" he said again, and poked his head around the door.

*No.*

*No!*

His heart froze but then restarted, seeming to fire instead of beat, going off in a swift burst of explosions. *Bap-bap-bap, bap-bap-bap-bap.*

"Kim?" God, it didn't sound like his voice, but it looked like her, sitting in a chair in the small office. There was the familiar golden color of her hair, though the woman he was staring at wore it in a confining bun instead of loose. There was the familiar fineness of her skin, as clear and sweetly colored as Iris's. There was the familiar, gut-clenching beauty of her face.

And then there was the familiar, desperate sense of shame he felt at looking at it, at wanting her.

"Kim?" he said again.

He'd never seen her move so fast. She rocketed out of her chair. She brushed past him, her shoulder knocking into his chest.

She ran out of the store.

Greg couldn't find his breath or his feet or his way to the front door. His heart kept on with those uneven blasts—*bap-bap-bap, bap-bap-bap-bap*.

When he realized she wasn't coming back, he finally commanded his feet to move. It took him a long time to return to his car, because he kept stopping every couple of feet to catch his breath and survey the street, willing her to show herself to him.

But she didn't.

He put the box beside him on the Land Rover's passenger seat, not even remembering what it contained or what he was supposed to do with it. Then, somehow, the engine was idling and he backed the car out of the parking space and started driving. If there were stoplights, he didn't see them. If there were pedestrians, he hoped they got themselves out of the way.

"Kim." He said her name out loud, and it stabbed him like a knife. His belly clenched, cramping against the pain, but it still came, more pain, again and again, in sharp, burning bursts. Tears stung the inside corners of his eyes.

Some months—years?—from now, when his sanity returned, he'd have to call his agent. Maybe he could play a character like Ned Smith after all. Because seeing again the first woman he'd ever loved, the only woman he *would* ever love, hurt like hell.

On his way to Jilly's shop, Rory maneuvered his Mercedes through the dusk and the late Saturday afternoon traffic, the large box holding that damned dress beside him on the leather passenger seat. Greg had surprised the hell out of him a few hours ago by stalking into the library and tossing the box onto the desk without explanation. Greg's face, tight and pale, had surprised him even more. There was a glitter in his brother's eyes that had warned Rory right away to keep his mouth shut.

So Rory had bent over the stacks of paperwork on his desk. Wrapped up in his work, he had ignored the box, too.

For about nine minutes.

But, like a quarter burning a hole in a little boy's pocket, the box refused to be ignored.

Telling himself it was a preemptive strike—if she *did* come to get it herself, God knew how long she'd want to swish around the house, distracting him, irritating him—he'd grabbed his keys and headed in the direction of West Hollywood. He had a vague recollection of the area where he would find Jilly's shop. Ten years ago it had been a seedy collection of bars, secondhand stores, and rooming houses. He assumed it was different now.

And when he turned onto Freewood Drive, he realized it was different, all right. A neon sign arching over the street flickered to life just as he drove beneath it. FREEWEST, it proclaimed in startling blue letters. As exclamation point, a palm tree burst into chartreuse green.

The colors hurt Rory's eyes. He winced and looked away, taking in the odd collection of shops and businesses. Christ. Tattoos and tarot cards. A shop specializing in motorcycle leathers, and a dance club advertising Saturday night was "Boogie in Bubbles Night . . . Bring Your Own Towels."

Boogie in bubbles. What the hell was that? he wondered, shaking his head. It was L.A., he answered himself. Admittedly, his adopted city of San Francisco had its share of eccentricities, but a layer of Old World, tongue-in-cheek chic softened all the edges like the fog softened the northern California air.

In L.A., everything was neon-bright, unabashed, and in-your-face. And, Rory thought as he pulled into a parking space and noted the sole type of stock in the shop beside Jilly's—condoms—in L.A. everything was about sex.

Which was all he could think about when he spotted Jilly at the back of her shop. With darkness now fully descended, the windows of Things Past were lit like a TV screen. Rory's gaze skipped over her window display to land on the woman herself, standing beside a rack in another of her improbable outfits.

Her compact body was dressed in a hot-pink

skirt with a matching short jacket. A round hat of the same color was perched on her head, with a veil that hung over her eyes to brush the bridge of her pert nose. The outfit should have looked ridiculous, but instead, as she bent over a rack to adjust some hangers, Rory stared at her round butt and thought it looked raunchy.

Christ. He rubbed the back of his neck. Face it. It didn't matter if Jilly was dressed like Janis Joplin or Jackie Kennedy; to him, her body was Sexyland and he itched to get in line for all his favorite rides.

Tightening his jaw, Rory grabbed the box and forced himself out of the car. *Just give her the dress and get out.* Now wasn't the time to be thinking of what he could do with a bonus admission ticket.

He'd been steering as clear of her as he could, and doing a good job of it, damn it, because he knew that somewhere between her uncontrollable hair and her unbelievably small feet he'd find his downfall. But not if he controlled his lust.

It just never had been so damn hard to manage.

After leaving L.A. almost a decade ago, he'd certainly not cut women out of his life. He'd enjoyed them and bedded them with pleasure. But cautiously. Temperately. He hadn't been looking for high passion, only mutual satisfaction, and he'd found it with women who saved all their passions and their focus for their careers. But Jilly didn't strike him as the cautious or temperate type.

Bells jangled brightly when he pushed open the door to Things Past. Jilly jumped, her hand flying to her chest as she twirled in his direction.

"Oh," she said, and swallowed. "We're closed."

Her lips matched the bright pink of the dumb hat she wore. "I'm not here to make a purchase, Jilly," he said. "And the door was open."

"Well, oh, all right." She swallowed again. "What are you doing here?"

The air of the store smelled light and sweet, like the scent Jilly brought into Caidwater. The scent that chased away the heavy dread of old memories. "I've brought you something."

"Yes?" she said warily, her pink lips pursing. "What?"

Rory stared at her mouth. He didn't know why he didn't mention the dress. He didn't know why he didn't just take the box from under his arm and lay it down somewhere, anywhere, and leave. But something about her discomfort in seeing him and her near-truculent suspicion . . . amused him.

As he approached her, she backed around a circular rack of clothes, toward the door he'd just come through. Yes, for the past two days, ever since she'd lit into him after the canoe incident, he'd been avoiding her. But now he wondered if it wasn't the other way around.

He halted and his eyebrows rose. "Are you going somewhere?"

Her shoulders hit the plate glass of the door, and she glanced behind her, as if surprised to find herself there. "Uh. No. Of course not." Her hand turned a lock. "Just, um, locking up. We're closed."

"You already said that." Rory didn't also point

out that she'd just locked him inside. With her.

Though God knew it was an infinitely appealing idea, it was also one he should be running from. But as he watched her nervously lick her full lips he relaxed a little, enjoying her tension. After a few days of living at Caidwater with her scent, her presence constantly teasing and tempting him, it seemed only fair to give her a taste of her own medicine in her own territory.

He started toward her again and she immediately sidled away from the door. When he changed direction to follow her, his hip brushed against a rack of clothes, and he had to grab the metal rod to save it from going over. The dresses hanging from it continued to swing, though, and a fluttering price tag caught his eye.

"Whoa." He grabbed the hand-lettered ticket to recheck the dollar figure. "Whoa," he said again.

That much? He set the box he held on the floor and pushed at the hangers to get a better look at the white, lightweight dress. The thing was decorated with lace on the neck and sleeves and a bunch of other places. Rory noticed there were several similar dresses on the rack. Astonished by how much she was asking for someone else's castoff, Rory looked over at Jilly. "You sell much of this stuff?"

A little smile lifted the corners of her mouth. "As much as I can find. That's what's known as a lingerie dress, and it's from the early 1900s."

He frowned. "But it's still someone else's old clothes."

She laughed. "To you. To someone else it's a

collectible antique. To someone in the movie or TV business, it could be a costume."

The top part of the dress was very full, but the waist was tiny. "Who could wear something sized like this?"

Jilly shrugged. "Collectors don't generally wear their clothes, and a costumer might just use it as the basis for a pattern. But I—" She clamped her mouth shut and her cheeks turned pink.

Rory looked from the dress to Jilly, then back to the dress again. Yeah, she'd fill out the full bodice sweetly, but even with her small waist . . . "This wouldn't fit you."

"Not without a corset," she agreed, her cheeks even pinker.

A corset. Rory remembered that intriguing category listed on her Web site, "Victorian Undergarments." As if it burned, he dropped his fingers from the dress, but that didn't stop a vision of Jilly, her waist made even smaller, her breasts thrusting forward. And what was burning was him, burning with the kind of lust he'd promised himself to control.

Drawing in a breath, he swung his gaze in the opposite direction of that devilish dress and Jilly. Clothes filled the store—dresses and blouses on racks, stacks of sequined sweaters on shelves against the wall. Hand-lettered signs indicated time periods and types of clothing. There wasn't a Victorian undergarment in sight.

Thank God.

Damn it.

But he wasn't ready to look at Jilly yet. He wasn't ready to leave yet either. He needed the camouflage of the racks to hide what the idea of a corseted Jilly had done to *his* body.

Taking another deep breath, he turned his back on the clothes and looked out the window into the evening darkness. Across the street was another neon sign, this one a moon and stars announcing the presence of an astrologer's parlor.

"So, um, what made you settle on this location? Another suggestion of your astrologer's?"

"Another what?" she asked, her voice puzzled, but then she caught herself. "Oh. Oh, no. This had been my mother's shop. I inherited it when she passed away."

Rory looked at her now. "I'm sorry."

"I was really sorry, too." Jilly dropped her gaze and brushed at something on her skirt.

He tried to change the subject. "So . . . what made your mother go into the vintage-clothing business?"

Jilly brushed at her skirt again. "I don't know exactly. I never had the opportunity to ask her." She looked up at him, that pink veil masking the expression in her eyes. "I was raised by my grandmother. She didn't quite . . . approve of my mother. I'd guess you'd say they were estranged. I never knew my mother until . . . until I opened the door of this shop, I suppose."

Something lurched in his gut. "When was this?"

"Four years ago. Four years ago I left my grandmother's." Her thumb jabbed in the direction of the ceiling. "I live upstairs."

"So you just came here on your own and took over your mother's business?"

"Yep." She absently straightened a blouse on a nearby hanger. "I was twenty-one and determined to prove something."

She'd been just a kid, Rory realized. A kid who hadn't known her mother, a kid who'd opened the door to a different world and then stayed there.

Not so different from himself.

He shoved the thought away and tried to ignore the spurt of admiration he felt for Jilly, too. As similar as their stories might appear, they'd chosen different worlds. Unbridgeable worlds.

He leaned over to pick up the box that held the dress. "I came to give you this," he said, moving toward her.

Her brows drew together, then lifted. "The dress!" A smile broke over her face. "Thank you. I was in such a hurry to leave yesterday, I forgot all about it."

She moved toward him now, her mouth soft and her eyes bright as she held out her hands. A lick of annoyance burned in his belly and he drew back the box. "Why in such a hurry yesterday?"

"What?"

"Did you have a date or something?"

She made a face and grabbed one end of the box. He didn't let go. "Well?"

She tugged on the box. He still held on. "Did you?" he repeated.

Jilly rolled her eyes. "Did *you*?" she asked.

When he didn't release the box or answer, she made that face again. "Anyway, I'm under no obligation to explain my personal life to you."

He still didn't let go, because, yeah, she did

need to explain her personal life to him. Because, dammit, when he'd wanted to think of her only as sex candy, she'd gone ahead and shown him the soft center of her, that part of Jilly who had been a young woman who hadn't known her mother until she'd opened up a door. Someone who brushed away nonexistent lint instead of letting him see that her mother's death still saddened her. Someone who had taken a business and run with it.

Thinking of her as sex candy was safer. Thinking of her as some other man's sex candy was safer still.

"Tell me if you had a date last night, Jilly," he said quietly.

At his new tone, the exasperation left her face. But she tightened her grip on the box and lifted her chin. "What about you?" she said. "Did *you* have a date last night?"

Something tickled the back of his mind. Jilly, hovering in the doorway of the library at Caidwater yesterday. He'd been talking on the phone to Lisa, a woman he casually dated in San Francisco. He'd been trying to coax her into taking the next plane out and then a limo from LAX to Caidwater. If she got there by five, he'd promised her dinner at Spago's.

He narrowed his eyes. Sometime in the middle of that phone conversation, Jilly had disappeared from the doorway and then later had been in such an all-fired hurry to leave before five o'clock that she'd forgotten the dress they were now playing tug-of-war with. "Are you jealous?" he asked.

She gave him a look that should have eviscerated him. "Of what? Of whom?" she said. "Of some woman you took to Spago's?" With a vicious tug, she jerked the box from his hands, then obviously realized that she'd also just given herself away. Her fingers fumbled, and the box and its contents fell to the floor.

Jilly looked down in dismay, her face a brighter pink than her skirt and jacket. He knew she knew he knew she'd been listening to that phone call. "Now look what you've done!" she said.

Rory bent to retrieve the dress, trying not to laugh. She looked so put out with him for catching her. He should tell her it didn't matter, that he'd always known the attraction ran both ways. It didn't take a genius to figure out that the kind of heat they generated required two. As a matter of fact, he'd made that phone call to Lisa only to prove to himself he could think of a woman other than Jilly.

He picked up the dress by the shoulders—it was black and rustled—shaking it out as he straightened. His gaze met hers and in her eyes was equal parts embarrassment and awareness. He bit back his smile again. Jilly flustered was kind of . . . cute. Sweet.

God.

He thrust the dress at her. "Put this on for me," he said.

She closed her arms around the garment and held it against her. "What?"

"Put the damn dress on."

Cute. Sweet. What was he thinking? Thoughts like those were as scary as the dimple. He had to remember that she was dangerous to him. She was potential disaster, his downfall, the symbol of all that could go wrong if he let down his guard in L.A. Hell if he was going to start thinking of this walking taste of sin as anything less than lethal.

He glanced down. The dress looked bare enough. A little glimpse of Jilly's flesh and he'd remember all over again why he couldn't touch it. Why he shouldn't touch her.

He groaned inwardly. God, he hoped she wouldn't ask him to explain all that, because it wasn't making sense to him either. He just knew it had to be done.

"Go on," he said, softening his voice. "I want to see what the fuss is about."

Obviously puzzled, she cocked her head. He wasn't going to let himself think of her confusion as cute, too. "Go on," he said again. "Show me what makes this dress so special."

She seemed to accept that explanation. Still clutching the dress against that hot-pink suit, she retreated in the direction of a couple of shuttered dressing rooms. "I'm pretty sure this one isn't a costume," she said, as if he really cared. "Though it looks like something Audrey Hepburn might have worn."

He stopped listening as she went into more detail. Instead, he concentrated on watching her withdraw behind those shutters. She was so short that once she stepped out of her high heels, her curly hair completely disappeared, and he had only her curvy calves to contemplate as she changed clothes.

But it was enough. He caught a quick glimpse

of pink netting when she lifted the hat from her head. Her voice lowered as he imagined her tucking her chin against her chest to undo the buttons on the suit jacket.

When the pink skirt dropped to the floor of the dressing room, his blood started to pound. She had him thinking of undergarments again. His eyes nearly bugged out of his head when a lacy-cupped bra fell on top of the skirt.

Good.

This dainty sex goddess was safe from him, and safe to him, as long as he only lusted after her. He just couldn't let himself like her.

Or touch her.

Crossing his arms over his chest, he watched her step into the black dress. It even sounded naughty, its rustle like a woman's sexy, hoarse, whispering demands. *Stroke me here. Yes. Just like that.* Rory shifted on his feet, imagining Jilly's voice, the heat of Jilly's skin, the places she'd want him to stroke.

She was sex, all right. He could feel the warmth of it, smell its scent. It slipped under the dressing room door and oozed out the tilted slats of the shutters.

Rory let it wrap around him, sex and anticipation. Hot tentacles of soft, scented temptation. The dressing room doors slowly opened and he held his breath.

Jilly stepped out. She'd said Audrey Hepburn, but to Rory's mind, the black dress was like something a ballerina might wear—tiny sleeves that fell off her shoulders, the top of the dress fitted like second skin to her waist, and then the full skirt a bell that ended just above her ankles.

Christ. He tried to suck in some air, but his lungs wouldn't work, because when he'd wished for bare flesh, the devil must have been listening.

Sweet, pale skin from her wrists to her shoulders. Then those nothing-to-speak-of sleeves, and then the wide, scooping neckline that somehow exposed and somehow lifted Jilly's nearly naked breasts.

Rory didn't know whether to light a candle in appreciation or cross himself for protection.

Then she turned, and his Adam's apple dropped from his throat to land at his feet. The dress was unzipped, leaving a vee of pale Jilly-flesh from an inch or so below her waist to her shoulders. His gaze ran over the swath of her nakedness, bumping slowly down each vertebra of her spine from the ends of her curling hair to the hint of the curve of her ass.

"Help," she said. "The zipper's stuck."

Rory swallowed. "Just take it off, then." He'd seen enough. Plenty. He was all lust again and that was what he'd wanted. Keeping his distance was safe. Anything more was dangerous.

Remember? He wasn't supposed to touch her.

"I can't," she said. "With the zipper where it is, I can't get the dress on *or* off."

*Oh, great.*

His feet were stuck, too. But after a minute he could force them to move, though he could almost hear the squelching sounds as the floor tried sucking him back to keep him from going to her.

Because he shouldn't touch her.

But, hey, the zipper was stuck, he told himself, trying to mollify his good sense.

Her shoulders tensed as he approached, and her voice was breathy. "Just jiggle the tab a couple of times. I can handle it once you get it free."

"Whatever you say," he murmured.

And then he was close enough to feel the warmth of her body. Steeling himself, he reached toward the misbehaving zipper and her heat grazed his knuckles. He thought of the women he usually let into his life. Tall, Nordic females like Lisa, whose classy coolness he enjoyed melting in slow degrees. But Jilly was different. Jilly was already burning-hot. The representatives of the Blue Party would go blue in the face if they knew the kind of fever he was exposing himself to.

When he grasped the zipper, one knuckle stroked the small of her back. She jerked, goose bumps breaking out over all that creamy pale, hot skin.

Rory closed his eyes against the sight and gingerly wiggled the metal tab, willing the damn thing free.

She looked over her shoulder at him. "Any luck?"

He opened his eyes and his breath stirred the coffee-brown curl at her temple. No. No luck.

No luck with the zipper, no luck ignoring the fire coming off her body, no luck controlling his lust for her.

And with those green eyes on his face, he was having no luck remembering that she was only spicy hot sex and also not something else, something more, something sweet.

She licked her lips.

No luck at all.

"Jilly," he said, leaning toward her mouth.

A car horn blared angrily outside the shop.

She started, he started, their combined movements started the zipper working.

Jilly stepped forward. Rory stepped back.

Without looking at him, she dashed into the dressing room.

Without saying anything, he headed for the shop's front door.

*God bless impatient L.A. drivers*, he thought, turning the lock and slipping out. Because if he and Jilly hadn't been interrupted, anyone caring to look through the brightly lit shop windows would have had quite an eyeful.

Rory didn't let himself think of what he might have had.

"You better see this, Rory," Greg said.

Rory focused on his computer screen and opened his mouth to tell his brother to go away. It was Monday morning and he had approximately twenty more minutes before Jilly arrived and destroyed his ability to concentrate. Without her in the house, Sunday had been peaceful enough, if he didn't count the unbidden images of her naked back that kept flashing through his mind.

"Rory," Greg said again. He'd crossed to the fifty-two-inch projection TV that Roderick had installed in place of a leather-bound set of Shakespeare. Grabbing the remote, Greg flicked on the TV and selected a channel. Even more mysterious, he slid a videotape into the VCR. "RECORD" flashed on the TV screen as it briefly displayed a logo: *Celeb! on TV*. Schlocky theme music swelled through the Bose speakers in the corners of the library.

Rory looked back at his computer. "Hey, if you like the publicity, good for you, Greg. But I don't have time to watch right now."

"This isn't about me, Rory."

He looked up again, and an image on the TV screen struck him like a fist in the gut. A grainy, picture-of-a-picture type image, but a familiar one all the same. It had replayed in his own mind over and over since Saturday night.

Jilly's naked back.

Something cold slithered against the nape of his neck and that hovering, portentous cloud he lived with lowered about six feet.

Rory slid down in his chair, closed his eyes, opened them, and stared at the TV again. He knew what had happened. Her Web cam. Jilly's naked back caught by her own Web cam. And just in camera range, *his* back, his hands reaching toward her. Christ, even with the poor quality of the picture, he could see his own damned hands were shaking as they appeared to be undressing her.

He curled his fingers into fists when Jilly looked over her shoulder, completely exposing her face to the camera. Her eyes were dreamy, and just as the scene had replayed in his mind, she licked her full, pouty lips.

"Fuck," Rory said.

"That's what everyone will be thinking," Greg agreed.

Rory frowned. "But why the interest in Jilly? What would—" But then the "why" struck him like a second belly-blow, as what was the back of his head, leaning toward her nakedness and her mouth, jerked around—that horn blast, he remembered—and it was Rory's own face that was caught on camera, completely exposed.

*"Fuck."*

"An activity made even more interesting when the would-be candidate of the Blue Party—the party that wants to put honor back in politics—appears about to do said activity in front of the Internet masses." Greg flicked off the TV's sound as the screen was filled by a big-toothed woman who apparently hosted the piece-of-crap program.

He raised his eyebrows and held up the remote. "Unless you'd rather hear the speculation?"

Rory closed his eyes and waved the nauseating thought away. "Believe me, I can guess what it is." He groaned. "What the hell am I going to do?"

He thought of his good buddy, campaign director Charlie Jax, and groaned louder. The man was going to skewer him, and who could blame him? Sexy Internet interludes didn't enhance Rory's reputation or that of the Blue Party.

"You need to do something quick," Greg said. "I hate to break more bad news, but it was Mrs. Mack who alerted me to the program. She also said the press is gathering at the gates."

Rory groaned again. "And Jilly's expected any moment."

The phone on his desk started to ring, and Rory eyed it as if it were a poisonous snake. "Don't pick that up. And go tell Mrs. Mack we're not answering the phone today." He belatedly looked at his brother. "Please."

There was sympathy on Greg's face. And a trace of something else—glee?—that made Rory think of countless games of hide-and-seek and cops and robbers when two boys had the run of a house filled with adults, but still the most responsible person in the huge place had been Rory himself.

He shrugged away the memories, shrugged away the resentment that he hadn't experienced any boyish glee in a million years, and vaulted out of his chair. With Jilly almost certainly nearing the house, he needed to run interference.

# ℚ Chapter 6

Rory approached the gates at the bottom of the Caidwater driveway just as Jilly's red woody was trying to nose its way through the milling throng of reporters and paparazzi on the other side. Christ. Southern California, politics, and the Kincaid name brought them out in droves.

Both types of vultures were there, piously earnest journalists in cheesy jackets and gleeful paparazzi in jeans and T-shirts so rumpled, it looked like they'd slept all night in the bushes.

Which they probably had.

He set his back teeth as they lifted their cameras—each complete with a powerful lens that seemed as monsterish and threatening as the eye of a Cyclops—in the direction of Jilly's car. If her windows hadn't been tinted, they would have had her.

Of course, the rattling, flashy red car was damning enough.

He pressed the button on his side of the driveway and the gates opened, giving one inattentive reporter a gratifying slap on the ass. Keeping to his side of the drive—the private property side—

he waved to encourage Jilly through, all the while ignoring the *whirr-click* of camera shutters and the shouting voices of the carrion-eaters come to pick his bones clean.

"Rory!"

"Mr. Kincaid. A question about the Blue Party—"

"What's your stand on Internet pornography?" Snickers.

*Hit the gas, Jilly*, he thought impatiently. But still she inched along, apparently a lot more worried than he would have been about bruising kneecaps or crushing cameras.

Finally he couldn't stand it. "Get the hell out of the lady's way!" he yelled.

And immediately realized his mistake. *The lady*. The throng surged around the car, their interest diverted from him and focused completely on the cherry-red wagon that was now forced to a complete halt.

Of course, because he wasn't the only one who could make a dumb move, Jilly rolled down the window and stuck her head out.

*click click click click click click click click click*

She blinked in consternation, her wild hair zigging in every direction and her mouth, painted the same sin-red as her car, falling open. Her gaze ping-ponged over the crowd and then found him. "Rory?"

He moved toward Jilly, pushing into the reporters who surrounded her, six deep and five across. Through the car's open window Rory could see she had a kind of Annie Hall look going. There was a tie around her neck. She wore a man's vest in a red paisley pattern. But she'd forgotten a shirt, he thought with resignation, staring at her bare arms.

But then she shifted to lean farther out the window and he spotted a white sleeveless T-shirt beneath the oversized vest. Oh, great, he thought, resigned again. The T-shirt was a tight one.

He sighed, shouldering his way past a skinny kid who smelled like he'd been sifting through garbage cans. Well, there was one thing you could say for Jilly. She was never a disappointment. This week's tabloid readers had a treat in store.

The reporters were shouting over one another, some calling her name and asking questions about herself, others asking questions about her political views. Rory tried moving faster through the crowd, afraid of how she might respond. The paparazzi continued clicking away, too, and when one called out, "Lick your mouth, Jilly, baby," Rory saw a red deeper and hotter than the shade of Jilly's lipstick.

Using his shoulder like a linebacker, he shoved the dirty-minded asshole away and finally found himself beside her door.

She bit her fat bottom lip. "What's going on?"

He shook his head. "We gotta get out of here." But there wasn't any place to go. They were surrounded, reporters and photographers pressing against them so closely that Rory couldn't get out a private explanation let alone get the car door open.

"Come on." He reached into the window and

grabbed her upper arms to urge her from the driver's seat.

She pulled back and her voice rose. "What are you doing?"

*click click click click click click click click click click*

"Jilly, just cooperate with me here," he said through his teeth. Ignoring another protest, he reached for her again, then hauled her light weight out the window and into his arms.

To realize he was stuck with her. The press had no intention of giving him any room to set her down.

Or even to take a breath.

Hitching her closer to him, he gritted his teeth and turned, battering through the crowd with his back, making his way in the direction of the gates. Though he was expecting the worst, something about the sight of the woman in his arms seemed to alter the group's mood. As he carried Jilly, walking backward so he could make certain they weren't followed, the reporters' aggression died and their shouted questions did, too.

Rory was still afraid to put her down, afraid she'd try to get back in her car or get snatched by one of the overeager reporters for a one-on-one exclusive. Maybe she was worried, too, because she had her arms looped tightly around his neck.

Her light, gentle perfume was in his lungs and even under the press's rabid eyes he appreciated the ride of her round butt beneath his hand. Jeezus, but she was one sexy armful. And this was the closest he'd been to it, with thirty-plus overinterested parties as witnesses.

Not to mention the—what? thousands? millions?—who would see what they wanted to in that replay of their Internet escapade.

*Damn*.

He paused by the button that would slam the gates shut on the intruders. To free a finger to press a button, he shifted Jilly against him. His mouth inadvertently brushed the smooth, hot skin of her temple.

*Hot*. She was so damn hot.

"Hey, Rory!"

This voice was friendly, and for some reason, he looked toward it as his finger reached for the button.

The reporter wore an appreciative, between-us-guys grin. "You got something special going on with her?"

Rory looked down at Jilly, and he saw her as the reporter did—her wild curls, her lush mouth, the abundance of her breasts. He couldn't help a smile from breaking over his face. He couldn't help it, because, hell, he *was* holding the sexiest, hottest armful in memory. Why shouldn't he appreciate it? Especially when their hand had been dealt the minute they'd been caught on the Web camera, and especially since he'd already determined how they were going to have to play out this disaster.

"Oh, yeah," he called back to the grinning reporter, his gaze not leaving Jilly's surprised—no, stunned—face. "Something special. Something *really* special."

And then, as if it were the most natural thing in the world, as if he'd not been planning it from about two minutes after he'd seen that goddamn segment of *Celeb! on TV*, Rory dipped his head and kissed Jilly's tempting, sin-colored mouth.

*click click click click click click click click click*

The sound of another round of camera shutters barely penetrated Rory's consciousness. He'd meant to make it a playful, good-to-see-you kind of kiss, but Jilly's full breasts were pressed so softly against his chest and her mouth was as hot and sweet as melted candy. He pressed harder, for a deeper taste, and she obeyed his need, her lips softening enough for him to press them open with his tongue.

Fire.

It was licking at his feet, burning through his veins, as he thrust his tongue inside her mouth again. She moaned, and her fingernails scratched the nape of his neck.

Rory dipped deeper into her mouth.

Red hots. Jilly tasted like red hots and he had an unquenchable craving for their cinnamon-spice heat.

*Clang.*

The sound of the gates closing broke their kiss. Her chest heaving, Jilly stared up at him, then at the reporters now locked out. She dried her wet mouth—made wet by him—with the back of her hand.

"What's going on?" she said hoarsely.

He let her slide down his body and her right hip brushed his aching erection. He bit back a groan. Every one of his muscles felt hard as a rock.

"*What* is going on?" she asked again.

But not nearly as hard as it was going to be to break the news of their little . . . dilemma to Jilly.

" 'Little dilemma'?" Jilly tasted the words because it was better than tasting Rory's kiss, that demanding, world-spinning kiss still lingering on her lips. Even now they continued to throb. "What 'little dilemma' are you talking about?"

Rory sat on the edge of his desk in the library, looking delicious and maddeningly calm in a pair of chinos and a crisp white shirt with the sleeves rolled to the elbows. He was spinning a videotape with his long fingers and didn't look like he even *remembered* kissing her. Which meant he'd probably forgotten entirely about coming to her shop late Saturday afternoon.

Fine. That meant he'd also forgotten how she'd made a fool of herself by letting on she'd known about his Friday night plans. Maybe he'd forgotten too, how she'd nearly jumped through the ceiling when he'd touched her naked back.

She breathed out a little sigh of relief. She'd been embarrassed about giving away her sensitivity to his touch and worried how he might react to the knowledge. But it didn't seem to be on his mind at all. It appeared her worries were over.

She frowned. Except for this "little dilemma" he was talking about. "Okay, Rory, spill."

A strange expression moved over his face. Then, without a word, he crossed to a television and VCR. The videotape went in, the TV went on. *Celeb! on TV* splashed onto the screen, and then the image changed to her naked back. Rory's hands. Her face, looking back at Rory and wearing a clear expression of yearning. Then Rory's gorgeous blue eyes and exotic cheekbones.

"No." Her first thought was to deny what she was seeing. "That's not . . . How the heck—"

"Your Web cam," Rory said shortly. "I assume you forgot to turn it off, just like you forgot to lock your door when you closed that night."

*Oh, crud.* Jilly flushed, guilty. He was right. She hadn't remembered to turn the camera off right away and then Rory had arrived, driving everything rational from her head. A little groan escaped her mouth as their images began replaying on the television screen. She looked away, unwilling to see that kiss-me expression on her face one more time.

"No," Rory ordered. "Keep watching." Now a big blonde appeared on the screen to speculate on what the famous Rory Kincaid had been getting ready to do.

They already knew whom he was getting ready to do it with. Jilly Skye. The big woman said her name three times, identifying her as a "secondhand-clothing dealer."

"*Vintage*-clothing dealer," Jilly spit out at the stupid blonde, welcoming in a bit of anger. It sure beat distinct embarrassment.

One of Rory's eyebrows edged up. "If you've finished your rebuttal?" When she sighed, he flicked off the TV, then nodded toward it. "That's our dilemma," he said.

Jilly swallowed, still trying to comprehend that a private moment in her shop Saturday evening had been shown on a nationally syndicated television program. "Oh, so," she said, rolling one shoulder and trying to pretend she wasn't experiencing a terrible uneasiness.

Rory lifted that eyebrow once more. " 'Oh, so' . . . uh, what?"

She swallowed again. "So who cares? Who cares what anyone thinks?" Oh, man. Jilly stared down at her shoes, ignoring another flush of heat crawling up her face. How many people had seen her bare back . . . and worse, much, much worse, the bare longing in her eyes when she'd looked at Rory?

And, worst of all, had he noticed it?

"*I* care what people think," Rory said, his voice tight.

Jilly looked up. He paced away from the TV, striding across the mellow-toned Oriental carpet covering the floor.

She bit her bottom lip. "It's not so bad. It's not as if we actually *did* anything."

Rory sent her a look.

Okay, so it had looked pretty much like they were about to do *everything*, but still . . . "We know what happened. Nothing. So what's the big deal?"

"The big deal is there's a contingent of media types camping at my gates now. Before, they'd just drop by once or twice a week. But the big deal is, now I can guarantee they're going to make the next few weeks hell." He sent her another angry look. "All thanks to your Web cam, by the way. If I remember right, you called it a 'little piece of fluff.' Well, your fluff just seriously impacted my life, thank you very much."

Guilt again rushed through Jilly. Then her eyes narrowed. The media types, he said. *Wait just a minute.* She crossed her arms over her chest. "Hey, I'm not the one who fanned the flames of speculation out there by kissing me."

Still pacing, Rory shot her another glare. "Do me a favor," he said, his voice even tighter than before. "Don't bring up flames. That's where this whole thing started."

She stared at him. It seemed he was blaming her. It seemed he thought something was *her* fault. Well, the kiss certainly wasn't. "What's that supposed to mean?"

He halted, standing in front of the library windows. "C'mon. You know you're hot, baby."

Jilly's eyes widened. "I am?" *She was? Rory Kincaid, above-the-title star of her wanton fantasies, thought she was hot?* She bit back her smile, but the surprising idea thrilled her all the same. "I'm hot?"

He started pacing again, as if he'd already answered her question. "So here's the deal. We have something special going. That's what that reporter asked—if it was 'special.' I like that. We'll stick to it."

Her chin dropped in surprise, though the thrill was still running strong. "What?"

He appeared not to have heard her, he was so lost in thought. "I'll issue a statement about your mistake with the Web cam. I'll say I thought I was alone with my special . . . friend."

"Issue a statement? 'Special friend'? Is this an upgrade from the 'uh friend' I was to that political creep?" Jilly shook her head. "Really, Rory, who cares that much what people think?"

"The Blue Party cares. The Blue Party cares what people think."

Jilly froze, as suddenly everything he'd said, everything he'd done, came together. " 'Dilemma,' you said!" Really mad now, she stomped over to him and halted his incessant pacing by standing directly in his path. " 'Dilemma,' my behind!"

His eyebrows rose.

"You said we had a *dilemma*. A dilemma would be something the two of us needed to figure out together. But you'd already decided all by yourself, hadn't you? Before I even drove up, you knew what you were going to do. Statements, special friends . . . kisses!"

He'd said she was hot. Hah. Now she knew that was as big a lie as their supposed "dilemma." It was something he'd said to put her off her guard, to control her. She recognized it from a childhood full of disapproval and demands to follow certain rules. Rory wanted to manipulate her into doing what would work best for *him*.

She crossed her arms over her chest. "I'm not going along with it."

He stared down at her, his eyes a burning blue. "Yes, you are," he said quietly.

She shook her head. "No. It doesn't matter to me if we cause the biggest scandal this side of Monica and Bill."

Rory grabbed the end of the Gucci tie she had around her neck and hauled her closer to him. "There won't be another Kincaid scandal, do you understand?" he said through his teeth. "I don't want anything to screw with my Blue Party nomination. And you—do you want people to think you undress for any man who comes in off the street?"

Jilly hesitated. There was one person who would surely think that of her. One person who had thought that about her mother and who had predicted that Jilly would follow in her footsteps if she didn't do as she was told.

Follow the rules. Listen to the nuns. Live a gray-and-white life. Control. Control. Control. All under the guise of "loving" her.

"I don't care," she said stubbornly. "So what if someone thinks that?"

She wondered for a minute if Rory might use her tie to strangle her. But then he released Mr. Gucci's best silk and grabbed her shoulders instead.

"Damn you," he said. "Damn you, Jilly. I care if someone thinks that. And I'm not going to let it happen to you."

And for some stupid, unexplainable reason, the rough note of concern in his voice made her sway toward him. Then a flash came through the window, like sunlight reflecting off metal or maybe glass. Startled, she tried drawing back.

Rory wouldn't let her. He drew her closer, then up on her toes and toward his mouth. "Promise me you'll cooperate," he ordered roughly.

Just like that, his eyes became the intense, burning eyes of her fantasy desert prince. A Sahara sun was heating her skin and she felt his belt buckle press against her stomach and his hard thighs graze hers.

Maybe that was why she answered, "Promise," before his mouth came down, fierce and satisfying, against her mouth.

But the kiss ended unsatisfyingly early when someone else entered the room.

"Oops," Rory's brother said. As Rory and Jilly broke apart, Greg was turning to leave.

"Don't go," Rory said abruptly. "It was just for the snoopy paparazzi. I saw the sun flash off a telephoto lens."

For the second time, Jilly tried swiping away his kiss with the back of her hand. *Just for the paparazzi.* When was she going to learn?

With a sympathetic smile in her direction, Greg handed some papers to Rory. "Faxes for you," he said.

Jilly had seen the machine that sat in the housekeeper's alcove office adjacent to the kitchen. As Rory bent his head over the sheets, she edged back, thinking this was a good time to make her escape.

But he instantly looked up. "Don't move a muscle."

His commanding tone made her want to do jumping jacks or run in place. Perform a few handsprings, maybe. Something that moved every muscle she owned. She settled for crossing her arms over her chest once more and sighing.

"Domineering devil, isn't he?" Greg grinned at her.

Recognizing a kindred spirit, Jilly found herself grinning back. "Very Pattonesque."

"How about Sherman?" Greg countered. "Like the tank."

She pretended to consider it. "Or Schwarzkopf, maybe? But no, he seems too nice."

"MacArthur, then."

"Machiavelli."

"Would you mind?"

They both turned innocent faces toward Rory. "Yes?" Jilly asked sweetly.

Rory rattled the faxes in his hand. "The special relationship is out."

"Thank the Lord," Jilly said instantly. "Indeed, some prayers are answered."

"Instead, we're going to be engaged."

Jilly blinked, then looked at Greg. "He didn't say what I thought he said, right?"

Greg looked like he was holding back another grin. "Depends on what you thought he said."

Rory impatiently rattled the faxes again. "You two can practice your comedy-club routine some other time, okay? I'm serious. This is serious. The senator faxed me. Charlie Jax faxed me."

Greg shot her a look. "You remember Charlie Jax, right? Campaign director Charlie Jax."

The political creep. Jilly swallowed. Rory's political ambitions.

Greg looked back at Rory and sighed. "I take it they already caught a glimpse of your Internet escapade?"

Rory ran his free hand through his hair. "Jax did. The senator is taking his word for it. They advise that I do something about the situation right away. Something that makes it appear respectable." His voice lowered to a mumble. "They seem to assume I can."

Jilly thought of her naked back and that look

she'd recognized in her own eyes. *Respectable* didn't seem a real option. She tried again. "This is *your* problem, Rory. Not mine."

He glared at her. "Caused by *your* Web cam. Jilly, we've been over this before. It's *our* problem. Especially with this kind of B.S. already pouring forth." He shoved the topmost fax into her hand.

Reluctantly, Jilly directed her gaze at the paper. It seemed to be a printout of a gossip column posted daily on the Web. The Kincaid name came up a lot, in bold print. And then there was hers, along with a lot of wild and almost creepy speculation about the kind of woman she was and the kind of relationship they had. "Ew," she said in disgust and quickly passed the fax back to Rory, who passed it on to Greg.

"Convince her, Greg. Tell her how it will only get worse if I don't put a ring on her finger."

"A ring!"

"An *engagement* ring. And only temporarily. We can break it off when I leave L.A."

Greg looked up from the fax and briefly met Rory's eyes. Something passed between them, an exchange of pain, or perhaps of remembered humiliation. "I'm with Rory on this one, Jilly. You both will be protected by calling yourselves engaged. Sorry."

She bit her lip. "It can't be that big a deal."

"Yeah. It can," Greg said. He glanced toward Rory again. "It can get really, really ugly."

Jilly thought of the decadent parties rumored to have taken place at the Caidwater mansion. Of the eleven wives in the Kincaid family. Of the fact that Rory apparently wanted something different for himself. Finally, she had to be honest and admit it *was* her fault they'd been caught on camera.

"No," she said one more time anyway.

"For God's sake. It's not like it's really going to change anything between us. And don't forget, you promised," Rory said. Then his face set and he crossed his arms over his chest. "The bottom line is that I won't let this happen to you, Jilly. I refuse to let you be hurt by what the media can do with this."

Jilly toyed with the end of her Gucci tie. It was such a nice, heroic sentiment, wanting to protect her. But she knew it came with a price. Her grandmother had said she wanted to protect Jilly, too. And that protection had meant she'd never known her mother. That she never could look at love the same way again.

But the implacable I'm-the-general-here expression on Rory's face told her she didn't have much choice. Which made it just that much harder to comply.

The only good side to the whole mess was the possibility that if she cooperated, Rory might feel like he owed her something. Once she thought of how best to bring up Kim and Iris, that is. After witnessing Kim's anguished reaction when Jilly had told her of Rory's intention to take the little girl away from southern California altogether, she was only more committed to reuniting mother and daughter. Maybe agreeing would make him look more kindly upon her plea.

Rory's eyes suddenly narrowed. "There's not something else I should know, is there?"

Jilly flinched guiltily. "What do you mean?"

There was no way she could come clean about why she was here now, not when he blamed this entire headache on her and her Web cam.

"You're not already married? Or hiding some skeleton in your closet that might come out to haunt us?"

Choking off a laugh, Jilly shook her head. "No husband. And the Jilly Skye closet is quite empty, I promise you." It was a fairly new closet, too, since Jilly Skye had lived as Gillian Skye Baxter until she was twenty-one. There wasn't any way to connect the two, not even through Things Past. She'd made that clean a break from her grandmother.

"Then you'll agree," he said, as if it were a given.

And she supposed, after all, it was. "Oh, fine," she said grudgingly.

Rory's expression didn't flicker. Instead, he immediately headed toward the far wall of the library. He pressed something in the paneled woodwork and a section slid back to reveal a safe.

Still without looking at her, he pressed some numbers on the keypad. "So. What do you like when it comes to engagement rings? Roderick kept an assortment of women's jewelry on hand. Rubies? Diamonds? Or my personal favorite, emeralds?"

Greg watched his brother shut the safe door and slide the wood panel closed. Jilly had left the room, heading to the east wing and Roderick's stash of clothes, uneasily twisting on her finger the emerald ring Rory had insisted she choose.

"Do you know what you're doing?" he asked.

Rory shrugged, then turned to meet his gaze. "What has to be done. You saw what was written. You and I both know it will only get worse unless Jilly and I make our relationship dully respectable."

Greg shook his head, but decided to keep from wondering aloud if "Jilly" and "dully respectable" should be uttered in the same breath. "It's getting kind of complicated, though, isn't it? This whole thing with the Blue Party?"

Rory stiffened defensively. "This kind of attention isn't just because I'm a potential candidate. It's because I'm a Kincaid."

Greg couldn't disagree. The legacy of their name, of their grandfather's and father's actions, had taken a toll on them both. It had made Rory obsessed with redefining the family name as something straitlaced and squeaky-clean. Thinking back to Rory's concern that Jilly might be hiding something, Greg realized that Rory also still couldn't shake his deep wariness when it came to women. He was constantly at watch for any ulterior motives.

As for himself, what Greg couldn't shake was . . .

The memory of Kim. The pain of seeing her again. The agonizing question of where she'd been and what she'd been doing the past four years.

And he couldn't shake his lingering shame

either. It was what made him guess and second-guess his decision to battle Rory over Iris.

Mrs. Mack entered the library. "Mr. Rory, I know you didn't want to take any calls today, but this one's from Michael Riles. It's about the community tech—"

"I'll take it." Rory hurried toward the desk and the phone there, eagerness and relief written all over his face.

Greg shook his head. "See how quickly you dive into that, Rory? Community technology centers in low-income housing areas. There's your next project. Not Washington, D.C."

Rory paused, his hand on the phone. "Go away, Greg."

"You can't really want to be a senator."

"*Go away*, Greg."

Greg smiled at his brother. Rory hadn't denied it, had he? But then his smile died. Jilly had denied that there was anything more Rory should know about her, but Greg couldn't believe coincidence had brought the proprietor of the shop where Kim worked to Caidwater.

He sighed. More than four years ago he'd moved into Caidwater—just temporarily, he'd thought—after his Malibu house had been demolished in a mud slide. He'd met his grandfather's newest wife. In less than a year she'd been gone from his life, yet he'd been trying to forget about her and their history every day since. There were a few things he couldn't deny either.

And one of them was this sudden, compelling urge to head for the FreeWest district and the shop called—it seemed a strangely ironic name now—Things Past.

Kim stood in one corner of the shop, her gaze glued out the right window. A camera crew was filming outside and she held herself motionless behind a concealing rack of 1940s housedresses, ready to disappear up the back stairs if necessary.

There were no public records to connect her to the business—her agreement with Jilly was verbal as a way to protect them both from Roderick's vindictiveness—but she couldn't afford to take chances. Not even when she didn't think she much resembled the too-young woman who had married so long ago.

Kim was so engrossed in watching the media bustle that she didn't notice anyone approach until the air beside her stirred.

She jumped. "Wha—"

Greg. He must have slipped like smoke through the front door. Her skin turned cold and her leg muscles tightened, coiling for flight. But, gritting her teeth, she forced herself to remain still.

Even though Greg was here again.

They stood there silently, just staring at each other, and she prayed her gaze wasn't hungry. It felt hungry, *she* felt hungry, as she absorbed what changes four years had wrought.

It wasn't that he'd been a total stranger to her since she'd left Caidwater. During that time she'd been to every one of his movies. It was one of her most intimate secrets, that she saw those particular films, and it was one of the very few secrets she kept from Jilly.

But it was different, seeing Greg in person. Different, and so heartachingly the same. They were eye to eye, both of them being five-foot-eleven, but his shoulders were wider, his body more muscular than it had been when they both lived at Caidwater. His features were even, All-American really, different from the exotic cast of the other men in his family. But if Greg didn't exude the legendary, compelling sexuality of his grandfather and father, he possessed something Kim valued much more—decency.

His medium-brown hair still had that boyish cowlick at the front, even though his hair was cut very short. That Christmas, the only Christmas she'd been married, she had teased him about that uncontrollable wave by gift wrapping a huge box stuffed with dozens and dozens of hair gels and tress tamers. In a ratty pair of sweatpants and a ripped T-shirt the color of his Kincaid-blue eyes, he'd sat on the floor beside the tree and laughed until tears ran down his cheeks.

Maybe that was when her husband, his grandfather, had first begun to suspect.

Her legs tightened again, all her instincts commanding them to run. But she controlled herself once more, ruthlessly ignoring her screaming nerves. Running would be the easy way, and the easy way was something she'd vowed to give up.

"What do you want?" she asked him. It was only a whisper, but she considered even finding her voice a victory.

His mouth kicked up in a ghost of his sweet,

crooked smile. Kim bit the inside of her mouth to mask the pain in her heart.

"I don't know," he said. One corner of his mouth lifted again, but there wasn't anything close to a smile in his eyes. "I'm not sure."

Kim briefly looked away, steeling herself. If he didn't know, then it was up to her. She had to be sure. *She* had to be sure he never came here again. That she never saw him again, except for those secret matinees and late-night showings when she sat alone in a movie theater and pretended all his good-guy smiles were just for her.

A woman deserved to pretend, didn't she, even when she didn't deserve anything else?

"I—"

"I—"

They both spoke at the same time, then broke off. He reached out a hand, and she quickly stepped back. "No."

God, no. He couldn't touch her. She'd never let him touch her, not even when his desperate heart had been in his eyes and hers was crying out for him.

Maybe she'd spoken too loud, because the few Monday morning customers were staring. Kim took a breath and turned toward her office in the rear of the shop. "Why don't we go somewhere less public?"

She didn't wait for his answer but headed in that direction, praying that when push came to shove, she wouldn't ditch the whole awkward situation after all and run out the back door. Stress and fear did funny things to her though. When she was eighteen and dumped by her stepfather on the streets of Hollywood with a D-plus grade point average and fifteen credits short of a high school diploma, she'd gone ahead and done what he'd always said was the only thing she was good for. She'd traded her young body and her blond beauty for the security and money a man could give her.

But she hadn't made her trade with just any man. Oh, no. Kim had brokered what she thought at the time was an awesome deal with an eighty-five-year-old Hollywood icon. Maybe her stepdaddy would have been proud after all.

To be fair to herself, she'd gone into the marriage with every intention of being what Roderick wanted, a beautiful young wife who could prove that he still had *it*, that he was still virile.

In return, she'd thought she would attain the security she'd been desperate to possess. She'd said "I do" without a qualm, never once considering that she was giving up marrying for love. It wasn't as if she'd thought Roderick loved *her*, of course.

And he hadn't. No one ever had. At eighteen years old, she'd never expected anyone would.

That was why she'd been thrilled about her pregnancy. Someone to love! Someone to love her!

She pushed these painful thoughts away and, by some miracle, found she'd made it to her office. She sat down at her desk and gestured for Greg to take the other chair. But he remained standing, his hands shoved in the pockets of his jeans as he looked around the small room.

"You graduated from high school," he remarked, gazing at a framed diploma.

Jilly had given that to her as a "graduation" gift three years ago. "My G.E.D.," she corrected.

He leaned toward another frame and she couldn't stop herself from staring at him. She liked his very short hair. It looked thick and warm and she wondered how soft it was. Her hands had never touched it. Not her hands, or her cheek, or her mouth. They never would.

He turned his head to look at her. "And your A.A. in Computer Science?" He didn't sound surprised, and she found herself astonishingly grateful for that.

"Yes. And in June I'll have my Bachelor of Science degree. I'm already doing a little Web-site building on the side." She hoped she didn't sound proud. She was, of course, extremely proud, but Greg was fully aware of all her faults and probably thought she didn't deserve any pride at all.

"So, including school and working here, you do a little Web-site building?" He sounded surprised now. And maybe impressed.

"I don't just work here, I'm a partner," Kim said, then instantly wished the words back. For a thousand reasons.

"A partner," he repeated slowly. "You're a partner in Things Past? That doesn't happen overnight."

Her hands curled into fists. He'd just put his finger on one of the thousand reasons why she should have kept silent. He spun around and inspected her A.A. diploma for a second time. She knew what he was looking for. It was from a local college.

He spun back. "You've been here all the time," he said. He didn't make his words sound like an accusation, but he didn't have to.

"Yes," she said.

He lifted a hand, let it drop back to his side. "I thought ... I always assumed ... Roderick said you were leaving L.A. for Vegas. Phoenix, maybe."

"Yes," she said again. She didn't want to tell him she hadn't had enough money to get that far.

Greg had been out of town on a shoot when Roderick sprang the divorce papers on her. Greg was to have been gone only five weeks, but on the second day of his absence, her husband had told her calmly, quietly, to get out. She'd been feeding their infant daughter a bottle and Roderick had been on the phone with the sheriff's department, just in case she refused to leave without a fuss.

Apparently Greg assumed that Roderick had given her something to start a new life with, but in fact, he had locked her out of the house with a small suitcase and the cash she'd had in her purse.

Nineteen dollars and twenty-four cents.

She'd even laughed—sure, a bitter laugh—about it at the time. Nineteen dollars and twenty-four cents. Nineteen for her age. Twenty-four for Greg's.

He ran a hand over his hair. "But if you've been here, you could have seen—"

"No!" For some reason, she couldn't bear to hear him say her daughter's name. "Roderick—the prenuptial agreement—"

"I know all about that, Kim," he said softly. "He told me what you'd signed."

Kim nodded. She'd been so naive. So stupid. She hadn't even read the agreement.

"What I meant," Greg continued, "was that you could have seen *me*."

She was so astonished she just stared at him.

An expression crossed his face, something she didn't dare put a name to. Then he turned his back on her.

"I looked for you, Kim. I looked for you in Vegas and I looked for you in Phoenix. Other places, too."

*Oh.* She bit the inside of her mouth again, tasting blood. He'd looked for her.

But she ignored the traitorous softening in her chest. Where would he have gone to look for the Kim of four years ago? Would he have looked for a showgirl? A waitress? Would he have looked for a woman bought and paid for by another old, wealthy man?

Sometimes she still hated herself.

"You need to go, Greg." She put every ounce of her strength in her voice. "I don't want to see you." She swallowed and said it once more. "I don't want to see you ever again."

Greg turned to face her, so slowly it felt like she died four times before she could see what her words had done to him. The bones of his face were stark and his eyes almost empty. Almost. "Not before you explain something. There's something I don't understand."

She waited, unable to say anything to that stark, beautiful face just yet.

"What's going on? Why is Jilly at the house? What does it have to do with Rory?"

Jilly. Rory. Kim's heart slammed against her ribs. Oh, God. *Oh, God.* Her fingers gripped the edge of her desk as if she could squeeze some answers out of the wood-embossed plastic. She'd been so caught up in being near Greg again that she hadn't seen this question coming.

Greg could ruin everything. If he warned Rory before Jilly had figured out a way to get him to see Kim's side, then she might never get her daughter back.

She stood so abruptly her chair crashed to the floor. "Please, Greg." Her voice cracked. "Please don't say anything to Rory. Or Jilly. I've never told her about—about—that you and I even know each other. But Jilly and I, we're not trying to hurt anyone."

She couldn't tell if he believed her. His expression was stony, his eyes chips of blue ice. Oh, God.

Kim swallowed. "We're not doing something bad. Please, Greg." She knew she sounded desperate. "Please, please don't say *anything.*"

If possible, his face became even harder. "I remember you saying those exact words before. Four years ago, in fact."

She latched onto what he'd said, unheeding of the grim look on his face. "And you didn't. You didn't say anything then."

She'd been six months pregnant when he'd called her name from across the Caidwater library. She'd looked up from her book, instantly sensing his feelings and his intent to tell her of them. But they were in his grandfather's house and she was his grandfather's wife and her belly was round with his grandfather's child. She'd known that speaking of it would only torture Greg more. Both of them. Then, like now, silence was best.

In her panic she moved forward, toward him, but her hips smacked into the desk. She looked down, as if the furniture had sprung out of nowhere, and then back up at the glittering blue of Greg's eyes. "You never said a word to Roderick or anyone else about . . . us. I should have thanked you for that."

He stared at her from those hard and empty eyes, then shook his head. "Shit, Kim." There was pain and confusion but mostly a savage anger in his voice. "Should you have thanked me? Should you thank me now? Should you really?"

He walked quickly toward the door. But then he paused and slowly turned back around. "Don't worry," he said wearily. "For . . . for old time's sake, I'll keep your secret."

Her heartbeat still thrumming in panic, Kim watched him go. Secrets again. She was so tired of them.

# ♪ Chapter 7

Seated in a corner of the Bean & Leaves beverage bar, surrounded by a few of her favorite members of the FreeWest Business Association, Jilly stared into the dregs of her cup of Cosmic Comfort tea and sighed. She was stalling.

The last Wednesday of every month, the business association met at 7 A.M. to discuss shared concerns. As the association secretary, Jilly was required to take the minutes and she never missed a meeting. But Ina, the association president as well as the owner of the Pilates exercise studio on the corner of Freewood and Fourth, had concluded the meeting with a clack of her mug against the tabletop nearly an hour ago.

"Got a problem, Dink?"

Jilly looked across the table into the warm gaze of her good friend Dr. John. At six-foot-seven, Dr. John had nicknamed her "Dink," short for "dinky," just about the first moment they'd met.

"Oh. You know." She tried smiling as she reached up to scratch her eyebrow. A gold ring pierced Dr. John's ebony skin at the far corner of his left eyebrow. Looking at it always made her itch. "It's that big job I have at Caidwater."

Knowing she could trust her friends, she'd told them days ago the truth of the "engagement" Rory had announced to the press. She had to admit he'd been right about that. The press interest had died quite a bit, especially since he'd said the wedding date was indefinite. She occasionally saw reporters around, but so far had managed to avoid them.

Dr. John's gold eyebrow ring hitched higher as he widened his eyes. "Are you falling behind?"

Jilly rubbed at the spot on her nose that was tickling. "No, I'm making a lot of progress on the clothing." Dr. John's diamond nostril stud caught in the gleam of the overhead light and winked. She rubbed her nose again. "It's something else."

The "something else" was the fact that, despite the engagement, she hadn't made any progress with Rory. In trying to avoid being caught with him by any spying, kiss-inducing telephoto lenses, she'd managed to also avoid the man himself.

Rubbing the prickling skin on her upper lip, Jilly gazed at Dr. John speculatively. "How would you go about acquainting yourself with a man?"

The blond-haired one sitting beside her laughed. "Why are you asking *him*, Dink? You know Dr. J is strictly hetero."

Jilly swiveled in her seat, smiling at Paul, one half of Paul and Tran's Catering—a new venture in the neighborhood—who was also one half of Paul and Tran the long-committed couple. "Okay, then you tell me, Paul. Say you want to spend a little time with a man. Let him get to know you. What would you do?"

From his seat on the other side of Paul, Tran leaned across his partner and answered for him. "Paul would cook, of course. Lots of finger food. Oysters." Tran rubbed a hand over his washboard abs and winked. "Yum."

"Or go to the movies." The ring piercing Dr. John's upper lip and matching the one in his eyebrow wiggled as he spoke. "And I happen to have free passes." From the inside pocket of his elegant, ash-colored Armani jacket, he slid out two tickets and placed them next to Jilly. "*Among the Pillows* is guaranteed to get you closer."

She picked up the passes, considering. Dr. John had a quarter interest in their local art-movie house, though his main occupation was running The Cure, his shop specializing in piercings, tattoos, and mehndi body art. "I don't know . . ."

For one thing, Rory didn't seem the type to appreciate visiting her neighborhood, let alone art films. The other, bigger reason was the shiver that ran down her spine when she thought of being alone with him in the dark. She wiped her suddenly damp palms on the front of her jeans and sighed. "I can't seem to make up my mind about anything."

For the first time since this conversation had begun, another of Jilly's friends, Aura, looked up. "Why didn't you say you were having problems earlier? I would have been happy to help."

Jilly smiled at the older woman. Aura wore her slightly graying sandy hair styled in a somewhat mussed pageboy. It went well with her comfortable, conservative clothing, mostly denim or khaki with the occasional Irish knit sweater thrown in.

Pursing her lips, Aura consulted the book she carried with her everywhere. Eight inches thick and its cover a plain celestial blue, it had gilt-edged pages filled with equations, notations, and drawings made in Aura's angular and undecipherable handwriting.

She tapped a page with her finger. "Aquarius," she murmured to herself, then addressed Jilly again. "You don't know whether to zig or to zag because of all the extra energy coursing through you. Blame the recent eclipse. But the restlessness won't go away until you find a way to relieve some of your stress."

Dr. John snickered and Aura sent him a frosty look. "Yes, John. That could very well be the kind of stress Jilly needs to relieve."

Jilly inwardly groaned as Paul, Tran, and John laughed outright now. Aura, who had once confided over a couple of glasses of wine that she'd dropped the initial L from her real first name when she opened her astrology parlor, couldn't be stopped from giving guidance any more than Dr. John could stop finding body parts to pierce.

Though Jilly didn't take Aura's astrologically based advice seriously, she did give the older woman her respect. Aura, who bore an uncanny resemblance to Martha Stewart but who talked about astral projections instead of apple pie recipes, had been Jilly's mother's best friend.

And then Aura had come to San Francisco four years ago with a packet of letters, and become Jilly's friend, too.

Only Jilly, her grandmother, and the minister had been in attendance as they interred Jilly's mother in the marble mausoleum on the cemetery's cold and windy hilltop. But then Aura had approached with her warm smile and warm hands and pressed into Jilly's numb ones the letters her mother had written to Jilly during the past twenty years. Letters her grandmother had returned unopened. Letters she'd never mentioned to Jilly.

Those letters had led her to L.A. Jilly had come here to get to know her mother, even though it was too late to meet her. She'd come here to escape her grandmother, even though it was too late to escape an unshakable fear of what people could do when they knew you loved them.

Aura's voice brought Jilly back to the present. "You just ignore these buffoons, Jilly, and let me see how I can guide you." She bent her head to consult her book again.

Jilly pasted on an expression of expectant interest, doing as Aura suggested and ignoring the gibes and innuendos the three men were tossing back and forth. It was imperative to find a way to establish some kind of friendship with Rory— necessary to plead Kim's case when the time was right—so she might as well listen. It wasn't like she had any bright ideas of her own.

Aura looked up once more. "Tran was right. It's food. Get Paul to make you up a basket of something."

Jilly mulled over the suggestion and took of sip of now-cold tea. "Maybe . . ." Maybe it was a good idea. She could bring a picnic lunch to Caidwater today. She would invite Iris along as a chaperone and then she could also gauge the progression of Rory's relationship with his aunt, too.

She smiled at Aura and jumped to her feet. "Can you do it, Paul?" The man was already nodding. "A lunch basket for three, to be ready in, say, an hour?"

Scooting out of her place in the corner, Jilly beamed at all of them. Before arriving in FreeWest, she hadn't known what it was like to have a family, as "family" in the truest sense of the word—a group of people who looked out for your welfare because they cared about *you*. You as yourself, not as a reflection of them.

"Thanks, everybody. You may have just solved my problem." She had a plan, she had a picnic. For the first time in days, her natural optimism surged, rising like little bubbles of carbonation in her blood.

"Not so fast, Jilly."

Aura's small frown couldn't check her desire to skip rather than walk out of the beverage bar. "What?" Jilly said, still smiling. "I'm listening."

The older woman held up a finger. "Be careful of what you say, because misunderstandings will come easily today."

"Gotcha." Jilly started to turn, but Aura caught her eye, so she obediently turned back. Sharing a patient and amused look with Dr. John, Jilly rubbed at her itchy eyebrow. "What else, Aura?"

The woman's expression was serious. "Everything you expect to happen will be the opposite," she said ominously. Then she smiled. "Now go have fun."

On the drive to Caidwater, a quilt and the picnic basket beside her, Jilly pondered how to get Rory to agree to join her for lunch. What if he didn't fall right in with her plan? She sensed he'd been keeping out of her way just as much as she'd been keeping out of his.

While she was coughing away the dust her tires kicked up on the dirt road—after her first and last run-in with the press, Rory had shown her an inconvenient but secret approach to the house—she came up with the answer. Iris.

Rory wanted to please Iris. More than that, he was knee-quaking, face-paling, spit-scared of her. And she could manipulate him with a skill that females seven times her age didn't possess. The little girl could get the job done.

So just around noon, Jilly hid her smile as Iris walked onto the back terrace of Caidwater, leading Rory by the hand. Maybe they should send the little girl to the Middle East. Give her a few marshmallows to squeeze and then see how fast those peace talks progressed.

As Rory came closer, Jilly's mental smile fell away and she caught her breath. Sand dunes popped into her brain. Naked male limbs beneath flowing robes and heat, heat, heat. No wonder southern California was experiencing another drought. Rory was here.

Coming to a halt in front of her, he eyed Jilly, then sighed. It was a resigned, almost strangled sound. Apparently the sand dunes didn't go both ways.

"Why are you dressed like a refugee from a bad production of *Grease*?" he asked.

She refused to be insulted. Along with her jeans and white blouse, she wore black-and-white saddle shoes and a Hollywood High letterman's sweater she'd ecstatically unearthed at a garage sale. "This is authentic vintage-fifties wear, I'll have you know."

Feeling the warm sunshine on her shoulders, she shrugged out of the sweater and looped it over her arm. "What's it matter how I'm dressed, anyway?"

Rory shot her another, unreadable glance. He sighed again. "It doesn't. That's the problem."

"Hey, Rory," Iris piped up. "You know what? You look at Jilly funny."

They both transferred their gazes to the four-year-old. Jilly had forgotten all about her.

Rory frowned. "What did you say?"

"You look at her funny."

"I do not," he answered, but he was getting that green-around-the-gills expression he always wore when he was interacting with Iris.

"You do."

Jilly thought this was pretty interesting. She sidled closer to Iris. "He looks at me funny how?"

"When you know he's looking, or when you don't know he's looking? He looks at you funny both times. But he looks at different parts of you."

Bristling, Jilly shot Rory a quick glare. "*Which* parts?"

"Your—"

"Iris," Rory quickly interrupted, "I don't have much time to spend on a picnic. Perhaps we should get going."

Jilly gave Rory another look, but surprise, surprise, he suddenly seemed hell-bent on grabbing the picnic basket at Jilly's feet.

Straightening, he glanced at the two females again, though he avoided Jilly's eyes. "Are we going to stand around yakking, or are we going to have this picnic you promised?"

And before anyone could answer, he was hurrying down the steps and toward one of the eight garden gates cut into a tall, massive hedge surrounding the rear terrace. With a shriek, Iris tore after him. Jilly grabbed up the quilt she'd brought and followed more slowly, promising herself to interrogate the child later. Not that she was really that interested in where and how Rory looked at her, of course. She pushed open the gate Rory and Iris had disappeared through—

To gasp at the sight spread out before her. This was only one of the wedge-shaped gardens that surrounded the Caidwater mansion, and Jilly had yet to explore them. But she couldn't imagine another being quite as remarkable.

The size of a small park, it was a garden obviously designed for children. Gently rolling grass led past climbing trees, berry bushes, and a pond with a fountain in the middle and a tiny bridge at one end. Jilly walked across the soft carpet of grass. Croquet was set up on a flat expanse of lawn, the colored stripes on the miniature wickets and child-sized mallets gleaming in the sunshine. Mounting a small rise to join the waiting Rory and Iris, she noticed the buildings nestled in the two far corners of the garden's pie shape. On the left sat a small red schoolhouse, complete with bell tower. On the right, a thatched cottage with a steeply pitched roof and ivy-covered walls.

Jilly stared at Rory. "Oh, my," she said. "It's—it's—"

"Just another example of how far people take fantasy in southern California," he answered dryly.

She blinked, trying to take it all in. "Who did this?"

"Caidwater's original owners, a pair of silent-film stars." His mouth twisted. "An adult's overblown notion of a kid's playground."

Before she could reply, or even begin to read the expression on Rory's face, Iris skipped away again. "Follow me!"

They let the little girl decide the exact location of their picnic. His face a mask of resignation, Rory positioned and repositioned the quilt under Iris's direction, never once seeming to realize she was deliberately trying to goad him. Jilly finally took the matter into her own hands by setting her bottom firmly in the middle of the pastel-shaded quilt.

She sent Iris a woman-to-woman look. "Just right," she said.

As usual, the little girl was perfectly reasonable when it came to anyone but Rory, so Jilly also made it her business to hand around the food in Paul and Tran's basket. With a melon wedge and

two finger sandwiches cut in the shape of butterflies on her plate, along with sparkling cider bubbling in a plastic champagne flute, Iris seemed
quite content.

Rory didn't relax so easily. His gaze on his little
aunt, he spoke in a hushed undertone to Jilly. "Do
you notice what she's doing? She's biting the
wings off those butterflies."

Jilly passed him his own plate, more sandwiches, melon, and a helping of a salad of cab-
bage and walnuts. "She's *supposed* to eat them,
Rory. That's lunch." She looked over at Iris in
time to see little-girl teeth sink into an "insect"
with obvious relish.

Jilly laughed. "When I was her age I would
have loved the chance to eat bugs." Not that her
grandmother would have allowed anything so
frivolous. "Don't you remember being a kid?"

"Being a kid? Oh, I remember, all right." With a
faint, not-quite-amused smile, he looked off into
the distance as if the past were just on the other
side of the tall hedge. "Everyone at Caidwater
was a kid. From my grandfather to my father to
whatever woman they were involved with and
whatever friends they had hanging on at the
time."

Not knowing quite how to respond, Jilly made
one of those "mmm" sounds that she hoped
would encourage him to talk.

And he did, after biting into his sandwich and
chewing. "Life here was just one party after
another for a passel of adult-sized, spoiled-rot-
ten, I-want-what-you-have kids."

The words came out matter-of-factly, as if he'd

analyzed his childhood and compartmentalized his feelings toward it a long time ago. Jilly admired this ability at the same time that it chilled her blood. "That doesn't sound so terrific," she said lamely.

He surprised her with a grin. "Are you nuts? It was a hell of a lot of fun for a long time." He glanced at Iris, but she didn't seem to be aware of the conversation. "Nobody made Greg and me sit down for meals. Nobody gave us a bed time. Nobody cared if we went to school or not."

Jilly blinked. "But how did you . . . why . . ." She began again, trying to imagine two boys left to fend for themselves. "That sounds like something out of *Lord of the Flies*."

"Nah." He shook his head. "Nothing so gruesome. More like Tom Sawyer and Huck Finn."

Jilly still couldn't reconcile what he had said and who he was. Greg and Rory had been two neglected little boys who had gone on to build successful careers. "At some point you two started going to school, though, right? How did Tom and Huck finally get civilized?"

He shrugged. "Sometimes you become the opposite of what—who?—you're raised to be, if that makes any sense."

*Oh, how much that did.*

"But I can actually pinpoint the day I realized *someone* at Caidwater needed to be an adult. Fifth grade. Mrs. Russo's class. We were to do a science experiment that day, something with wires and electricity." He smiled, clearly caught in the memory. "Man, I didn't want to miss that."

Jilly made another "mmm" sound, which was rewarded when Rory continued to talk.

"There had been a big bash here the night before. I got up early to make sure I had plenty of time to rouse someone to drive us to school. I carried a pitcher of Roderick's famous hangover remedy—screwdrivers—as I walked around. I knew better than to go into bedrooms, so I looked for someone passed out on the floor or a couch. But it was deathly quiet around the place, except that the lights were on in the room with the indoor swimming pool. I went inside."

Jilly tried interpreting his expression, but it was beyond her. Just as was a child carrying around a pitcher of vodka and orange juice. She swallowed. "And inside?"

"Inside was empty. Except for a pair of women's panties floating on the surface of the pool. The rest of her clothes lay on the bottom like a drowned body. Something about that . . . the discarded clothes, the image of someone drowned . . . I just knew I didn't want Greg to see that."

Rory looked away from her. "So I chucked the hangover remedy, ran to the utility closet, and grabbed the lifesaving hook, in a hurry to drag those clothes out. As I scooped them from the water, I remember realizing it was up to me. It was up to me to save both of us."

Jilly's bite of sandwich tasted like dust. "S-so what did you do?"

Looking back at her, Rory shrugged. "Well, though I missed that day of school, I never missed another one. I made sure Greg didn't either. I bullied whoever I could, from Roderick to one of the gardeners, to get us there. I hoarded cash, so if I was really desperate, I called a taxi."

Jilly glanced around at the miniaturized, impeccably cared-for garden. She swallowed. "It seems hard to believe childhood here wouldn't be idyllic."

Rory's smile had a cynical edge. "That's because you're still caught up in the fantasy. But I realized when I was eleven that fantasies aren't dependable." He smiled again. "And that I'm the kind of person who needs to be absolutely sure of what's real and what isn't."

That chill trickled into Jilly's blood again and she twisted around her finger the gorgeous but too-large emerald engagement ring. "Rory—"

"I want to go to school," Iris suddenly said. "Greg says I have to go to school next year when I'm five, and I want to."

Rory turned toward the little girl as if just remembering she was there, but then smiled approvingly. "And you will, Iris. I promise. At my house near San Francisco, remember? And maybe Washington, D.C., after that."

Jilly swallowed. At his house near San Francisco. And maybe Washington, D.C., after that. Where would Kim and Iris's relationship be then? As if a cloud had passed over the sun, the air around Jilly cooled. Her appetite completely gone, she could only stare at her plate as Iris and Rory worked through the food in the picnic basket. Once Iris was down to the crumbs of her cookie dessert, she jumped up and ran toward the red schoolhouse.

"My compliments to the chef," Rory said, handing her his empty plate and glass.

"Chefs," she corrected him automatically. "It's a brand-new catering business in FreeWest, run by my friends Paul and Tran."

Rory stretched out on the quilt, stacking his hands beneath his head and closing his eyes. "Your turn," he said.

She closed the lid of the picnic basket. "My turn for what?"

"Tell me something about Jilly Skye and how she grew up. I gave you the condensed version of the Caidwater Chronicles. Turnabout is fair play. You must have some interesting stories to tell."

Interesting stories to tell? Licking her lips, Jilly stared down at him. He was going to be sorely disappointed if he thought her past held any excitement. Because Jilly's mother had been a rebellious, then pregnant teen, Grandmother had guarded Jilly from anything interesting happening at all. Protecting Jilly, Grandmother had said, and again in the name of love, from her own "bad blood."

His eyes opened. Their blue was stunning, and such a contrast to his olive skin and black hair. "You can't be shy?"

"Shy?" Jilly didn't think it was the least bit shy to be suddenly floating away again on thoughts of long Arabian robes and what a man wasn't wearing under them. Her gaze ran down the lean length of his body and she wondered what his skin would feel like against her palms. She wondered how it would be to bump her tongue over the intriguing ridges of his chest and stomach.

Wiping her palms on her jeans, she cleared her throat. "I'm not shy. I just don't have anything to tell."

He chuckled and closed his eyes once more. Jilly found it easier to breathe when he wasn't looking at her. "You said your grandmother raised you," he prompted. "In a house of gray and white."

"And then when my mother died I came to L.A.," Jilly said. "I took over her business, I became involved in the FreeWest Business Association, and I built up the store in a way that I hope my mother would be proud of."

His eyes opened again. "That's important to you?"

"That my mother would be proud of me?" Jilly nodded. "Yes. It's my way of connecting with her. My grandmother was certain my mother would come to nothing. And then even more certain that I would make a disaster of my life. But . . ."

"You showed her?"

"And maybe myself," she said slowly. "You know what I mean, right? With your business? You did that, too. Made it yourself. Made yourself."

He took his time sitting up, all the while looking at her, deep inside her, Jilly thought. Then he smiled. Her breath disappeared again.

"Made myself," he said, and one of his big hands lifted to cup her cheek. "You're right. We both did that."

Jilly didn't think it was a good idea for him to be touching her, but she couldn't have moved away even if his fingers were burning her. Which they were. Oh, a sweet, shivery burn.

A dangerous burn. *Sister Bernadette*, Jilly thought to herself as a warning against the seductive, tempting prickles that rushed across her flesh.

Rory's gaze sharpened. "What did you say?"

Oh, boy, had she whispered it aloud? Her eyes widened and she tried scooting back, but Rory instantly slid his hand into the hair at the back of her neck to keep her close.

The heat from his palm made her scalp tingle. "I didn't say anything."

"You said, 'Sister Bernadette.' Who's that?"

"She—she was one of my teachers." Jilly swallowed, trying to control all the secret places that were suddenly warming in response to something as simple as his long fingers tangled in her hair. "When I was in high school at Our Lady of Peace Academy. She taught a class for seniors called Deportment and Discipline."

He grinned. "And you said you didn't have anything interesting to tell. It sounds like something to do with S and M."

"No!" Jilly's eyes widened in amused shock. "Sister Bernadette would pray for your soul for thinking such a thing. It was a class on . . . on male-female relationships."

Rory shook his head. "C'mon. You want me to believe you took a class on male-female relationships when you were, what, seventeen or eighteen? Isn't that a little late?"

"It's true. Our Lady of Peace is a school housed in an old convent. Girls only. Believe me, with the way we were sheltered, seventeen was quite early to be discussing sex education."

Rory looked like he might fall backward in shock if he weren't still gripping her hair. "Someone . . . you . . . that looks like . . . you were raised in a *convent*?"

"I was raised by my grandmother and taught by nuns. At a very strict school."

She saw him swallow, the long muscles of his tanned throat moving smoothly. He shook his head from side to side in amazement. "I don't believe it," he said. "Taught by nuns, then settling in FreeWest, of all places. I'll bet you couldn't wait to make up for lost time."

His gaze dropped from her eyes to her mouth.

Oh, no. Oh, no, twice. Once, because that speculative look on his face was making her all shivery and burning again. Twice, because she couldn't have him thinking she'd wanted to "make up for lost time." Not in any sexual way. Quite the contrary. She'd come to L.A. determined to disprove her grandmother's dire predictions.

*Be careful of what you say, because misunderstandings will come easily today.* Aura's prediction. "No," Jilly said hastily, alarmed by the way his gaze remained focused on her lips. "You don't understand."

But he didn't seem to be listening. Instead, he kept looking at her, touching her, and she felt that indescribable pull toward him. "You know," he said almost absently, "I've been fielding questions for days about why we don't appear in public."

She swallowed nervously. "I'm in public all the time. Why, I was just at the grocery store yesterday."

His small smile didn't reach his intent eyes. "*We*. Why *we* don't appear. Together."

She had a bad feeling about where this was going. "No. You said our engagement wasn't going to change anything between us."

"And it hasn't. I'm still impossibly intrigued." He leaned toward her. "How about you?"

She leaned back. This wasn't supposed to happen. The picnic was supposed to establish a friendship, not anything more passionate. Oh, but she *was* intrigued.

"You make me crazy, you know that?" he murmured, coming closer.

Jilly's pulse jumped, but then she thought of their small chaperone, the one she'd been so smart to bring along. "Iris . . ." she said warningly, then put her hand on his chest—ignoring its interesting hardness—and pushed.

He didn't budge.

"Iris!" she called out now, desperate for the child's presence to dash cold water on what was happening between them.

Then, thankfully, Rory's gaze flickered, and he suddenly lifted his head. "Damn. Greg's here."

As if from a far distance, Jilly heard Iris's shrill welcome and then her excited chatter as she filled Greg in on the picnic. It was obvious that Iris saw the younger man as the father in her life.

But the thought flew away as Rory's fingers twisted in Jilly's hair and tugged gently. Reluctantly she met his intense gaze again.

"Tonight," he said. "Tonight we'll go out. Away from the house. Just the two of us."

*No.* That was what she was supposed to want to

say to such commands. But instead, she licked her dry lips and told the truth. "You don't want to go out with me. I make you crazy. You just said so."

"But we're engaged, remember?"

"Just for the press," she said hastily.

"And for all the Internet junkies and tabloid readers." With his free thumb he stroked her cheek. "Since everyone believes we can't keep our hands off each other, what would it hurt?"

Jilly searched her mind for an answer. Because there certainly were fifteen good reasons, at least, not to agree.

*Think, Jilly, think.* She needed to remember why she shouldn't say yes. Except she could think only of Rory, of his blue eyes, of his warming touch, of his sexy mouth that had kissed her so passionately.

But he'd kissed other women, too, no doubt. His type of women, the type who wouldn't make him crazy. Leggy, classic, Grace Kelly blondes who knew more about men and what would please a man like Rory than one nun-led class had ever taught Jilly.

"No," she said, grabbing at the first thing she could think of. "It's a full moon." She cleared her throat and scooted away from his hands. "My astrologer has, uh, warned me to stay away from the opposite sex during the full moon."

Rory looked amused. "That's for werewolves, sweetheart."

"Well, sure, but—" She broke off as Iris approached them, towing Greg. "But I remember now," Jilly said, looking at the little blond girl. "I already have something to do tonight. I'm going to the opening of a new FreeWest art gallery with my business partner."

Sighing in relief, she transferred her gaze to Greg. He was such a nice, relaxing presence after the heated intensity of Rory. This kind of man would take no for an answer. She smiled at him.

And Greg smiled back. "You'll be at a gallery opening in FreeWest tonight? With your partner?" He swung Iris up in his arms and the little girl clung to his neck like a monkey. "That sounds great. Rory and I enjoy supporting new businesses. And art! We love art, too. We'll meet you there."

Rory looked from Greg to the surprised-into-silence Jilly, then back to Greg. He grinned. "By Jove, I think you did it. For once, she can't think of anything to say. Good work."

Jilly gaped at the two obviously smug, satisfied males and started sputtering. *Everything you expect to happen will be the opposite*, Aura had said. "Uh. Oh. *Oh, no*—"

But Rory had jumped to his feet and the brothers were already walking away, giving her no more time to protest, refuse or, excuse.

*Oh, no.*

# Chapter 8

Greg leaned against one of the few unadorned patches of wall in the art gallery, occasionally taking a sip from the glass of white wine in his hand. He didn't know if the sour taste in his mouth was due to the shitty Chardonnay or because he had to watch Kim interacting with, even *touching*, other men.

Wearing black jeans and a loose-tailed men's dress shirt, she was turned in profile to Greg and surrounded by a small group of apparent friends. Her heavy golden hair was twisted against the back of her head, held there magically by two black-lacquered chopsticks. She reached forward to give a casual tap on the forearm of a huge black man, and when she smiled at his response, the gleaming color of her hair caught the light, and caught Greg's undivided attention.

From the beginning, he'd always watched her. Four months into Kim's marriage to Roderick, he'd returned to live at Caidwater. Temporarily, he'd thought then.

He'd been between movies, and with time on his hands and someone young and sweet livening the rooms at the mansion, he'd started to watch Kim. He'd catch her swimming in the indoor pool, cutting roses in one of the gardens, painting her toenails in the sunroom.

She'd been shy around him at first. Excusing herself when he came into a room, not looking him in the eye even when he coaxed a few words out of her, gripping her bottles of fingernail polish like a lifeline.

But then she'd changed. After discovering she was pregnant, books had quickly replaced the bottles of polish. He'd continued to watch her, fascinated by the way she had blossomed as her body had. She'd smiled, laughed, teased, and talked to him. About pregnancy, babies, and anything else that had caught her fancy, because she'd started to read *everything*. The Caidwater library had finally found a resident worm.

In those months he'd watched her grow up, grow into motherhood, grow into womanhood.

Watching her now, though, watching her chuckle and then gently bump the person next to her with her shoulder, Greg felt that sick sense of shame rise in his belly again. He let it fill him.

He *was* still ashamed. But it was no longer because he loved his grandfather's wife. And it wasn't because four years ago he'd let her get away.

He was just goddamn ashamed he hadn't gotten over her by now.

While Roderick's legal papers had forced her to stay away from Iris, Kim could have contacted Greg. But during the four years that he'd wondered and waited, she never had. She'd made it absolutely clear last week that she never wanted to see him again.

So tonight he'd crashed the gallery opening to convince himself that it *wasn't* love he had for Kim. Just a bad case of wanting what was forbidden.

That made sense, didn't it?

"What are you doing over here by yourself?" Rory's shoulders hit the wall beside his with a thump.

Greg forced his gaze away from Kim to look at his brother. There was an edge to Rory tonight, too. He was dressed all in black, his eyes the only color relieving the darkness.

"A better question would be why you wanted to come at all," Greg countered, then took another sip from his glass, envying Rory, who appeared to have found the only beer in the room.

He pretended to survey the nearby avant-garde sculpture—a tower of egg cartons sprinkled with wood shavings. "Is an appreciation of the arts approved by your Blue Party masters?"

Rory narrowed his eyes, then glanced at Greg's wineglass. "That swill must be worse than I thought to put you in such a nasty temper. And whether or not the stuff here is 'art' I will leave to someone who cares a hell of a lot more about it than me."

Despite his lousy mood, Greg had to laugh. Rory always had a one-track mind.

His brother's gaze roamed around the room. "Have you seen Jilly?"

"The one track," Greg murmured.

"Huh?"

"Haven't seen her."

Rory impatiently pushed himself away from the wall. "I think she's avoiding me." He drained his bottle of beer, then shoved the empty into Greg's free hand. "I'm going to find her."

Shaking his head, Greg remained where he was. As usual, Rory's need for immediate action always impressed him. It was what made him think the political life was going to be a disaster for Rory. It was what made Greg always feel less than a man himself.

In a sudden pocket of silence, a laugh sounded. Greg looked in the direction of the pretty sound, though he knew whom it came from. Kim. She'd drifted to a corner of the gallery. Then she half turned, catching sight of Greg.

Jilly hadn't warned her he'd be there.

Expressions chased themselves across her paling face. Surprise. Fear. Neediness. Across the room, their gazes held. Greg remembered the dark warmth of her brown eyes.

The wineglass she held slipped bonelessly from her hand and landed with a crash against the polished floor.

Kim snapped her gaze away from his. Color flooded her face, and he could tell she made an excuse to her companions. The black man leaned down with a napkin to grab up most of the mess.

When he straightened, Kim almost jerked the napkin out of his hand. And then, without another look in Greg's direction, she hurried away.

Maybe he was more like his brother than he

thought, because Greg couldn't suppress the sudden urge to start after her, not thinking of anything but catching up to her.

He followed her until she made her way into a small galley kitchen. She had her back to the narrow entry and her head was bent as if she were inspecting her hands.

"Did you cut yourself?" Greg asked.

Her shoulders jerked at the sound of his voice. She shook her head. "I'm fine."

He took a step toward her, and as if she sensed him, she whirled and retreated a few steps of her own. Staring at him from the distance between them, she worried her bottom lip. She wasn't wearing lipstick or any other kind of makeup. When she'd lived at Caidwater, her mouth had been a soft pink and her eyelashes dark, to make her eyes that much richer.

That much more forbidden.

But she looked just as beautiful to him now.

And she'd said she never wanted to see him again.

So the way in which she made his heart pound, like the slam of a fist, *had* to be because she was forbidden to him. That was all. Nothing more.

Now. Then. Forbidden.

"I was damn noble when I was young," he said, his mood spiking to new, angry heights. "And stupid. Maybe if I had kissed you, touched you even, I wouldn't have wasted the last four years on some dumb-ass dream."

Hugging herself as if in fear of his touch, she took another step back.

It only made him angrier. "Damn it, Kim. I'm

not going to try to now, for God's sake. You've made it clear you don't want me to even get close to you. And maybe I've finally figured out that this is your game, that this is what gets you off."

She shivered, but kept silent.

He wanted to prod her, push her, make her cry. Make her want him with all the pain-filled longing that he'd felt four years ago.

That he felt now.

"How many other men have you played like this, Kim? How many have you made fall in love with you, only to demand they don't speak of it to you or to anyone? How many haven't you let touch your skin or kiss your mouth?"

With every angry question he stepped closer to her and she moved back. Now it was *her* shoulders against the wall, and they stood toe-to-toe, but her face remained a pale, unreadable mask. It was as if she were frozen inside.

The cold stunned him. "God, Kim." His anger leaching away into tiredness, he quieted his voice and looked down at the toes of his scuffed cowboy boots. "Don't you ever feel anything?"

"No," she said. "I try not to."

He looked up.

There were two spots of color on her face, one on each cheek.

Greg swallowed. No, he thought, his anger reheating. This had to be just another of her manipulative games. "Why not?" he asked suspiciously.

Her chin jutted toward him. "You know. Because of the bad thing that happened before."

He frowned. The bad thing? What the hell did

she mean? "But *we* never did anything bad, Kim. We never did anything before."

She looked at him like he was two years old and short of sense. "No. Not us. *Me.* I did the bad thing. Marrying Roderick. Marrying your grandfather when I didn't love him."

Greg shook his head, trying to understand her, trying to believe her. "So the rest of your life is punishment for that mistake?"

She shrugged. "The rest of my life is up in the air right now."

Shaken by the sadness in her voice, Greg stepped back. "Kim . . ."

She took that chance to make a break for it. She was around him and at the doorway of the kitchen in a flash, but then she turned. "Just so you know . . ." She licked her lips, then rushed the rest out. "With you—with you it was never a game."

The words hit him like nine separate blows. He absorbed each one, "never" *bam* "a" *bam* "game" *bam*. His eyes closed against the hurt. For the past few days he'd been trying so goddamn hard to pretend he hated her.

Taking a breath, he opened his eyes. Looking at her only intensified the pain. "I know," he said. Deep down, he *had* known.

Their gazes met, and it was like four years had never happened. It was just like those months at Caidwater when she grew round with Iris in her belly and the only intimate communication they had was with their eyes.

*I cared about you.* He read the words clearly. Nearly heard them. *I never wanted to hurt you.*

Greg sighed, trying to tell her everything. *And I never knew if my feelings were impossibly wrong or just incredibly right.*

*I'm sorry.* Kim slowly came toward him.

Greg froze, unsure of what she intended, but knowing any sudden movement of his would spook her.

Then she lifted her hand and touched his hair.

*God.* Lightning seared him, a crackling heat that cut like a firebreak through his brain and traveled down his body, hardening his shaft in one rocketing, desperate upthrust.

He reached for her. "Kim—"

But she ran before he could return the touch.

Jilly took a pinch of Rory's shirtsleeve—she was leery of actually grabbing hold of his arm—and tried pulling him toward the far end of the gallery. "Let me introduce you to some of my neighbors," she said loudly.

Rory didn't seem to hear her, and he had no trouble resisting her forward movement. Despite her tugs, he held his ground and continued to stare after Kim, who had just bolted from the gallery's small kitchen. "Who's that?" he asked.

Jilly craned her neck and pretended not to know whom he meant. "That's Mackenzie, the manager of the condom shop."

Rory winced. "You had to remind me of that place, didn't you? But I mean the tall blond woman. The one who appears to have just done the Riverdance all over my brother's ego."

"Oh, her." Oh, he'd noticed that, too, Jilly

thought nervously. She'd been hoping Rory hadn't seen the scene between Greg and Kim the way she had. But Greg *did* look shell-shocked after talking with her partner, and Jilly had no idea why.

"Do you know her?" Rory asked again.

Jilly cleared her throat. "Well, um, yeah. She's my business partner. You know, the one who handles the Web-site side of things."

"What's her name? She looks familiar."

Beneath her 1940s beaded sweater, Jilly felt a drop of sweat form. It trickled toward the waistband of her straight, black, knee-length skirt. "Kim." Kim had made it absolutely clear she'd never met Rory, that he probably wouldn't even know her first name, let alone the last name she used now.

But Iris was the spitting image of her mother.

Rory rubbed his chin and glanced over his shoulder again, as if to get another look at Kim. But thankfully, she had disappeared. He looked back at Jilly and shrugged. "Is she married?"

A second bead of sweat pricked Jilly's spine. "Are you interested?" *What the heck would she do if he said yes?*

He grinned and chucked her under the chin. "Jealous?"

She pretended not to be and rolled her eyes. "I was merely going to point out that your political image might take a beating if you so quickly moved on to a new conquest."

He laughed, drawing glances their way. Jilly sent a silent warning to a woman standing nearby who had suddenly taken a good look at Rory and was sidling nearer. Getting the hint, the woman smiled knowingly and backed off.

Jilly crossed her arms over her chest. "Well?"

Rory's gaze dropped to her sweater and he groaned. "Don't do that," he said. "When you do that, I can't think."

Jilly looked down to see what he was talking about. And quickly unfolded her arms. Pearl buttons marched up the front of her light pink lamb's wool sweater and she'd left the top three unbuttoned, which should offer a completely modest look. But with the sweater's tight fit and her abundance of . . . *ahem* that filled out sweaters, it wasn't wise to make moves that pushed any more of her forward.

He took a deep breath. "Now. What were you saying?"

Jilly hoped her skin didn't appear as warm as it felt. "You were showing undue interest in another woman."

Rory glanced across the room at Greg, who still stood in the kitchen. "I just wondered if your partner was already involved with someone. Looks like she just gave my baby brother the I-have-to-wash-my-hair-tomorrow night speech."

Jilly smiled in relief. Of course, that must be it. Greg had asked Kim out, and naturally, she'd refused. "Sorry, Rory, but there actually *are* some women immune to Kincaid charm, with or without another man in their life. Kim isn't involved with a guy, and I can tell you she's definitely not interested in becoming involved with one."

His eyebrows went up. "Oh? So that's the way

it is." He regarded Jilly with new interest. "Are you the woman in her life, then?"

Jilly blinked. "Am I the—?" His meaning dawned on her and her jaw dropped. "I am not . . . what would make you think . . ." Not knowing whether to be embarrassed or outraged, and if either response was anywhere near politically correct, she settled for sputtering.

Then she looked at Rory more carefully and noticed the wicked amusement gleaming in his eyes. She smacked him in the chest. "You stop teasing me."

He started laughing outright. "You should have seen your face."

Jilly huffed. "Well, just consider the look on your face if what you suggested was true and the press found out about it. What would the Blue Party think about a candidate dating a woman who . . . liked women?"

"Okay, okay." He stopped laughing. "But just for the record, though the Blue Party might want upright candidates, it's not interested in legislating morality." He leaned closer to her. "Which means it's perfectly acceptable that a *potential* candidate like myself spends time with his beautiful, sexy fiancée on a Friday night."

Jilly thought maybe he'd sucked the air right out of the room with that tempting mouth of his, because she couldn't breathe. "I'm not sexy or beautiful," she said. But it sounded nice. More than nice. Tantalizing.

One of his eyebrows lifted devilishly. "Want me to prove it to you?"

"No!" Though she had to catch herself from

swaying toward him. "I told you this afternoon. My astrologer advised me to stay away from the opposite sex during the full moon," she said piously. "We're already pushing it."

It was best to get all her armor out, because some tide had turned at the picnic today. Obviously Rory had come to some decision, and this teasing, charming, and yes, even sexier side of him was the result. A side that was way, way too lethal to one of Sister Bernadette's best pupils.

Jilly turned her back on him, desperate for a way to cool him down and keep him at a distance. The contrast of the bright blue of a book cover against the tan color of a sensible dress caught her eye in the crowd.

Perfect.

She slanted him a glance, keeping all amusement out of her expression. "Come on," she said sweetly. "Let's circulate."

He gave her another one of those teasing grins. "Call it whatever you want, I'm game."

Oh, bad, seductive, sinful man. "Stop that," she said. "I don't know what's gotten into you all of a sudden."

His eyes seemed to consume her. "The truth of the situation. Your naked back, with my hands all over it, has been shown to millions. Then we kissed, quite convincingly, I might add, for those pestilent tabloid shutterbugs, to prove we have a *special* relationship." He shrugged. "So we might as well have one."

She stared at him. So *that* was what he'd decided at the picnic. "Just like that? You said it's so, so let's make it so?" She put her hands on her hips. "Maybe I don't want to."

He leaned toward her, resting that full, sheik-of-the-desert mouth against her ear. "Give me a chance, baby. I can make you want to."

Jilly closed her eyes as temptation ran like water over her body.

"God." His voice whispered hoarsely in her ear again. "Your skin temperature just jumped fifteen degrees."

Doing her best to ignore him, Jilly rallied her common sense and pushed him away. "Because you're standing too close!" she said. "This room is crowded enough as it is."

He chuckled knowingly and she tried pretending it was annoying instead of beguiling. Even more desperate than before, Jilly turned back toward the crowd and almost wept with relief when she got another glimpse of that blue book cover, even closer now. "Aura!" Jilly called to her friend.

Aura and Dr. John paused in their progress through the room. Spotting Jilly—who was waving wildly—they changed course and headed toward her. They made an odd sight, the huge, bald black man, with his many piercings and fierce tattoos, alongside the Martha Stewartish Aura, in her conservative dress and low-heeled shoes. She carried her book in one hand and used the other to push back her sandy-gray hair.

"Is that who I think it is?" Rory looked stunned.

Jilly smiled. "That's my astrologer, Aura, *not*

who you're thinking of. With our local tattoo artist."

Rory was still staring at the celebrity look-alike Aura. "Your astrologer," he repeated. "And a tattoo artist." Then he sighed as he continued to watch them approach. "Of course they're your astrologer and a tattoo artist," he grumbled. "Just some of southern California's finest and freakiest."

"And two of my very best friends," Jilly said cheerfully. Two friends bound to direct Rory's line of thought away from the passionate. She could only hope it would work for herself as well. "So be nice."

"Nice?"

"Just think of them as potential voters," she told him, and then her friends arrived and she was making introductions. Dr. John gave Rory a hearty handshake, and Aura not only shook Rory's hand but continued to hold his palm in her own, turning it face-up for an inspection.

With an intent expression on her face, she handed over her thick, gold-edged book to Jilly and used the fingers of her now-free hand to trace the lines on Rory's palm. He surprised Jilly by taking the attention without rancor or ridicule.

"Hmm," the older woman said, almost in appreciation. "Success, long life, good health. You're a very lucky young man."

Rory shot an amused look at Jilly. "Not lucky tonight," he said.

Aura glanced at Jilly and her mouth turned up in a secret smile. She ran her fingers over

Rory's palm again. "Tsk, tsk, tsk. The night's not over yet."

"You're right." Rory chuckled. "I've never met a fortune-teller, but I'm beginning to regret that fact."

Jilly made a face at him. "She's an astrologer, not a fortune-teller." She turned to Aura, frowning, as she watched the older woman continue to hold Rory's hand. "I didn't know you read palms."

A mischievous smile broke over Aura's face and her eyes twinkled with glee, Martha Stewart planning another impossible-for-humans-to-reproduce cake decorating project. "You caught me. I don't. But it's not every day I get to hold the hand of such a delicious-looking man."

Rory and Dr. John laughed.

Jilly shook her head. "Aura, his ego is already too big. You're supposed to be helping me cut him down to size."

Aura released Rory's hand and took back her book. "I'm sorry, hon, but I fell in love with this young man's grandfather when I was a little girl, and his father not many years later."

She turned to Rory again. "I was sorry to hear of your grandfather's passing. It seems like the end of an era. But your father, is he well?"

The expression on Rory's face cooled. "He's living in France."

"Ah." Aura nodded, as if he'd actually answered her question. "You Aquarians are passing through a long period of trouble with family."

If possible, Rory looked even more distant. "Is that so."

Aura nodded again. "Yes. Jilly told me the two of you share a birthday."

Jilly had forgotten that.

Rory perked up. "She talks about me?"

Jilly gritted her teeth. "As little as I can."

Dr. John laughed and shook his head. "Dink, Dink, Dink."

By rights, the glare Jilly sent him should have pierced a few more holes in the big man's skin. "What?"

But Rory saved her from any secrets Dr. John might have spilled. " 'Dink'? What's this about 'Dink'?" he asked.

Dr. John laughed again, his deep bass almost shaking the floorboards. "Dink, as in dink-y. Dinky and demure, that's our Jilly."

Rory looked like he might fall over in a faint. "Demure? You think she's demure? We must know different women."

Aura reached out to touch his arm. "That's just *so* Aquarius of you. You air signs get so confused by the wrappings that you never look at the package itself."

She flipped open her book, ran her finger down a page, then told Rory, "But you'll have a chance to do better next month. On the fourteenth, when Venus and your ruler, Uranus, join together. Take advantage of it."

Rory just stared at her. "Excuse me?"

Instead of explaining, she merely shook her head and snapped shut her book. "Oh, and you Aquarians are so stubborn, too. You're much, much too unwilling to alter your course once you've decided on one. Jilly's like that as well."

"I've noticed." Rory smiled at Aura, suddenly oozing charm. "Maybe you have some advice for her on that. It seems she listens to you quite a bit."

Aura's eyes rounded. "What?"

Rory gestured at her book. "Maybe there's something in there that can persuade Jilly to . . . soften a little. To . . . well, it's a personal matter, but I'm sure she'd listen to you, as you *are* her astrologer." He wore the kind of indulgent look that said, while he didn't buy anything Aura had in that book for a minute, he was willing to tolerate the whims of the dinky little featherbrain beside him.

Jilly went hot again. First, because of his patronizing, smug, it's-all-B.S. attitude, and second, because . . .

Jilly didn't buy anything Aura had in that book for a minute either.

Call her too pragmatic, or unimaginative, or not in touch with her intuitive side, but when Aura offered her advice and pronouncements, Jilly usually let them slide right through one ear and straight out the other.

So when she'd told him that day on the boat that it was inauspicious for them to kiss according to her astrologer, and when she'd said that kind of stuff at the picnic and then again tonight, she'd just been giving him a convenient excuse.

Dr. John was laughing so hard he was in danger of popping a nose ring. Aura looked from Rory to Jilly in total bewilderment.

Jilly swallowed, trying to save the situation. "What Rory means is, he knows how much I treasure you, Aura. After all, you've been like a mother to me." As if her gesture were completely impulsive, she reached out and hugged Aura, while urgently whispering in her ear, "I'll explain later. Just pretend I come to you for consultations."

Some people are the type to not question urgent whisperings. Some people quickly catch on to the gist of situations. Unfortunately, Aura was not one of them.

She pushed away from Jilly, her hair quivering as she shook her head. "But, dear, you *don't* come to me for consultations—you're aware of that. Why, I happen to know that when you turn to page E-seven of the *Los Angeles Gazette*, it's strictly for the daily crossword puzzle. You don't even glance at your horoscope!"

*Busted.*

Jilly couldn't think of anything to do but chew her bottom lip and avoid Rory's direct gaze. But out of the corner of her eye she saw that one of Rory's eyebrows had winged up in that devilish way again.

He crossed his arms over his chest. "As I recall, you told me several times that this was 'inauspicious' or that was 'inadvisable' according to your astrologer."

Dr. John's laughter resurged, with such strength that his guffaws turned into eye-watering coughs. Coughs that absolutely required a glass of water, claimed Aura, as she took John's arm and led him off. Jilly stared after the two, suspecting they'd deliberately left her alone with Rory.

Traitors.

"I'm thirsty, too," she said, shuffling backward.

He reached across the distance between them and grabbed a handful of her hair. "Not so fast, Dinky." Gently, firmly, he pulled her closer to him, slow inch by slow inch.

Jilly's heart started up a bossa nova in her chest. He wasn't the kind of man who would like to be made a fool of, and she was afraid that was exactly what he'd think she'd been trying to do.

Maybe she could render him brain-dead with that sweater-arms-breasts move again! But no, her Sister Bernadette training prevented her from doing something so out-and-out sleazy. There was nothing else but to face the consequences, whatever they might be.

And then something redirected his attention. He glanced over her head, and his disgruntled expression instantly became one of puzzlement. His hold on her hair loosened absently and she scuttled back. Reprieve!

That was what she thought, until she turned to see what or whom she had to thank.

Kim.

"Where do I know her from?" Rory murmured. He narrowed his eyes and rubbed his chin. "She's so damn familiar."

Jilly's bossa-nova heartbeat sped to merengue rhythm. *No.* He couldn't put Kim and Iris together *now*. Yes, it was all going to have to come out sometime, but that sometime was some time much later. Sometime when he wasn't already irritated by her little astrology deception. Sometime when they could have a calm, rational discussion about Iris and the custody issue. When that happened, Jilly wanted him to know her, like her, trust her.

Definitely not now. So what could she do to distract him?

He rubbed his chin again, drawing Jilly's attention to his wicked, midnight-at-the-oasis mouth.

Did she . . . did she dare?

A little thrill of excitement rushed through her as the inspiration struck. It was all so simple, really.

"Now, who—" he began.

Jilly rose up on her toes. She threw her arms around Rory's neck.

And then she kissed him.

# Chapter 9

His mouth burned Jilly's. She made a little sound and tried escaping the raw heat, but his arm came around her like a vise. The silk of his shirtsleeve pressed against the bare flesh of her back, exposed where her sweater had ridden up.

Then, abruptly, his arm slid off her skin. He grasped her upper arms and jerked her away from him. "Not here," he said hoarsely.

Certain they'd been scorched, Jilly touched her lips with trembling fingers. She gulped in a breath, but the oxygen it provided was quickly used up as he starting towing her across the gallery, his hand shackling her wrist.

From the corner of her eye she caught sight of the bright gold of Kim's hair. *Good.* Kim was far away, in the opposite direction to the one Rory was heading in. At the moment, though, Jilly couldn't think why that was so important. She frowned and pulled back on the arm Rory was using as a leash.

He swung around. "No." His eyes pinned hers, then dropped, to focus on her mouth. "Don't even think about it. You're coming with me."

Jilly's stomach lurched. She should resist, she thought vaguely. But there was his mouth's rough heat and the cunning way it had of stealing into other parts of her body, warming her so deliciously.

He pulled her forward again, and she let herself be led astray. For just a few minutes, she told herself, she could indulge this strangely wanton impulse. One kiss, two at the most.

He'd already slayed her with three when she found herself outside, fighting for breath, her head whirling. Some sort of male instinct had unerringly directed him to the gallery's back door. He'd pulled her through it and out into the tiny, deserted delivery area. Then he'd pushed her against the stucco wall and proceeded to sear away any sensible thoughts.

"Jilly," he whispered, his voice as tempting as a secret. "You need to open for me, sweetheart."

In the near-complete darkness, he was an inky shadow. His body was barely touching hers, but with the cold stucco against her back and his hot presence just grazing the budded tips of her breasts, she felt erotically caged.

"Open for me," he commanded again.

Jilly just couldn't think clearly enough to obey. "The door?" she said, bewildered.

His big hands left the wall on either side of her head to cup her face. "Your mouth, sweetheart. Open your mouth."

"Oh—"

That was all he needed. His lips touched hers again, soft as a child's kiss this time, but then his tongue slipped inside. The tip of his tongue met hers.

Jilly's body jerked.

He groaned, and leaned into her, supporting her suddenly Jell-O knees with his heavy, hot weight. His tongue boldly stroked, sliding against hers, and she jerked again. Rory caressed her cheeks with his thumbs, as if to soothe her, but the touch only stoked the strange fire coursing through her body.

His tongue left her mouth, and she wanted it back, desperately. The urgent need made her push toward him, made her rub against his big body.

He groaned again and his hands dropped to her hips. He pulled them against his, tilting her into him. His arousal pressed into the vee of her thighs, making her blush, but then his tongue plunged back into her mouth, and the warmth of her skin was nothing compared to the sinful fire burning in her blood, or to the wet heat that suddenly rushed, liquid, between her thighs.

Jilly heard herself moan, and she had to grab onto his shoulders to keep herself upright. Her fingernails dug into his hard muscles as he pressed in a deliberate rhythm into her mouth with his tongue, and against her body with his hips.

Shuddering in reaction to the overwhelming stimulation, Jilly could only open herself more to him, widening her mouth, widening her stance. Rory's tongue plunged again and he pushed his leg between hers. His hard thigh found the source of all the warm wetness, and he pressed.

Jilly jerked so strongly, the back of her head struck the stucco and broke their kiss.

"Easy, easy," he whispered. His thigh continued its delicious, tingle-inducing pressure as he gently explored the back of her head. "Are you okay?"

"I'm dizzy," she said. The tingles were everywhere, legs, arms, flesh, brain.

He chuckled. "Me, too, honey." Then he bent his head and kissed her neck.

Jilly moaned again, the suction and heat of his mouth and the feel of his leg between hers too much to keep quiet about. She turned her head against the wall to give him better access, and his mouth traveled downward. He licked the skin over the pulse at her neck.

Clever, naughty tongue.

Then it licked lower, heading between the buttons of her sweater. Jilly's muscles stiffened and her nipples hardened into even more aching points.

He pressed harder against her with his thigh, setting fire to all those wild tingles, and his hand came up to the fourth button of her sweater.

Jilly's hand grabbed his.

It startled them both.

"Honey," he said, his voice that seductive, hoarse whisper. "Let me."

She didn't let go. In Jilly's mind, an image of Sister Bernadette was pacing before a green blackboard, her habit whirling around her ankles to expose her black orthopedic shoes. *Stop them*, the stern sister urged. *This is what the bad boys want.*

Jilly gulped, her heart racing. Sister Bernadette had never covered what to do if the good girl wanted it, too. And she wanted it so badly, with every pound of her heart, with every pulsing ache of heat between her legs. But Jilly knew she had to stop him from touching her breasts, because—

He kissed her again, hot, soft, and wet.

Because . . . she had no idea why.

Then he lifted his head, his breath ragged. "Please, sweetheart. Don't go nunnish on me now."

*Nunnish. Sister Bernadette.*

"No." Jilly twisted away from him, stumbling out of his persuasive reach. She'd taken vows, almost nunnish vows, and if Rory touched her breasts she knew she'd completely forget them. From the start, he'd brought out the bad in her. "I'm sorry," she said. "But no."

Desperate to get away from him, she whirled, searching in the darkness for the knob to the back door.

"Jilly—" He came toward her.

"No!" Her hand found the knob, twisted it, then she dived inside the gallery, losing herself in the noisy crowd.

At the entrance to a large walk-in closet, Rory stared at the delectable sight of a sweetly rounded backside covered in denim and embroidery. He gritted his teeth as Jilly bent over to retrieve a hanger at her feet.

"There you are," he said.

With a tiny shriek, she jumped two feet into the closet, falling on her knees.

Rory crossed his arms over his chest and didn't feel the least bit guilty for having startled her. This room had once been his father's and was thickly carpeted, even the closet. Anyway, a little discomfort was nothing compared to what she'd done to him. Three nights ago she'd left him harder than a flagpole, so hard he'd spent fifteen minutes in the cool night air getting himself under control.

Long enough for her to get away.

Not long enough for him to come to his senses. He'd been dead set on getting her back in his arms.

But when he'd finally cooled down a little and ventured back inside, the flash of a photographer's camera had returned his good sense. Christ, they'd been *this* close to becoming even more tabloid fodder. If he'd gotten his hands on Jilly's spectacular breasts, no doubt he would have had her tight skirt pushed up and himself pushed inside, right there against the goddamn wall.

*That* would have given *Celeb! on TV* quite a ratings boost.

And would have brought him as low as his grandfather and father. The thought made him sick. The last thing he wanted was for Jilly to be further compromised.

As he watched, Jilly shook herself free of some tangled silk garments on the closet floor and got back on her feet. With a slow turn, she faced him, her eyes kitten-wide and wary. "What do you want?"

*You.* Because beneath those wide eyes was

enough sexual dynamite to blast this entire ghost-filled monstrosity sky-high. Which was why he shouldn't allow himself within a spark's distance from her again, engagement or no engagement.

He sighed. "The minute I saw you, I knew you were trouble." And that gray cloud above him just continued to darken. Because, despite the danger of an explosion between them, he was going to beg a favor from her.

She retreated deeper into the closet, sucking on her lower lip. Sighing again, he ventured closer. The small area was well lit, and he could detect her fast, nervous breaths as her chest moved in and out beneath an embroidered denim shirt. She made a vague gesture that sent some of the clothes on the rack swaying. "I guess—I guess I should have talked with you first thing this morning."

Still enjoying her obvious discomfort with not a particle of guilt, he raised one brow and leaned his shoulder against the jamb of the closet door. "Yes?"

Her hand gestured again. "We should talk about that night."

*Hmm.* He hadn't really considered what her reaction would be after running away from him, but now he could see she was agitated. Nervous.

"I'm sorry," she said.

And sorry. He mulled the sentiment over. Sorry could work for him, perhaps even give him the upper hand with her, something he desperately needed. Especially because he needed her to agree to this favor. "What—"

Clattering and yelling from the hall outside the room interrupted him. Greg, Iris, Mrs. Mack, and God knew who else were running around this wing of the house, calling out the name of that cursed escape artist of a chinchilla.

Rory muttered under his breath and stepped inside the closet, half closing the door behind him to block out the search party's noise. "What exactly are you sorry about?"

Hesitating, she sucked on her bottom lip again, giving Rory time to examine today's selection of wacky vintage wear. The flared jeans were embroidered in a nature theme, and, he had to admit, quite spectacularly. Three decades ago some young woman with way too much time had hand-stitched vibrantly colored trees, flowers, and butterflies, almost completely covering the denim. Rory narrowed his eyes. Some young woman with way too much time and a sense of humor. A green-leafed tree grew up the left pant leg, and one of its branches stretched right across the front of the jeans. It was an apple tree.

And a juicy red piece of the fruit was embroidered to hang right over the bottom of the zipper placket, right over the vee of Jilly's thighs.

*God*.

"I shouldn't have let you do that," Jilly said suddenly.

His gaze jumped away from the apple to her face, which was a little red, too. He frowned. "Do what?"

"Kiss me." She hesitated again. "And, you know . . . against the wall."

"I agree." He couldn't stop his slow smile.

"Against black satin sheets would have been a huge improvement."

Her eyes rounded. "What? *No!*" He could tell she was thinking about it, though. Her cheeks turned even redder. "Bl-black satin?"

She was made for black satin. He could see her pale skin and her dusting of gold freckles against the sleek darkness. "Honey, you need to find yourself a better class of lovers. Black satin is a definite yes."

She was silent for another moment, and then she shook her head, as if freeing herself from a fantasy. "No. You don't understand. I'm trying to tell you I don't want to do that type of thing at all. It's just not fair."

Not that he was so sure doing "that type" of thing with her again was wise either, but the "just not fair" roused his curiosity. "What are you talking about?"

Her mouth, that lush, sweet mouth, primmed. "Sister Bernadette—"

"We're not going to talk about your convent upbringing again, are we?" It gave birth to all sorts of unholy fantasies of his own, mostly centered around Jilly's luscious curves molded by a naughty corset and then covered by a gray school uniform.

She lowered her eyebrows and plodded on. "Sister Bernadette told us about . . . about men. Well, she told us about boys, but I'm certain the same thing applies."

This was getting curiouser and curiouser. Suddenly Rory found himself enthralled. He rocked back on his heels. "Go on," he prompted.

She shuffled her feet. She was still standing among some fallen clothing and he thought he saw one of the disarrayed piles shift strangely.

"The sister explained that when you let—" Taking a breath, Jilly began again. "The sister explained that when you let a boy, a male, touch your—"

"Kiss! Kiss!" Whistles, more calls, and little smacking sounds penetrated through the half-closed closet door as the chinchilla search party made another pass near by.

Determined not to be interrupted just when things were getting interesting, Rory leaned back against the closet door, closing it with a solid click. "Touch your what?" he asked innocently.

"Touch your . . ." With her hands, Jilly gestured in the vicinity of her shirt. "You know."

Rory narrowed his eyes. That shirt was a piece of erotic suggestion, too. Clouds floated and robins flew in the shirt's sky-blue "air." The birds carried cherries in their embroidered beaks, and two of the succulent pieces of fruit appeared to be falling through the air, right over Jilly's nipples.

He shuffled himself now, shoving his hands in his pockets to ease the fit of his jeans. "Touch your cherries, you mean?" With his chin, he indicated her shirt.

Jilly looked down, blushed redder, looked quickly back up. "Yes," she said faintly.

Rory couldn't help himself. "But I *didn't* touch your cherries," he pointed out.

"Well, yes." She cleared her throat. "That's exactly right—"

"But I *did* touch your apple." So sue him, but

this was getting fun. And paying her back with a little teasing was almost worth the discomfort he was causing himself. "Some might consider it even *more* intimate, by the way."

"My apple?" Jilly said blankly. Then she froze. After a moment she shifted her legs and looked down.

Rory looked, too, then had to bite back a half laugh, half groan. Because he saw something new. Crawling up the inside of Jilly's right thigh was an embroidered snake, its forked tongue and lascivious eyes focused on the apple just out of its reach.

"Oh, my," Jilly said, sounding faint again.

Rory's lips twitched. "What would Sister Bernadette say about that, do you suppose?"

Jilly took a deep breath, as if coming to terms with what she'd seen. "That I should look a little more carefully at what I put on in the morning."

*Amen*.

Then she crossed her arms over those cherries and glared at him. "Anyway, you did *not* touch my . . . my apple."

He looked back at her with mock outrage. "I most certainly did touch your apple! I had my thigh right against that very sweet, very juicy piece of fruit!"

Maybe he'd gone too far. Jilly just stared at him, her lips moving but no sound coming out.

A little guilt pierced him. And good sense. He couldn't make her so uncomfortable in his presence that she'd refuse to go along with the request he had to make. "But let's talk about something else."

She swallowed. "Not until you accept my apology for the, uh, state I left you in the other night. Are you okay now?"

Since the "state" he thought she referred to was something he'd been in and out of—mostly in—since the first moment her high heel had hit the Caidwater driveway, he wasn't sure why she was apologizing now. "Okay how?"

"How long does it take to subside?"

That depended on how long it took him to get his mind off her. "Isn't this a bit personal?"

She blinked those big kitten eyes. "Oh. You're right. I'm sorry. It's just that Sister Bernadette explained the whole thing about boys getting blue, uh, you knows, if you let them get too close to your, um . . . cherries." She sighed, as if glad to have gotten all that out.

Rory just stood there, hoping she wouldn't exhale too hard, because the slightest movement was bound to knock him flat. He opened his mouth, closed it, opened it again. "Are you talking about blue balls? The nun told you boys got *blue balls*?"

Again she went as red as the apple. "Um. Yes. That's the term, I believe, though I think it was another student, not the sister, who actually used it."

Rory was *seeing* red. Not only had some woman given out a bunch of misinformation to impressionable teenagers, but not one man Jilly had been with since then had bothered to straighten out the biological facts for her. He could see this little sexpot in her naughty high heels floating from Hollywood party to Hollywood party, making love to men she thought she owed because they'd gotten too close to her— fruit.

The idea made him sick. *"Damn it all to hell!"*

In response to his loud curse, the clothing at Jilly's feet exploded. Something gray and furry erupted. As the creature took scampering laps about the walk-in closet, Jilly backed herself into a corner. When Kiss finally disappeared on a shelf above one clothespole, Jilly nervously eyed the shelf and the stack of boxes on it that the chinchilla had dived behind.

"There's Kiss," she said unnecessarily. She also didn't need to tell him the animal still made her uneasy.

Rory shook his head. That damn chinchilla. It could spend the rest of its life in a shoebox, for all he cared. Laying out the truth for Jilly was more important. "Forget that stupid rodent. Listen to me, Jilly, and listen to me good. There's no such thing as blue balls."

She blinked.

"I wasn't in any more pain or under any more strain than you probably were Friday night. You don't have to go around thinking you're hurting a man if you say no. Got that?" He knew he sounded surly and mean, but, dammit, he felt surly and mean. Why had the men Jilly had taken to bed let her go on thinking this kind of crap?

"You're just being nice."

"I'm *not* being nice." He took a step closer to her, ignoring the ominous rustling from the boxes over his head, exasperation spurring him on. "Why would I be nice to you? You have a weird profession and weird friends. You make me talk about cherries instead of your breasts and apples instead of your p—" He found he couldn't say it. "Instead of your apple."

"I don't want you to think I used . . . I don't want to be a tease," she said.

Rory relaxed a little. "Oh, honey, I know you're not a tease. Honest to God, I know more about teases than you could ever dream of."

She looked doubtful.

Rory hesitated. But then he thought about the men who had shared Jilly's bed in the past, and then he thought about the men who would share Jilly's bed in the future. He'd been given this opportunity to have an influence on just the type of men they might be.

"Listen, Jilly, don't you ever let anyone say you teased them and so you have to pay up. You might have a great body and you might look undeniably enticing in anything you put on, but I've never met a woman who is less a tease. You wear your feelings on your sleeve and in your eyes and in the shade of rose your skin turns when you talk about anything to do with sex or men."

She didn't look like she believed him.

He made a rough, impatient gesture, and his hand met one of the hanging garments. Rory fisted the silk material and pulled the robe from its hanger. It still held the scent of his father, Daniel Kincaid. The scent of power and selfishness. He stared down at the paisley material, astonished that he was considering telling Jilly about that night. The Kincaids had paid big to keep it private.

But her safety was worth more than that price and his pride. "Let me tell you, honey, that after the lesson the man who wore this taught me, I know teases and I know users."

She swallowed. "Who does it belong to?"

"My father. He swears Hugh Hefner stole the smoking jacket look from him," he said, and laughed without real amusement. "Anyway, I introduced dear old Dad to the sweet young thing I'd met in line at the DMV. A nice, un-Hollywood, uncute meet, right? She lived in the Valley and wanted to become a day-care teacher, she said. I melted on the spot. Day-care teacher. Nice, normal. So damn wholesome. I asked her to marry me. She was the kind of woman who could give to our children all I didn't have growing up."

"You wanted children?" Jilly said softly.

"Oh, yeah. And with her. I gave her a big ol' ring and she gave me the big ol' Yes I wanted to hear more than anything."

"And then?"

"Like I said. I introduced her to the family. Grandfather, Dad. Had a real old-fashioned engagement party. And two days later I came home unexpectedly and found my father in bed with my sweet young thing. My fiancée. Only she was nastier than she looked. And she didn't really want to be a day-care teacher after all. She wanted to be an actress on the daytime soaps."

Jilly swallowed again. "I'm sorry," she said.

Rory released the silk in his fist and let the robe fall to the floor. "I didn't tell you that to get your pity, Jilly. I said it so you'd know I know you're not a woman like that. I've got a finely honed radar for those types. You're not a tease or a user, even though you might be a little weird and you might dress a little flakily."

"So I'm just flaky and weird. Thanks." She made a face. "I think."

Rory shifted uncomfortably on his feet. Now that he'd dumped that story on her, he wasn't quite sure what to say next. "Well, anyway . . ." He cleared his throat. "I hope you're free next weekend." Better just tell her straight out. If she saw it as a choice, she might think she had a say in the matter.

She blinked at the sudden turn of conversation. "What?"

"We're going on a trip."

She repeated the order slowly, patent disbelief in her voice. "We're going on a trip."

He held firm. "Yes. I have to meet with some of the Blue Party people in San Francisco. The man who's sponsoring my Senate bid wants to be introduced to the woman I'm going to marry."

What he didn't say was that it had been merely a casual mention. He could easily have made excuses, but for some reason, Rory had liked the idea of having her with him.

But Jilly was shaking her head. "I agreed to let you say we're engaged. I never said I'd play your fiancée."

"Too bad," he answered. "Unfortunately, some

additional footage of us showed up on television over the weekend. You kissing me at the gallery opening. So the tabloids and the talk shows have heated up again on the subject of us. The leaders of the Blue Party want to meet you."

All true. And the prospect of hours-long meetings had seemed so much more palatable with Jilly nearby.

"Grrr."

He lifted his hands. "Hey, what can I say? It's not my idea."

She narrowed her eyes. "That's right. I'm certain *you* wouldn't choose to travel with, let alone marry, a woman with 'a weird profession and weird friends.' "

Rory set his jaw in response to her stubbornness. "Yeah, well, at this point we're both out of choices. I have this meeting up in San Francisco, and you are going there with me."

"Over my flakily dressed body."

"Listen, Jilly, the senator wants to meet you. You need to help me out."

"I don't need to do any such thing."

Gritting his teeth instead of throttling her stubborn neck, Rory admitted to himself they weren't getting anywhere. "Never mind. I'll give you the details later," he said, retreating toward the closed closet door.

"I'm not going to change my mind," she answered, bristling.

He ground his molars. Damn it. San Francisco was for her own good and for his peace of mind. "Later. For now, I'll just—" He turned the knob.

Nothing happened.

He turned it again, shoving with his shoulder at the same time.

Still nothing happened.

"What's wrong?"

He couldn't face her. "The door is locked or jammed, or something."

She groaned. "Mrs. Mack warned me that some of the doors will do that."

Great. Now he was locked inside a closet with a woman who looked like a sex goddess and who was acting like an irritable donkey. "Well, you could have warned *me*."

"How did I know you were going to shut the door?"

He swung around, pissed because she was right, and pissed because, as usual, disaster continued to dog him whenever she was near. Fighting his frustration, and losing, he gazed at her and her garish, Garden of Eden outfit. "For God's sake. You should have known when you started talking about your stupid cherries and apples!" Desperate to get out of her vicinity now, he kicked the uncooperative door with his foot.

The useless thump unleashed sudden chaos.

With frightened squeals, Kiss jumped up from his latest hiding place, sending boxes tumbling onto Rory's head. Jilly laughed, the sound cut short when the creature dived from the now-cleared shelf to the floor, where he scuttled over and around Jilly's feet. She gasped, then jumped away from the critter, bumping against Rory's chest. He automatically put his arms around her, twisting so that her back was against the door and he could shield her from the chinchilla's frantic dashing.

The rodent circled the closet once. Twice. There was another mad scrambling pass, and then the animal suddenly quieted, having nestled away in another hidden location.

Rory's arms still encircling Jilly, they both froze, holding their breath against another violent chinchilla scurry.

After a moment, Rory let out his air. "I think we're safe."

Jilly didn't immediately move out of his arms, and he didn't let go. She felt warm again, too warm, and her breath smelled sweet. "Maybe we should just stay put for a while," he said.

She took him seriously. "You don't think we should bang on the door and call out to someone?"

Inwardly smiling, he shook his head with an almost imperceptible movement. "I think they've moved their search to another wing. They'll be back here eventually, but I don't want to give Kiss another rodent panic attack."

She tensed again, her eyes widening. "No. Let's not do that."

"Anyway," Rory said softly, "it'll give us another chance to talk about this weekend."

"No." She said it automatically.

"C'mon. Say yes."

"No."

He smiled down at her. "If you don't, I'll kiss you again."

"No!"

"I'll touch those cherries."

*"No."* She studied him through suspicious green eyes. "Anyway, you wouldn't do anything I didn't want you to."

He smiled again. "But after I kiss you, you'll want me to."

She tried to jerk away, but he tightened his hold. "Easy, easy. Remember the crazed chinchilla."

She immediately refroze. "I hate that smugness of yours, do you know that?" She lowered her voice in a lousy imitation of his. "I'll make you want me to."

He laughed softly, disturbing the curls around her forehead. "Believe me, sweetheart, your revenge is that despite how much trouble you cause me, I want to, too."

She looked up at him. "There you go again. I don't know whether to be complimented or insulted."

"I'm just being honest. I don't know how the two of us got into this situation, or why the two of us even *met*, when it comes to that, but for the moment, we happen to be engaged. And for the moment, I don't mind holding you in my arms."

Her gaze narrowed. "I'm still not going to San Francisco with you."

He sighed. "It won't be that bad. It's a beautiful city and we'll have a suite at one of the best hotels. You can play around during the day, find more goofy stuff for your shop, I'm sure. Then we'll have dinner with Senator Fitzpatrick."

"Senator Fitzpatrick?"

"Yes. Senator Benjamin Fitzpatrick. He's the one pushing me to be the Blue Party candidate.

He's the one who wants to meet my fiancée. It's . . . it's a kind of command performance, you see." Just a slight embellishment of the truth.

"Senator Benjamin Fitzpatrick." She said the name slowly, as if this were the first time she'd ever heard it. "Maybe I . . ."

A thrill of victory sped through Rory's blood, joined by a last-minute worry. "Now listen, these are the final few meetings before I announce my candidacy. If you could just manage to, uh, tone yourself down, it would be really great."

"Tone myself down?" she asked softly.

He swallowed. "I just think the senator might be offended by any clothing too outrageous, you understand? And if you could keep any talk of aromatherapy or astrology or anything else you might or might not be interested in to a minimum, I'd really appreciate it."

"Hmm." She sucked her lower lip as if lost in thought, but he wondered if she might really be holding back a smile.

His heartbeat quickened. He wanted *something* to go right in these last few weeks before he became the upright, respectable Blue Party U.S. senatorial candidate. And the day he kicked off his campaign, he'd savor the image of his profligate grandfather rolling over in his grave.

"Hmm," Jilly said again, apparently still musing.

"Is that a yes?" he asked, trying not to sound overeager.

She sucked a moment longer, then looked up at him, a little smile curving her mouth. "Yes."

And if he saw an odd gleam in her green eyes,

he ignored it, because he couldn't afford to be suspicious. And he was so relieved, he leaned into her, his palms flat against the door. Only a small thank-you buss on that well-sucked lower lip, he swore to himself. But just as his mouth reached her mouth, the door gave way.

Jilly stumbled back. Rory stumbled forward. His forehead whacked her chin. She cried out, he grunted, and then Kiss squealed in delight as he dashed up Rory's back, leaped from his shoulder onto Jilly's hair, and from there swan-dived to the floor.

As Rory rubbed his smarting head and Jilly gingerly touched her chin, they both watched the rodent escape from the room.

With another long-suffering sigh—not the last he'd ever release in her presence, he feared— Rory shot her a sidelong glance. "Has it ever occurred to you we bring out the worst in each other?"

# Chapter 10

In the small office at Things Past, Kim frowned at her computer monitor, trying to concentrate. Thoughts of Jilly kept intruding, though. She'd left early that morning for her San Francisco weekend, and the mischievous smile she'd worn didn't bode well for Rory Kincaid.

At the knock on the open door, Kim lifted her head, welcoming the interruption.

Except when she saw that the interruption was Greg. Her palm instantly itched with a ghostly tickle, a trace of the memory of his hair against her hand. She swallowed. "No, Greg, I—"

A little girl appeared from behind him, peeking around his thigh even as the rest of her stayed hidden. Her small hand gripped Greg's worn jeans and she observed Kim with eyes that startling shade of Kincaid blue.

The child's hair was a familiar gold.

*Iris.*

She popped out of sight. Kim blinked, then rubbed her eyes. Maybe she'd imagined her . . .

But Greg was watching Kim closely as he reached behind him to pull the small figure back into view. He had a hand on each one of her little shoulders and she leaned trustingly back against his legs. "Kim," he said quietly. "This is my aunt, Iris Kincaid." He cleared his throat. "Iris, this is—"

"Kim." She didn't even know she could speak, let alone move, but she found herself out of her chair and hunching down to child level. "Hello, Iris." Kim's heart was racing, yet she forced herself to be calm as she smiled at the little girl.

Greg tugged on Iris's long hair. "Say hello, sweetheart."

Iris ducked her head instead.

Kim looked up at Greg and he shrugged. Then he cleared his throat again. "We wondered if you wanted to come to the beach with us."

Kim wondered if this was a dream. She was thinking of pinching herself when Iris muttered. "What's that?" Kim asked.

The little girl stuck out her lower lip, then raised her voice. "*He* wants you to come to the beach with us."

*Pinch.* Oddly enough, Kim found her lips twitching. "Ah," she said, holding back her smile. She welcomed any of Iris's moods. It was enough to watch the child breathe, the child she had given birth to, the child she'd so lovingly tended for the six weeks she was allowed to be a mother. "But you're not so sure you want to share him."

"Iris," Greg said warningly.

"It's okay," Kim said, standing to give herself some distance before she scared Iris to death by grabbing her up in her arms. "I'm just happy to have met you." Kim met Greg's eyes. "That's enough," she lied.

Greg gently tugged on Iris's hair again. "Give me a break here, bug," he said lightly, though his expression was serious and his eyes so darn watchful.

Kim tried to appear uncaring.

"All right," Iris said grudgingly, looking down at her red sneakers. "She can come."

Kim almost cried.

The drive to the coast was quiet. Kim was afraid to say anything, Iris apparently didn't feel like talking, and the traffic occupied Greg. Once they reached the beach, he filled his arms with a Mexican-striped cotton blanket and a huge bucket filled with sand toys. "Hold Kim's hand while we cross the parking lot," he told Iris calmly.

Apparently used to the "hold a grown-up's hand" rule and maybe distracted by the nearby promise of the white sand, Iris lifted her fingers toward Kim without protest. Kim hesitated, half terrified and half elated. She could *touch* her daughter.

"Hurry *up*." Impatient with the delay, Iris matter-of-factly grabbed Kim's hand herself, to immediately start dragging her in the direction of the low wall separating parking lot from sand.

The muscles of Kim's hand cramped in an effort not to squeeze her daughter's too tightly. Such a small palm, she thought with amazement, and such little fingers. But so much bigger than the little fists that baby Iris used to hold close to her infant cheeks. The wonder of the changes had barely registered before Iris dropped Kim's hand and hopped over the wall. She ran straight toward the crashing waves, twenty-five yards of sand away.

"Iris!" Kim heard the fear in her voice. She started in her own dead run.

"She'll be fine." Greg called out, halting her. "She's not going anywhere."

Her heart still pounding, Kim took in a long breath of salty air and had to admit Greg was right. Once Iris neared the sand packed hard by earlier waves, she spun around and ran back toward them, smiling with glee, her arms flapping in the breeze.

With her gaze Kim traced the curve of her daughter's smile. "She looks . . ."

"Just like you," Greg said. He trudged past her for a few feet and dropped his load down onto the sand.

She hurried to help him unfold the blanket, always keeping one eye on Iris, who swooped and hopped across the beach like a creature half-seagull, half-sandpiper. With the striped cotton stretched between her and Greg, the fringe fluttering like the excitement in Kim's belly, she met Greg's eyes. "Why?" she asked. "Thank you, but why?"

Why had he offered her this gift of an afternoon with her daughter? Why would he do such a thing when she'd hurt him?

His gaze cut away to the pounding waves and he didn't answer.

Once the blanket was laid out and the bucket

upended, Iris danced around the beach for just a few more minutes before she settled onto the sand with the toys. Kim looked over at Greg for a clue to what to do, but he'd stretched out on the blanket and closed his eyes.

Swallowing hard, Kim edged toward Iris slowly. Sitting down a few feet from her daughter, she slipped out of her ratty running shoes and socks and dug her feet into the sand. The top inch was warm, while just below, it was cold and damp. Winter sand. For the past four years Kim had been just like that. Only an inch of her warm and alive, while just below, the rest of her had lain cold and untouched.

Iris glanced at her. "Aren't you going to help?"

Kim started. Her daughter wanted her help. "Oh. Okay. What are we building? A sand castle?"

Iris curled her small upper lip. Kim bit back another smile, because the forthright gesture reminded her of Jilly. Forthright was good. Kim had the feeling she could learn a lot from her daughter. "No castle?" she guessed.

Iris made another moue of disgust, her face clearly asking if she had to explain *everything* to grown-ups. "I *live* in a castle. What I like to make is sand houses."

Sand houses. Kim scooted closer, blinking away the sting of tears in her eyes. The princess in the castle wanted to make sand *houses*. She didn't trust her voice, so she merely followed Iris's orders for a while, filling the bucket with saltwater, collecting bits of shells and seaweed to decorate the small cottages that Iris molded and patted into shape.

In a circle of sand about eight feet in diameter, she industriously constructed a whole community of houses, some close together, some farther apart. Each one was built and decorated slightly differently, though the most elaborately adorned house was also the smallest, standing in the center of the circle. The wind whipped Iris's long hair across her face, but she didn't seem to notice as she carefully placed the last shell into the small house's side.

"There," she said finally. "Done."

At the pronouncement, Greg opened his eyes and shifted closer to Iris's community. "Looks good," he said. "Why don't you tell Kim about it?"

Something in his voice suddenly scared Kim. "Oh, I can just enjoy the pretty sight," she said quickly. Lord knew she was good at protecting herself from the hard stuff.

Iris was staring at her. "You don't want to know about my houses?"

Kim briefly closed her eyes. "Of-of course I do."

The little girl spread her slim arms. "This is IrisLand."

Kim swallowed. "You mean, like Disneyland?"

Iris curled her lip again. "Nuh-uh. Like . . ." She looked at Greg for help.

"It's not an amusement park," he said, his eyes fixed on the child. "It's where Iris would like to live . . . and how she would like to live, I guess. More like Mister Rogers's neighborhood."

Iris jumped to her feet. "I have a house for everyone I like. See—" She pointed to a large cottage near the center. "This one is for Mrs. Mack. I make it plenty big because she likes to clean."

Kim remembered the Caidwater housekeeper. "I'm sure she'd thank you for all that space to keep tidy," she said seriously.

With a nod, Iris skipped to some other houses. There was one for her former nanny, the maids, the gardeners, even one for Greg's agent. A big house, yet unclaimed, stood by itself, almost completely out of the boundaries of Iris-Land.

"Who gets that one?" Kim asked curiously, pointing to it.

Iris made an unnameable face. "That one is for my nephew Rory."

Greg choked out a laugh. "You keep making his farther and farther away, Iris. How nice is that? You know you like him a little bit."

Iris ignored him, instead skipping to the center of the circle to drop down beside the smallest, most lovingly built house. "And *this* one belongs to me and Greg."

Kim stilled, her feet deep in the cold, damp sand. "You and Greg?"

"We'll live in it always, me and Greg, happy ever after."

Kim smiled a little, obviously the little girl had a big-time crush on him.

"I'll call him Daddy."

Daddy. This wasn't a little girl's romantic crush after all. She wanted to live in a small, normal house and she wanted Greg to be her daddy.

"*Iris.*" Pain filled Greg's voice.

Kim stared at him. She'd thought all the hurt in regard to Iris was her own. But it etched his features, too, even as the wind toyed with his boyish cowlick. Suddenly he didn't look so young any-more.

Just add this, Kim thought, to her collection of sins.

Iris chatted the rest of the afternoon away. At some point she even warmed up enough to give Kim a pick of houses in her neighborhood. Kim noted, however, that Iris limited her selection to one of three that were almost as far-flung as Rory's.

But Kim well knew that all good things came to an end, so when Greg announced it was time to go, she didn't cry like Iris did, though she wanted to.

The sun was setting and the late afternoon breeze was cold, but it was toasty inside the car. Within minutes Iris was asleep in the backseat and even Kim felt deliciously warm, almost all the way to her heart. A quiet song played through the car's speakers, and Kim let the softness wash over her.

No matter what, she had this memory. She could smell the salt air in her hair and if she closed her eyes, she could—miracle of miracles—still feel the sensation of Iris's hand in her own.

"We're here." Greg's voice startled Kim awake.

She blinked. It was full dark now, and they were parked outside Things Past. She whipped her head around. No. It hadn't all been a dream. Her daughter still lay curled in the backseat, sleeping heavily.

In the glow from a streetlight, Kim memorized her daughter's features from the small, almost turned-up nose to the half-moon curves of her eyelashes. Without thinking, Kim reached out to touch her, but then she snatched her hand back. Maybe it was better not to ask for more. Never to want more.

"You asked me why I did it." Greg's voice was quiet and sure, like a shoulder to lean on in the darkness. "You wanted to know why I brought her to you today."

"Yes," Kim whispered. She continued to memorize the beauty of her daughter. It was easier than looking at the only man who had ever touched her heart.

"Because I love her," he said.

Kim flinched, her knees drawing toward her chest as if to reflexively protect herself. Then, damn him, he made it worse.

"Because I love you. I always have."

She froze and all the coldness came rushing back into her body. Stiff and unable to move, she was completely unaware of the tears coursing down her cheeks until Greg unbuckled her seat belt and turned her to face him. He had his hands on her shoulders, then her arms, and then he was wiping the tears away with his thumbs. But his touch didn't penetrate her numbness.

He loved her.

Crying about it was only going to confuse Greg and cause him even more hurt, yet the tears kept coming. She stared at his beautiful and bewildered face through them. He was still wiping her tears away and she still couldn't feel his hands.

*He loved her.*

Nobody had ever said he loved her before.

*     *     *

Dressed in his tuxedo, Rory paced outside the closed door of the second bedroom in his suite at the Ritz-Carlton Hotel in San Francisco. His head hurt from too many cups of coffee during the day-long meeting with the Blue Party strategists.

His jaw hurt, too, from gritting his teeth every ninety seconds or so, which was how often the image of Jilly had popped into his head—the image of how she'd looked this morning when he'd picked her up on the way to the airport. In a leopard-print coat and matching round hat, she'd ducked into the passenger seat of his Mercedes wearing a little smile that announced she didn't care what he thought of her outfit.

He'd thought it was nuts.

No, he'd thought *he* was nuts.

How had he hoped to successfully pull off this dinner with the senator and the other Blue Party bigwigs with Jilly in tow? It was an idea as ridiculous as whatever get-up she was likely wiggling into at this very instant. He cleared his throat. "Are you almost ready?"

*Oh, please God, nothing leopard-spotted or tiger-striped.*

A muffled response came through the other side of the door.

He closed his eyes, his gray cloud weighing heavily on his shoulders. If she walked through that door in something outrageous, how would he explain her to the senator? Rory cleared his throat again. "Um. Jilly. I don't know if I made clear how imperative it is that we make a good impression tonight."

"You mean, that *I* make a good impression." Her voice was clear as a bell this time. Wry, too.

Rory ignored the wryness. "The senator is naturally interested in the woman I've been . . . spending a lot of my time with. He's put a lot of confidence in me, and I've got a lot at stake with him."

There was a pregnant pause on the other side of the door, then Jilly spoke again. "Speaking of what you have at stake, I'm curious as to exactly what entices you about the political life."

He stiffened. Not Jilly too! He'd had enough of his brother casting doubts on his ambitions. "I don't have to explain myself to you." Jesus, hadn't he already spilled his guts to her in the closet the other day? Jilly knew his past. She didn't need to know his intended future.

"Fine." He heard a shrug in her voice. "But as your, hmm—what would you call it?—oh, yes, your *intended*, I thought you might like to fill me in on the party line."

She wasn't taking this seriously, damn her. "Listen, whether you appreciate it or not, it's a hell of a coup to get the nod from the Blue Party. They're committed to bringing principles back to politics. And I'm a Kincaid, remember?"

"And that's important because . . . ?"

His hands fisted. "Because, dammit, I've spent my entire life as a member of a family that has had its garbage gone over and its dirty laundry exposed by every two-bit gossip rag and every overpaid talk-show host for the last half century. I'm tired of the Kincaid name being either a Leno punch line or a four-column, salacious headline."

"Not to mention your eagerness to serve the American people in general and the voters of California in particular," she added sotto voce.

He ran a hand through his hair wearily. "Yeah, and all that, too." Not that he didn't see what she was getting at with such a complete lack of subtlety. But, hell, he wasn't going to fool himself and say that public respect wasn't as important to him as the opportunity to effect a change in the negative attitude toward public office. "And I don't want tonight to mess up my chances."

From the other side of the door, another ominous, perhaps even offended, pause.

*Uh-oh.* Better quickly change the subject. Rory looked desperately around the parlor, decorated in soft grays, and his gaze snagged on the small mountain of bags Jilly had staggered in with after her day of shopping. He rubbed his chin. "So it looks like your time was spent well, if that load of purchases is any indication. What did you get?"

"It's what I *didn't* get that I think I'm regretting." She sighed audibly. "I was considering another tattoo, but I'm leery of anyone but Dr. John working on my skin."

Rory's blood froze. Did she say *tattoo*? Did she say *another* tattoo? With astonishing recall, he flipped through every image of Jilly he'd stored away in his mind. A tattoo. Was it possible she had one he'd yet to see?

Of course it was possible. He swallowed. "What you're wearing tonight, it's . . . um . . . it covers you up, right?"

She laughed. "Of course it covers me up."

But who knew what her definition of "covered" was? He thought about that flesh-colored dress, those plastic-wrap jeans, the delicate, vulnerable curve of her bare back. At least he knew there were no tattoos from her neck to the twin dimples at the base of her spine.

He swallowed again. She wouldn't really have marred that pale, gold-dusted skin, he told himself. Dr. John wouldn't have inked a butterfly or a rose on her flesh, let alone some man's name or something even more indecent. *Wild child. Sex kitten. Vixen.*

At the sound of Jilly's voice, Rory shook himself free of the distracting images. "What?" he said hoarsely.

"I was just asking your opinion on how many rings I should wear."

He still couldn't stop himself from imagining the smooth flesh just to the inside of her hipbone. Was its only decoration a freckle or two and a delicate tracing of veins? "Earrings?" he asked absently.

"Well, those, too, I suppose. But I was really thinking of my other piercings."

*No.* No? Rory dashed to her door and tried the knob. Damn. Locked. He took a deep breath and told himself to be calm. But, God, disaster was always just a heartbeat away with Jilly nearby.

"Are, uh, those 'other piercings' of yours going to"—he had to swallow to get the word out of his suddenly dry mouth—"show?"

"Only the one in my tongue."

Rory swallowed his. He was choking on the thing when she finally took pity on him.

"I'm kidding, I'm kidding!"

He caught his breath.

"About the tongue."

She was going to kill him. No, that was much too simple and too quick. But no doubt about it, his life was spinning out of control. Before the night was over, something terrible, something unimaginable, was going to happen. He would bet his not-yet-won Senate seat on it.

"*Jilly*," he said warningly. "I'm not in the mood."

She only laughed, then opened the bedroom door.

He instinctively stepped back. And back again. Because whatever he'd been expecting, it wasn't this.

Jilly held out her arms and spun on the high heels of black, nasty-girl, velvet-strapped sandals. The notion of a career in shoes whirled through his head again.

She made a neat 360. "What do you think?" she said.

"You're covered up," he managed to get out. And she was. In a black tuxedo that mimicked his own, even to the satin stripe running down each pant leg. Except she wasn't wearing a cummerbund, or a bow tie . . . or a shirt either. This tuxedo was designed for a woman, obviously, with the jacket's waist nipped in and the buttons reaching to a point that only hinted at Jilly's awe-inspiring cleavage.

He ran his gaze from her hair—neatly controlled by a velvet band—past her ears, discreetly studded with one pearl in each lobe, to her toenails—painted a classy shade of gold.

When his gaze moved back to her face, she stuck out her tongue and wiggled it. "See? Told you I was kidding. And the tuxedo is a perfectly respectable Bill Blass, circa 1970."

Rory stared into her completely serious eyes. *Perfectly respectable*? Did she really believe that? Because, yeah, she had on more than he expected, and probably more than several of the other women would be wearing tonight, but not one of them would be sending out fiery sexuality like smoke signals. Only Jilly. Always Jilly.

"C'mon," he said gruffly. "We're going to be late."

She scurried after him as he strode down the hall to the elevators. "Are you all right? I thought I looked okay."

He sighed, punching the button that would take the elevator down to the lobby so they could reach the other elevator that led to the penthouse restaurant in the opposite tower. "You look great." He couldn't tell her how great. He couldn't tell her she looked like an orgasm in high heels.

As the elevator whooshed them down and the other whooshed them back up, he pinched the bridge of his nose, trying to imagine the senator's reaction to the chocolate-and-cream-filling cup-cake standing beside him. He wanted the older man to like Jilly, he realized. She might not be the right type of woman for a senatorial candidate, but she had sparkle and sass and charm. She'd created friends and a life and a business for her-self out of nothing, and he could only admire that.

A private maître d' met them at the top of the elevator. He nodded at Rory and sent an approving, less-than-professional smile at Jilly.

She let loose a quick glimpse of that lethal dimple of hers. Rory pressed a possessive hand to the small of her back and gave the guy a sharp look to get him moving in the direction of the private room the Blue Party had booked for the evening.

In the twenty steps that it took to get there, Rory tried to think of how to explain Jilly or how to defuse her or at the very least how to shield her from the Senator's almost-certain disapproval.

The murmur of voices and the clink of glasses and ice drifted from the entrance to the room. Rory slid his hand from Jilly's back to her waist, cupping it to check her progress. She slowed, but didn't stop.

"Jilly . . ."

She glanced over her shoulder, a little smile playing across her full, pretty mouth.

"No matter what happens," he said urgently, "I—"

"There you are!" a male voice interrupted. "Come in, come in!" Charlie Jax, apparently lubricated by a martini or two, gestured them forward with an almost-friendly smile.

Jilly followed his command, Rory just behind. There were several groups in the room, circles of people in evening dress holding cocktails. But the biggest circle was directly in front of them, and as they came forward, the group parted to reveal at its center Senator Benjamin Fitzpatrick.

Jilly paused. The senator looked up from the woman at his side. Rory held his breath.

His lined face unreadable, the older man handed off his drink. Then he started smoothly and quickly forward, for once not hindered by the arthritis—the result of his years on cramped Navy subs—that usually plagued him. Rory saw Jilly's shoulders tense and he wanted nothing but to whisk her away.

What had he been thinking? He didn't need to put Jilly through some sort of respectability gauntlet. This was all his fault. He'd forced the "engagement" on her and forced this weekend on her, too.

The older man stood before Jilly, his gaze inspecting her from head to toe. The senator had a strong core of morality, but he'd better not find Jilly wanting in any way. Rory didn't give a shit if the old man hated her on sight. He cared only that he kept his mouth shut about it.

Then the senator smiled, his face creasing in an elated, very genuine grin. "My God," he said. "Gillian Baxter."

To Rory's astonishment, Jilly seemed to recognize the name. She smiled back, dimple ample evidence to her own pleasure. "I go by Jilly Skye now, Uncle Fitz."

The senator reached out. "Whatever you call yourself, welcome back, sweet girl." He swept her against his chest, and Jilly laughed, hugging him back.

*Sweet girl? Uncle Fitz?* Stunned, Rory stood dumbly by while they exclaimed over each other.

An icy and welcome glass of scotch on the rocks was pressed into his palm. "You looked shell-shocked," Charlie Jax said. "I don't have a clue who your fiancee is to the senator, but it looks to me like you don't know who you've been cavorting with all this time either."

With the light of the streetlamp shining into the car, Greg searched Kim's face for further tears. She'd cried when he'd told her he loved her. But she wasn't crying anymore.

Without an excuse to stroke her cheeks, Greg hesitantly placed his hands on her shoulders. Under his palms she was stiff and unyielding, just like the expression she wore.

Had she already and so easily dismissed his admission? He gave her a little shake. "I said I love you."

She licked her lips. Swallowed. "Don't," she replied, her voice hoarse.

"I've tried that," he confessed softly. "Doesn't work for shit."

"Oh, Greg." She sounded so damn sad.

He refused to panic. "C'mon, Kim. This can't be a news flash. You knew I loved you four years ago. You had to see nothing has changed."

"*I've* changed." Her voice was stronger now. "I'm not the same person I was then. Thank God. Thank Jilly."

He thought of the diplomas on her office wall. He was proud of them and proud of her, but he wasn't surprised. He'd seen them coming in the stacks of books she'd dragged out of the Caid-

water library all those years ago. "I understand," he said.

"Do you?" She narrowed her eyes. "At that
time you were a decent, honorable man. The
same man you are today. But do you have any
idea what it takes to change yourself? To stop
giving excuses and blaming everyone else for the
choices you made?"

"It wasn't your fault, Kim."

"Like hell."

He blinked. He'd never heard her swear
before. "It wasn't," he repeated.

"I knew you didn't understand." She shook
her head. "Of course it was my fault. Both the
marriage and losing my daughter. Because not
only was I willing to sell myself, but I was stupid
about it. I'd have more respect for myself if I'd
been smart enough to read the prenuptial agreement instead of taking Roderick's word for what
it contained."

Greg squeezed her shoulders. "He was a bastard."

"And maybe exactly what I deserved," Kim
said fervently. "But not anymore. Now I have an
education, a career, a growing business."

A sudden thought clawed at Greg's belly. "And
a man? I didn't think . . ." He dropped his hands
from her shoulders. "Is there someone else in
your life?"

She looked out the window. "It's not that simple."

Simple? Greg didn't know whether to laugh or
stick his fist through the windshield. *Nothing*

about them had ever been simple, and the idea of her with someone else was so damn complicated it made him nuts.

Who was he kidding? The idea of her with someone else made him sick with jealousy, as sick as he'd been when they'd lived in the same house, every day knowing she was his grandfather's wife.

"Kim." He grabbed her upper arm and jerked her around to face him. "Tell me there's no one else," he said harshly. "Goddamn it, *tell me*."

"There isn't someone else," she said calmly. "There won't be anyone for me."

"What the hell is that supposed to mean?" His voice was still rough, but the bitter waves in his belly were calming.

"It means I don't want a man . . . I don't want sex."

His fingers loosened, releasing her arm. "What?" he said in surprise.

"I don't have those feelings. Sexual feelings." Her voice was so matter-of-fact he thought perhaps he wasn't hearing right.

Greg shook his head, completely at a loss. She was twenty-three years old and telling him she was without sexual feelings? "What are you talking about? I remember at Caidwater you wouldn't let me touch you—"

"Then it was because it seemed wrong. To touch or even talk about what was going on between us would have been an even bigger betrayal of your grandfather. But now . . ."

"Now?" he prompted.

She looked away from him and her voice lowered to a whisper. "Once I had to leave Iris, I just seemed to lose my sense of . . . of touch, I guess. When people touch me, when I touch people, I don't feel anything. It's as if my nerves are dead. My skin is numb."

A smile flickered over her face and then she cast a glance toward the backseat. "Except for today. I felt her hand today. I'll always be grateful to you for that."

Greg stared at her. "I still don't understand. If your—your skin is numb and you don't feel anything, why have you still been trying to avoid my touch?"

"Because." Her whisper scraped like a razor across his heart. "Because I thought—I hoped, maybe—it might be different with you."

*And she hadn't wanted to know if it wasn't any different*. That was what she didn't say. And what she also didn't say was that it *wasn't* different. Greg wiped his palm down his face. God.

Pain filled his belly, head, heart. When her touch felt like a crack of lightning against his skin, she felt nothing when *he* touched *her*.

His hands started to shake. To lose her, to find her, to find out that he couldn't arouse her. Why had this happened? Was this his punishment?

Cool air blew across him as she opened her door. He leaned toward it. "Kim . . ." He didn't know what to say. He didn't know what to think. "Are you sure?"

Her small smile twisted the knife in his gut.

"I'm sure. No matter what my heart says, my body's just not in it." Then she looked at her daughter a last time and was gone.

Once again he'd let her get away.

# Chapter 11

Close to midnight, after too much talk with too many people, Rory pulled Jilly down the hallway toward their suite.

"Wait, wait, you're going too fast," she protested.

He didn't slow until he reached their door. Unwilling to let go of her, he slid the card-key in and out one-handed, then jerked open the door. Once inside, he slammed it shut and grabbed Jilly above the elbows, spinning her to face him.

"I should spank you," he said.

She lifted her chin. "Why?"

"You know exactly why. All this time you knew the senator and didn't tell me."

She shook her head vigorously. "But I didn't know who he was to you. I avoid politics like other people avoid heights. Honest, I had no idea what he had to do with the Blue Party or with you."

Rory didn't let go of her arms. "Until the closet."

Even under the dimmed lights, he could see her flush. "Until the closet. But come on. I had to listen to all your warnings about what I should wear and how I should behave. Admit you deserved just a *little* torture."

He didn't want to. "You should have told me right away, right then in the closet, dammit, that Senator Fitzpatrick was 'Uncle Fitz' to you. That he was your dear old family friend. The one who's an 'ex-Navy man,' " he said through his teeth.

"Why? You were having so much fun worrying about what kind of detriment a woman like me might be to your political career."

Rory took a deep breath. "I never said that."

Jilly stomped on her bad-girl high heels toward her bedroom. Then she spun to face him. "But it's what you've always thought, right?" There was an unfamiliar glitter in her eyes.

"I never said that," he repeated, feeling cornered. To get more air, he quickly loosened his bow tie and unfastened the top button of his tuxedo shirt.

"Humph," Jilly said, her toe starting an annoyed—and annoying—tap. Curling tendrils of her hair had escaped the velvet band and were dancing against her forehead. "You know, this weekend of playing fiancée was *never* part of our deal. As a matter of fact, I'm suddenly aware that I'm getting nothing for all this trouble." Her mouth set moodily.

"Oh, yeah?" Rory said softly, feeling more than a little moody himself. Because, speaking of nothing, she'd been so occupied with the senator for the entire evening that Rory had seen little of her. He'd told himself he was mad and getting madder by the minute over the joke she'd played on him, but he admitted now that he'd hated giving her up to the senator and the others. He'd wanted to watch her mouth as she talked, watch her breasts rise and fall with each breath.

But she'd seemed to have forgotten she was there as his woman, his *fiancée*.

"So you wish you were getting some . . . thing?" he asked, unfamiliar, dangerous heat in his voice. The need to punish her was rising in him again, uncontrollable and as wild as she looked in that black, satin-striped tuxedo.

Her eyes narrowed and she took a step back. "Y-yes. No."

"Which is it?" Rory stepped closer. "Yes or no?" She was corruption, temptation, every dark sin and every secret desire. And he was damn tired of denying himself.

She put her hand on his chest, but she didn't push him away. "Rory . . ." Her eyes widened as he took her in his arms and pulled her against him.

"Yes or no, Jilly?"

Her little body was hot against his. He could feel her trembling and she parted her lips, swallowed, parted them again. "Rory . . ."

"Yes or no?" he whispered. His hand slid beneath her hair, cupping the bare skin of her nape with his palm.

At his touch, she jerked. Then her pupils dilated, her arms slid up to circle his neck, and she pulled down his head.

Jilly's mouth was a drug. Rory promised himself to outlaw it, once in Washington, and once he'd had his fill of it. The taste of her chugged through his blood, moving with fierce, steady purpose, turning him on hotter and harder than he'd ever known.

Sweet punishment.

His tongue was deep in her mouth, her body was plastered against his, yet she twisted against him restlessly. He slid his hands up and down her back to soothe her, to slow himself, but Jilly moaned so erotically that he had to lift his head to catch his breath.

Her head dropped bonelessly back. With her eyes closed and her mouth wet, she looked on the brink of orgasm. Rory's head spun, and he groaned and ground his hips against her. Jilly's eyes opened to slits, glittering greenly, greedily.

Their light lit him on fire. He bent his head, kissing her neck, biting it, sucking it, no taste enough. Startled by the thought, he lifted his head again, reining in the impulses that were driving him.

She opened her eyes slowly, as if coming awake. "How do you do that?" she whispered. "You make me so hot."

He laughed, the sound strangely shaky, and he held her with one arm so he could draw the cruel velvet band from her extravagant curls. "It's you," he said, tossing the band away. "You're the one making it hot."

She shook her head and her hair fanned out. Then she slid her hands from his neck to his shoulders, to push off his jacket. It fell to the floor behind him. "Maybe this will cool you down."

But he didn't think so, because then Jilly started plucking at the studs fastening his shirt.

His heart slammed against her fingers, and she made a face as she awkwardly managed to undo them. Then she pulled out his shirt—delicious agony as it slid over his erection—from his pants. The tails fluttered to his thighs.

"There," she said, taking a tiny step back.

There? *There*? Two could play that game.

With a slow smile, he reached toward the buttons of her tuxedo jacket. He heard her suck in a breath, but he didn't dare look at her face, or anywhere else. He concentrated on his fingers, freeing the buttons without touching her skin.

Once unbuttoned, the jacket parted to show only an inch of her pale flesh and a small strip of tantalizing black lace, right at the point of her cleavage. Rory let his hands fall to his sides. "There," he whispered.

Her breath exhaled in a small moan, and the edges of the jacket inched farther apart. Rory looked up, into Jilly's green eyes. "I'm still hot," he said, holding her gaze as he shrugged out of his shirt.

Her hand crept toward his bare chest. Jilly's gaze broke from Rory's to watch her own fingers as they moved toward him. Rory's belly clenched in anticipation. God, she was good at this.

Four fingertips met the wall of his chest, just below his shoulder. He clenched his teeth, his muscles, locked his knees to keep perfectly still as her fingers stroked downward, burning four separate trails, and leaving four separate swaths of goose bumps behind. The nail of her middle finger bumped over his pebbled nipple, and he was so hellishly tense his groan couldn't fight past his tight throat.

Her fingers met the waistband of his pants and fell away. Her gaze moved up to his. There was something in her eyes—uncertainty? nerves?— but both must be wrong. Even though she was trembling, she played these sexy games too well to be nervous.

He ran his fingers down her hot cheek anyway, a comforting gesture. "My turn," he said. His fingertips slid inside her tuxedo jacket at her shoulders. He meant to go slow, he meant to build the anticipation just like she had, but God, he didn't have her control. Suddenly he couldn't wait anymore.

In one quick movement, he jerked the jacket off her shoulders.

She gasped.

He thought he just might die. She'd been working up to killing him since the moment he'd met her, and if her hooker high heels or her decadent taste didn't do him in, the heaven-sent abundance of her breasts would take care of it. They spilled over the top of a black, lacy bra, plump and pale, their color as pure as snow dusted with freckles of angel gold.

Oh, but before they buried him six feet under, he needed more. See more, taste more, have more.

His hands shook as he grasped the black bra straps and pushed them down her arms. Air dragged in and out of his lungs, rough and painful, as he then pulled on the straps to drag the lace cups over her stiff nipples until the bra settled at her waist.

She swayed. "Rory," she breathed.

"Shh." He slid one arm around her back and cupped one breast in his other hand. Its full weight settled hot and sweet into his palm.

"Rory."

"Shh." He bent his head, his heart pounding in an unholy, reckless rhythm, and licked her nipple. She cried out, her body arching in a genuine, generous response that wound his arousal even tighter and set his erection throbbing against the black wool of his pants. He licked again, her taste and scent entering his bloodstream, that addictive drug that drove every other need but the need for her from his head.

His body shook as he bent her over his arm and took her breast in his mouth, sucking on her nipple as if he could fill himself with her taste. In the distance he heard her cry out, and he felt her skin go even hotter.

His heart was slamming around his body, moving like a pinball from groin to wrist to chest to throat and he needed more Jilly to satisfy it. He lifted his head and gently squeezed her wet nipple between his thumb and forefinger as he moved to take the other in his mouth.

Her hands buried in his hair, she was rubbing against him, her hips pushing on his arousal, and he felt her movements quicken, thrusting against him in an unmistakable rhythm. *God*, Rory thought. *She's almost there.*

He palmed the tender bud of her nipple one

last time, then released the breast he'd been toying with. But he kept sucking her other breast,
listening to the beat of his blood, the beat
strangely synched to her sinuous movements. His
fingers trailed past the bra still fastened about her
waist. Flattening his hand, he moved his fingers
between their bodies until the tips brushed the
vee of her thighs. She was so far gone she didn't
even seem to notice, but he shuddered at the heat
there and at the telltale dampness.

"Oh, Jilly," he murmured against her full, hot
breast, and then, knowing what she needed, he
cupped her firmly, pushing his fingers hard
against her.

Her body jolted. She cried out. Her body shuddered again and again and again.

He knew when she came back to earth. His
mouth drifted reluctantly from her breast up her
throat, and he pressed a kiss against her soft, surprised mouth. He looked into her eyes and ten-
derly stroked her cheek. "Good flight, angel?"

She looked stunned. "What?"

He laughed softly, even though his body was
aching with the need for a journey of its own.
"Are you always so responsive?"

She blinked. "What?" She shuffled back and he
let her go, because her bewilderment was so cute
and he enjoyed the idea that he'd shaken up the
sexpot. Her arms crossed over her magnificent
breasts. "Oh, my God, Rory." Her face flushed
bright red.

He tweaked her nose. "It's okay. I can make it
happen again."

She shook her head, obviously flustered, and backed away. "Oh, no, you can't."

Now he really laughed, even though the peek of her rosy nipples he could see through her fingers was making the throb in his groin even more painful. "Not your convent sex ed again? Jilly, honey, your choice of partners has been decidedly average if no one has ever proved to you your unlimited, um, capabilities."

She still looked shocked.

He reached out toward her. "C'mon, sweetheart, let me take you to bed."

"No. I told you. I can't." She bent down and picked something up from the floor, throwing it over her nakedness. His shirt. "I took a vow."

"What?"

"I said I took a vow."

Without warning, that gray cloud that was his constant companion once again took on an anvil weight. It fell on his chest, hard and ominous. "A vow? What the hell kind of vow are you talking about?"

She looked away. "Um. Well. You know."

Rory sensed southern California in the air, and, of course, disaster. *"What kind of vow?"*

Jilly licked her lips, still reddened from his kisses, then met his eyes. "A vow of celibacy. Four years ago I took a vow of celibacy."

No. No way. He refused to believe it. He also couldn't believe she'd even said such a stupid thing.

"Damn it, Jilly! If you don't want to have sex, just say so." He was mad at himself and mad at her and mad at how difficult it was to ignore the pulsing insistence of his erection. "Just because we—you . . . fooled around, you're still under no obligation. I thought I explained that. No elaborate excuses are necessary."

Of course, he was going to have to find the ice machine and then find some way to stuff all six feet of himself inside it, but he meant what he said. Damn it.

Despite his reassurance, her expression was miserable. "I'm sorry, but it's not an excuse. It's a lifestyle. My lifestyle."

She couldn't be serious. But she looked serious. Her *lifestyle*.

"Why? No." He pinched the bridge of his nose against a sudden headache. "Don't tell me. This is something you cooked up with your astrologer, right?"

"No, it's not like that at all." Jilly slipped her arms into his shirtsleeves and wrapped the garment tightly around her body. "Maybe you won't understand, but it's like what you said before—about becoming the opposite of what you're raised to be."

He narrowed his eyes, still not sure he was buying this. "Yeah, but your grandmother sent you to convent school. To—what was her name?—Sister Bernice or whoever. Your grandmother *raised* you to be celibate."

"But then expected the opposite when I moved to FreeWest. In her mind, I was my mother all over again. I wanted to prove to her how wrong she was about me. About both of us. Being celibate takes all the guesswork out of a sex life, you see. No disease, no unwanted pregnancy. No emotional mistakes either."

Rory just stared. To his mind, what Jilly needed was to take her sex a little less seriously. A long weekend on a soft bed with a hard man should do it.

But he wasn't volunteering for the job, because he could tell by the determined set of her shoulders and the serious pleat of her brow that getting her there would take more effort than he was willing to put forth. Especially for some crazy woman from southern California who'd become the bane of his existence.

And maybe he even understood a little her fear of emotional mistakes.

He stalked toward the suite's front door, kicking his tuxedo jacket out of the way in frustration. Really, he should have seen this whole thing coming. He *had* seen it coming. But she was just so damn difficult to stay away from.

"Um, Rory."

He paused. "What now?"

Her voice was soft, apologetic. "Well, if you need to . . . if you want me to do something for you . . ."

*Hell.* He kicked his tuxedo jacket again and continued on his way to the door. "Gee, thanks, but no."

"Where are you going?" Jilly asked.

He didn't spare her a glance. "To find the ice machine."

Jilly squinted against the afternoon glare coming through the Mercedes's windshield, then slid a glance at the man driving. Despite Rory's quasi-calm exit the night before and his current impassive expression, she could feel his annoyance. He'd spoken only two words since emerging from his bedroom this morning, one being "come" and the other being "on," as a way of telling her it was time to leave for the airport to catch their flight home.

Now on the way to Things Past from the L.A. airport, she squirmed in her seat, wishing for something to break the monotonous, ominous quiet besides the subdued hum of the luxury car. She cleared her throat.

Rory didn't take his gaze off the road ahead.

Jilly couldn't stand the silence, and the tension, any longer. "Aren't you going to say *something*?"

There was a long pause. "Like what?" Only his mouth moved.

Jilly made an impatient gesture. "I don't know. You could say you understand. You could accept my apology. You could yell at me. Something. *Anything*."

"Maybe I'm still trying to take it all in."

She didn't believe that for a minute. He'd taken it all in last night, every word. He just didn't get it. "Can you understand what I have to prove? When I said I was going to take over my mother's business, my grandmother tried to prevent me from leaving her house by saying she loved me and that she needed me. When I still insisted, she instantly predicted all sorts of vile things. Utter failure. Abject poverty. That I'd turn into a tramp like my mother and end up back on her doorstep, pregnant."

Oh, she'd recognized the desperation in her grandmother's words. The old woman knew she was losing Jilly. But in the name of "love," she had kept Jilly's mother from her and then tried to control her life. This was why Jilly had broken all ties with her grandmother. And why she'd had a private chat last night with Uncle Fitz to make sure that no one in the Blue Party would try to reconnect them.

"There are ways to prevent pregnancy and disease, Jilly," Rory pointed out.

"I know that." But there were some lessons not easily undone. After years of nun-training, she couldn't abruptly enter into a casual sexual relationship.

He shook his head in disbelief. "And in the last four years you've never been tempted?"

"Never," she answered emphatically. "My friend Kim and I took the vow of celibacy together. Sure, it started out as a pathetic giggle over a cheap bottle of wine, but there was a rightness to it the next morning. And all the days after. No, I can honestly say I've never been tempted."

"What about last night?"

*Oops*. She couldn't quite figure out a way to explain last night . . . and all the other times with Rory.

"You let me undress you," he reminded her. "You undressed *me*. And then you let me—"

"Okay, okay! I remember it perfectly well." His clever mouth on her breast, his lean cheeks hollowing as he took that part of her inside him. His too-wise fingers finding, touching, pressing, creating perfect pulsing waves of delicious, heated pleasure.

She squirmed against the soft leather of the seat and cleared her throat again. "It must be an allergic reaction or a nutritional deficit."

Okay, so that explanation sounded goofy even to her ears, but she had to say something to return their relationship to a less intimate footing. "Maybe I need more leafy green vegetables. Would you mind a quick stop at the whole-foods store so I can stock up?"

There was an astonished pause, and then he muttered under his breath.

"What was that?" she asked innocently.

"Just a prayer. That as soon as I'm out of L.A. the Big Quake hits and dumps this half of the state straight into the Pacific."

She made a face at him. "You don't mean that."

"Sweetheart, you don't *know* how much I mean that."

He sounded so sure, and so surly, Jilly scooted closer to her window and welcomed the silence that followed. She needed to get away from him. With her nose to the cool glass, she wished for light traffic and a quick trip home.

Rory turned up the Mercedes's air conditioning and tried to muster up some contrition over needling Jilly about the night before. But, dammit, the sex-free package of sensuality beside him deserved a little discomfort for what she'd done to him. Despite all her La-La Land celibate looniness, and even after the roller-coaster ride of the past twenty-four hours, she had a way of insinuating herself into his blood.

And then turning him upsidedown. Insideout. Though he'd grabbed control of his life ten years ago, it took only this one woman with her wacky curls and even wackier lifestyle to loosen his grip. God, he had to find a way to deal with her before his entire life spun out of control.

Even now he could feel the sleek heat of her skin against his fingertips and taste her berried nipples against the roof of his mouth.

*bap bap bap bap*

Rory cursed. The car had drifted to the left and was riding the lane bumps. He quickly jerked the wheel, steering into the lane's center.

Inhaling a calming breath, he checked the rearview mirror. A battered Chevy was riding the Mercedes's butt. Glancing to his left, he switched lanes, then checked the rearview mirror again. The Chevy had changed lanes, too, and was practically kissing his bumper. "Damn," he muttered.

Watching the cars around him closely, he speeded up and switched lanes again. *"Damn it all to hell."*

He could feel Jilly's gaze on him, but he didn't want to take his focus off the traffic. Another car—a Dodge truck—gained on the right, keeping level with them. "We're being followed," he said.

"No!"

"Yes. My guess is they picked us up at the airport." Freelance photographers were known to stake out LAX, hoping to catch surprise shots of surprised celebrities. Rory gritted his teeth and pressed on the accelerator. The late Sunday afternoon traffic was thickening and he didn't like the way the Chevy and its buddy the Dodge were boxing him in.

"The guy over here is gesturing for me to roll down my window," Jilly said.

"N—" But smoggy L.A. air poured into the car before he could get out the word.

The Dodge veered dangerously close to Jilly's side. Rory's gut clenched, but with the Chevy behind him and the traffic in front of him, he had no place to go. "Dammit, Jilly. Roll up your window!" He didn't dare take his hand off the wheel to use the driver controls.

"They need to get out of our way," she said over the wind. "My exit is coming up."

The Dodge inched even closer. Rory's leg muscles tensed. If the asshole driver caused an accident, if something happened to Jilly, he'd break the guy in two. Rory was counting on the chance to strangle her himself.

She leaned out the window. "What do you want?" she shouted.

*Oh, Christ.* Rory's heart bucked in his chest. The driver was taking photos with one hand while steering with the other. Without thinking, Rory grabbed Jilly's arm and hauled her close. "He wants to get us killed, you idiot. Now *roll up your window*."

"They're going to make us miss the exit," Jilly insisted. "We *can't* miss the exit."

Rory gritted his teeth again. "To hell with the

exit. You're going to Caidwater with me anyway."

"I want to go home!" But she leaned over to lever up the window and it was suddenly quiet in the car. "I need to go home," she said again.

Rory's gaze flicked from the Chevy behind him to the Dodge on his right. The damn paparazzi weren't giving up. "No," he said. If the photographers followed them to Things Past, Rory could guarantee only one thing. "If we all end up there, at least one of those bastards will get a camera in *his* face. Right after my fist."

At Caidwater, at least, he could put some locked gates between them and Jilly.

Something—the threat of violence, maybe— shut her up after that. It gave him time to concentrate on maneuvering through the traffic. The back of his neck ached with coiled tension as he tried to ditch the cars following them as safely as possible. But the photographers drove so recklessly that several times Jilly gasped, echoing his own fear.

She grabbed his thigh when he made a last-minute lane change to exit the freeway. They lost the Chevy, but the Dodge found its way behind them.

"Damn," Rory muttered. Thinking quickly, he made a fast left. "Say a prayer, honey."

Holding his breath, Rory sped through a stale yellow light. The blare of horns and the squeal of brakes behind him clearly indicated the other car had tried to follow.

"He didn't get through," Jilly said. Rory

instantly checked the rearview mirror. Cars were stopped in the middle of the intersection. The Dodge was blocked from following them.

Jilly's head fell back against the seat and she closed her eyes. "I think I aged from twenty-five to eighty-five in the last half hour."

Rory couldn't begin to say what the car chase had done to him. Driving more slowly now, he looked at Jilly again and reached out a shaking hand to stroke her hair. "You sure you're okay?"

"Fine." Her fingers caught his. "You?"

Something inside Rory's chest twisted, wringing out a strange mix of relief and tenderness. He couldn't speak.

"Rory?" She turned her head and opened her eyes. "Are you all right?"

At her impossibly sweet, impossibly concerned expression, his mouth went dry. He swallowed. "I'm fine, too. Thanks for asking." Not many did.

Still gripping his hand, she drew it down her soft, warm cheek. "I think someone knotted every one of my muscles."

Each one of his was kinked, too. "I know just what you mean." He shot her another sidelong look. Her face was pale and her mouth was set in a strained line. She'd obviously been clenching her teeth. He could kill those bastards.

"How about a soak in the hot tub when we get back to the house?" he said suddenly.

"Rory . . ."

He gently disentangled their hands, hating the way his continued to tremble at the thought of Jilly in danger. "Just the hot tub," he assured her.

"And just long enough to make sure those photographers get tired of waiting for you at home."

He forced a grin he didn't much feel, because she needed to relax as badly as he did. "You don't need to worry. I'm not interested in older women anyway."

She looked blank, then laughed and slapped his arm. "Oh, fine. You talked me into it. We eighty-five-year-olds don't get such invitations every day. Hot, bubbly water sounds blissful."

And the hot, bubbling water felt blissful, Rory thought half an hour later, leaning against the tile. He sighed, and the sound echoed in the cavernous room that housed the hot tub. It was dark outside now, and running along the eastern wall of the room were windows that reflected the adjacent Olympic-size pool and the soft glow of the few lights he'd turned on.

The patter of footsteps made him look up. Jilly was wrapped in a voluminous bath sheet, though he could see the strap of a bathing suit tied around her neck. "Did you find something to fit you in the changing rooms?"

She cleared her throat. "Well, um, yes. One thing."

Her obvious nervousness put Rory on instant alert. But he'd promised an unthreatening, uneventful soak, so he dropped his head back against the tile and pretended to close his eyes. "Come in, then." Through his lashes he watched her hesitate.

After a moment she dropped the towel, then dropped instantly into the hot water.

Unfortunately, the "instantly" wasn't quick enough. The image of Jilly in a tiny black string bikini burned itself into Rory's brain. He stiffened and sat up. "What the *hell* are you wearing?"

She slid lower into the bubbles. "I thought you weren't looking!"

He forced himself back, trying to relax, though the water had just jacked up forty degrees. "I wasn't looking, I just happened to see." Liar.

"It was the only suit that fit me," she said defensively. "Believe me, it wasn't my first choice."

Rory muttered under his breath, every thought, every promise of relaxation quickly evaporating.

"What?"

"I said you *must* be my curse."

Even in the dim light he could see her eyes widen. Then she glared at him. "Well, I think you're my curse, too."

"You curse me worse than I could possibly curse you."

She slid along the underwater bench, closer to him. "I doubt that. I really doubt that."

"Think about it." He pointed his finger at her gold-dusted nose. "That damn camera of yours forced me into kissing you."

The mouth he'd kissed—so well, and so many more times than once—turned down. "Well, I was forced into accepting that kiss."

"And now, now I'm engaged to you." He crossed his arms over his chest.

She blinked, and slid even closer. "*What*? Well, I'm engaged to *you*. That's an even bigger curse."

Lost in their argument, Jilly had apparently forgotten the brevity of her bikini. She was sitting up straight, and the tops of her plump breasts were wet but completely exposed to his eyes. Rory's shaft stiffened as he watched the bubbles tickle at the nipples barely covered by the small black triangles of fabric. He remembered all that beautiful flesh filling his mouth and, groaning, closed his eyes.

"I'm cursed by wanting a woman—wanting her so bad that I ache—who's celibate. Beat that."

There was a long pause. "But I can," Jilly answered quietly. "Because you tempt me every day, every minute, to break my vow."

Rory's eyes slowly opened. The steam rising off the hot water had tightened the curls around Jilly's face and there was a sheen of moisture on the creamy skin of her face. She was staring at him, her eyes wide. She took a long breath and her breasts rose from the water.

Rory's palms itched. His penis throbbed. He'd been trying to figure out a way to handle her, to defuse the curse, and he suddenly had the answer. Not suddenly, by God. But inevitably. It had been coming to this since the first moment he met her. And he was so damn tired—years tired—of always considering the consequences. Of always being so responsible. Forget about all her protests of last night. It was his turn to play.

Slowly, slowly, he reached under the water and found her leg. He drew his finger down her thigh.

She shivered. "Rory . . ."

"Think about it, honey. Especially now that you're finally admitting you're tempted, and not just nutritionally challenged." He made another enticing pass over her leg. "It's going to come to this every time we're together unless we do something about all this . . . tension between us."

"What exactly do you mean?" she whispered.

He drew his hand out of the hot water and cupped the delicate curve of her shoulder. He saw goose bumps spread across the tops of her breasts. *God.* His mouth was so dry he had to swallow before speaking. "Listen. Why don't we forget about your pesky celibacy for now? And then when I'm gone, well, when I'm gone you can pick it right back up again."

He smiled, because it sounded so damn reasonable to him. And satisfying somehow, to think of her celibate again after he left L.A.

"Oh, Rory." She sucked in her bottom lip and he knew she was tempted again.

And, thinking of the night before, he knew it would take hardly any effort on his part to persuade her. After all, she was finally acknowledging her own desires. He leaned forward, focused on seduction.

"It's difficult . . ." she whispered. Her eyes had turned dreamy.

"I know," he said soothingly, leaning closer. She was millimeters away from letting temptation take her.

"Especially since I've been celibate my whole life."

Rory stilled. "Celibate your whole life," he repeated stupidly. *Celibate her whole life.*

The full truth hit him with the heart-stopping force of a cold Pacific tidal wave.

He wanted to scream in frustration. He wanted to smack his forehead against the hard tile. He wanted to lock Jilly up someplace where she couldn't confound him again.

What the hell had he been thinking? Of course she'd been celibate her whole life. She'd told him about the nuns and about her strict grandmother.

This woman who lived next door to a sex shop, this woman who oozed sex through every innocent pore, was not just celibate.

*She was a virgin.*

His mind whirling with the implications—no man had touched her, ever—Rory inched away from her, trying to ignore the devilish voice urging him closer. What did it matter? the devil whispered in his head. Rory was hot, she was hot, *somebody* had to be her first. Have her first. Rory shuddered.

"Rory?"

But he couldn't do it. Not like this.

Now he *really* wanted to smack his forehead against the tile. Why couldn't he, just this once, have the Kincaid conscience as well as the Kincaid last name?

But he didn't. And he couldn't let a celibate— albeit easily aroused—virgin have sex with him on a whim born out of a black bikini and a car chase. It didn't seem fair, especially not when he knew how easily he could make her say yes. With the undeniable and undeniably combustible attraction between them, and with his experience and her lack of it, he could kiss her and touch her breasts and have her underneath him on that towel she'd dropped in seven minutes flat.

"Rory?" she whispered again, her voice equal parts hesitation and temptation.

Four minutes.

Forcing his gaze away from her, he pulled himself out of the water and wrapped his towel around his waist to hide his erection. "Not tonight, Jilly," he said. God, he should be elected a saint in heaven for this sacrifice. "Go home and think about it. When and if you really want to— to break your vow, then we will." His penis went even harder at the thought. "But not like this. I want you to be sure."

The devil snickered, not in the least impressed with his nobility.

Rory walked stiffly away from the hot tub, his body giving him hell. So much for the relaxing soak. He hoped to God she'd decide in the affirmative by morning, because he couldn't survive in this state much longer. "I'll get dressed and then drive you home."

# Chapter 12

Rory prowled around the library, pausing at the windows to see if Jilly's cherry-red rattletrap was anywhere in sight, then resuming his prowl when the morning was as distinctly Jilly-less as it had been a few minutes before.

Damn her. She hadn't told him last night she'd be late this morning. When he'd taken her home, her hair had still been damp from the hot tub's steam and her expression serious. Had she been considering his offer? He couldn't guess then and he didn't know now.

He hadn't slept at all, his mind cluttered with images of voluptuous angels in tiny black bikinis and saintly men tortured by fires of desire. Dammit, he should have let the devil in him have its way with her. At least then he'd be able to sit down without poking himself in the belly. Christ, he'd been hard for days now. *Weeks*.

Yet he was glad he hadn't taken her to bed the night before. Because the experience was going to be that much sweeter when Jilly came to him on her own terms.

*If* she came to his bed.

And if she ever came back to the house. Where the hell was she?

He supposed he could check out her Web site. It wasn't as if he were so pitifully interested in what the woman was doing that he was really resorting to tracing her whereabouts via her camera. Iris had been asking for her this morning. If he spotted Jilly in her shop, he could tell his little aunt to stop prowling, er, *waiting* for her to show up any second.

It took him only a few moments to click into the Web cam image of Things Past. The shop was empty—he suddenly realized it was still a few minutes before opening time—but they must have turned the Web cam on early. The door of the shop's rear office was open and he could see movement in there, a shoe, then part of a woman's leg, and he squinted, trying to determine if it belonged to Jilly.

But it didn't, because Jilly suddenly appeared in the camera's line of sight from a different direction. He guessed she had just come from her apartment upstairs, because she had a purse slung over her shoulder and she was yawning.

A little spurt of satisfaction soothed his impatience. Maybe she hadn't slept well either. He leaned back in his chair and crossed his arms over his chest, regarding her dispassionately. She had on ankle-length pants, flat black shoes, and another of those glittery little sweaters.

Without thinking, he found himself leaning closer to the screen again, frowning. Was this an I've-come-to-be-seduced outfit? As much as he wanted her clothes to scream "To hell with celibacy!" he just couldn't tell. Everything she wore made him hot, hotter than he could ever remember.

Startled by the thought, Rory forced himself back against the cushy leather chair. No need to get carried away. Jilly certainly was appealing, but his feelings toward her were nothing more than run-of-the-mill lust, after all.

She crossed the shop's floor, clutching a mug of coffee. He studied her rationally. She had nothing particularly special.

Except her breasts.

Well, yeah, there were those incredible, wet-dream breasts. But this was L.A. Breasts were everywhere. Breasts were as common as palm trees and taco stands. And if they didn't come naturally, then the just-as-common plastic surgeons were happy to implant them.

In other parts of the country, little girls saved up their allowance to buy Barbie dolls. In southern California, little girls saved up their allowance to buy Barbie's cleavage.

But Jilly Skye wasn't just breasts. She was sass and savvy business sense. She was vintage clothes and nunnish vows. If she was a curse, she was a damn cute one, and he was finding it difficult to remember why he'd tried so hard to resist her for so long.

As he watched the screen, she leaned into the office and appeared to speak to the shoe and the leg he'd observed earlier. Rory grinned and slid down in his chair, focusing on the tight curve of her ass.

"—stop—that—" Jilly's voice abruptly sounded close by.

Rory jumped guiltily and swung his head around. "What? I wasn't do—" He broke off as Jilly's voice sounded again.

"—what—you—now?" The words came through his computer speakers and clipped on, off, on.

Another female voice answered. "Audio fea—not work—"

Hmm. Someone—the owner of the shoe and the leg—was fiddling around with an audio feature that wasn't work—

"I just can't seem to get it." The voice was suddenly clear and smooth. And apparently the woman speaking didn't realize that she had got it working just fine. "But I want to try your idea of on-line fashion shows soon."

Hmm. Rory rubbed his chin. On-line fashion shows sounded like a great idea. There was that savvy business sense again.

"Maybe you should try getting some sleep," Jilly said. "Were you at it all night? You know you only make mistakes when you're tired."

The other voice muttered something about being too worked up to sleep.

"I hear you, babe," Rory answered. "And I'll wager it's man trouble."

"You'll find a way," Jilly said cheerfully. She still had her back to him, but Rory imagined her sweet, one-dimpled smile. "I have faith in you."

Rory's mood shot optimistically high. "I have faith in you, too, honey," he told Jilly's digitized figure. It was kind of a hoot to insert himself into their conversation. "Now, my little nun, tell your nice friend good-bye, get in your car, and come to

Papa." He grinned. *So you can come* for *Papa*.

He'd missed what the shoe and the leg had been saying, but then Jilly answered. "Don't hold your breath."

The other voice sounded like it might be doing just that. "Are you having trouble?"

Jilly looked down at her feet. "I don't know how to bring it up to him. The time never seems quite right."

Rory sat up straight. Him? Him who?

"You were going to wait until he was your friend."

"Well, I think he likes me." Jilly hesitated. "At least he feels *something* for me, that's pretty certain. But does he consider me a *friend*?" She continued to stare at her feet.

"Time's running out," the other female said. The tinny sound of fear in her voice sent a trickle of apprehension down Rory's back.

"I know," Jilly said. "But I need to make sure Rory trusts me before I ask anything of him."

He gripped the edge of the desk, and the trickle of apprehension turned into a chilly waterfall of superstition. *Shit*. Had he fallen for some sweet thing's line again? *What the hell did Jilly want from him*? And he didn't think it was for him to put an end to her celibacy.

She looked up and spoke to the woman in the office. "But I promise I'll get him to listen to me about Iris."

Iris? Rory shook his head. This was about *Iris*?

"Honest, Kim," Jilly continued, "I'll do anything to make this right." She shuffled back and Rory saw the shoe and the leg shift, then both shoes and legs. The other woman was coming out of the office.

The camera showed her fully, a tall blond woman with classic features. Rory recognized her as Jilly's partner, and that sense of familiarity struck him once again. The blonde was frowning. "Don't . . . don't do anything rash, Jilly."

"Rash? Me?" If he wasn't feeling so sick—no, angry—he might have laughed at the note of false bravado in the deceitful cupcake's voice. "I promised I'd take care of this. And I will. That's why I took this job, remember? So we could get what we want."

Rory didn't stop listening, but their conversation quickly wrapped up and Jilly left the shop. He continued looking at the blonde, though, his mind running over the women's exchange even as the sense of betrayal turned his breakfast to bile.

Iris . . . Jilly . . . the familiar-looking blonde, Kim.

*Click.* Everything suddenly fell into place. Iris, Jilly, and the familiar-looking blonde. Kim, who looked just like Iris. Dammit, that was it. Jilly's partner was Iris's birth-her-and-abandon-her mother.

*That's why I took this job, remember? So we could get what we want.* Jilly had said that. Along with, *I'll do anything to make this right.* The birth-her-and-abandon-her mother apparently wanted something.

So in order to help out her partner, Jilly had been using him. Celibate. Ha. Virgin. Ha-ha. Every word, every kiss, every hot inch of flesh had been calculated to twist him around her little finger. To get him to "trust" her.

This was what he got for straying from the straight and narrow. For forgetting his responsibilities. It had all been a wicked, wicked game.

Oh, sweet, cheating little cupcake.

He couldn't wait to take his first bite out of her.

"Ouch!"

The sound of Rory's painful exclamation coming from the library made Jilly pause on her way into Caidwater. She'd planned to lose herself in her work this morning because he was more dangerous than ever, now that he'd put forth the tantalizing idea of breaking her celibacy—and then left the decision entirely in her hands.

If he'd instantly tried seduction as soon as she'd admitted temptation, she would have found it far easier to refuse. But he hadn't tried to manipulate her. Instead, he'd insisted it was her choice. Knowing she would have to come to him and ask him to take her to his bed sent shivers rolling down her spine. The idea became just that much more exciting.

"Ouch!" Rory exclaimed again.

Giving in to her curiosity, Jilly peeked around the library door. And had to smile.

"Doctor" Iris was at work on Rory. He was seated in a chair, a black doctor's bag at his feet. The little girl wore a real-looking doctor's coat—probably a costume she'd discovered in one of the rooms—that was folded back at her wrists and trailed to the floor. In her hand, she held a very authentic rubber mallet.

"Hold still," Iris said bossily. Her face had that mulish expression she seemed to wear exclusively for Rory. She lifted the mallet and then bonked him on the knee.

Rory grimaced and kicked up his leg. "Go easy, will you?"

Without answering, she dropped the mallet into the bag and then rummaged through it for something else. "You need a bandage," she said decisively. When she straightened, she held a thick roll of cotton gauze.

He eyed it suspiciously. "*Where* do I need a bandage?"

Jilly didn't know whether to laugh or cry. The only thing the past few weeks had done for his relationship with the child was to ripen the distrust they had for each other. Kim was right. Time was running out and Jilly needed to discuss the situation with Rory. Closing her eyes, she rubbed her temples, trying to ease a sudden headache.

"You're here."

Jilly's eyes popped open. Rory had spied her in the doorway. She cleared her throat. "Well, um, yes."

"Come in."

His voice was charged with something, something dark, maybe even angry. Jilly hesitated, then told herself she was being silly. It was probably just the gauze that Iris was tightening around his forehead that made him sound strange.

As she approached him, he glanced at his aunt. "Iris, could we finish this later, please?"

"No." She continued winding the headband. "You said you'd play with me."

"Later."

"No. You're dying."

"What if I promise not to kick my toes up until you're here to enjoy it?" he suggested.

She didn't budge. "I'm keeping your brains in. Thank me."

"Thank you."

Jilly could tell he was clenching his teeth.

"It sounds like Rory wants to talk to me alone, Iris," she said, trying not to squelch her nervousness at the thought. His face was stiff and his eyes were unreadable. "I'm certain he'll play with you later if you go away now."

Iris cocked her head. "Hmm. Okay, but I'll just play over there." She pointed toward a boxed game sitting by the windows, then retrieved a pair of scissors from her bag and leaned toward Rory's face.

Jilly dashed forward to take the scissors from her hand. "I'll do that." She cut the gauze.

The little girl tucked in the end of the bandage, then skipped over to the windows, her white coat dragging across the carpet. She sent Rory a pointed look. "I'll operate on you while I'm waiting," she said.

Jilly's eyes widened. But then she realized that Iris was sitting beside a game of "Operation." She vaguely remembered commercials for the kids' game. The player—er, doctor—used tweezers to remove parts of a little man. If the doctor fumbled, the "patient" got a loud zap and his nose lit up.

"She calls it Rory, huh?" Jilly gave the real Rory a sympathetic smile.

He didn't smile back. "Sit," he said, pointing to his desk.

Jilly's pulse jumped at the barked command,

and she slowly followed him there and took a seat. He eased his big body behind his desk and pinned her with his eyes. There was tension everywhere—in his gaze, in the rigid set of his broad shoulders.

"I know what you're doing," he said.

"Wh-what?"

"I know you've been using me."

Jilly stilled, struck frozen by the Arctic chilliness in Rory's eyes. "What?" She couldn't think of any other response.

"You had a reason for wanting this job. You've had a reason for every move you've made. You and your partner, Kim. My grandfather's seventh wife. The woman who bore Iris." He laughed, a sound so harsh it hurt to hear it. "God, what a fool I've been."

She wanted to clap her hands over her ears. She wanted to close her eyes. She wanted to run away and turn back the clock and start the whole world over again.

"You—" She licked her lips and tried again. "You don't understand." How did he know? *What* did he know? She was afraid to ask.

"I heard you talking about it this morning. You can tell your partner the audio's just fine at your Web site. And, baby, I understand perfectly. I've been through this before, remember?"

Jilly grew even colder. She remembered the afternoon they'd been locked in the closet. *User.* He'd said she wasn't a user. Not like that woman who said she loved him but then jumped into bed with his father to make a career for herself. *"No,"* Jilly said. "This isn't like that at all!"

"Because you haven't screwed dear old Dad?" he said crudely.

Jilly flinched.

"But my father can't give you what you want. Only *I* can do that, right?" He shook his head. "What a nasty game you've been playing, sweetheart."

She flinched again. He thought . . . he thought she'd been *playing* with him. "Rory . . . no . . ."

He sneered, and the vicious expression was more frightening than any words he'd used. "I'm not going to buy any of it, sweet thing. Not anymore. Not your little celibate-virgin act, not your breathy protestations."

Jilly closed her eyes. This was bad. Very, very bad. "It was my idea, not Kim's," she said dully. Reuniting mother and daughter had seemed so right, so fitting. Such a wonderful way to ease Jilly's own regrets. "Don't blame her."

"What do you two want exactly?" he asked casually. "Don't answer that. Money, right? To not sell your story to the tabloids?"

"No—"

"Two hundred and fifty thousand was the going rate ten years ago. A cool quarter million to keep out of the *Enquirer* the sordid threesome my dad and I had going. But I can't imagine that your Kim has anything as salacious, so I'll give you half that."

Jilly stared at him.

*Zap!* From the other end of the room, Iris had started her surgery. "Oops, Rory," she called out. "I had trouble with your ankle bone."

His eyes didn't even flicker. They stared Jilly

down, flat, and oh so hard and cold. "Take it or leave it," he said.

She swallowed. "No money. We don't want money."

He looked ready to sneer again, or worse, to let out another of his raw laughs, and she gripped the arms of her chair. "I'm not kidding, Rory. She wants to see her daughter."

He went ahead and laughed anyway. *Zap!* Another sound of surgery gone awry punctuated his bitterness. A tight smile curved his mouth and he nodded toward Iris. "And I'm my aunt's favorite nephew."

Jilly rubbed at her throbbing temples. How had it come to this? How could she have messed up something she'd begun with the best of intentions? How had she caused pain when she'd only wanted to assuage her own?

She gazed at Rory, bandaged as if he were truly wounded. But he *was* hurt, she realized. She had hurt him by her dishonesty.

Her stomach churned. This man, this man who had rescued her from a chinchilla—twice—who had made her laugh and made her ache, whom she'd teased unmercifully about pierced tongues and secret tattoos, who had lit fire to a thousand sheik-and-harem-girl fantasies, hated her.

And she—oh, no. Her stomach churned again. She . . . loved him.

But this wasn't supposed to happen! When Jilly had finally been given her mother's letters, she'd realized how vulnerable love could make someone. Her grandmother had used her mother's love for Jilly to keep them apart. She'd used Jilly's desire to be loved to keep her under strict control.

Jilly had promised herself then and there that she would never give her heart.

And yet she was in love with Rory. She loved him for making his own way, as she had. She loved him because, despite how much he detested Caidwater, he'd taken responsibility for it. She loved him because, when his four-year-old aunt continued to be uncooperative, he continued to try to build a relationship with her.

And it wasn't every man who could look daggers at a woman below a disheveled, unnecessary bandage.

And still make her shiver with desire for him.

*Zap!* In the opposite corner, Iris cackled to herself as she tortured poor patient Rory. Jilly glanced over at the child, then stiffened her spine. She steeled herself against all the emotions, the hate, the desire. The love. She couldn't think of it now. She certainly would never speak of it.

Only one thing mattered anymore. Kim and Iris.

"I swear to God, Rory," she said fervently. "I swear to you that Kim doesn't want money. She wants Iris. At least some time with her, some kind of visitation." Jilly's voice broke, and she took a breath to regain control of it.

His eyes narrowed. "She can't come traipsing back into Iris's life. I won't let her do that. It happened to Greg and me. In and out, now and then, sometimes June, sometimes March. It's hell."

Jilly's hands were shaking. Did this mean he believed her about the money?

"Enough of the histrionics. Just name your price, honey."

*Zap!* Jilly glanced at Iris, and controlled the sudden need to zap the real Rory herself. "What can I do to make you believe me?" she asked, struggling to keep her voice quiet. "How can I make you at least *consider* what Kim's asking?"

He was already shaking his head, looking bored, so she smacked her palm on the desk to get his attention. "It wasn't her choice to leave Iris," she said through her teeth. "You can check that out yourself. There was a prenuptial agreement."

Rory stared at her. "What kind of prenuptial agreement?"

"The kind that an eighteen-year-old girl would sign, not realizing it left everything with your grandfather should their marriage end. Everything. Money, houses . . . children."

He leaned back against his chair and crossed his arms over his chest. One eyebrow lifted. "Maybe Roderick already knew what kind of person his seventh wife would turn out to be. He had the right to protect himself and his future progeny."

Jilly closed her eyes, opened them. "Rory. I don't think you're unfair. Please listen. Please think about it."

"I *think* you have something else up your sleeve. Another scheme."

Tears stung the corners of Jilly's eyes. Oh, how betrayed he must have felt ten years ago to be so bitter and distrustful now. But the honest truth was, she *had* schemed. Stupidly, stupidly schemed, not knowing what she was up against. Not thinking how badly it might turn out. Not ever guessing in a million years that she might fall in love with him.

She swallowed. "How can I make you believe what I'm saying? What do you want from me?"

He rubbed his chin, and then a little smile played over his mouth. "Hmm . . ."

She was so desperate to make the situation right that just his little "hmm" had her spirits lifting eagerly. "What?" She slid to the edge of her seat. "What do you want?"

His smile widened, but there wasn't any humor in it, just a kind of satisfaction. "You know what I want."

"What? What?"

"You."

*Stupid.* She hadn't seen it coming. "Me," she repeated.

"You. In my bed." His blue eyes glittered. "In my bed until I leave L.A. If you're there every night—hmm, let's make that any time I say—then, my sweet little 'virgin,' and only then will I look into your friend Kim's claim."

Jilly's whole body trembled as she stared into Rory's eyes. She couldn't tell if he expected her to agree or to refuse. She could sacrifice her sexuality for her friend or she could let Rory take Iris away forever. Which choice made her the whore and which choice made her the nun?

Her head hurt. Her heart hurt. She didn't know which to choose.

But, oh, how right she'd been to be afraid of love. Because here she was, in love with Rory and forced to yield to his control.

She gripped her hands together. Unless...
unless she went into this bargain and his bed just
for herself. For the opportunity to experience,
truly experience, the exciting, no-holds-barred
living she'd always promised not to pass up.
Wouldn't it be the thrill of a lifetime to allow herself the chance to love this man with her body the
same way she loved him with her heart?

If she kept quiet about her feelings, she could
even be safe from his power over her. Wouldn't
that mean victory even in surrender?

The pain in her chest eased a little.

But the words still came out slow. "All right,"
she said.

His body tensed. "All right?" he repeated
warily.

She nodded, just a little breathless. "Your bed.
Until you leave L.A."

He blinked.

*Zap!* "Hey, Rory," Iris crowed, "I just took out
your heart!"

Then he smiled, cool and confident, his eyes
glittering, glittering. Jilly shivered.

He didn't take his gaze off her face. "That's just
fine, Auntie," he called back. "Because I won't be
needing it."

# Chapter 13

Jilly was able to duck any further discussion of their bargain because Caidwater was suddenly overrun with people. Party planners arrived to go over last-minute details for the Blue Party fund-raiser Rory was hosting in less than two weeks. Then the caterer appeared for a final consultation as well.

Jilly's own responsibilities kept her busy, too. Workers from the museum that was receiving the most valuable of the costumes showed up as previously scheduled. She spent the afternoon transferring the plastic-bagged clothes onto the museum's rolling racks, then wheeling and securing the racks in the museum's truck.

It was dusk before Jilly waved the drivers down the curving Caidwater driveway. Blowing out a long breath, she reentered the house and heard Rory and several others—the party planners, she guessed—in the near distance.

*Not yet*, she thought. She wasn't ready to face him without a little suck-up-her-courage time. As their voices came closer, she quickly slipped through the door to Caidwater's movie theater.

But she wasn't alone here either, though the room was dark. An old black-and-white movie was playing on the screen, the sound turned off, and the flickering light from the film revealed Greg in the first row of the hundred or so seats.

His head turned. "Jilly Skye, come on down," he called out softly.

She smiled and walked slowly along the gently inclined aisle between the plush velvet seats. Her smile softened when she saw that Iris was in the seat beside Greg, her head against his shoulder, obviously asleep. Jilly dropped onto the soft cushion on Greg's other side and tilted back her head to look at the screen.

"What's this?" she asked. Two men were apparently arguing in a tent lit by the quavering light of a lantern.

"Roderick Kincaid in *Desert Life, Desert Death*."

"And we're watching without sound be-cause—?"

His palm stroked Iris's long blond hair. "Puts her to sleep every time."

"Ah." She wiggled more comfortably into her seat. It *was* strangely soothing to watch like this. The lack of sound distanced her from the action on the screen, and when one man pulled out a gun and shot the other, she didn't even blink.

"You hiding out from someone?" Greg asked.

At that moment a new character rushed into the tent, wearing the robes of a desert sheik. Jilly tensed. "Roderick?" she asked, already knowing the answer. Finally. Here was the source of all her desert-prince-and-ingenue fantasies. She must have seen this movie at one time or another, and

Rory's face had the same stark handsomeness of his grandfather.

"They say our great-grandmother was the princess of a nomadic tribe in the Sahara," Greg told her. "I always thought it was a load of studio-generated bullshit, but when you see the old bastard in those robes, you have to wonder."

Jilly looked at him curiously. "You didn't like your grandfather much either?"

"Hated him, especially . . . later. But he was a damn good actor, I'll give him that."

Nodding in agreement, Jilly slid lower in her seat and rested her head against the back of the chair. The story unfolded silently on the screen, but she hardly took it in, thinking only of how Roderick Kincaid had changed her life. She'd never even met the man, but his choices had irrevocably affected her.

Without Roderick Kincaid, she would never have met Kim. Things Past wouldn't be the same—or maybe even a success—without Kim. And, of course, Jilly would never have met Rory.

She would never have fallen in love.

Oh, one day she might have taken a chance on some gentle, mild-mannered guy who wouldn't try to command or dominate her, but she would never have loved such a man.

That path wouldn't be half as scary as the one she was stepping onto now, though. What she was considering doing with Rory, what she'd already agreed to do, was going to be short-lived. It would most likely end with her heart breaking.

On the screen, Roderick Kincaid was galloping across the sand dunes on a white horse. Suddenly he reined in the horse, slid off its back, and fell to his knees. Apparently anguished, he dug his hands into the sand, then lifted them. The camera closed in on the grains sifting through his fingers.

Jilly's stomach clenched. That was she. Reaching for something, touching something she wasn't going to be able to hold onto. "Have you ever felt, Greg," she whispered, thinking aloud. "Have you ever felt like a dream is slipping away, slipping right through your fingers?"

There was a long silence and she thought perhaps, like Iris, he'd fallen asleep. But then he spoke, his voice slow and quiet. "Maybe we just need to close our hands, Jilly. Close our hands and refuse to let the dream go."

As she turned to look at him, the door to the theater abruptly swung open. Without even cursing her cowardice, she just as abruptly slid further down in her seat, hoping whoever it was—and she knew exactly who it was—wouldn't see her.

Greg glanced over his shoulder. "Uh-oh. I think here comes my cue to leave."

She considered begging him to stay, but that wouldn't change the fact that she'd made a bargain with Rory. "See you later," she mumbled.

In the darkness she saw the white flash of Greg's smile. "Buck up. His bark is worse than his bite." He lifted Iris into his arms and was gone.

Her heart starting to thrum against her breastbone, Jilly waited for Rory to take Greg's place.

Instead, it was the seat directly behind her that squeaked as he settled into it. "Greg's right, you know," Rory said, his voice dispassionate. "I actually think you'll like my bite."

Jilly's womb clenched. *Oh, my God.* Just his voice in the darkness could seduce her. Swallowing hard, she mentally scrambled for some modicum of self-preservation. *Tell him you've changed your mind.* She'd find another way to get him to listen about Iris. *Stand up and say you won't barter your body.*

Then he touched her, his hands light against her shoulders. He pressed his long fingers into her tight muscles, gently massaging them, persuasively working at the kinks.

Jilly tried pretending his touch relaxed her. But every second of his hands on her body coiled her tension tighter and tighter. Her breasts swelled, her nipples went so hard they ached, and between her hips there was a heated heaviness that wasn't going to be satisfied like this.

He lifted the hair off her nape, and Jilly held her breath. Then his hot, bare palm touched the naked flesh of her neck. She almost shot off the plush velvet cushion. Biting back a moan, she tried holding onto the arms of the seat, but then he stroked her skin gently once more and she surged to her feet.

"Now, Rory," she said hoarsely. She couldn't take any more anticipation without exploding from the lethal cocktail of nerves and desire. "I want it to be now."

Clamping down on his lust, Rory eased his grip on Jilly's wrist as he led her up the stairs to his bedroom. *Now*, she'd said. Surprise, surprise, he thought angrily. He should have known she would just want to get it over with.

He took a calming breath, forcing himself to slow his pace up the stairs. She'd used him. And when she'd been caught, she'd used her body to get what she wanted. Yeah, he was the one who'd proposed the deal, but still, she'd betrayed him.

He wanted to punish her, he wanted to ravish her, he wanted to *ish* her in every possible position until the little sex kitten had completely lost her strength to scratch. Maybe then he could sleep. Maybe then he could think of her saying, "I need to make sure Rory trusts me," without feeling so damn sick inside.

It seemed that ten years older hadn't made him that much wiser after all.

Once inside his room, he slammed the thick door shut behind them. Jilly jumped at the sound, but the sun had gone down and his bedroom was blacker than the theater. He couldn't see her face.

He dropped her arm and put his hands on his belt buckle. "Get undressed," he said.

She sucked in a breath, the sound ragged in the gloomy atmosphere.

Rory paused. His eyes were adjusting to the darkness and he could make out her outline. Her head was lifted in the direction of his bed, an outrageous affair of gruesomely carved wood that hulked in the corner like a monster from a horror movie.

Hell, the thing gave *him* nightmares sometimes.

"I call it Quasimodo," he said.

He felt her gaze leap to him. "Wh-what?"

"Quasimodo," he said again.

He heard her swallow. "You call your ... your—part Quasimodo?"

Oh, shit. He was in trouble here. She thought he named his penis after the hunchback of Notre Dame? An urge to laugh, to cup her cheek in his palm, to kiss away the aghast expression he imagined on her face, threatened to eclipse his anger.

But she'd made a fool of him. "No, cupcake," he corrected her wryly. "That's what I call the *bed*."

He could swear he heard her sigh in relief. "It *is* big."

"And so's the bed."

There was another heartbeat of silence, yet suddenly he couldn't bear for her to say anything else. Looping his arm around her neck, he drew her to him. "Jilly," he said against her curling, tickling hair. "You're going to kill me."

She pressed her forehead against his shirt. Tension hummed in her taut frame. "Rory, I—"

"Shh." He kissed her forehead, her cheek, her ear. She shivered. "Give me and Quasimodo a few minutes of your time, honey."

He should be stripping her down, laying her flat, filling her with himself. Hell, she'd agreed to it, asked for it, and he'd been wanting to do all that, only that, since the moment she'd put her cherry-tipped toes on Caidwater land. But instead, he found himself playing with her hair and lightly brushing his evening whiskers against her soft cheek. He lingered, kissing, at that tender, scented spot behind her ear.

Her dark curls clung to his fingers and she made this sweet, uniquely Jilly half hum, half moan. His groin tightened like a fist. *Do it*, his devil prompted. *Strip her, take her, drive the ache away.*

Yet something else inside him ignored the voice and he lifted her hair so he could bend his head and kiss the back of her neck.

She shuddered, like a leaf rattled by a stiff, hot Santa Ana wind, and he closed his eyes. With as much control as he could find, he bit down.

Her body jerked and she moaned, sharp and needy.

He licked the spot. "I said you'd like my bite," he whispered against her ear. He chased the goose bumps running down the side of her neck with his tongue.

Then he touched the tiny button at the throat of her tight, sequined sweater. "How many?" he said.

She clutched his upper arms and he knew desire spoke for her. "How many do you want?"

He squeezed shut his eyes. She was really, *really* going to kill him. "How many buttons?" By some miracle, he managed to get the words out.

And should have saved his breath. "Buttons?" she repeated dazedly.

He wanted to laugh again. To kiss her with tenderness, even though she'd deceived him. Instead, he unfastened the first button and kissed the inch of skin revealed there, right below the notch at her throat.

"Oh, God," she said.

"Keep praying, baby."

Beneath ten pearl-sized buttons was something of satin and lace. White. It gleamed in the darkness and he unhooked it with an easy flick of his fingers, his knuckles grazing the inside curves of her breasts.

"I want to see." He made to move away to turn on a light.

"No!" She caught his hand and softened her voice. "Please, Rory. I like it . . . dark."

He shook his head, though he curled his fingers around hers. "Hasn't someone told you, sweetheart? You're wasting a lot of impact with the lights out." The men who'd shared her bed—

"Please, Rory."

He didn't want to think about them anyway. "Fine." Her fingers released his.

So it was time to do it. He had her half naked, he had her permission, he had the darkness she wanted.

So why the hell was he hesitating? Annoyed with himself, he reached out and efficiently pulled the sweater off her, catching her bra straps at the same time to bare her quickly. Her clothing fell to the plush carpet with an almost soundless *thwat*.

She sucked in another nervous breath.

Rory found himself slowing again. He cupped her shoulders with his hands, palming her hot skin, then stroked down to her wrists. Her breasts were pale in the darkness, he couldn't see them as clearly as he wanted to, but they lifted as he drew up her hands.

He ran his tongue across the bumps of her knuckles. She gasped. Lord, she was erotically charged in the most unlikely places. His erection pressed hard and tight against his pants as he thought of undressing her and discovering each one. He licked again. She gasped again. "Do you like that?" he whispered.

"I—I like what you like."

The tiny, artful break in her voice stilled him. Then he remembered. *Dammit.* She might sound as unsure as a prom date in the backseat of her boyfriend's car, but this was a woman built like a sex toy—and because she wanted something from him, she'd given the go-ahead to play.

Determined to keep control of the situation, he stepped back and crossed his arms over his chest. "Strip," he said harshly.

She looked around, a bit wildly.

"Not the wallpaper, sweet thing. Yourself. Take the rest of your clothes off."

She shivered.

The show of vulnerability almost made him pause again. *Goddamn it.* "You're cold," he said, knowing she wasn't. "I'll light the fire." Because *he* wanted to see her, see the body she'd bargained with, see the expressions crossing her face, he moved toward the room's tiled fireplace. In the winter months Mrs. Mack kept a fire built and match-ready.

The scratch and hiss of a wooden match sounded loud in the darkness. As the flames started to lick the wood, he turned.

And nearly sank to his knees. His erection surged against his belly. She was naked.

With nothing covering her curves, he could finally, fully, appreciate her luscious body. Delicate shoulders led to her full, pink-tipped breasts. A tiny waist, curvy hips, a triangle of dark hair at the vee of her thighs.

He crooked two fingers, hoping she didn't know they were trembling. "Come here, honey."

She walked toward him slowly, the fire's yellow-and-orange light flickering over her pale skin. He wanted to feel the fever of her nakedness, taste the burn.

When she stood in front of him, he snagged her gaze and, holding it, deliberately licked the pads of his thumbs. Then he brushed them against her tightly ruched nipples, once, twice.

Her back flexed and her eyes closed.

He palmed the weight of her breasts, using his still-damp thumbs to circle the points, not touching now, but teasing her, teasing him. Her spine flexed again, a kitten stretching toward the sun, and he bent his head and took one nipple into his mouth.

He groaned at the sweet taste and the aroused tightness. Grabbing her hips, he jerked her against him, taking her breast in deeper, sucking as if he could fill himself up with her.

Her fingers speared his hair, holding him to her, and she protested when he lifted his head. "Easy," he whispered against her smooth, hot skin. He moved to her other breast, licking the point and then taking it into his mouth, toying with her nipple until she squirmed.

He bit down.

She gasped, her body slamming against his,

her fingers digging into his scalp. He soothed her with warm laps of his tongue, and moved his hands from her hips to the sleek, smooth roundness of her bottom.

"Kiss me," she whispered.

But he didn't want to. He only wanted her body, he only wanted to bury himself in her heat, to ease the ache he'd been forced to live with since he'd met her. Kissing her would give her something of himself, and he wasn't going to let her get that close again.

He licked up her neck, followed the curve of her ear, bit again, this time on her earlobe. Her skin heated with each pass of his tongue, each nip of her skin, even though he'd turned to protect her smooth flesh from the brunt of the fire's warmth.

She grasped his face, trying to bring their lips together, but he eluded her mouth. Instead, he lifted her hair again and bent over her shoulder to circle his tongue around her nape, circling his hands on her soft buttocks in the same pattern.

His breath rasped in and out. The flames and the shadows were like the two of them, heat and darkness rubbing against each other. His fingertips traced the back crease of her thighs and moved between her legs.

"*Jilly.*" He groaned her name because she was slick and wet and her inner heat was just inches away from his touch.

Now. He stepped back from her to throw off his clothes, his gaze drinking in her dreamy eyes, the new darkness of her nipples, and the fine trembling of her body. Her mouth was wet and parted and he wrenched his gaze away from it. Her body, he wanted her body.

"Ahhh." He pulled her against his nakedness. She twined her arms around him and lifted her face to his. The reflection of the fire lit her eyes. Everything about her was warmth and arousal. He could smell the perfume of her hair and, even headier, the scent of her skin. Grasping one of her thighs, he pulled up her leg so he could push himself against her, hard.

She moaned.

He smiled and bent to kiss her neck, then found her hand so he could press into it the foil-wrapped condom he'd taken from his pocket. She drew back, stared at it, stared at him, and licked her lips.

He wasn't going to kiss her.

Not even when her fingers fumbled so awkwardly to open the package. Finally, impatient, he took it from her, ripped it open with his teeth, and handed it back. His heart slammed against his chest as she slowly drew out the latex sheath.

God, it was almost as if she didn't know what to do with it. But he knew her virgin act was just that . . . an act. She looked at the condom, looked at his erection, and took another step back. Her breasts quivered as she drew in a long breath.

His life wasn't long enough to wait. He grabbed the condom out of her hand, slipped it over his throbbing erection, then grasped her wrist to draw her to the bed . . .

But the fire was here, its light jumping against her breasts, her belly. Bending his head, he traced the colors down her body, licking nipple, ribs, swirling his tongue in her belly button as he sank to his knees.

"Rory . . ."

He pressed his mouth right above the triangle of curls, then rubbed his cheek against the sleek give of her belly. Her knees buckled and he caught her hips to ease her down to the carpet. The dark curling ribbons of her hair spread out around face and her mouth was dark, too, an almost bruised-looking pink, though he hadn't allowed himself to touch it, taste it.

He pushed her knees up and apart and came between them, teasing himself with the wet curls at the apex of her legs. Closing his eyes, he fought for control, forcing himself away from the slick softness.

"Please, Rory," she whispered.

"I will," he promised. "But first, first let me—" He stopped. No, not *let me*. She was his for the taking. The way he wanted to.

He traced her soft folds and watched his thumb disappear between them. He pressed.

She gasped, but her body gave, and her eyes closed as he pushed deeper.

Her hips rose off the carpet. "Rory, kiss me," she pleaded.

But he wouldn't. Not when the inner muscles of her body squeezed down on his thumb so tightly. He drew it out, pushed it in again. Her hips lifted again, too. *"Rory."*

He glanced at her face. Her eyes were closed and she bit down on her lower lip, hard. He drew his thumb out, and painted her folds with the wetness, finding and circling the small, hard nub. Her thighs opened and he looked at her pretty, pretty body, revealing and softening and glistening in the firelight.

For him.

Holding himself in check, he continued playing with her prettiness, stroking, circling, dipping into her ever-opening body to test the wetness, until finally her hips lifted, her back bowed, and she cried out.

Tremor after tremor shook her, but he held fast, his thumb firm against the pulsing nub.

And then her body quieted and he positioned himself against her wet, open place, and drove inside her body.

She cried out again.

*Hell.* Rory froze, her body pulsing hotly against his erection. Tightly. Too tightly.

He looked at her face, locking his jaw against his need to keep pushing into that exquisite heat. She was biting down on her lower lip again, her entire body fighting against the pain of his intrusion.

*Pain.* Oh, God. She *had* been a virgin.

She'd tricked him yet again.

Then, suddenly, her body relaxed. Her inside muscles still clung to him firmly, but her thighs opened and then came around his waist. He slid deeper. "Jilly—"

"Yes," she whispered, her voice husky with new satisfaction and renewed desire. Her hands clutched his shoulders. Her hips lifted and he slipped deeper still.

Nothing could stop him now from driving

inside her again. From closing his eyes and finding the rhythm that stoked the heat and teased higher the fire in his blood. Her hips rose to meet him with each thrust, taking him in, in, in.

At the very last instant, he opened his eyes. The firelight had turned Jilly's cheeks to gold and she glowed like a tempting, sexy angel. Pleasure gathered in his body, coiling for its final leap. As it took off, Rory fused his mouth to hers and tasted heaven.

When it was over, he rolled off her small body, sucking in harsh, rapid breaths. "Why, Jilly?" he asked hoarsely.

She shook her head, staring at the ceiling. With a sigh, he stood and picked her up in his arms, struggling to control a dangerous mix of tenderness and anger. Once beside the bed, he drew back the covers and set her on the sheets.

She was trembling again, so he pulled the blankets around her. He raked his fingers through his hair, studying her face. "Why, Jilly?" he asked again, his voice harsh. "Why the hell now? Why me?"

She just shook her head. Rory wanted to pound the walls in frustration. Was nothing the way it should be in this cursed place? Winter was as warm as summer. Grown men had four-year-old aunts.

A conniving, deceptive little kitten turned out to be a virgin. The convent school, the nuns, the celibacy vow had all been true.

"I want to go home," she said.

And because Rory suspected it was the only thing she *would* say, he let her go.

* * *

Jilly held onto the truth of why she'd agreed to Rory's bargain as tightly as she held onto her tears. Letting herself think only of the beauty of his lean strength in the firelight, of the heated glide of his touch, of the erotic sting of his bites, she made it home, made it through the night, made it through the entire next day at Caidwater.

She made it back to Rory's bedroom, too. That evening, and four more after, she promptly knocked on his door when she was done for the day. They never spoke, not beyond his low groans and her soft moans. But each session of lovemaking was sweeter and wilder, and each time he made her body shudder, she bit her bottom lip to make sure the words "I love you" would not escape.

Rory liked control and power and she knew he'd sap hers if he suspected she loved him. Domineering people did that. They could use your feelings to manipulate your actions. She couldn't, wouldn't, let him. She could let him use her body so beautifully, but she dared not let him have her heart. Her grandmother had taught her never to give that up.

On the fifth day, she was approaching Rory's door when Greg came out, shutting it behind him. He paused, staring at her.

Jilly self-consciously ran her fingers through her tangled hair. It was dusty, her skin was gritty, and she was so tired she couldn't think of an excuse to explain why she was obviously heading for Rory's bedroom. That morning, Mrs. Mack had directed her to a small attic previously overlooked, and Jilly had spent the day foraging through old boxes and trunks.

Greg seemed to grasp the situation in one look. "He's going to hurt you," he said quietly. "Maybe he won't want to, but what happened before has hardened him."

Jilly rolled one shoulder as if she didn't care and refused to see if there was pity in his eyes.

"Jilly, you can't know what it was like for us growing up. Photographers everywhere. Parties, drunks, drugs. Kids would talk about it at school. Hell, some of them were constantly angling for invitations to the next Kincaid orgy."

Her heart clenched. "Rory hated it."

Greg nodded. "It was so damn sleazy. And he always tried to protect me from the worst of it. But there was no one to protect him."

"So he . . ." Jilly swallowed. "He was hurt." By what people said, by what people thought about his family, by that woman who had pretended to want to marry him. By his father.

Greg met her gaze. "So now he protects himself. He won't let himself care for you."

She checked out the grimy toes of her pink, high-top sneakers. "What makes you think I want that from him?"

"Takes one to know one," she thought he murmured, but then his voice sounded louder. "Do you understand? Rory's stubborn and Rory's cynical."

Jilly sighed, suddenly so darn weary. She couldn't think now of what she'd pay later for loving Rory. "I know what he's like," she said. "I just want this time for . . . myself. Can't I have that?"

Avoiding Greg's gaze, she started to take the remaining few steps toward Rory's door.

But Greg wouldn't let her go. He touched her shoulder. "Are you sure you know what you're doing?"

She smiled faintly and held out her hand, palm up. Then she slowly made a fist. "I'm closing it Greg, and holding on for as long as I can."

He didn't stop her this time, and when she knocked on Rory's door, Greg had disappeared from the hall. Then her pulse leaped as she saw the knob turn and the door ease open.

Rory leaned one shoulder against the jamb, his casual pose at odds with his intense expression. She recognized what she saw on his face now, its stark planes made even starker by desire. Despite her tiredness, heaviness and heat pooled between her legs. Her breasts ached.

Last night they'd barely had the door shut before he was pulling off her clothes and taking her against it. The memory made her shiver, made her sensual aches sharpen. Like always, just one look, and he brought out the bad in her. She swallowed.

With his knuckle he slowly rubbed at a spot on her cheek. "You have smudges all over your face," he said softly.

Her eyelashes drifted down in response to the unexpectedly tender touch. She swayed.

He caught her upper arms with his big, hard hands. "Let's get you in a bath," he said.

"No, I can—"

"Shh." He half carried her into the bathroom. The mosaic-tiled room was as decadent as he made her feel, and as he filled the huge sunken tub, he slowly undressed her.

Jilly trembled and licked her lips. His touch was so gentle that each stroke of his hands felt like a caress. "Rory." She tried to put her arms around him, but he forced her hands away and lifted her into the tub full of deliciously warm water.

Then he knelt on the floor beside her and rolled up his shirtsleeves. He washed her skin, drawing a thick bar of Rory-scented soap over and over her.

Tears pricked the corners of her eyes. He continued stroking and caressing, his fingers slipping and sliding everywhere: between each one of her fingers, over her ticklish toes, around each breast.

This was worse than making love—more intimate, more dangerous, she thought. This sweetness, this gentle solicitude, was going to be her undoing. He lifted the coiled hand nozzle and thoroughly doused her hair. Then he washed that, too, massaging her scalp with his strong fingers until she wanted to purr.

He pulled her from the water just moments before she fell asleep and gently dried her with a towel. Then he carried her, nearly boneless, back into the bedroom and laid her across Quasimodo's sheets. When she languidly reached for Rory, he ignored her, tucking the covers around her.

She closed her eyes. "Just for a minute," she murmured.

His hand was so achingly tender against her cheek. "Take all the minutes you need."

Greg watched Iris stuff a pink toy rabbit and her hairbrush into a purple backpack. "You're only going to Mrs. Mack's for dinner, bug, not a decade. Do you really need all that?"

She ignored the question, frowning as she pushed the bare feet of a baby doll into the pack's opening. Frowning deeper, she pulled the doll free and tucked it under her arm. "I'm not putting Daisy in there," Iris muttered to herself.

She named her dolls after flowers, as she had been.

Four-plus years ago, he and Kim had been in one of the Caidwater gardens. Kim had been wandering with a book in her hand, using it to identify the different kinds of flowers. He'd been pretending to be interested, when the only true fascination he'd had was in watching Kim. Suddenly she'd gasped, her palm flying to caress her round belly. Then she'd smiled—he'd never forget its glow—and looked at him.

So excited, so certain, so . . . damn happy. "Her name is Iris," Kim had said. "She just this moment picked it out."

As at just that moment his heart had picked out the woman he'd love for the rest of his life.

Now the baby named that day was sitting on her bed, cuddling a fluffy-haired doll. "You're my own special bug," Iris whispered, then kissed a rosy, plastic cheek.

Greg briefly shut his eyes. "Bug" was his pet name for Iris, and hearing his own special girl use it for her own special baby cut through him.

She looked up. "Will you be here when I get home?"

He kept his voice upbeat. "When you wake up in the morning, for sure. Mrs. Mack will bring you home and put you to bed after you have dinner and watch a video with her granddaughter."

Iris kissed the top of Daisy's head, then looked at him again. "Where will you be?"

He smiled at the daughter of his heart. "Since my best girl is going to be busy, I thought I'd drive over to Malibu and check out the new house." He was finally rebuilding on his beach property. Four years too late.

Iris played with the baby doll's hair. "What about my room?" she asked offhandedly. "Did you paint it yellow? I want yellow."

Greg sucked in a sharp breath. They'd been over this before. She knew that she was supposed to leave Caidwater and go with Rory to northern California. Greg hadn't given up hope of convincing his brother—there was indeed an airy, creamy yellow room at his Malibu house—but he wasn't going to make promises to Iris that he couldn't guarantee.

"Rory still wants you with him, honey. But no matter what happens, we'll see each other *lots*."

Iris squeezed Daisy against her chest. "I want *you*," she whispered.

The world ending couldn't have stopped him from taking the little girl in his arms. He held her tightly, Daisy's plastic heels digging into his ribs. "I want you, too, bug," he said. "So much."

"Then tell Rory he can't have me," she said fiercely. "Don't let me get away."

*Don't let me get away.* The words tumbled into Greg's brain as he sat on the edge of the bed and rocked Iris back and forth. He'd tried to reason with Rory several more times in the past month. But it was clear his brother took his responsibility toward Iris seriously and Greg couldn't fault him for that. On each occasion that Rory had refused to consider leaving Iris with Greg, he'd bitten his tongue and told himself to bide his time.

But time wasn't going to change Rory's mind.

Closing his eyes, Greg accepted the truth of that. He'd been too patient. He'd acted—once again, and just like always—the laid-back, easy-going character who used hope instead of action to get what he wanted.

He'd hoped Rory would see that Iris belonged with him.

He'd hoped Kim would come back one day and love him. He'd told her he'd searched for her—yes, he had—but once again he'd given up too easily.

Too soon.

And still he struggled with the hardest question of all. How much of this predicament was his fault, his punishment for loving Kim?

Mrs. Mack came to stand in the doorway of Iris's room. "Is there a little girl in here who wants French fries?"

Greg reluctantly loosened his embrace. Iris slipped away from him after one backward glance and a wave of her small hand.

He rubbed his palms against his thighs, thinking about his choices and his past. When events at Caidwater had turned against Rory, he'd left and made his own way. When Kim had found herself alone and homeless, she'd built a new life for herself.

Why didn't he have the same kind of courage? Dammit, why couldn't he take what he wanted?

Kim. Iris. *Don't let them get away*. Not this time.

Greg turned his hands palms-up and deliberately curled all ten fingers into two fists. *Don't let them get away*.

# Chapter 14

The door to Kim's apartment was at the top of a flight of steps cut into the stucco side of the Things Past building. Both Jilly's apartment, "A," and Kim's, "B," sat on the second floor over the shop itself.

A smile and an autograph had been all Greg needed to worm that information out of a Things Past salesclerk the day after Kim had left him in his car. *No matter what my heart says, my body's just not in it.*

Those words had frozen him then, but now, now they gave him hope—at least her heart wanted him. But as he'd promised himself earlier that evening, he wasn't relying on mere hope any longer. He raised his hand and knocked briskly on the door.

As if the occupant welcomed an interruption, it swung open quickly. "Jill—" Kim broke off.

"Surprised to see me?" Greg asked. She looked stunned, actually, and even tried to shut the door in his face.

He stuck his foot against the jamb and the door bounced off his cowboy boot instead.

She stared down at the scuffed leather, then stared back up at his face. "What do you want?"

With his palms flat to the wood, he pushed the door open wider and let himself in. When he closed it, he locked the two dead bolts and leaned back, his shoulders against the cheap raised panels and his arms crossed over his chest.

"I want what's mine."

Kim took a step back. For once, her long blond hair was down, and it slid over the shoulders of her T-shirt. His gaze followed it, and he could tell her breasts were braless beneath the thin cotton.

He set his jaw and raised his gaze to her face. "I'm tired, damn tired, of playing this same role over and over again."

She shuffled back another step. It almost made him laugh, because in baggy sweatpants and bare feet, she looked so achingly young and vulnerable that he found it hard to believe he'd been more than half scared of her since the moment they'd met. But that was over.

He raised his brows. "Aren't you going to ask me what role?"

She wet her mouth with her tongue. "What role?"

"I've played the guy who doesn't get the girl so many times, I have all the lines memorized. And every single one of my cues." He pushed away from the door. "I realize it's a role that's come too damn easy."

Kim shuffled back again.

He smiled. "I let Roderick cast me in it. I've let your guilt cast me in it again. But no more." Thanks to Iris, Jilly, Rory, even Kim herself. "I'm holding out for the lead role this time, Kim." *I'm holding onto you.*

She licked her lips nervously. "Greg, I told you—"

"But this time *I'm* telling *you.* After you were gone, I spent four years in that house, living with Roderick and the truth festering between us. But I didn't tell him how I felt about you. I wouldn't give him that excuse to throw me out. I spent four years there for Iris. First, because I loved her as your daughter, Kim. And second, because I loved her for herself."

Kim's hand flew to her chest as if to halt a sharp pain. Tears sprang into her eyes. With a visible effort, she blinked them back, then crossed her arms, hugging herself, and rubbed at the goose bumps on her arms.

Maybe she was feeling something after all. She opened her mouth, but nothing came out.

Good. Because it didn't matter what she said. Only what he knew. "For four years I lived in a kind of hell that I wouldn't wish on anyone, and you know what? I don't give a damn if you don't think you deserve any happiness. After these past years, *I* do."

"Of course you do," she choked out. "Of course." She rubbed her arms again.

He smiled and came so close to her that he could see the pulse racing at her throat. "I'm glad you think so. Because I won't get it unless I have Iris . . . and unless I have you."

"No!" She shook her head vigorously, her golden hair swirling around her shoulders. "Oh, no."

"Oh, yes," Greg said, not the least deterred by her denial. He slid his hand into her long, silky hair and closed his fingers, holding it, holding her. He pulled her head back and leaned toward the mouth he'd never touched . . . never tasted.

That pulse in her throat thrummed wildly against her skin. "But I can't—I don't—"

"But you will," Greg said with certainty. "And I'll keep trying until you do. After four years, I've earned this."

He touched her mouth with his.

The sensation blasted his senses. Groaning, he pressed harder, felt her mouth open, and he pushed his tongue inside as another explosion rocked his nerve endings. The heat, the blinding light that her mouth brought to his soul, burned away the years of pain. The years of shame.

Releasing her hair, he pulled her to him, her body aligning itself sweetly, so rightly, against his. Through their shirts he could feel her nipples harden. "Kim," he murmured against her mouth. "All my life I've waited for this. This is what I deserve for loving you. Just this."

She melted against him. There were tears running down her face and their saltiness only increased the poignancy of their kiss. He'd waited all his life to have her. Every day, every minute, every breath had led to this moment, this moment when she gave to him the strength that he needed, the strength to be the man whom he wanted to be.

He lifted his head and stared down at her wet mouth. She was trembling. "Maybe, long ago, we were wrong to feel the way we did. But we've lived through the pain it caused us. It made us different. Stronger. Wiser, I hope. And maybe even deserving."

Another tear rolled down her cheek.

"It's made us better, Kim," he whispered. "And you make me better."

Her knees buckled and he tightened his arms around her. "You're hurting me, Greg."

He didn't know if he was hurting her body or her heart. He eased his hold on her, then lifted his hand to palm her breast. Her nipple was still hard. "Do you feel that?" he whispered.

But she was already shuddering. "Yes, yes, *yes*."

And Greg took that as the answers to all the other questions he had. Her bed was soft and warm, but she was softer and warmer, and when he felt her come and heard her cry out with shock, with joy, he wasn't surprised to find his own face wet with tears.

Jilly's eyes slowly opened. She blinked against the soft daylight, and blinked again. It was morning. She was in Rory's massive bed, whose sheer white hangings were draped over its canopy and then tied back with tasseled cords to the heavily carved posters.

She'd slept the whole night with Rory. Naked. Every other time she'd left immediately after lovemaking, but last night he had bathed her, put her to bed, and then let her sleep.

Turning her head on the pillow, she blushed as she looked at him. He was fast asleep, his lashes dark crescents against his high cheekbones. The sheet was pushed down to his waist and he slept on his back, one arm flung across the wide bed, the relaxed fingers of his hand just inches away from her breast.

With her gaze she traced the heavy muscle of his shoulder and then the hard expanse of his chest. Dark hair edged down its center to disappear beneath the sheet. Her body tingled and she felt her skin go even hotter as she imagined the intriguing shapes and textures hiding below.

But this beautiful man she'd made a bargain with had let her sleep—only sleep—beside him last night. She shivered.

Then jumped when he spoke, his eyes still closed. "You're looking at me, aren't you?" He let out a long, resigned sigh. "You can tell me. How bad is it?"

She scooted farther away from him and pulled the sheet up to her neck. "What are you talking about?"

"I can't help it," he said.

She frowned. "Help what?"

One eye opened. "Morning hair. Really bad bedhead. It's my curse." He ran a hand over his dark hair.

It looked fine to Jilly, a little rumpled, but fine. "I thought *I* was your curse." It was almost pitiful, how she wanted to be something of his. Even that. Then her thoughts suddenly jumped to her own hair. It had been wet when he'd brought her to bed.

She slid down farther under the covers and tucked a curl behind her ear. "But, uh, speaking of bedhead . . ." she mumbled self-consciously.

His other eye opened and he rolled onto his side so they were facing each other. He reached out to untuck the curl and played with it, pulling it straight, then releasing the tension so it twisted back to its natural spiral. "Your hair is perfect."

Jilly's stomach developed a bad case of the jitters. "It's too wild."

"Mmm." His gaze transferred to her mouth and he moved closer.

Jilly scooched back, nervous. For the first time ever, she'd woken up with a man. The sun was shining. Rory had just complained about bed-head. This was way too intimate, even more intimate than his slow touch in the bathtub the night before.

He slid his hand beneath her hair to caress her neck. "What's the matter, honey?"

She fought off her shiver. He knew so well how to touch her, that was the matter. "It's just so—so light."

He smiled indulgently. "I'll fix that." In one smooth movement he jackknifed up. The covers slid farther down and Jilly's gaze stuttered at the sight of his naked hips. As he reached toward the softly draped bed hangings, she remembered their hardness cradled in her palms.

With a flick of his hand he loosened the tasseled cord nearest him, releasing the sheer over-hanging fabric. Then he leaned across her to do the same on her side of the bed, cutting the sunlight in half and cocooning them in an almost tent-like atmosphere.

The sheik and his slave girl . . .

Jilly scooted farther away from him.

"Where are you going?" he asked softly. "Another few inches and you're going to fall off the bed." He shortened the distance between them.

Her body instinctively moved back.

He frowned. "Am I going to have to tie you up?"

Her breath caught. A white horse galloped across the sand. The desert prince was coming. Her breath caught again.

His eyes narrowed and his mouth twitched. "You *are* wild." Without taking his gaze from her face, he reached back to snag the tasseled drapery cord from the bedpost. "Is this what you want?"

Her eyes widened and she inched away again. "Of-of course not."

"I don't believe you." Before she could protest, he grasped her nearest wrist and hauled her close. The hand holding the cord found her other wrist, and he wrapped it with the cord and stretched it over her head.

"Rory!" She was shocked. Shocked at how excited just the very loose binding could make her.

He lifted her free arm and pressed her hands together, twisting the cord around both of them. Then he pressed the tasseled ends to her palms. "Hold it," he ordered, his voice quiet but firm. "Hold it just like that."

Jilly's fingers automatically closed over the cord, and then they clenched spasmodically as Rory began to draw the sheet slowly down her body. She started to bring her arms down, but Rory clapped one big hand over her two bound ones. "Trust me, Jilly," he said.

When he released her hands, she kept them

over her head. They'd made a bargain, she thought dizzily. Yeah, that was why.

The sheet rasped over her nipples. They were stiff already, and she felt his gaze on them, and then his warm breath. When his mouth closed over one, she involuntarily tried to bring her hands to him, but Rory foiled her again. He firmly lifted her arms back over her head and held them there as he licked her breasts, then blew cool air over the aching tips.

Her legs shifted restlessly and he dropped his hand to caress her sheet-covered thigh as his mouth slid down to her navel. When he encountered the edge of the sheet, he grasped it with his teeth, and pulled, taking it past her hips, the tops of her thighs, her knees.

Goose bumps burst over Jilly's skin. Her hips twisted and when Rory dropped the sheet, he smiled. "Pretty," he said. Then he placed his hands inside her knees and pushed her legs apart.

Jilly closed her eyes. It was so much, the erotic trick of being "tied," Rory's so-knowing touch, his obvious desire as he looked at her body.

He positioned her and she didn't resist, letting him splay her legs wide and then lift her knees so her feet were flat against the mattress. She kept her eyes squeezed tightly shut, so aroused and so embarrassed by her arousal she didn't think she could look at him.

Her skin was hot and tingly and she knew he was looking at her, but she held herself still until she felt something wet and soft between her legs. Her stomach jumped and she immediately tried to close her thighs, but his wide shoulders were there, holding her open for . . . his mouth.

*"Rory."*

His touch was merciless. He ruled her, controlling her responses, licking softly, blowing cool air gently, then exploring her body avidly as if he couldn't hold himself back.

Her hips rose to his mouth and he held them in his big hands as he kept up the intimate, glorious play. She'd never known . . . she'd never thought . . .

And then she couldn't think, because all the warmth and all the tingles converged where his mouth tasted her body and she found herself flying forward, her body lifting off the bed. *"Rory."*

Without a hesitation, he kept kissing her, loving her, but his hand reached up and pushed her down onto the bed. Her hands twisted against their soft binding, passion twisted tighter in her belly, and under Rory's controlling hand and his commanding tongue she flew forward again, but only her passion and her spirit this time, flying somewhere where only he knew to find her.

He caught her as she fell, and she grasped him by the shoulders to pull him up to her.

"No," he said, spreading her thighs wider. He slowly drove two long fingers into her and bent his head once more. "Again."

When he was through with her this time, she could only moan as he slid up her body and teased her with the hard tip of his arousal. She tilted her hips to lure him deeper and linked her still-joined wrists around his neck. His chest just brushed the tips of her breasts.

His blue eyes glittered as he looked down at her. "I have you," he said, pressing home.

And, oh God, he did. Jilly shivered, suddenly so afraid of all the ways that he did have her . . . her body, her heart. She pressed her lips together to stop herself from blurting it out.

His mouth found her ear, traced it with his tongue. He pressed deeper still. "Do me, baby," he said hoarsely.

Jilly closed her eyes, the dark words lifting her higher. She raised her hips and matched his rhythm, letting desire take her one more time. He was relentless, coaxing her slow, then fast, insinuating his hand between them to add another teasing pressure.

Their gazes met. There was wonder in his, she thought. Something beyond desire. Something that made her heart slam against her chest. Something she wanted so badly to believe in. *Trust me*, he'd said. Then he closed his eyes and bent his head to bite the curve between her shoulder and her neck. Jilly cried out his name, and their bodies shuddered against each other.

She was still shivering when he rolled off her and onto his back, throwing one forearm over his face. Jilly fought for breath, still stunned by what he'd wrung from her body and even more by what she'd seen in his eyes.

"Jesus, Jilly," he said hoarsely.

Her heart speeded up again. Maybe—

"You're one hot fuck."

Her heart stopped. Her skin went cold. She looked down at her hands, still bound by the tasseled cord. *Trust me*, he'd said.

She'd been taught better. With a wrenching movement she shook free of the cord and then slid out of the bed, pushing the sheer drapes to one side. "I'll be going now," she told him quietly.

He grunted. "See you later."

"No. I'm done."

He opened his eyes and found her with his gaze. She didn't even flinch or attempt to cover her nakedness. "What?"

"I finished yesterday. Everything is cleared out and accounted for. I have a few boxes I'll take away in my car, but other than that, it's finished."

"*We're* not."

"Our bargain's off." She couldn't do it anymore and survive. Not when she had to work so hard not to tell him she loved him, and he only wanted a . . . a "hot fuck" in his bed. If she kept coming back here, she'd end up spilling her feelings to him, and God knew she didn't want to give him that kind of power over her.

Not when she knew he was never going to love her back. He wouldn't want to. Rory saw her as some*thing* to enjoy, but not some*one* to truly care about. She'd been oh, so wrong. There was no victory in this kind of surrender.

He sat up slowly, his expression hardening. "I won't listen to your friend Kim. I won't help her."

Jilly drew in a long breath. "You should. You're wrong not to. But I'm not going to sleep with you anymore. Not even to get you to do the right thing. Good-bye, Rory."

With quick footsteps she walked toward the bathroom for her clothes. She was half dressed when he appeared in the doorway, dangerous and gorgeous in a black silk robe. Even now, that slice of his tanned chest she could see had the power to make her fingers clumsy.

"Not good-bye." His voice was harsh. "There's still the fund-raising party. You're expected to be there as my fiancée."

She shook her head and awkwardly slipped her arms into her shirt. "Expected by whom?"

"By me."

"Too bad." She grabbed her shoes, unwilling to take the time to put them on.

When she brushed past him in the doorway, he grabbed her arm. "I—I need you there at the party."

She paused, then steeled herself to deliver the ultimate wickedness, the ultimate lie. "You're a good fuck yourself, Rory, but not that good."

He dropped her arm as if it burned him, and she ran out of his room and ran out of the house, and wished she could run away just as easily from the futility of loving Rory.

Kim wandered about the floor of Things Past. The shop wasn't due to open for hours and she wasn't scheduled to work at all, but her apartment upstairs had seemed too . . . empty without Greg in it and in her bed. She hugged herself, not quite able to believe it hadn't all been a dream.

He'd left when it was morning, yet still almost dark, whispering something about wanting to be at Caidwater before Iris woke. "Don't think too much" had been the last words he'd said before giving her a kiss that had sent a sweet, sharp ache through her womb.

Greg had made her feel again.

She entered her small office, crossed to the pot of coffee she'd started brewing earlier, and poured herself a mugful. She cupped it in her palms, astonished at the heat pouring through the ceramic. Nearly burned, she quickly set the mug down and held her hot hands to her cheeks.

Heat, aches, desire. One kiss from Greg and it had all flooded back. No, that wasn't quite right. It had happened when he'd talked about his love for Iris, when he'd told Kim he'd stayed at Caidwater for her little girl. At that admission, pain had pierced her, nearly doubling her over. He'd loved Kim that much. No. He'd loved Iris that much.

She sat down, unable to trust her suddenly trembling legs. What was going to happen now? What would all this feeling do to her?

The sound of the locks turning on the front door and the cheerful jingle of the bells had Kim twisting in her seat to see Jilly slip into the shop. Her friend looked exhausted and Kim jumped to her feet and rushed toward her. "What's wrong?" she asked.

Jilly's eyes were shadowed. "Oh."

*Oh?* Kim's stomach dipped. Jilly had never merely said "Oh" in her life. "How bad is it?" she asked. "What happened?"

"It's that obvious?" Jilly said glumly.

"You without a forty-word answer for the color of the sky is enough to terrify me," Kim said. " 'Oh' is a nine-one-one call."

Jilly looked down at her feet. They were bare and she was carrying her shoes. "Oh," she said again.

"You're scaring me, Jilly," Kim said. She grabbed her by the arm and led her into the office, where she pushed her down into a chair and poured her a cup of coffee. Three packets of sugar, the real stuff, and then she handed the mug to her friend. "Drink some, then tell me everything."

Jilly obediently sipped, then stared into the liquid. "I broke our vow."

Relief coursed through Kim. She laughed shakily. "Is that all?"

"And Rory knows who you are and he was really mad because he thought I was using him for your sake, so then we made a bargain and I was sleeping with him until he told me I was a good f—the 'F' word—and then I couldn't do it anymore because I actually, truly, really l-love him and I don't want him to see me just as a good f—the 'F' word—and so I walked out on him and I refuse to play his fiancée anymore and he's so angry I don't know what he'll do and I f—effed up everything."

This remarkable explanation was punctuated with one, tummy-deep sob. Jilly hastily set the mug on the desktop and buried her face in her hands.

Jilly in love? Kim had known her friend long enough to appreciate how much she feared the emotion. This truly *was* disaster. Kim waited for panic to set in, even as she put her arm around Jilly's shoulders. But instead, she felt undeniably calm as she murmured words of comfort. "It's going to be okay. You were foolish to make such a bargain for me, though."

Jilly looked up. "I did it for me," she whispered brokenly. "I wanted him, if just for a little while." She swallowed. "What are we going to do now?"

Kim blinked. The question was to her? Jilly was always the one with the plans. Always certain, always forging ahead. Kim just went along, or, at most, tweaked a detail here and there.

"Greg will probably be back soon," she said uncertainly. Surely he would know what to do next.

"Who?" Jilly asked.

Kim groaned, all that she'd kept from Jilly pinching her with guilt. "I broke our vow, too," she confessed. "With Greg Kincaid. You see, we . . . knew each other a long time ago. I was ashamed to tell you about it."

Jilly's face went paler as Kim related the details of the situation with Greg. When Kim was done, Jilly rubbed a shaking hand over her eyes. "You spent the night with your ex-husband's grandson? Rory isn't going to like this, Kim. I just know it."

*Now* the panic welled. Kim swallowed, trying to ease her suddenly tight throat. Once more that question rose up in her mind. *What are we going to do?*

Kim grabbed Jilly's supersweet coffee and gulped it down. Someone had to think of something. Greg. Maybe he could come up with a plan. Someone definitely had to come up with a plan.

That someone should be Kim.

Her throat tightened again at the thought. *But it was true.* For all these years she'd let someone else rescue her, first Roderick, then Jilly, and now she was turning to another person—to Greg—to solve a problem she'd created herself when she'd made the choice to marry. Once again she'd been resorting to the easy way.

But maybe she could face her own demons now. It certainly wasn't fair to expect anyone else to do it. "I'm going to talk to Rory myself," she said.

Jilly's hand jumped to her throat. "Y-you're going to Caidwater?" She knew how the house symbolized Kim's feelings of pain and power-lessness.

Kim paid no attention to Jilly's shock and grabbed her car keys off the desk. "Yes." It was time for her to face *all* her demons.

The bells hanging from the shop's front door shook as she exited, just as her hand quivered while she unlocked the car. But she was able to ignore her body's nervous response on the drive from FreeWest to Caidwater. Not until she reached the wrought-iron barriers at the bottom of the driveway did fear finally overtake her.

Twenty feet from the gates, Kim halted under the partial cover of an overgrown clump of scarlet bougainvillea. "You can do this," she whispered to herself, mustering the courage to pull up to the button that would announce her return.

As if sensing her presence, the gates suddenly began swinging open. Kim gasped, but then a low-slung Mercedes took the final curve of the driveway and came flying through them. She couldn't see the driver, but she guessed it was Rory.

Meaning she could go home. Her insides melted with relief. Some other time—

*Coward.*

The accusation lashed across her mind. The time to face Caidwater was now.

Biting her lip to stop the trembling, she met her eyes in the rearview mirror. "Do it," she whispered to herself. "Drive up to Caidwater and wait for Rory to return."

With a determined twist of the key, she started her car. Her foot slammed on the gas, accelerating the vehicle through the slowly closing gates. They shut silently behind her.

Kim braked, peering anxiously up the curving driveway. The house wasn't yet in sight, but its image hovered in her mind anyway. Like Roderick himself, Caidwater had become a vengeful, angry, and suspicious presence.

But her daughter was there.

Kim pressed the accelerator again, and the car slowly climbed the narrow blacktop. Then the house came into view. Kim shuddered, its salmon color reminding her of raw flesh. Gritting her teeth, she pulled into the curve that swept past the front door and parked.

It took all her willpower to open the car door and step out. She stared at the imposing entrance, trying to remember a time when the place hadn't terrified her. The front door was open, and it seemed like a voracious and greedy mouth, ready to swallow her up.

Kim walked forward reluctantly, with each step ticking off a mistake or weakness that had brought her to this point. She'd traded her body for security. She'd lost her daughter. She'd relied on Jilly to address her own mistakes. Cold waves of shame washed over her and she hated herself and her failures all over again.

How could a woman like her think she deserved a night of joy with Greg, let along a lifetime with her daughter? The past had tainted her.

Courage shredded, she abruptly spun back to her car. Pain sliced through her, but she ruthlessly ignored it. She'd left Greg and Iris before, dammit. She could do it again.

Then a commotion from the interior of the house made her glance around. "He's out again!" someone yelled. Little-girl squeals joined more shouts.

"Mrs. Mack! The front door's open!" The sound of pounding footsteps drifted through the open doorway.

Kim swiftly turned her head, anxious to get in her car before someone saw her. She rushed away from the house to the tune of more tumult coming from inside Caidwater. With her hand on the car's door handle, she glanced back nervously once more, just in time to see Greg—with Iris perched on his shoulders—erupt through the front door. The little girl clutched a big butterfly net.

But Kim didn't have time to puzzle that out. Intent on getting away, she fumbled with the door handle as the pair rushed toward her.

"Kim!" Greg called. "Kim, wait!"

Still fumbling to open the door, she closed her eyes to the sounds of his voice and the too-near footsteps, which was maybe why she couldn't avoid something furry and gray that reached her first. The creature scrambled up her clothes to perch, unbelievably, on top of her head.

Her head was then, just as unbelievably, completely covered with netting as Iris yelled, "Gotcha!" and swung her butterfly net to capture her prize.

Kim froze. Greg grinned. Iris shook her forefinger. "You're not supposed to be running away." Kim supposed she was talking to the furry thing.

Yet Greg's gaze met hers. "That's right. You weren't, were you?" he asked softly.

Iris was still scolding her pet. "Don't you love me?"

"Don't you?" Greg's voice, soft and low again. "Don't you, Kim?"

Oh, God, she did. She loved both of them so, so much.

"And you belong to us," Iris continued crossly.

"That's right," Greg murmured. "You do."

And, oh, Kim wanted to.

"Now, you be good, Kiss," Iris said.

Kim frowned. "Kiss?"

"Certainly," Greg answered, and with one smooth movement he deposited Iris on the ground, plucked the creature and the net off Kim's head, and handed them both to the child. He leaned forward, his mouth near Kim's. "Your wish is my command."

Then he kissed Kim. Kissed her in front of her daughter. Kissed her in front of the household help who were trailing out the front door. Kissed her in front of the Caidwater mansion, where all the pain—and all this joy—had begun over four years ago.

Kim clutched Greg's shoulders. Wasn't this a mistake? Shouldn't someone rescue this good, decent man from her wickedness?

But then a plan blazed in her mind, the first real, Kim-initiated, Kim-rescue plan she'd ever had. It poured out of the deepest part of her and blazed so sun-in-the-heavens bright that it eclipsed the dark force of Caidwater and the shadows of her fear and shame.

She broke the kiss and looked at the house, the daughter she'd longed for, the man who'd waited for her. The only thing truly powerful here was love. And it was *her* power. It was a gift she had to offer to Iris and to Greg that didn't come from her body or her mind, but from the unsullied, pure goodness of her heart. Nothing, no one, no choice made in the past, had ever tainted that.

"Marry me, Greg," she whispered. "Marry me and let me make you happy."

For once in her life, she thought she could do it. She thought she deserved to try.

# Chapter 15

Rory strode in the direction of Things Past, moving quickly despite the weight of the damn cloud that seemed to be following him more closely than ever. Though Greg had minimized the hubbub around the house by disappearing two days ago with Iris, leaving a note about a quick trip to Vegas, bad luck continued to dog Rory.

With the fund-raiser just three days away, he was without food for the party. The contracted caterers had been forced to cancel because of a hepatitis outbreak, and every alternate was booked solid due to the Valentine's Day weekend.

Desperation had drawn him to the memory of Jilly's picnic, the one provided by her friends with their new catering business. Maybe new enough to be available over the holiday weekend.

But first he had to get Jilly to give him their number.

Jilly. Anger at her flared for a moment, then died out. When she'd reneged on their bargain the other morning, he'd barely remembered they *had* a bargain. He'd barely remembered his own name. Sex with Jilly blew his mind and that morning the pieces had been so scattered it had taken him several minutes to gather them together before he could talk to her.

She'd been angry and he knew why. No woman liked being treated as a lay instead of a lady, but he couldn't take back the word then. He wouldn't now. The danger for him had always been in controlling how he felt about her. Using that harsh word had done it for him.

Reaching her shop, he glanced at the display window, then dug his feet into the sidewalk. The person behind him plowed into his back, but Rory didn't move or acknowledge the muttered insult. Taking a deep breath, Rory closed his eyes, then opened them again.

No, it was real. In the window of Things Past— the window he'd never paid any attention to before—Jilly had hung an image of his face in a plastic bubble over a kinky-looking bathtub setup. Worse, she'd put words in his mouth. A cartoon bubble of white cardboard, affixed to the plastic bubble. And the words springing from his lips in bold black letters shouted, "Cast a vote for safe sex! Visit French Letters!" An arrow pointed to the place next door.

His stomach sinking lower, Rory let his gaze slowly follow the arrow toward French Letters. He blanched, and then, zombielike, walked toward the condom store's window. No. His mouth soundlessly formed the word as he watched what was happening.

But this was real, too. A strangled moan— something close to a calf's bleating—slipped from his throat. The woman the world consid-

ered his fiancée was dressing a window in a condom shop.

And, oh, my God, how she was dressing it. He
pushed his sunglasses more firmly onto his nose
and glanced around the street. It seemed bless-
edly paparazzi-free for the moment, but the
vipers had the habit of trolling likely locations. It
wouldn't surprise him to discover Jilly's shop on
the scandal-seekers' list.

Trying to breathe through his lung-squeezing
anxiety, he stepped up to the window. Certainly a
gentle reminder of her position—well, *his* position as the would-be Blue Party candidate—
would coax her out of the condom shop. He
tapped on the glass and she looked up.

Without thinking, he drew a finger across his
throat. *Cut it out*! he mouthed.

So it wasn't quite as gentle as he'd planned.
Neither was the look she gave him in return. He
didn't need an accompanying finger gesture to
know exactly what her response to him was.

She went back to adjusting the window display, which exhibited a kitchen scene, complete
with a mannequin in a June Cleaver dress,
starched apron, and pearls. "Vintage wear from
Things Past," announced a small placard. Both
June and Jilly stood beside a small table, and as
Rory watched, Jilly bent her head over a fruit
bowl and the bunch of bananas she was currently
outfitting with condoms.

Rory blew out a long breath as he watched her
roll an apple-green, ribbed Trojan over one of the
yellow fruit. That calf-bleat slid through his

throat once more. He tapped on the glass again. Impatiently.

Vigorously.

She just as vigorously ignored him, picking a cucumber from the bowl and then dressing it with a purple, nubby-sided rubber that looked more like a Koosh ball than a safe-sex tool.

He could imagine what the Blue Party would think about *that*. He knocked on the glass. She pretended not to notice as she rummaged through a basket of foil-wrapped condoms, biting her lip as if mulling over which one would look best on the obscene-appearing spaghetti squash in her hand.

Rory saw red. He hated the idea that anyone glancing in would assume Jilly to be some kind of sexpert, for God's sake. After all, who had taught her how to use a rubber? He had. Who had taught her everything she knew about sex, dammit? He had. Despite everything that went right and everything that went wrong between them, who had missed her like hell the past few nights in his bed? Rory had.

Not even attempting to draw logic lines among the three thoughts, he stomped into the shop, a series of trumpet notes—*ta-da da da da daaaa*—announcing his presence. He ignored the sound. He ignored the gender-unspecific salesclerk who rushed up to him in an overabundance of pierced body parts. He leaped into the display area and grabbed the squash and the unwrapped latest latex choice out of Jilly's fingers.

"What the *hell* do you think you're doing?"

She tried grabbing them back. "I'm putting together a window display for a friend."

"This—this isn't . . . seemly."

"*Seemly?*" She choked out a laugh.

Red was tingeing the edges of his vision again. Any Tom, Dick, or Harry could walk past and assess her condom technique, for God's sake. Coupled with her hot little body in those tight jeans and a bowling shirt—"Angel" embroidered over the pocket—and she was asking for trouble.

He ground his teeth together. "I don't want people to get the wrong idea about you."

She made another grab for the condom and managed to get her fingers on it. "You mean, like you did?"

Hell, yes, that was exactly what he meant. He didn't want some La-La Land Lothario to seduce innocent Jilly into his bed just because "Angel" looked devilishly sexy. With a tug, he pulled back on his end of the latex and the thing started to unroll. Rory stared, shocked. The flesh-colored rubber was embedded with red, green, and blue rhinestones. "Ugh. Who would wear something like this?"

"I don't know. Someone who can't afford diamonds?" she snapped. "Give it back." She tugged, and it unfurled some more.

He hung on. "Jilly, this just doesn't look good. You—"

She cut him off impatiently. "Why are you here?"

"You should be glad I am. Someone has to make you see—"

"That doing something for a friend can end in

disaster?" she asked. "You already proved that to me once."

His muscles tensed. "I remember a few times when you appeared to think it was delightful."

She didn't even blink. "Just cut to the chase. What do you want?"

He sucked in a calming breath. "Short of a cure for the disasters that continue to befall me, I need a caterer." He jumped on her sudden look of interest. "Let's go discuss it somewhere."

"Nice try." She pulled on her end of the rhinestone condom, and it got even longer. "I told you, I'm doing a favor for a friend here. Let go."

He didn't. "But I could do a favor for *your* friends. Those caterers. Do you think they could use a job Saturday night?"

The tension on the condom relaxed and Jilly's eyes gleamed. "I'm sure they could."

"Terrific." He tried to draw the latex out of her hand. "If you agree to come to the party, I'll agree to use them." He hadn't planned on suggesting such a trade, but he liked the idea now that it had popped out of his mouth.

Her eyes narrowed. "You need *them*, you don't need me. I don't want to come to your party."

He pulled. "Yes, you do."

She pulled back. "No, I don't."

"This is ridiculous." He yanked.

"I agree." She yanked.

Rory glanced out the window. Their shenanigans had drawn a small crowd, and a trickle of apprehension rolled down his spine. He could see it now, sequenced photos of their squabble splashed across papers and television screens.

One never-to-be-forgotten year, his father had been the star of no less than seven televised brawls. "Jilly," he said through his teeth, pulling again.

"Why don't you just let go?"

Because, dammit, she was besting him at every turn. Every time he thought he had things figured out, *them* figured out, Jilly put in a convenient niche where he could leave her, or leave her alone, she did something else unpredictable, something else surely designed to make him nuts.

Like leaving his bed.

Staring her down, he pulled harder on the condom, the rhinestoned latex stretching to anatomically unbelievable lengths. "Come to the party."

Narrowing her gaze, she hung on, her face and her grip stubborn and angry. "No."

"You owe me. You used me." If he could hold onto that, maybe he could hold onto his sanity.

Her mulish expression didn't soften and she lifted an eyebrow. "You used me back, remember?"

*No.* But before he could get a word out, from the other side of the window there came a flash.

Startled, Jilly released her end of the long, taut condom and it snapped like a rubber band, catching Rory across the placket of his khakis.

"Oh!" Her eyes widened. "Are you okay?"

It took all his willpower not to double over as more flashes went off, announcing the paparazzi had indeed arrived. "You *really* owe me now," he said when he could breathe.

Jilly glanced quickly at the two photographers on the other side of the window. "Rory—"

"No. Listen to me. The only way to neutralize what's going to come of this latest round of pictures is for you to be at the party."

Her hand had moved to cover her mouth, but then she took it away, her voice strangely breathless. "Why should I care about your latest PR problem?"

He ground his teeth once more. "Because you were the start of them all. Please, Jilly."

She was still resisting and she still sounded strangely out of breath. "Maybe it won't be so bad. Maybe people will think they put our heads on someone else's bodies."

He snorted. "Nobody has a body like yours."

Her gaze drifted from his face down to the condom he still gripped. Her hand lifted to cover her mouth again. "Yours either," she said from behind her fingers.

Suddenly suspicious, he ducked his head to follow her gaze. At belt level, the overstretched, garishly bejeweled condom hung limply from his hand, trailing nearly to his knees like the tired tongue of a dog.

Oh, right. Like the tired tongue of a dog. "Shit," he muttered, tossing the thing onto the table. *"Now you really owe me,"* he said through his teeth.

Odd, muffled sounds came from behind the hand she had clapped over her mouth. "Okay, okay," he thought he heard her say. "I'll be there."

And then she giggled. Peals of the stuff that he swore annoyed the hell out of him, even though the bright, amused sound seemed to momentarily push his dark, hovering cloud away.

Still seething, he held his own emotions in check as he ducked out the back door of French Letters and passed through an alley to an adjacent street crowded with shoppers. But then he caught sight of his reflection in the window of a holistic veterinary clinic.

He paused, his confrontation with Jilly replaying in his head. The condom-covered bananas. The rhinestoned rubber stretching, stretching, stretching between them. The flash, the snap, the limp thing lying against his leg.

And Rory laughed.

Out loud, outright, with his head thrown back and with their entire tug-of-war rerunning in his mind once more. A passerby—in motorcycle leathers and dog collar—gave him a wide berth, and Rory laughed all the harder.

Who knew looking like a fool could make him feel so free?

Three evenings later, Rory struggled to remember that fleeting feeling of liberation as he fought off a more familiar sense of dread. He stood by the windows of the playroom adjacent to Iris's bedroom, impatiently fingering the folded-up paper in the pocket of his white dinner jacket. Tiny white lights decorated the terrace below. An orchestra was tuning up in one corner and a bar was set up in another. A few small tables were scattered around the edges, but the middle was left open for dancing and for the toast Senator Fitzpatrick planned to give once Rory formally announced his candidacy.

In addition, there were some other, splashier

surprises planned to follow his announcement. Surprises that had kept workmen roaming the Caidwater roof and canoe pond for the past two days. The hoopla was all a bunch of PR nonsensical hype, of course, but Charlie Jax had shown an odd penchant for the dramatic.

Rory touched the paper again, reassuring himself it was still in his jacket. It contained the text of his speech—if you could call the few, strangely difficult-to-find words expressing his intention a speech—and he hoped like hell that once it was uttered to the several hundred expected guests, his sense of impending doom would finally go away.

"Iris! Aren't you ready yet?" he called out. Greg and the little girl hadn't returned from their Vegas jaunt until late in the afternoon, and Rory had done his best to charm her into getting dressed quickly. "Iris!"

"It's Auntie to you," she shot back through the connecting door, her voice sulky.

Rory sighed. As usual, his brand of charm fell flat when it came to Iris—Auntie.

Even after living with her the past few weeks, he wasn't any closer to understanding what she needed or wanted from him. He sighed, hoping that as soon as they moved away from L.A., they'd become more comfortable with each other. She was a duty he was bound and determined to manage well.

He looked back out the window, checking for something that might account for his underlying, unquenchable anxiety. But from here he could see that the gates to the eight gardens surrounding the house were opened as they should be, each garden illuminated by more tiny lights strung in the trees and through the hedges.

Caidwater's first-floor rooms, cleared of clothing thanks to Jilly, were also ready for visitors. The caterers, Jilly's friends, had arrived first thing in the morning. The delicious smells emanating from the kitchen assured him that at least the food was going to be disaster-free.

Rory rubbed the back of his neck. He had a small, legitimate concern about the catering staff, however. Paul and Tran's business, until now, hadn't needed any additional servers. So to meet the demands of this emergency job, they'd been forced to recruit a good number of FreeWesters to pass the food and drink.

Rory rubbed the back of his neck again, uneasy about mixing the staunch Blue Party supporters with the kind of people he'd met at the FreeWest gallery opening a few weeks before. He could only hope that Paul and Tran had drafted the least loony of the bunch.

There was no more time for second-guessing, though. He'd done everything he could to ensure that the evening went smoothly. Remembering previous Caidwater bacchanalian revels—resulting in drunken brawls and ménages à trois that had made morning headlines—he'd hired a phalanx of security guards to prevent any possible scandals.

That had been the worst part of being twelve, sixteen, twenty-two. His gut still clenched when he thought of those headlines. They were sleazy, they were titillating—God, the Kincaid men were sleazy and titillating—and he'd looked so much like them that everyone had expected more of the same. For so many years it had brought him both unwelcome attention and undeserved censure.

But tonight wouldn't be like those other parties. Thank God he'd convinced Jilly to be in attendance. As predicted, within hours those damn condom-shop photos had hit the Net and the tabloid TV programs, but had quickly been eclipsed by another brouhaha involving the male lead in Greg's last movie and his horse. With Jilly on Rory's arm, the entire rhinestoned episode would be quickly forgotten. Nothing would mar the long-awaited events of this evening.

On that thought, Iris strolled through the connecting door. At the sight of what she was wearing, Rory's jaw dropped. "No," he said.

She raised her eyebrows in an imperious manner that uncomfortably reminded him of himself. "Yes," she answered.

Mrs. Mack had bought the little girl a blue-on-blue, velvet-and-ribbon two-piece outfit for the party. Iris had claimed she could dress herself, which left Mrs. Mack free for the thousand other details she needed to attend to. But looking at the child, Rory had to accept that either Iris was not capable of dressing herself, or she was intent on sending him to a padded room.

She had donned the prescribed clothes, all right, but donned them all wrong. The elastic-waisted skirt had been drawn up under her arms like a tube top. The shirt was buttoned around her waist. And the matching blue tights had been pulled over her blond hair, the legs wrapped around her head like some kind of turban. She had her black patent leather shoes on the wrong feet.

Rory closed his eyes, struggling for control. She was testing him, of course. There was a book on his nightstand, *The 4-Year-Old's Fearsome Mind*, and it predicted battles just like this one. He tried to remember its advice, but when none of it came quickly to mind, he opened his eyes and pointed toward the bedroom. "Go fix it." Then he belatedly added, "Please."

"No."

Rory shoved his hands in his jacket pockets and squeezed his speech into a ball. "Yes. Right now. We don't have time to fool around. Guests will be arriving for the party any minute."

"I don't want to go to the party."

"I don't care what you want. Tonight's important and you need to be there," he said loudly. Then he softened his voice. "Just for a little while. I have a baby-sitter coming a bit later."

"No *baby*-sitter."

"Four-year-old sitter, then. Now go get dressed properly." He cleared his throat, trying to find the words to persuade her. "C'mon, Iris. I want to show you off as my little girl."

"I won't." Her blue eyes glittered and her voice rose with each word. "I won't. I won't go to the party, I won't live with you, and I'll never be your little girl!"

Rory struggled for calm. "Iris—"

"Is there a problem?" Greg said from the playroom doorway.

Rory spun toward him. "Hel—heck, yes,

there's a problem. You wore her out on your Vegas jaunt and now she refuses to go to the party." He narrowed his gaze, taking in his brother's jeans and cowboy boots. "And where the hell is your dinner jacket?"

"I don't want to go to the party either," Greg said. He looked down at Iris, who had rushed over to his side, and tweaked the tights-turban. "A *Blue Hat, Green Hat* moment, huh, bug?"

Rory frowned. "What are you talking about?"

Greg shot Rory a look. "I'm talking about Iris's favorite book, *Blue Hat, Green Hat*. It's about animals who dress themselves, and the turkey who always gets it wrong."

Rory shuffled his feet. Okay, so he didn't know the kid's favorite book.

Looking down at the little girl, Greg shook his head. "You know, this makes *you* the turkey, Iris."

She pouted. "I'm not a turkey."

"You are, dressed like that." He pushed her gently toward her bedroom. "Now go fix yourself up while I talk to Rory."

She gave Greg a half-pleading, half-pouting look, but he ignored her, and after a moment she walked toward her bedroom. "I still hate you," she hissed in Rory's direction, then slammed the bedroom door shut.

"Sorry about that," Greg said. "I'll talk to her about not using the word 'hate.' "

Rory shook his head. "You're not responsible for her."

An odd expression crossed Greg's face. He squared his shoulders. "Yes, in a way I am. Day before yesterday I married Iris's mother in Vegas."

Rory stared. "What?"

"I'm married."

Rory tried grinning. "I don't believe it." This had to be some kind of joke.

But Greg didn't grin back. "I married Kim Sullivan, who is Iris's mother."

*"What?"*

"We all lived here together before Iris was born. Roderick, Kim, and I. I fell in love with her then."

Something cold and slimy slithered down Rory's spine. "Are you telling me you're Iris's fath—"

"No!" Greg took a quick step forward, then halted, drawing in a deep breath. "I want to kill you for thinking that about Kim, about me, but we're going to have to get used to it. Iris is absolutely Roderick and Kim's child. When they were married, I never touched Kim. She wouldn't even let me tell her how I felt."

Rory slowly shook his head. "I don't understand."

"I know you don't." Greg looked him directly in the eye. "But more than four years ago I fell in love, without considering the consequences or the complications. Hell, I'm not sure I had time to consider them." His mouth briefly turned up in a rueful smile. "And to be honest, I wasn't very good at hiding my feelings. I'm certain that's why Roderick threw Kim out. He hated the idea we were in competition."

Rory made an impatient gesture. "The old man

married an eighteen-year-old girl. He finally woke up to the truth. She was out for his money or his influence. Something. That's why he threw her out."

At his sides, Greg's hands fisted. "And I'd like to hit you for that, too. But Kim wouldn't thank me for it. She'll tell you herself that she made a bargain with Roderick that she regrets. She was young and desperate, but she won't use that as an excuse either. Five years later, however, she's built up a business and built up herself."

Rory still couldn't take it in. "Jesus Christ, Greg," he said slowly. "Do you hear what you're saying? You married our grandfather's ex-wife. The mother of his child. Even our father never went *that* far."

Greg nodded. "It's true. And we want you to give us custody of Iris."

Rory's jaw dropped again. "You've got to be kidding! Roderick gave custody of her to me!"

"But I've lived with her for her entire life. I'm the closest thing she's ever had to a father, and I want to *be* a father to her." Greg's eyes went steely. "Roderick choosing *you* was his revenge on me. Not the best choice for Iris."

"Yeah, right. You're an actor, Greg. As flaky and irresponsible as Daniel and Roderick."

There was a long pause, and then Greg's face settled into cold, implacable lines. "*Damn you*, Rory." His voice was full of quiet fury. "Damn you for not looking beyond the Kincaid last name and seeing the man I am."

Rory tensed, just as furious. "Not looking beyond the Kincaid last name? Damn you back,

Greg, because I've been trying to *get* beyond the Kincaid last name my entire life. I want it to stand for—"

"Something different," Greg finished for him. "Well, I'm not ashamed of who I am or of my career, Rory. And I'm not our father, who only looks after his own selfish needs, or our grandfather, who manipulated people to feed his power. If you want to know the truth, that sounds more like you."

"What the hell do you mean by that?"

A muscle jumped in Greg's jaw. "Just think about what you've done lately in the name of the so-honorable Blue Party. There's your so-called engagement. And then there's Iris. If you *really* want to make the Kincaid name stand for something different, maybe you should think about what she needs and stop using her like our grandfather or father would."

Anger poured into Rory's blood. His brother was lecturing him. His Hollyweird-based little brother was trying to tell him what was right and wrong. His little brother who wouldn't have known the difference between the two if it weren't for Rory. "I—"

"Mr. Rory!" Mrs. Mack's voice called from the hallway. "Guests are arriving!"

Rory closed his eyes. Shit. The party. He'd completely forgotten about it. Heavy with thunderclaps, his doom-cloud descended, weighing heavily against his shoulders.

"Mr. Rory!" Mrs. Mack called again.

He opened his eyes. "I'm coming!" Then he

pointed his finger at his brother. "You I'll talk to later."

"I won't give in, Rory." Greg folded his arms over his chest. "Not this time, and not about Iris."

Ignoring the remark, Rory quickly brushed past his brother. He hurried down the staircase to discover that his first guest, standing uncertainly in the foyer, was Jilly.

His immediate, flooding sense of pleasure at the sight of her set his hackles rising once more. He scowled at her. "You're late." He had no idea what the hour was. He had never told her a particular time to arrive.

Her chin shot up and her pretty green eyes narrowed. "You didn't tell me what time to come."

She was always smarter than she looked. And she looked—God, she looked like a Valentine fairy. A bosomy fairy, but a fairy all the same. Her long skirt was a soft pink, and a filmy fabric lay over a stiffer one, so that it belled out gently. A tiny, cap-sleeved fuzzy sweater in the same pink covered her from modest cleavage to her waist. Her mouth was painted a deeper shade of pink and her dark hair hung in semi-tamed ringlets to her shoulders. And there were jewels in her hair.

He blinked, dazzled by them. Dozens of tiny rubies appeared to be sprinkled through her curls, like mini-kisses. Without thinking, he reached toward them. She stepped back, and the movement exposed a small slice of her stomach between the navel-grazing band of her skirt and the hem of her sweater.

A dime-sized ruby nestled in her belly button.

Lust, like a hot fist, sucker-punched him. Another emotion, unnameable but undeniable, also hit him. Hit him someplace else, someplace deeper. For a moment he couldn't breathe. Then he found his voice. "Jilly—"

"Oh, Rory, there you are! Where should we go?"

He couldn't take his eyes off the woman in front of him. "What?" he asked absently, not even registering who had spoken. His senses were completely tuned to Jilly. He could smell her perfume and, even from here, feel that telltale heat of her skin.

He wanted to lick her. He wanted to kiss her, consume her, take her into him and drive himself into her, as he'd done the last morning they'd been together. He wanted them so close that nothing would untangle them.

A hand prodded his arm. "We're looking for Paul and Tran."

Rory glanced toward the voice, looked back to Jilly, then did a double take. It was Aura. Aura and Dr. John, and a gaggle of others, all wearing matching red vests over their own idiosyncratic get-ups. He swallowed. "What—" He swallowed again. "Why are you here?"

"We're here to help Paul and Tran, of course," Aura replied, smiling. Her blue-covered book was tucked beneath her arm. "What do you think of our vests? I dragged out my sewing machine and made them myself. French seams. They're completely lined, yet I think dry cleaning won't be necessary. Just the gentle cycle and a cool iron."

Rory gaped at her. Not only was Aura a ringer

for Martha Stewart in the looks department, but apparently she could talk like the domestic doyenne at times too. "The vests are fine," he said faintly.

She smiled. "Now, where are Paul and Tran? We're here, all of us, to help this evening."

As he ran his gaze over the entire group of oddballs, Rory's momentary pleasure in Jilly fizzled out in a cold wash of dismay. Knowing the FreeWesters would be helping tonight, he should have been more prepared for this. But instead, he'd chosen to delude himself that he'd already paid and paid and paid in the what-could-go-wrong-next department.

The light from the foyer's massive ironwork-and-stained-glass chandelier gleamed off the bald pate of the equally massive Dr. John. The light also caught the several hoops the big man was wearing in multiple locations for the occasion. Someone—Rory thought he recognized the gender-unspecific salesclerk from the condom shop—smiled sunnily from behind the big man's shoulder.

Rory stared. The salesclerk's two front teeth were each decorated with a faithfully rendered American flag. Rory didn't want to think about the sort of process that kind of result required. Behind the salesclerk stood several others, all but the last sporting a startling hairstyle, hair color, tattoo, or all three.

Dragging his gaze off the sight, Rory rubbed his temple. "Paul and Tran are in the kitchen. That way." He pointed in the general direction, then watched as the group turned and shuffled off in a ragtag line. That calf-bleat he'd recently found himself capable of slid past his lips when he noticed that the last FreeWester—the only one who'd appeared seminormal from the front—wore his hair in waist-length dreadlocks.

*Oh, God, oh, God, oh, God.* Rory couldn't even think of a swear word strong enough to cover this situation. And the hell of it was, there was nothing he could do about it. Any moment, guests were expected to arrive. Little did they know it was for a "Come as Rory's Worst Nightmare" party.

Once the FreeWesters disappeared from sight, he swung back toward Jilly, a red-and-pink target for all his frustration and foreboding. "This is your fault," he said.

"Oh, no." She shook her head. The jewels in her hair flashed. "You're not going to pin your problems on me."

Oh, yes, he was. Because she'd descended on Caidwater like a plague, upsetting, tormenting, turning upside down and sideways every plan he'd made. "I wouldn't be in this fix if it wasn't for you."

She narrowed her eyes. "Which fix would that be?"

He made a wild gesture with his hand. "Scandals, oddballs, freaks, flakes! Just when I'm getting my life in order, you surf in and curse it with your do-gooder schemes and your dopey friends."

"Friends so dopey they gave up their evening to help you out of a jam. You needed them, remember?"

He hated that she had a point. "If I'd been thinking clearly, I would have put tuna salad on Saltine crackers and served it myself instead of letting those loons into the house. What the hell are the guests going to think?"

Jilly shrugged. "Maybe they'll surprise you and look below the surface to see the good people they are. You could stand to do a little of that yourself, you know."

He clenched his teeth. "A little of what?"

"Looking deeper." Color rose up her throat and cheeks. "I bet you haven't spent two seconds in the last ten years scratching beneath the surface. Why don't you devote a couple of minutes to self-improvement and try to see inside my friends, me, yourself even."

His blood was starting to heat. "What's your point?"

"My point is that if you look beneath the surface, Rory, you might find something surprising."

He said the first thing that came into his head. "The only thing that's surprised me lately is finding a woman who turned away from a whole aspect of life—from sex—because she was afraid one old lady's prediction would come true. You let that fear control you for years. How's that for scratching the surface?"

She sucked in a sharp breath and then looked away. "Forget it. Don't even bother looking inward, Rory. I'm suddenly certain there's nothing inside you. Not flesh, not blood, not heart. Nothing."

That he thought he might have hurt her made him even madder. His blood heated another few degrees. "Oh, you can dish it out, darling, but you just can't take it, can you? I've looked inside you, my sweet, and see a woman so trapped in the past and so caught up in proving something to someone else that she doesn't have a clue what she wants for herself."

Her gaze instantly snapped back to him. "And I can say the same thing of you," she retorted. "Do you really want to hold public office? Is all this concern over propriety and perfection something you *really* care about? Or do you just want people to think 'senator' instead of 'scandal' when they hear the Kincaid name?"

His blood boiled over. "I'm sick of that question, dammit. All that I care about is supposed to come true tonight. The name Kincaid, for once, is supposed to be associated with something honorable and worthwhile. But I see it slipping through my fingers, thanks to you."

She flinched, and all the starch left her spine. Her hand pressed against her stomach—right over that crazy, distracting ruby. "Fine," she said, her voice now quiet and suddenly devoid of emotion. "If it's really what you want, Rory, then you can have it. That's what I've heard, anyway. *Just close your fingers*. Hold on tight and don't let go."

# Chapter 16

Trying to ignore the new bruises on her broken heart, Jilly watched Rory's mouth open. But before he could get out another word, Uncle Fitz and his Blue Party entourage surged through the front door. Rory was forced to move forward to greet them and Jilly used his distraction to slip away.

Unsure of what to do next, she escaped in the direction of the soft, calming strains of a violin. She found herself on the back terrace, where white fairy lights were wound around the stone balustrades. The gardens below were lit as well, turning the Caidwater grounds into a magical, romantic kingdom.

A champagne glass was placed in her palm, cold liquid sloshing a little to drip on her fingers. "Congratulate me," Kim said.

Jilly turned. "You're back. And—" The twinkling lights caught in the fire of the diamond on Kim's left hand. "You did it. You're married." Despite how sick she felt inside, Jilly smiled.

Kim touched the edge of her glass to Jilly's. *Clink.* "Yes." She grinned. "We actually did it. I can't believe how happy I am."

"That's wonderful," Jilly whispered, emotion tightening her throat. "That's so, so wonderful."

With twin movements, they both took big gulps of the champagne. Kim laughed almost giddily and Jilly blinked, startled by the light-hearted sound. Kim's brown eyes sparkled and her face was flushed. She looked . . . she looked *alive*.

"Greg must be good for you," Jilly said.

Kim nodded. "And I'm going to be good *to* him. Iris, too." She hesitated. "We haven't told her I'm her mother . . . we're talking about how best to do that, but she's going to know the truth. I promise that. No more secrets."

Jilly frowned. "Has Greg talked to Rory—"

"Don't worry." Kim put her hand on Jilly's arm. "It's our problem now. I should never have let you go into my battles for me. I see that. But we'll handle it from here."

Jilly stared down at the tiny bubbles rising to the top of her glass. "I'm sorry I messed up," she said.

*"No."* Kim patted Jilly's arm. "That's not what I meant. But you should be living your own life, not trying to fix mine."

"What life?" Jilly whispered. When she'd talked her way into the job at Caidwater, she'd thought reuniting Kim and Iris would make her life complete. She'd thought it would be like reuniting with her own mother. But Jilly realized now that it wasn't going to work. Big pieces of herself were still missing.

"Oh, Jilly." Kim's forehead pleated in concern.

"Why are you here tonight anyhow? I thought you and Rory had parted ways."

Jilly opened her mouth, but no good answer came out. Three days ago she'd been absurdly happy to see him outside the window of French Letters, then absurdly angry at the way he'd instantly ordered her around. In the end, though, she'd agreed to attend the party. Maybe because it *was* the end. She had to witness it.

After tonight, whatever it was they'd had together would be like a dream. A fantasy. "I just had to see it through," Jilly said. "To see it really be over."

"Why don't you tell him you don't want it to be over? Why don't you tell him how you feel?"

"What?" Jilly's eyes widened. "Rory doesn't want the love of a woman like me."

"Oh, sure," Kim scoffed. "That's why he insisted on that engagement. That's why he bargained you into his bed."

Jilly bit her lip. So maybe he wanted her, but it was in the way that someone wanted what was worst for himself. And there was another reason for not telling Rory the truth. The most important reason of all.

"What if he used my feelings against me?" she whispered hoarsely. That was her grandmother's lesson. Love could be used to hurt, to manipulate, to humiliate. She wouldn't give someone that power over her again.

"Jilly . . ." Kim said. There was an ache in her voice that matched the ache in Jilly's heart.

Movement caught her eye and she took the

champagne glass out of her friend's hand. "Greg's over there trying to get your attention. You better go see what he wants."

With one last concerned look, Kim hurried toward her new husband. Jilly leaned against the balustrade and watched her walk away. Kim was really walking toward a new life, she thought. That also was the result of this interlude with Rory.

She'd lost Kim. For four years it had been Jilly and Kim against the world. Their business and their friendship had given Jilly a focus and a purpose. But now, now Kim had Greg and her daughter. Jilly didn't begrudge her that, not for a second, but it meant that their lives were going to change. It meant that she was alone again, just like all those years growing up in that gray-and-white house.

She closed her eyes tightly, suppressing a cold wave that threatened to sweep her away. Loneliness was like that, dark and engulfing, but she would find a way to fight it.

It was silly to feel so sad, she told herself. Silly, because she'd been alone most of her life. Surely she wouldn't have trouble managing it again.

Taking a deep breath, she opened her eyes. Caidwater was filling up with guests and many had already spilled onto the terrace. Through the French doors she could see Rory standing in the library with the senator. Obviously at ease in his evening clothes, he looked expensive and accomplished, and his exotic features made him only that much more compelling.

She shivered, remembering his warm hands moving slowly on her skin, the laugh in his voice when he admitted to his bedhead affliction, the way his body fit hers like a key in a lock. Despite all her vows, he'd opened up her sensuality and her heart.

He turned his head as a beautiful blond woman, in an icy blue column of a dress, joined him. Rory bent and kissed her lips. It was nothing more than a casual salute, but it went halfway to squeezing the air from Jilly's lungs. The rest was taken by the less-than-casual grip the tall woman took on his arm. This was the type of woman Rory wanted. This was the type of woman who matched what he wanted for his life.

Jilly turned her back on the sight and looked out over the gardens. Well. There it was. The end. She'd seen it through and she'd survived. At least it couldn't get any worse.

But then a familiar, expensive fragrance drifted toward her. Someone called in her direction.

"Gillian." It was the old name in the unforgettable voice. It was the past rising up and the distinct feeling that yes, indeed, it could get much, much worse.

One hand braced on the solid rock balustrade, Jilly turned. That dark and engulfing loneliness rose up again, but she pretended she didn't feel its chill against her back.

"Jilly, Grandmother, not Gillian," she said, looking coolly at the woman who had raised her but never loved her. "My mother wanted me to be called Jilly, and that's who I am."

Rory disentangled himself from Lisa's clutches. He needed to check on the party's progress and, more important, on Jilly's whereabouts. Their argument had left him with a bad taste in his mouth and a cold heaviness in his chest. He wasn't sure whether he wanted to apologize or go a few more rounds, but he just knew he had to be with her.

"Excuse me," he said, politely smiling at the senator. "But I need to tend to a few things."

The older man bent his silver head. "But come back soon, son. And bring Gillian—Jilly—with you, too. I want your announcement as soon as possible and she should be at your side. Then tonight can be a celebration."

The announcement. Rory touched the crumpled speech in his pocket and beat off the cloying cloud that was descending lower. He pasted on another smile. "Soon, sir."

Thinking he'd caught a glimpse of Jilly outside, he hurried through the French doors and onto the terrace. But once there, he was immediately stopped by the head of the security force he'd hired for the evening. "Mr. Kincaid," the man said over the soft play of the orchestra. His expression was serious.

Rory frowned. "A problem?"

"There's some press at the gatehouse. They have credentials, but they're not on the list."

"Credentials? What pr—?" He broke off, his attention snagged by the sight of Jilly. She was standing at the far end of the terrace, against the balustrade, her posture tense and stiff. A small frown wrinkled her brow as she listened to a gray-haired woman in front of her.

"Rory?" Aura drifted toward him, holding a tray of canapés. "Would you object to me passing out my business card?"

His head swung toward her. "What?"

She nudged the tray into the hands of the security guard, who reflexively closed his fingers over it. Then she dug into the pocket of her red vest and drew out a small stack of cards. "I always carry them. Who knows when a person might need my kind of help?"

"Sir?" the security guard asked. "What do you want me to tell the team at the gatehouse?"

A too-thin woman with an oversprayed hairdo touched Aura on the back of her arm. "Are you the one doing readings tonight? I'm Gemini, Virgo rising."

Aura smiled at the lady. "Just a moment, dear. Rory? Do you mind?"

Rory was distracted from answering when the older woman talking to Jilly turned. Her familiar face gave him a jolt and he searched his memory banks for her name. *Ah.* Dorothy Baxter. The senator had introduced them at another fund-raiser several months before.

Dorothy Baxter was an old and generous friend of the senator's and therefore an important friend of the Blue Party as well. What was she doing with Jilly?

"Rory? Rory?" Aura again. "May I pass out my card?"

"Mr. Kincaid? The press?" The security guard still gingerly grasped the tray.

Rory's attention snapped back to the questions

at hand. The press. He thought swiftly. "If they're not on the list but they have credentials, they can come in. No cameras, though."

"Yes, sir." The guard nodded, then looked down at the tray of canapés in his hand and then over at Aura, who was lost in conversation with her wannabe client.

With a sigh, Rory took the tray himself. As the security guard moved off, Rory saw Jilly abruptly begin to walk away from Mrs. Baxter, but the older lady said something that made her reluctantly turn back.

He frowned, Jilly's obvious dismay setting off warning bells. *What was going on?* He took a step in her direction, but was halted by the Blue Party's Charlie Jax. The man put his hand on Rory's arm and spoke in his ear. "Now, Rory," he ordered. "The senator wants you to make that announcement now."

Rory tightened his fingers on the silver tray, Jax's tone and the knowledge that he had to pay attention to it grating on his nerves. "Okay. I'm on my w—"

Mrs. Mack rushed up to him, her expression anxious. "Mr. Greg is leaving. I—I don't know what to do. But he has suitcases. And Iris. I know you wanted her to be at the party."

Suitcases. And Iris.

Charlie Jax tugged on Rory's arm. "We want you to make that announcement *now*, Rory."

What the hell was Greg doing? Rory wondered. Shaking himself free of Jax, he shoved the tray toward Mrs. Mack. "I'll be back when I can," he said, then pushed Jax in Aura's direction.

Without missing a beat, the astrologer turned away from the Gemini, Virgo rising, she'd been speaking with and grabbed the politico's palm. Aura smiled serenely. "Let me see here . . ."

Rory ignored Jax's panicked look and dashed inside.

The senator caught sight of him rushing through the library and called out, "Rory! Don't you—"

"Just a minute, sir." Rory waved his hand and sped by. In the foyer, guests continued to pour through the front door, but there was no sign of Greg, or suitcases, or Iris. His stomach clenching, he headed down another corridor in the direction of the kitchen. Maybe they would use the service entrance.

Barreling through the kitchen door, he braked to a halt. A scene of controlled bustle greeted him, with Paul and Tran moving quickly between trays and the refrigerator. But at the far right of the room, the door leading outside was open and three people were preparing to exit, each gripping a suitcase. Greg, Iris, and Kim. Kim, Iris's mother.

The resemblance between them startled him now, and he was shocked he hadn't realized it before. As he watched, Kim untangled Iris's long blond hair from the strap of the small duffel she had slung over her shoulder. The little girl ignored the gesture and ignored the woman. But Kim's expression of patient yearning struck Rory like a blow to the chest.

As if she sensed his gaze, she looked up and met his eyes. Her jaw firmed, and she touched Greg on the shoulder. A loving touch.

Greg's head turned and he saw Rory. Greg and Kim slowly set down the suitcases they carried. Only Iris seemed unaware of the simmering tension among the three adults.

Rory strode toward them. "Where are you going?"

Greg rested his palm on top of Iris's head. "I'm ferrying some things to my new house. Kim and Iris are coming with me. We'll be back."

Rory narrowed his gaze. "You're sure about that?"

"I'm not running away. But I *am* taking control this time, Rory. I'm not going to back down."

"No." The low, clear voice of Jilly's partner, Greg's wife, broke in. "*I'm* taking control."

She walked toward Rory, then held out her hand. "Kim . . . Kincaid."

He heard her slight hesitation at the last name and wondered if it wasn't such a comfortable fit for her either, considering the past. Her grip was unhesitating, though.

"I need to make an appointment with you," she said.

Rory took a deep breath. God. This woman was not only his former stepgrandmother but also his new sister-in-law.

"Greg! Greg Kincaid!" Suddenly two men crowded the kitchen doorway. The discarded suitcases blocked them from entering, but still a flashbulb went off. "*Celeb!* magazine here. Is it true you were married in Las Vegas yesterday?"

"Is this your new wife?" Another flash. "Kim Sullivan Kincaid Kincaid?"

Rory automatically moved between Kim and

the reporters just as Greg drew Iris behind him, but not before the man with the camera spotted the child. He nudged his loud-mouthed pal.

The reporter's eyes actually gleamed. "This is the daughter, then? Roderick's . . . or yours?"

Though his brain froze, Rory's body went into action. Even as the words *Roderick's . . . or yours?* echoed in his mind, he bolted for the door. Greg bent and whispered something to Iris, who ran to Kim, and the woman hurried her daughter out of sight. Then the brothers faced the press again.

"It's time for you to leave," Rory said.

"We just want a few answers." The reporter gave Greg and Rory a smarmy smile. "It's not every day the grandson of a Hollywood legend marries his former stepgrandmother. You're news, Greg."

"Leave," Rory said, louder.

"And then there's the kid. Paternity is always a hot Hollywood issue."

"That's it." Greg kicked the suitcases out of the way.

"No." Rory caught his brother's arm and pulled him back, even while *the grandson of a Hollywood legend marries his former stepgrandmother* roiled in his brain and in his belly. "I'll deal with this." *Paternity is always a hot Hollywood issue.*

Behind him, a clatter of metal made him glance back. Paul and Tran, each holding a silver platter like a shield, had taken up places beside Greg. Behind them, several of the FreeWesters, including Dr. John, stood like a red-vested, weirdly menacing battalion. A flash went off again, nearly blinding against the metal platters.

"Get out," Rory said.

"Don't you have a statement, a few words maybe?"

Rory blocked his brother from surging forward again. "No." Once more he pushed Greg behind him.

"Just tell us who the kid's real father is," the reporter challenged.

This time, metal trays clanking against each other like weaponry, Rory and the troops took a step forward together. "Get the hell out."

With the FreeWesters and Greg backing him up, Rory grabbed the door. Under a barrage of flashes, he then managed to push it closed on the photographer and the reporter, and with a satisfying click, he turned the lock.

Shouted questions continued to sound from outside and the door trembled under a battery of knocking. But Rory ignored the noise and faced the odd collection of erstwhile volunteers. "Thank you," he said. "Thank you all." The trays rattled again as the "soldiers" exchanged satisfied grins.

Rory turned to the largest of them. "Dr. John, would you track down a security guard and have them escort our friends off the property?"

At the big man's nod, the red-vested soldiers dispersed. Grateful, resigned, and surprisingly half amused, Rory watched them return to their regular duties. Their inspired and automatic defense was going to make for some interesting tabloid photos. But most interesting of all was that they didn't appear shocked, dismayed, or even titillated by the accusations, as tonight's party guests would undoubtedly be.

He appreciated that. Admired it.

But then Rory had no choice but to meet Greg's eyes.

The questions and innuendos spread across his mind like newspaper headlines. ICON'S GRANDSON MARRIES HIS OWN GRANDMA. Bleh. Even worse, MAN FATHERS GRANDMOTHER'S DAUGHTER.

"Jesus, Greg," he couldn't help saying. "What the hell have you done to my life?"

Greg didn't bat an eye. "I've been trying to tell you. This isn't about you, Rory. This is about me, my wife, our child. Iris isn't here to make you look good to the voters."

Rory grimaced, the headlines and innuendos still running through his head.

Greg spoke again. "She cares about being loved. About being happy. Not what 'Kincaid' means. That's up to me and you now, Rory."

But he could still hear that reporter. *Just tell us who the kid's real father is.*

The kid's real father was Roderick. Roderick, who had left Iris in Rory's care.

But despite that, and despite the disgusting headlines that were about to explode into reality, as Rory stared into his brother's hard eyes, he knew Greg wasn't going to be satisfied with leaving it at that. With leaving Iris with him.

Rory shook his head. This certainty of purpose, this determination, was a new side to his brother.

And Rory respected him for it.

Remembering Kim's firm grip, he knew she was going to put up a good fight, too.

Rory blew out a long breath, that cloud hanging over him like a suffocating weight. "For God's sake, Greg. If I don't try to hold onto her, what will the Blue Party think? And the voters?"

Candidates with squeaky images, candidates who wanted to renovate politics into something cleaner and more honorable, did not give up custody of children to men who married their ex-stepgrandmothers. The ex-stepgrandmother who had birthed, then abandoned, said child. Knowing his grandfather, Rory had no doubt that when he did a little digging on that prenup, he'd discover that Kim had been without choice. But that wouldn't be how it played in the press.

"You have to think about Iris." Greg folded his arms over his chest, and for the first time, Rory forgot Greg was his younger brother and saw him as the man he had become. "You have to do what's right."

*What's right.* The words instantly touched off the mother of all headaches. Jilly had also talked about doing what was right, the morning she'd left him. Rory rubbed his forehead. He'd never considered himself someone who would do the *wrong* thing, for God's sake. Quite the opposite.

But the truth was, for the opportunity to be a Blue Party senatorial candidate, for a shot at respectability and for renovating the Kincaid name, he'd been doing the wrong thing over and over. Like Iris and her *Blue Hat, Green Hat* moment, he'd been willing to wear his family loyalty inside out and his sense of justice upside down.

*Blue Hat, Green Hat.* Iris's favorite book. And he hadn't even known it. He closed his eyes, disgusted with himself. All along he'd been thinking of her as just one more responsibility. A duty. Oh, yeah, Greg was correct yet again.

Though the decision Rory was about to make—had already made—was no doubt going to complicate his future plans, Iris should be with the ones who had cared for her the longest and loved her the best. It *was* time to make the Kincaid name stand for something different.

"Fine, then," he said slowly, his headache vanishing as quickly as it had come. "What's right, what's true, is that *you* are Iris's father. And I'll make certain that the three of you are a family." Rory held out his hand, even as he was keenly aware that he'd just set his whole damn world spinning.

Greg smiled and came forward, ignoring the proffered palm. He pulled Rory into a bearlike hug instead. "You've never let me down," he said.

Rory slapped his brother on the back. Despite the irrevocable—and maybe unrecoverable—blow he'd just made to his future, he thought his cloud of inevitable doom showed, for the first time, a spark of a silver lining.

Rory headed back to the party, the packed rooms and buzzing conversations a sure sign of the fund-raiser's success. Biting back a surprised laugh, he noticed Aura holed up in a corner of the living room, her waitressing duties long abandoned. A circle of tuxedoed men was gathered around her and her big blue book, and he thought he heard one of them mention the Nasdaq and Sagittarius in the same breath.

Passing through the library, he raised his brows as he caught Dr. John suggesting a dragon tattoo to a woman sporting a diamond choker and a smooth, tennis-on-Thursdays tan. Maybe he wasn't the only one who would never forget this night.

Crossing the threshold to the terrace, he paused. The senator was holding onto the microphone as if ready to give a speech, and partygoers were gathering close. Rory sucked in a breath. With his blessing, his four-year-old aunt was going to be adopted by his brother, who had just married his ex-stepgrandmother. What would the senator and the Blue Party think about that?

Those headlines popped back into his mind.

But they wanted *him*, not his brother or his family situation, he tried reassuring himself. Maybe he had a little ground to make up now, but Jilly had told him to close his fingers over what he wanted and hold on. And, dammit, he wanted this.

Didn't he? Yeah, like Greg had said, Rory was autocratic, impatient, and undiplomatic. He chafed under the control of party leaders like Charlie Jax. And yeah, the slow wheels of the political process might grind his patience into the ground. But for a man who wanted to change his image, being part of something that wanted to change the image of politics was ideal. Wasn't it?

Just then, the senator spotted him across the terrace and immediately lifted the microphone to his mouth. "May I have your attention. I've been on pins and needles all night, wanting to introduce you to our host . . . Rory Kincaid!" The silver-haired man gestured toward Rory with the mike.

Applause broke out and more guests poured onto the terrace. Rory made his way through the crowd, taking in the pats on the back, the scents of expensive perfumes, the names of the distinguished Californians in the audience. People he respected. People who respected him. But that cloud over his head was thickening again.

Funny, he was twenty feet away from the most important, satisfying moment of his life. You'd think that doom-cloud would finally disappear.

But the flash of something pink and red in his peripheral vision snared his attention. Jilly. He turned his head to see her whisk down the steps toward the gardens, followed by that older woman, Dorothy Baxter.

And suddenly, more than anything else, he had to know for certain that Jilly was all right.

Lifting his hands above the crowd, he made the time-out signal. Senator Fitzpatrick blinked in bewilderment and the applause petered out, but Rory ignored both and hurried after the two women. The orchestra gamely struck up another tune and he didn't feel the least bit guilty for leaving the older man to use his canny political skills to smooth over the moment. This was the senator's element, not Rory's.

And he didn't feel the least bit guilty for stopping just short of Jilly and Mrs. Baxter when he caught sight of them moving into the rose garden. Something about the stiff way Jilly was walking told him she might need him, though he suspected she wouldn't necessarily welcome his presence.

The heady scent of roses filled his head as he paused in the shadows at the garden's entrance. No other guests had wandered this far from the house, and in the light from the moon and the lights strung through the precisely cropped hedges, he could clearly see Jilly's tension.

"Grandmother, I don't care to discuss this."

*Grandmother*. He remembered now. In San Francisco, the senator had called Jilly by the name Gillian *Baxter*. Rory's brows rose, and he looked more carefully at Jilly's grandmother. Like Jilly, she was small and, like Jilly, she was apparently not afraid to speak her mind.

"I don't care whether you want to discuss it or not, girl. But you owe something to that man you're engaged to. More appropriate dress, to begin with."

"I like what I'm wearing," Jilly said.

The older woman sighed. "I'm sure you do. But you were trained to know better. Something less flashy, more understated, would better serve your position."

"What position is that?"

"Don't be stupid, girl. It's no secret that Rory Kincaid is going to announce his candidacy tonight. You're entering the political arena now. *My* arena. You should listen to me closely. Frankly, I'm shocked you've managed to get this far on your own, but I suppose those years in my home weren't entirely erased by your work at that . . . that . . . shop."

"That shop" wasn't a smart way to describe Jilly's baby, Things Past. Rory took a breath, waiting for Jilly to explode.

"Things Past," Jilly corrected her mildly. "That's the name of my mother's business. Now my business."

Rory stared, stunned by her quiet response. It was as if Jilly's grandmother's presence had extinguished the light, the energy, the joy that made Jilly so uniquely herself.

Joy. Rory examined the word in his mind and knew it was the right fit. Jilly had a joy in colors, in textures, in laughing, in *life*, that he hadn't felt since boyhood. Yet when he was with her, joy found its way into him, too.

"Your business. Yes, fine." Dorothy Baxter made a dismissive gesture, then reached out and patted Jilly's cheek, ignoring her flinch. "But despite that, you've done well. This engagement wholly meets with my approval. I can only imagine you now appreciate what I did to keep you from your mother and the kind of life she led."

Jilly appeared to absorb the words calmly, though Rory was sure each had to feel like a blow. She didn't want her grandmother's approval, and surely not for a sham engagement to *him*. He saw her hands slowly fist, and he knew she itched to throw the truth back at the older woman. Jilly opened her mouth, pressed her lips together, opened her mouth again.

Rory tensed, waiting for Jilly's response. If she

did indeed tell her grandmother the engagement was a fake—her grandmother who was a crucial contributor to the Blue Party coffers—it would be the final nail in his senatorial coffin. Without an engagement, their tabloid appearances became scandals that a woman like Dorothy Baxter wouldn't tolerate from a Blue Party candidate.

The loss of Dorothy Baxter's support, coupled with the likely headline—GRANDSON FATHERS HIS OWN AUNT!—would force Rory to surrender the candidacy. He sucked in a sharp breath, his cloud gathering darkly over him. There was no way his political aspirations could weather both storms.

# ℓ Chapter 17

Jilly battled a tumble of rising emotions. She'd fled the terrace to escape witnessing Rory's imminent announcement. When he truly entered the political field he would forever exit her realm. Watching that would be like watching his horse gallop across the dunes again, though away from her this time, leaving her alone in the desert.

But she hadn't been able to escape her grandmother.

Jilly bit her lip, swearing she wouldn't surrender to any of the words she longed to say or the tears she longed to shed. Grandmother hated tears. Jilly wasn't all that fond of them herself, but when her mother entered the equation, she wasn't confident of her control.

Grandmother suddenly focused on Jilly's belly. "*What* is that?" she asked in offended tones.

Jilly dipped her head to peer at her navel, exposed by the hem of her sweater. The ruby nestled there glittered. "Embellishment. Decoration." She'd donned the synthetic jewel as a wink-nudge joke to herself, assuming—rightly, she hoped—that it would make Rory nuts.

Her grandmother shook, literally shook, with outrage. "It makes you look like a . . . like a *tramp*."

Years ago Grandmother had said pierced ears would make her look like a tramp. Just as her hair unbound and free made her look like a tramp, as well as the God-given curves of her body. Nothing Jilly had ever done was good enough, proper enough, modest enough.

"Gillian." Grandmother's voice whipped at her. "That shop and your mother must have influenced you after all."

Jilly flinched. She pushed her fingernails into her palms, but the small biting pain was nothing to the claws at her heart. "Why?" she asked. "Why do you do this?" Her grandmother's expression became blank, but it did nothing to appease Jilly. "Why would you want to judge me, or hurt me, or criticize my mother?"

"Your mother is dead," her grandmother said coldly.

"That's right. But what you say about her hurts me because I know now that she loved me. You lied about that. You said she left me with you, abandoned me, when the truth is she was forced to give me up. Forced by you. If Aura hadn't come to her funeral, if Aura hadn't given me the letters she wrote me that you returned to her, I'd still be believing your version."

"Nonsense."

Jilly recognized the bluster in the woman's voice. Five years ago she would have been intimidated by it, but no longer.

"Her letters would have confused you."

Jilly fought the telltale sting of tears in her eyes. "Her letters would have let me know *somebody* loved me."

"What did she know of love?" Grandmother's voice. "She was a disobedient, wanton child."

Jilly blinked furiously. Her mother had been pregnant with Jilly—the father unknown or unrevealed—at seventeen. She cleared her throat, trying harder to suppress the tears. "So why didn't you encourage her to give me up for adoption? Or let both of us go?"

Her grandmother blinked. "What? When I had the opportunity—no, the *responsibility*—to make right with you the mistakes I had made with *her*?"

Jilly's throat was so tight she had to whisper. "The success to counterbalance the failure?" But it was more than that, she thought, seeing it all so coldly clear for the first time. Her grandmother was someone who didn't like to lose, and she'd paid back her rebellious daughter in the way that would hurt the most—by taking away her child. Hot tears spilled down Jilly's cheeks.

"Crying." The older woman shook her head as if appalled at the very idea. "Crying is a weakness. And you listen to me, Gillian. You wouldn't be in this position, and with this man, if it weren't for me and everything I drilled into you." Her arthritic finger jabbed toward Jilly's throat. "Think about that."

Jilly put her hands over her eyes. The movement wasn't going to stop her tears—they continued to flow down her face—but she wanted to hide from the knowledge that was creeping into her mind. Some people could not be swayed. Some people could not be reasoned with. There was no word, no gesture, no memory that could be invoked that would in turn evoke tenderness.

And whether her grandmother was evil or ignorant wasn't for Jilly to judge or to influence. A thousand business successes or a million vows of celibacy wouldn't change the old woman's opinion of her. There wasn't a thing she could do to prove herself worthy.

Jilly merely had to let go.

Rory was right. She had to step out of the past and stop living against her grandmother and just live. For herself.

Squaring her shoulders, she turned away to start back to the house.

"Foolish girl." Her grandmother's voice was no less certain than it had been all those years when she'd kept Jilly's spirit imprisoned in her austere gray and white house. "You think twice before turning your back on me. What about this engagement? I can mean a lot to your fiancé."

Oh. Oh, God. Jilly halted, and then spun around to face the older woman. Because of her new resolve to live her own life on her own terms, Jilly couldn't suppress the nasty urge to throw the engagement back in her grandmother's face. But that would be throwing Rory's chances back as well.

Grandmother was right, at least about that. She was an old, and moneyed, political influence in California.

"No, Grandmother," Jilly found herself whispering though. "Don't use Rory to get at me.

You've already done enough damage on that score."

Her grandmother's gaze narrowed. There was a calculating and cynical gleam in her eye. "What do you mean by that?"

And despite every resolve and every self-protective instinct, the words poured out of Jilly. "I've never told him I love him," she said, her voice hoarse. "And I do."

She brushed away the last of the wetness on her cheeks. "You made me afraid to admit to such a 'weakness.' You made me worry about how he could hurt me, manipulate me, with that knowledge."

Her grandmother had made her afraid of love. All along, she realized now, her vow of celibacy had never been a way to prove anything. It had been her way to protect herself from loving.

"Oh, fiddle."

Jilly almost laughed, it was such a ridiculous response. She shook her head instead. "Don't you see? Love is what you used against my mother and me. It's how you controlled my mother, and how you tried to control me. She loved me, so she didn't fight the more powerful you. When you didn't want me to move to L.A., when you didn't want me to take over my mother's business after her death, you used every threat you could think of, telling me you were being truthful because you loved me. I would fail. I would be promiscuous. I would come begging at your doorstep in no time flat."

"But Jilly did none of those things." The familiar deep masculine voice, then the familiar figure stepped out of the shadows and into the rose garden.

*Oh, God.* Jilly cringed. *Rory.* Her body, mind, heart, emotions, turned into themselves, trying to prevent the vulnerability that she was terrified he'd witnessed. Oh, God. Had he heard her say she loved him?

His footsteps crunched on the gravel path until he reached them. "And neither did she agree to marry me," he said. "Our engagement is a sham."

Jilly moaned. "No."

He ignored her pitiful sound. "When we found ourselves in a compromising position, Jilly agreed to pretend a relationship with me to preserve my scandal-free reputation."

Her thin lips pursed, Grandmother looked from Rory to Jilly. "This can't be true."

Shaking her head wildly, Jilly tried to find her voice. "He's joking. Ho-ho-ho. What a big kidder this guy is." And it wasn't altogether true. Their engagement had been to protect her as well.

Grandmother's gaze switched to Rory, who stood calm and relaxed beside Jilly. "Those kind of jokes aren't funny, young man," she said frostily, but then her voice warmed. "I'll overlook it, though, and tell you what I told my granddaughter. This engagement has my support and approval. Frankly, I'm more than pleased to find that someone could see through Gillian's apparent . . . frivolousness to what she has to offer. To the standards I raised her with."

Rory crossed his arms over his chest. "Unfortunately, ma'am, I can't say that I have that kind of vision."

Jilly cringed again. While she knew he considered her about as substantial as dryer lint, it wasn't easy to hear him say this to her grandmother. She made a quick move to get away, but Rory's hand snaked out and grabbed her wrist.

"Like you," he continued, "until now I didn't appreciate Jilly for who and what she is—a loyal, loving person. A person who always tries to do the right thing, despite the risk to herself."

Jilly stared at him. His expression was something—tender? bemused?—impossible to name. "What?"

"And, ma'am, she doesn't need my approval *or* yours. Neither does this engagement. I wasn't joking earlier. It was a hoax I coerced her into, something to save my reputation."

Jilly's free hand grabbed Rory's forearm. "No," she whispered. Didn't he realize he was a knife's edge away from cutting his own political throat? "Don't listen to him, Grandmother."

He didn't take his eyes off the frozen expression on her grandmother's face. "But she should, Jilly. She should listen to everything I have to say."

But Jilly couldn't. Not for one more second. By standing up for her with the truth, he would drive a stake through his dream. Grandmother would see to that personally.

"No," Jilly said again. Her feet scraped against the gravel walkway as she jerked her arm to break free of Rory's hold. "No." And then she turned and ran, because if she couldn't stop the death of Rory's ambition, she certainly couldn't stick around and witness it.

The air was thick with the smell of roses. She would never enjoy their scent again.

Without one thought but to escape the destruction rampaging behind her, she ran away from the party, away from the lighted gardens and into the darkness. In her own ears her breath was loud and her footsteps sounded panicked. Only trees and dark shadows were ahead and she dodged around them until one of the shadows materialized directly in front of her.

Jilly ran straight into a man's body. "Umph." She grunted and her heart jumped high in her chest before she realized it wasn't Rory.

Ducking around the winded man, she mumbled, "Sorry," and started running again. To her car. That was the direction she was heading in anyway. Her car was parked near the secret entrance to Caidwater.

Home. She could think all this through at home.

"Wait," the man called out. "Our cell phones aren't working. Did he do it? Is it over?"

Jilly slowed, but didn't stop to consider how this person knew what Rory was up to or why cell phones were involved. "Yes," she called back miserably, "Yes, I think so." And then she ran again, her mind focused on home. "I'm sure it will all be over in just a few minutes."

Her grandmother was elderly, but spry. Once Rory laid the truth on her, she'd make haste back to the party and finish the job he'd so foolishly begun.

To avoid dealing with the valet parking service that had taken over several nearby properties for the guests' cars, Jilly had left her own vehicle at the mouth of the dirt road that led into Caidwater via the neighboring estate. Once she reached the old woody wagon, her fingers scrambled underneath the bumper for the hide-a-key. She gripped it like a lifeline, finally allowing herself a moment to haul in a few much-needed breaths.

There was just enough moonlight to bounce dully off the shiny door handle, and once she had slid inside the driver's seat she automatically relocked the door and fitted the key to the ignition. She took one last look in the direction of Caidwater. By craning her neck, she could see the rooflines of the second and third stories.

Steeling her heart, she shifted around and twisted the key.

*Chug-chug-chug buzz.*

The engine didn't immediately come to life.

*Chug-chug-chug buzz.*

Not the second time either.

Jilly swallowed a small bubble of panic. The darn thing just *couldn't* pick now to go kaput. She'd walk all the way home before she'd go back to Rory's party and his shattered dreams.

*Chug-buzz.* She cursed in an unladylike way.

*Thump.*

The loud noise on the driver's door startled her. Jilly swung around to stare at a figure outside her window. Recognizing him, she cursed.

It was Rory.

She didn't want to see him, hear him, know anything about what had transpired after she'd left him and her grandmother alone. She didn't want to see or hear his anger and disappointment.

"Jilly!" His voice was muffled. *Thump*. His palms slamming against her window were not. "Open up!"

In response, she turned the key. *Chug-buzz-chug*. More foul language.

"Jilly, I need to talk to you!" *Thump, thump*.

She twisted the key again, her heartbeat frantic. She was the star of one of those low-budget, teen horror movies where the one-armed hockey player tries to get at the incredibly stupid and incredibly underdressed ingenue with his hook.

*Buzz.*

*Thump. Thump. Thump.*

*Buzzzzzzzzzzz*. Okay, so the car wasn't going to start. Breathing raggedly, Jilly forced herself to accept the idea. With a death grip on the steering wheel, she stared straight ahead. Maybe if she pretended Rory wasn't there, he would go away.

Instead, he leaned over the side of the car and his face loomed in front of her through the windshield. "Open up!"

Startled again, she squeezed the steering wheel and threw herself back against her seat. She also muttered several more bad words.

And then she rolled down her window. An inch. "Go away."

He braced his hands on the roof of the car. "Get the hell out of there," he ordered. "I want to talk to you."

She didn't like his commanding tone. Her head ached, her heart ached, her feet were jammed into a pair of satin high heels apparently made for a woman without toes. Her car wouldn't start, the jewel in her belly button was itching, and the man who had just destroyed his own dream on her behalf was looking at her like a serial killer with strangulation on his mind.

She hadn't asked for him to stand up for her, darn it, and she hadn't wanted him to. Suddenly all the emotions of the evening—of the past weeks!—sadness, anxiety, vulnerability, boiled into an unexpected and white-hot anger.

So he wanted to talk with her. Well, maybe the person who had a few things to say was she herself.

With a wild flick of her wrist, Jilly unlocked the door and threw it open, almost catching him in the belly. Then she stepped out of the car and shoved the door shut. Moving back, he stared at her, apparently surprised by her sudden capitulation.

She stalked him then, taking one long stride for each of his wary steps back. He retreated in a full circle until she finally had him backed up against the driver's side of her car. Her finger poked his chest. "Why?" she said. "Why did you mess it all up?"

That funny expression, half tender, half bemused, replaced the frustration on his face. "I don't think I messed it up. I think I finally got it right," he said mildly.

Jilly blinked. "But you ruined *everything*. My grandmother will—" She broke off, then brightened as a new thought occurred to her. "Did you placate her somehow? Did you come up with some story to cover . . ."

He was shaking his head. "I told her the truth."

That panic bubble rose in her throat again and

she swallowed, hard, to bring it back down. "Maybe if I talk to Uncle Fitz . . ."

He was shaking his head some more. "No, Jilly. I don't want what the senator has to offer."

Jilly could feel herself trembling. "Well, of course you do. I'm sure you've always wanted to be—"

He put his hand over her mouth. "You were right before. I didn't really want to be a senator, or hold any kind of political office. Though I might not have been half bad at it, I realize now that the idea only appealed to me because the way the Blue Party wants to change Washington is just the way I wanted to change the Kincaid name. I wanted to be respected. I wanted people to hear 'Kincaid' and not automatically think of shocking scandals and tabloid headlines."

Beneath his hand, Jilly grimaced. Then mumbled.

He took his hand away. "What did you say?"

"I said that what you did tonight won't help at all with changing the Kincaid image. Grandmother won't keep quiet about a fake engagement."

The corners of his mouth lifted in a little smile. "I don't know. It might not turn out as bad as you think."

Jilly was certain it was going to turn out exactly as bad as she thought. "Oh, Rory." Her shoulders slumped.

He smiled again. "Oh, Jilly," he echoed. "If I'd kept quiet and gone through with all of this, the respect of other people would have come at the price of my *self*-respect."

He draped his arms lightly over her shoulders. "I wasn't willing to do that. I couldn't let you compromise your spirit or your heart. The Blue Party isn't worth that to me. Especially when I realized that I want both of them, as is, to be mine."

She pretended she hadn't heard that last line, because surely, surely she was misinterpreting him. She also pretended not to notice the light embrace and hoped he would think the goose bumps rushing down her arms were from the night chill. "No. You could have had both. The candidacy, your self-respect. If you'd just kept your mouth shut around my grandmother."

"Nah, I told you I couldn't do that. Not once I heard you say you loved me."

Her mouth going dry, Jilly stiffened. "I didn't say that."

"Yeah, you did."

She shook her head frantically. "No. No. No." *Deny, deny, deny.* Never give him the chance to have the upper hand. Hadn't everything that happened with her grandmother tonight just reinforced that? "I didn't say it," she repeated.

He nodded. "Yeah. You did."

"No," she said firmly. "I did not name names."

He sighed, and that serial-murderer-considering-strangulation expression tightened the muscles of his face. "Who the hell else would you be in love with?"

She said the first name that popped into her head. "Greg."

He sighed once more. "My condolences, then."

"What?" Her brows came together. "Why?"

"Because that puts you at the bottom of a long list of women in his life."

"So?" she blustered.

He continued as if she hadn't spoken. "First, there's his wife."

"I—" Jilly stopped herself from saying "know" and replaced it with an innocent "Oh?"

"And then there's his daughter."

"Oh?" She blinked. *"Oh?"* She blinked again. "His daughter, you said?"

Rory nodded. "Iris." His hands found their way under her hair and stroked the nape of her neck. "It was the first right thing I did tonight. I made a promise to Greg and Kim that the three of them would be a family. Your grandmother gave me the chills, by the way. Thank God you and Greg made me see Iris not as a responsibility, but as a little girl to be loved."

Jilly stared. "Y-you gave up Iris?"

He grinned. "And the Blue Party candidacy, too."

"But you're smiling . . . no, grinning," she felt compelled to point out.

"I know," he said. "It's the damnedest thing, but the moment I told your grandmother about our sham, the moment I waved bye-bye to being senator, this black cloud that's been hovering over my head just . . . dissolved."

His hands slid to her shoulders and he gave her a tiny shake. "So give me something else to smile about, Jilly. Tell me you love me."

*Oh, no.*

She took a step back, but his embrace tightened. She looked up at him, at that exotic handsomeness that had fueled a thousand fantasies and probably would for the rest of her life. But to say she *loved* him. To his face. To let him know he had that power over her. *No, no, no.*

She trembled.

He must have felt her fear. "Oh, Jilly." His voice hoarsened. "I didn't grow up with love. I didn't go looking for it either. But you infiltrated my life and brought so much brightness, sweetness, and yes, chaos, I know I'll never be the same. I don't *want* to be the same."

Staring at him, Jilly thought she'd fallen into a fantasy again. But there wasn't a white robe or a sand dune in sight. It couldn't be, it wasn't possible, that he truly wanted her? But there was a look in his eyes, a look all at once sweet and surprised and tender and bemused, and her heart seemed to know what it meant.

"I don't understand," she whispered, not quite sure she was ready to believe the goofy, mushy thing in her chest that was beating so hard Rory must be able to hear it.

He drew her close, but she remained stiff and afraid. "Yes, you do. God, Jilly, I've resisted long enough for both of us. Please say it."

And give up her independence? Give up her autonomy? Let another strong, autocratic person have sway over her?

But then the truth hit her. He was offering her something she'd longed for all her life. Love. And it was going to take letting go of the past to have both hands free to hold onto it. Did she have the courage?

After another moment, she leaned back in his arms, looking into his eyes. "You first."

Being brave didn't mean being stupid.

His mouth twitched, but then he cupped her face in his hands. The moonlight gilded him, making him something real yet something magical all at once. "I love you, Jilly," Rory said. "I want you to be my wife. My one and only and forever Kincaid wife."

Her heart stuttered in utter, ecstatic Snoopy-dance happiness. It was true? It was true. Someone loved her. *Rory* loved her. He wanted her to be his wife. "You do?"

"I do." His lips twitched again. "Now out with it."

"Wait a minute." She pursed her lips, still trying to figure it all out. "If our sham engagement turns into a true engagement, does that mean—"

"That I run for senator? No. That you still have to fess up? Yes." He ran his thumb over her lower lip. "Now talk, woman."

"I—"

*Boom*. A deafening explosion sounded, and then a shower of red burst in the sky. *Boom*. Red. *Boom*. White.

Stunned, Jilly tilted her head back as more fireworks exploded. *Boom boom boom*. Man-made stars peppered the sky, then trailed white fire toward earth.

She glanced at Rory, but he was looking up, too, and the noise was so loud he wouldn't hear her questions over it.

*Boom. Pop pop pop pop. Boom. Boom. Boom*. Blue. Blue blue blue blue. Blue. Blue. Blue. The dark sky went bright with sparkly mushrooms and stars.

And just as the echoes from that died away, a loud hiss entered the air. Jilly gasped.

Then pointed over Rory's shoulder.

Without letting go of her, he turned his head to look back at the house. All along the roof-lines of the second and third stories, sparklers burst into flame, sparklers in the shape of four huge letters. The letters of a name that crawled across the Caidwater mansion, over and over and over.

RORY RORY RORY RORY RORY RORY RORY RORY RORY

He hung his head, then looked back up at her, sighing. "Ah, shit. The fireworks were supposed to happen *after* I announced my candidacy. Some-one must have jumped the gun."

*Oops.* Jilly remembered the man she'd run into with the non-functioning cell phone. Well. Maybe she'd tell Rory about that another day. Because right now she had something much more impor-tant to talk about.

"I do love you," she said. He'd given up that RORY RORY RORY for her. And all she had to offer in return was her heart.

The light of a million RORYs was in his eyes as he gazed at her. "What did you say?"

"I love you." He bent toward her, but she held him away with a hand on his chest. "Are you sure, though? Are you sure you don't belong there, back at the house, with them?"

"I belong with you. You make me crazy. You make me laugh. And I think with your help I might be able to find a heart inside me after all."

Jilly grimaced. "Sorry about that."

"I'm not. You were right. I'm just sorry that I took so long to start looking for it." He bent his head and kissed her, tender and sweet, and then his tongue swept across her lips and she opened her mouth for a deeper kiss. They groaned together.

Jilly tightened her fingers on his solid, very real strength. It wasn't the sheik and the slave girl, Jilly mused, somewhat dizzy. The final, healing, make-her-whole truth was that they were equals in this state called love. They were the sheik and the sheik-ess. The sheik and the sheik-ster. The sheik and the sheik-wife.

Something like that.

She pressed her body closer to Rory's and wrapped her arms around his neck. She'd figure it out later. Right now there were fireworks of her own she wanted to dazzle him with.

And the certainty that she'd never be lonely again to savor.

# ⟩ *Epilogue*

The last lavish Kincaid party at the Caidwater estate took place on the first Saturday in June. Standing on the terrace between two massive arrangements of flowers, Rory breathed in the sweet scent of orange blossoms—Jilly shunned roses—and breathed out a deep sigh of satisfaction. The vows had been said, his ring was on her finger, the minister had pronounced them man and wife.

She was bound to him forever.

Of course, Jilly being Jilly, that didn't mean he could keep perfect track of her. For some reason he couldn't fathom, he was standing alone at his own wedding reception while Kim was tasked with tracking down his bride so the wedding photographer could have at them for one final round.

But it wasn't so unpleasant to wait under the warm afternoon sun. Dove calls, mockingbird whistles, and the chatter of the wedding guests harmonized with the endless splash of the eight Caidwater fountains. The estate would be someone else's soon. Rory suspected its legends would live on, though, even with Kincaids living elsewhere. But they wouldn't be far.

Not when Jilly's business continued to thrive and they both wanted to be near Greg, Kim, and Iris. Rory even found himself with an appreciation of L.A. these days. Like Jilly, it was warm, bright, and free-spirited. A combination pretty damn hard to dislike, especially when he'd uncovered its loyal, generous heart.

Another few minutes passed, and he entertained himself by playing mental matchmaker with the eclectic and eccentric mix of wedding guests. Politico Charlie Jax with Aura, naturally. At this moment she had him by the champagne fountain and was studying his hand again. The experienced campaigner had yet to figure out she was snookering him with her palm-reading prowess.

The FreeWest Pilates instructor, Ina, he paired with Senator Fitzpatrick. The long-widowered man needed a woman in particularly good shape to keep up with him. Rory hadn't been the least surprised when the senator had decided to run on the Blue Party ticket himself. The pollsters were predicting a landslide win. Jilly said that Uncle Fitz had confessed to her he was relieved not to find himself facing retirement.

As for Rory, after some reflection, he realized he did actually like the idea of public service. But he was finding ways to make a difference through the private sector. He was armpit-deep in details as the new head of an organization that would create technology centers in low-income housing areas. He had contacts, favors to call in, and money, and he was determined to do something worthwhile with all of these assets. But he no longer needed the respect of anyone but his family and himself.

His gaze moving over the crowd again, he smiled as a group of FreeWesters broke into laughter. Jilly's friends were his now, too, and their exuberant, offbeat views of life kept him amused and on his toes. He liked them all. Well, to be honest, he still wasn't entirely comfortable with the gender-unspecific, American-flag-toothed salesclerk at French Letters, but everyone needed something to improve upon.

A stealthy movement nearby caught his attention, and he glanced down to catch Iris trying to sneak behind him. She'd played flower girl at the wedding, and in her old-fashioned lacy dress, button shoes, and straw boater, she looked the picture of innocence. Which was why he narrowed his eyes and snagged the wrist she was hiding behind her back.

Without a word, he pried her clenched fingers open to free a bright green grasshopper that, recognizing liberation when he saw it, immediately hopped away. Rory raised one brow. "Were you going to do something with that?"

She tried pouting, but then broke into a grin. "It was going down your pants."

He made his expression fierce. "Is that any way to treat your uncle?"

"You're *my* nephew."

"Your father is my brother. You're my niece."

Iris shook her head. "Nephew."

He nodded his. "Niece."

"Aunt," she corrected.

"Uncle."

"You're giving up?" she crowed.

"*No*! What I meant was, I'm your—" Then he did give up as she cackled at him again and danced away.

"Brat!" he called out. She went right on laughing. And probably went right back to looking for another grasshopper to torture him with.

He shook his head, thanking God that all that troublemaking was his brother's headache for the next fourteen years and not his. Jilly had been right—Iris had terrified him at first—but they'd reached a truce months ago. They continued to act out these little skirmishes purely for their own amusement. Rory could even see himself as a pretty good father one day.

But there was a lot of honeymooning to do first. Speaking of which—*ah*. Jilly was finally coming toward him through the crowd. His heart lurched—actually *lurched* in his chest—at the sight of her.

God, he loved her. When he'd overheard her tell her grandmother her feelings for him, when he'd realized that her spirit and her joy could be *his*, the world had righted itself. And even though it had been night time, the sun had come out in the light of the fireworks that were supposed to punctuate an ambition, but instead celebrated love.

He'd finally wised up, and the smartest move he'd ever make was recognizing that he needed her joyful spirit just as she needed his staunch reliability in order for them both to take a chance on happiness with each other. A chance that he intended to turn into a lifetime.

Jilly smiled as she reached him. Her romantic white dress looked so delicate, he hoped she wouldn't kill him when he tore it off her the minute they were alone. To be honest, he'd had enough of the wedding and was more than ready to proceed with the rest of their lives.

"Miss me?" she asked.

He frowned. "Don't look so smug. What were you doing? The photographer wants to take some final pictures and then we can leave the reception and get on with the good stuff."

Her smile turned secretive. "I was working on the good stuff."

"Oh, yeah?" His interest piqued, he put his arm around her to draw her close. Beneath the wedding gown, her body felt unusually stiff. "Are you okay?"

But before she could answer, the photographer descended, grouping Greg, Kim, and Iris around them for several shots. Rory tried bearing it gracefully, but when Jilly's hip brushed his groin, his fingers dug into her waist. There was that unfamiliar stiffness again.

He bent to her ear. "Are you okay? You feel kind of . . . rigid."

She lifted her mouth and whispered back. "I was afraid to put it on before the ceremony, just in case it made me feel faint."

"Huh?"

"It's a corset. You know," she whispered. "Those Victorian undergarments you're always so curious about."

"*Hu-uuh?*" he moaned. The person fainting was going to be him.

"What's up?" the photographer asked.

"Are you all right?" Jilly questioned.

"What's the matter?" Kim said.

"Don't lock your knees," Greg advised.

Rory looked at them all with a mixture of annoyance and exasperation. "Just finish up with the damn pictures."

But as the photographer grouped them for the last shot, the sound of chopper blades rumbled near. Everyone looked up as a helicopter drew overhead, descending lower and lower. A man leaned out the open side, a camera with a telephoto lens in his hand.

Then a high-pitched shriek pierced the air, even over the low roar of the helicopter. Looking toward the new sound, Rory caught sight of a flash of fluffy gray fur speeding across the terrace, and he groaned. One of the female guests jumped, then another and another, each trying to escape the rodenty partygoer that had just been startled into making an unexpected appearance.

Greg turned on Iris. "Did you bring Kiss to the wedding?" he demanded.

She pretended not to hear and ran off in the direction of her pet. "Kiss! Kiss!" she yelled.

With resigned eye rolls, Kim and Greg started after her.

Rory looked at the guests, scattering in the direction of the house. He looked up at the snooping helicopter. He looked down at his brand-new wife.

He remembered the Victorian undergarment.

No longer able to restrain himself, he hauled Jilly into his arms and kissed her. Deep and long and full of promise.

*"Rory."* Somehow she broke away from him, her face flushed and her skin already burning with that heat he knew so well. Burning for him. "The helicopter. They're watching us from up there. We'll be all over the papers and television."

He didn't spare a glance upward. Instead, he looked at his wife, who was his spirit and who was his joy. "C'mon, honey." Leaning close, he grinned. "Let's give them something to talk about."